Also by Bernard Jan

Novellas
A World Without Color
Look for Me Under the Rainbow

Novel
January River

CRUEL SUMMER

BERNARD JAN

Cruel Summer

by

Bernard Jan

Published by Bernard Jan, Zagreb, 2021

Originally and first published in Croatian as *Okrutno ljeto* by Dvostruka duga, Čakovec, 2014, ISBN 978-953-287-154-8

Copyright © Bernard Jan 2021

All Rights Reserved.

No part of this book may be reproduced, stored, or transmitted in any form or by any means, electronic, mechanical, photocopying, recording, scanning, or otherwise, without permission in writing from the copyright owner, that is the author of this book. The only exception is by a reviewer, who may quote short excerpts in a review.

www.bernardjan.com

This is not a true story.

All characters in this work are fictitious. Any resemblance to actual persons, living or dead, is purely coincidental.

Translated into English by Bernard Jan

Editing by Claudette Cruz, The Editing Sweetheart

Proofreading by the Hyper-Speller at wordrefiner.com

Cover design by Dean Cole

ISBN (Print On-Demand) 978-953-59581-7-8

Cataloguing-in-Publication data available in the Online Catalogue of the National and University Library in Zagreb under CIP record 001088479.

A Note from the Author (and Acknowledgements)

It has been over twenty years since I wrote *Cruel Summer*. A long period, imbued with waiting, hopes, discouragement, loss of faith . . . demolished trees, silence, ignoring, frustrations. Yet I kept looking into the future that was always there, somewhere far away, patiently waiting.

In the end, it turns out that there is nothing left for us to believe than that everything is happening for a reason, but in its own good time. For the safe space of time in which *Cruel Summer* had been so long stored did not hurt it; on the contrary, it rises again; it is reborn and embarks on its new journey, ready and bold to experience its second odyssey, and not a retreat. Over twenty years of dreaming is long enough for children to grow up to become adults, teens to develop into young men and women and mature people who will replace their skateboards with briefcases, thicker or thinner bank accounts, new commitments to themselves and others.

Over twenty years.

And it was as if nothing had happened.

Looking back on a long time ago when I was writing *Cruel Summer*, I did not intend to write a skateboarding manual. However, assuming that younger readers—those still in love with their magnificent boards on the wheels—would expect more than just a list of tricks, I took the liberty to explain the *basic things* about skateboarding.

Limited by space, I had to stick to the *tricks mentioned in this book*. To the best of my ability, I tried to satisfy both the majority of readers who are only interested in the story, or the plot, and who do not want their attention distracted by lessons of skateboarding. But I also wanted to please that minority, curious to read a little more about this sport—potential skaters. So I experimented a little with the introduction to each chapter, satisfying the curiosity of those who carry skateboarding genes with the technical aspects of skateboarding. In this way, the story itself remains intact and the readers' attention is not distracted.

I would like to reflect on some of the phrases in American slang I had to deal with that I would have to clarify here—for those who do not know them—to facilitate the reading of the novel. For instance, *boogie-board* has two meanings in American slang. In California, the term is used for a surfboard, while teens use it as a slang for a skateboard. To *skurf* means the same thing as to skateboard, and it is a compound of two words—skate and surf. *Johnny-be-good* is a common term in American slang for a cop or a police officer, while *G-man* and *feeby* or *feebee* are the FBI and FBI agents. *Fu(h)ggedaboudit!* is a typical Brooklyn pronunciation for *Forget about it!*, and so on.

As I said before, skateboarding terms like *tail grab* (where the back hand grabs the tail of the board) and *boardslide* (also like *tail grab*; in *Cruel Summer* it is used for snowboarding, and it is a slide performed along the obstacle) are explained under ordinal numbers of the chapters.

It all comes down to the fact that the jargon or slang used by skateboarders is the same wherever they are, and the roots in this case are from America.

It was a great pleasure to work on this project, to learn and to be taught to try something I have never done before in my life—to skateboard. The following people deserve my mention on these pages: Igor Piet Rešetnik, Valentina Mlinarić, Suzana Gjoni, Danijela Bušetinčan, Iva Rogić, Nikolina Baković, Sonja Kunović, Nives Tomašević, Verica Zorić, Goran, Neda and Vlatko Pavletić. My caring parents, my mother Ksenija and my father Dubravko, and my nana Anđelka—you have my love forever. I owe special thanks to Zagreb skaters Dario Pavlinić, Marin Kovačić, Tino Turk, Miroslav Petković, and Gordan Karabogdan. I hope and want to believe that you have replaced your retired skateboards with things that give you an equal dose of adrenaline, fervor, love, passion, freedom, and craziness in your life!

And to complete my Croatian team, Aleksandra Hampamer, my Croatian publisher, with Snježana Klopotan, my editor, and Melita Kravat, book cover and interior designer. Aleksandra, thank you for reviving us, me and my novel, when we have been hibernating for so long that we were half dead. A nice word of praise breathed life into us. The foreboding promise revealed a glimpse into the future. So little has passed from the promise to the realization. Sixteen years of waiting have come together in one beat of time, powerful and loud, a beat that was worth the wait. Thank you for that.

Seven years later, another circle is completed, and *Cruel Summer* is coming to life in English. My two friends Ozren Ćuk and Thomas Carley Jr., creator and owner of Tom's Music Place, Creative Realm, and Peacemaker, were the first ones to start this exciting adventure as my early English readers. Thanks, guys, not only for your valuable input but for your friendship past and present too. Angel Ramon Medina, author of many zombie books from Puerto Rico, was my first reviewer of the still unpublished and raw book that needed more editing. And still he had praises for it. Thank you for your support, my friend, we've been through a lot since then. The Editing Sweetheart, Claudette Cruz, was brave enough to tackle the editing job at such a short notice and in such a short period and did a great job with it! My respect and eternal thanks! The Hyper-Speller from wordrefiner.com refined and polished every word and punctuation, and I thank him for that. My thanks go to James Ventrilo from Readers' Favorite who helped me with writing a good query letter for literary agents and contacting them. I owe thanks to Derek Doepker, Founder of Bestseller-Secrets.com and Doepker Global, for the encouragement and ingenious advice on pre- and post-book-launch tips and tricks during his challenges. My thanks also go to Dave Chesson and Kindlepreneur for helping me with his knowledge on how to get our books in front of more readers and how to best choose Amazon keywords and categories. James J. Cudney, Nico J. Genes, and Stephanie Haddad-Wallace gave me their priceless, last-minute feedback after reading the advance reading copies; thank you, guys! Jonathan Hill, a great indie author, spilled again his magic over my blurb. Thanks for making it shine, J! Dean Cole did a fantastic job with my stunning book cover I am absolutely in love with. My thanks and respect, Dean, and thanks Aldina Šćulac, Boris Pecigoš, and Anita and Maitreya Euschen for giving it a big thumbs-up! And then, Michael Evans, another great indie author, who was and is incredible support to me as an author and a human being. We walk the same paths in the same shoes with the same dreams for a better world. Thank you, Michael, not only for writing over fifteen, fantastic science fiction, thriller and dystopian books in your teenage years, but for having so much understanding and for being an advocate for a better future and an inspiration to everyone. You absolutely rock!

Thank you all for your patience, support, and encouragement you have provided me during and after the writing of this novel. If you've enjoyed it at least a little as I did, then it was worth it.

Nothing was wasted. It was all worth it. For now, we embark on our second journey. And we travel and we go all the way.

I also want to thank many skateboarding brands, magazines *Transworld Skateboarding*, *Transworld Snowboarding*, *Thrasher*, and others, as well as Wikipedia and the information and articles all over the Internet for better understanding of extreme sports and for keeping this flame and love alive. Possible mistakes are only mine.

Based on events that could have happened at another time.

Chapter

1st: To do the *ollie* (the basic and, according to many, the simplest of tricks) follow these steps. Put your front foot across the middle of the board. Your back foot is in the center of the tail. The tail of the board extends from the back truck to its rear end while the nose of the board extends from . . .

HE IS SEVENTEEN. A FREE ENTITY of a six-and-something million New Manhattan population, panicky in their effort to keep up with the time and catch a break in short nightly intervals before the challenges of a new day. The fact that it is summer is of no importance to anyone. The pulse of New York City continues to beat in its wild, crazy, and exhausting way.

He is young, very young. Healthy, too, except for a swollen lip and a bruised eye. His face will soon become a specimen of various colors. That doesn't concern him much because he must think about other things. More important than just the one bruise.

The afternoon he finds himself in is sunny, but chilly—a story of this summer. This summer is cold, the coldest in this

century. New Yorkers have already come up with a name for it.
Cruel summer.

Cruel summer, Michael thinks, shaking with cold. His washed-out T-shirt, over which he had pulled only a hooded sweatshirt with a drawing of a grinning skeleton printed above the sign *Blind*, is doing a poor job in keeping him warm. If someone asked him, he wouldn't hesitate to take that pathetic sun out of the sky with one shot.

Or rather those who made it so . . . *uneconomic.*

This time, too, the main, alternative energy source dries up insidiously, opening the door wide to a new wave of pollution and new atmospheric changes.

A new climate *disorder.*

Michael grimaces. He imagines the reaction of the mayoress of the largest metropolis in the world, with hundreds of thousands of households reaching for heating in the middle of August, causing an overload of the power grid and triggering a new chain reaction of chaos.

Like he cares about it! *He* is not the Greenpeace green.

But the grass he stands on is *green*. Although slightly bitten by the morning frost. A perfect setting for his gloomy feelings and depressing thoughts.

The cemetery is empty and quiet, and it looks rather sad. Who would have thought of stumbling into a place like this during the biggest hustle and bustle of the city? Who but its tenants, perhaps some homeless people, thieves, human organ snatchers, or necrosadists . . . ?

Or maybe Michael.

Michael looks down from the sky wrapped in a haze of various vapors and particles of dubious origin. He stares blankly and seemingly absentmindedly at the marble tombstone in front of him. Elegant, not big, but enough to have the names of spouses with their birth and death years. And their children—assuming they will want it and that the rivers of life will not take them to other places.

Nothing more. Humble and simple. That's what Michael's mother wanted. Michael's father didn't object. Michael knows his reasons: Hank doesn't like to spend money on unimportant things. But this is another story that never questioned the greatness of Hank's love for his late wife. Michael is a living witness to this, isn't he?

Melanie Hope Daniels.

Melanie Hope Daniels—gold lettering carved in white marble.

A face surrounded by an aura of tenderness. Forgiveness. Compliance.

Modesty.

Modesty.

It was his mother, a self-effacing look full of love.

That's all Michael has from her now, with the promise he'd given her before she passed away: he will look after his sister and keep an eye on her.

Melanie Hope had high hopes for him, in reality still a boy. She believed in the power that lies behind his casualness, seeming disinterest, and defiant rebellion. She believed the contempt in his eyes with which he looks upon most of the world around him. She put her hopes in a "rebel without a cause" in a world that offers thousands of reasons for rebellion, into an unhappy child to whom even the unconditional maternal love has not dulled the blade of the evil fate of birth.

(Wrong place? Wrong time? Who would know?)

The mother's vision slowly fades, devoured by the cold marble.

The world is at its end. Or is it the beginning of something new?

Hope is dead. What will tomorrow's dawn look like? Toward the end of the millennium.

"Mother," Michael says dreamily.

One word. One sigh.

A warm cloud swallowed with haze. And grayness. In the city of light, money, success, and synthetic kitsch. That's how Michael experiences it—the intersection of contradictions and unimaginable extremes.

Yet . . .

. . . yet he still loves it in some bizarre way and still doesn't leave its harbor in search of a better life in the Old World. He has three good reasons for this. Three good reasons that still keep him here. For now.

The first lies at his feet; the second enjoys the blessings of school vacations in the wilds of Colorado; and the latter, though no less important, patiently waits for Michael to turn his attention to it. That's exactly what he does.

Leaving a fresh imprint in the damp earth, Michael takes his skateboard, adjusts a Creature flex fit baseball full cap all the way to his eyes, and sets off.

Toward the streets he will storm through. Toward the asphalt that will rattle under his wheels.

Thuuunderooously!

* * *

The apartment welcomes him in silence. Desolate and cold. Elegant, too big and too comfortable, equipped with state-of-the-art home appliances—a poor substitute for what his father *didn't* provide him.

But he leaves him a full refrigerator with a message, a magnet pinning it to the glittering, ice-blue door: *I'm afraid I won't be home until late at night. Have dinner without me. Don't wait for me. I'll eat something at work. SURPRISE me and come home before the small hours. I should talk to you. I really should talk to you about something. Dad.*

Instinctively, Michael touches his chapped lip as if trying to protect himself from the new pain. But the pain erupts again, accompanied by a torrent of boy's curses. *You can bet we'll have something to talk about!*

He washes his hands and face, but doesn't change into other clothes. He doesn't intend to stay long. Any longer than he should.

He pulls out a handful of ice cubes from the freezer and presses the cold compress on his face. Guys will tease *the hell out of him* when they see an ugly swelling. But Michael isn't in the mood for buffoonery and ridicule today. He feels lonely, his ships sunken and vulnerable. Rebecca's departure has affected him more than he is ready to admit.

The richness of colors, smells, and flavors overwhelm him when he opens the fridge. The rogue and the starving would have killed for this moment, illuminated by the light bulb. Suddenly, he is disgusted with the sight of so much food, and Michael gives up the sandwich his stomach is craving for. With deep regret he says *no* to ham from some of the genetic engineering farms.

(What would his father think if he learned that his own children are boycotting what he is doing for a living?)

Sighing deeply, he grabs the carton of milk and slam shuts the refrigerator door with his foot.

(That is what Michael thinks of his father's *important* work.)

He pours cold milk into a plastic bowl, stuffs it with strawberry-flavored cornflakes, and coats it with an excessively thick layer of brown sugar. Positioning himself in front of the big plasma TV, he sets to dinner.

Nervously changing programs at the pace of the snack, he is looking for something worth fifty dollars a month. Nothing interesting. A pile of garbage. Only the propaganda. Obvious and transparent lies. Old and repeatedly watched films.

Across the satellite, he runs into MC Solaar. Delighted by the unexpected luck, he summons his hologram, but his mood quickly fades with the first beats of the old hit of the Backstreet Boys. *Quit playing games with my heart!* Michael yells back and turns off the screen. He cannot understand how his sister can listen to such music.

He stops eating for a moment, his mouth still full of personally prepared mash and saliva. He can *feel* the flakes dissolve in his mouth, the sugar melting. Each cell of his body fills with a sweet strawberry flavor, irresistibly dragging him to his grandparents' ranch.

His sister's presence and closeness are more real than illusion. It is as if he has fallen into one of the games of virtual reality. Everything else is lost except that experience.

Rebecca is in a greenhouse, a large dome in the backyard of the estate. The air is saturated with sweet scents, and Michael unconsciously wrinkles his nose. The sight of Rebecca picking flowers catches his attention. Without a doubt, yellow roses will adorn the table tonight. Roses yellow like the sun. Roses yellow like ripe corn. Yellow like summer.

A cruel summer.

That brings him back to reality. Into the chilly Greenwich

Village, into a world of bohemians, artists, and streets swarming with all kinds of couples. Preoccupied with thoughts, he finishes the simple dinner.

For years, Michael questioned his mom why they were not moving out of this neighborhood, but he never got an answer that would satisfy his boyish curiosity. Melanie Hope did not know how to offer him the reason why they did not move, and this began to confuse him.

(Maybe she liked it here? Maybe she didn't mind male and female couples holding hands? Maybe she had more liberal views than him? Not really. Not his mother.)

He didn't ask his father about it. He never asked Hank about such things. In fact, Hank and Michael never talk *seriously*. Intimacy is a stranger to them, something alien, at least when they need to tell each other something.

Michael doesn't love his father. Nor does he respect him. Michael isn't sure if his mother was aware of the cold between them. But in reality, he doesn't *hate* Hank, except when the two of them get into a fight and there is a physical altercation. Michael couldn't stand it. He couldn't bear his father to *touch* him. So he avoids him whenever possible. That is how the streets of New York became his second adopted home.

Michael considers Hank a sick and disturbed person. A *very* sick person. And for that reason he doesn't hate him. Whenever Hank becomes unpleasant, Michael suppresses his true feelings and allows pity to overwhelm him. It isn't easy, but in a way, Michael feels sorry for him. But nothing more than that. This is as far as he could and is ready to go.

If Melanie Hope knew of Hank's dark side, Michael couldn't know for sure. But she *was* his wife, which is why she must have sensed how unpleasant Hank could be.

And Hank knew how to be unpleasant.

Very unpleasant.

Is that why she asked her son for a favor before she succumbed to pneumonia? Is that why she asked him to look after their treasure: a girl they both loved unconditionally and equally sincerely? Perhaps Melanie Hope knew, after all, that Hank was not capable of such love?

Taken aback by the sudden onset of feelings, Michael loses his appetite. The pain is back again, both mental and physical.

He takes his unfinished dinner to the kitchen and then, like a sleepwalker, heads to the bathroom and finds painkillers in his father's cabinet. He shakes two Darvocets out of the bottle and washes them down with tap water, then he repeats the whole process once more. His confidence returns, though not completely.

Urged by the overwhelming desire to call Denver, he drags himself into his father's study room and greets the electronic pet on his father's desk.

"Sergio Unit, please connect me with Denver, Colorado, the Creeks' Ranch."

Tapping his fingers on the polished surface of the desk, he waits for the Sergio Unit to digest the information.

"I am sorry, Michael. The number you requested is currently unavailable. Would you like me to try again?" the electronic voice answers.

(They are not in the house. They're probably in the greenhouse, or maybe in the barn. Or they went shopping.)

"No need, Sergio Unit. Thank you. Disconnect."

The screen dims and Michael heads to his room to retrieve his backpack. He checks out its contents: Rimbaud's *Collected Poems*, as well as a French-English, English-French Pocket

Dictionary and a Light-Cola, half-liter bottle refilled with fresh water are already in it.

Then he slides into the Alphanumeric windbreaker, tosses his backpack onto his back, and grabs a skateboard.

Before going out, he checks his appearance in the mirror once more. He isn't too crazy about the reflection staring back at him, but there is nothing he can do about it. After all, skateboarding accidents happen every day, and who cares?

Pulling the door behind him, he locks it well.

* * *

Rebecca abruptly reins in the horse. The ranch is right in front of her, down a gentle slope a little to the left. A lovely little, fairy-tale place, basking in the cold sun. If she galloped at it at this speed, her grandma would be terrified, and she would force her grandpa to forbid her to ride before she breaks her neck. But that won't happen, Rebecca knows. She knows her grandpa well and his mysterious smile that flashes with pride every time he sees her riding.

He would forgive her immediately, she is sure.

Such is her grandpa. An aging image of her mother, who didn't live long enough to enjoy her own grandchildren.

Rebecca's vision blurs. She blinks away the tears. Here, in the wild, no one will see her if she cries. But then again, if she lets her feelings take hold of her, if she lets herself cry . . . No, that won't be good. She knows it would be a relief for Michael and Hank to see her cry; she had not shed a single tear since her mother's death. At least not in front of them. Therefore, they would greet her tears with great relief, because that means that *she is okay*. But that's not how Rebecca expresses her feelings. She is a *Daniels*, after all.

The air smells of summer mixed with the fresh breath of winter. A strange combination.

Rebecca's riding hat lies still on her back, her thick, blonde hair glistening with the illusion of a fragile aura as her blood runs hot beneath a warm, faux-leather jacket, soaking her sweaty, plaid shirt. And the temperature keeps falling and approaching the freezing point.

Today, Rebecca and her mare have traveled a good chunk of the way. Vanity is in a great mood and in even better shape than Rebecca. She obeys all of Rebecca's orders, for which she will be abundantly rewarded.

Rebecca pats her neck gratefully, to which Vanity replies with a cheerful whinny. Rebecca clicks her tongue twice and allows her to go pick up her prize.

* * *

House. Home. Hearth.

The divided sense of belonging that has caused confusion in Rebecca's head since her mother died.

New York—Denver. House—home. Hearth?

(Or the other way around?)

She lives in New York; loves being in Denver. Not far from the Ken Caryl Ranch, fifteen miles southwest of Denver. Rebecca adores her grandpa and grandma, but she never stopped thinking about her father and brother who had stayed there since she left New York. Especially about her brother. She also knows that when she returns to New York *(too soon, much too soon, very much too soon)*, her heart will turn into an ocean of sadness that she had to leave her grandparents. That's how it was last year, that's how it was the year before. This year it will be even harder.

Because her mother won't be there to ease her the pain of parting.

(What remains of her consolation? What remedy to cure the pain?)

"Time heals everything," Grandma told her as she cried, her beautiful head resting in Grandma's lap. "And the rare moments of joy from which we emerge as winners become our signposts on the road of life."

But how many of these signposts will there be? How many clear ones? And how many times will we stray . . . lost in the jungle of life?

With the strength of her willpower, Rebecca shakes off the black thoughts. A car is parked in front of the house and it is just leaving. A black Lincoln Navigator, Rebecca recognizes it under a thick layer of dried earth and mud. She nods in greeting to the two men behind the dirty windshield and they nod to her in return.

Reaching the barn, she slides out of the saddle and takes Vanity into the barn. A familiar neighing welcomes her. It is Grandpa's black Darkfall and Vanity's mother, Josephine.

After taking care of her four-legged friend, Rebecca walks across the yard to the house. Not forgetting Vanity's prize—a handful of sugar.

"Who was that?" she asks her grandfather from the door, interrupting him in preparing an early dinner.

"Rebecca! Hello! I didn't hear you come in."

"I'm sorry. I didn't mean to scare you. You okay?"

"Sure, my child! How was the ride? It seems to be quite a long one. But is it wise considering you two haven't seen each other for a long time?"

"I know, Grandpa. Thanks for worrying, but it was great! Vanity was happy to see me again. You are not angry with me, are you?"

"Do I look angry?"

With the mound of chopped potatoes lying in front of him on the table and the sharp knife he holds upright like a flag, he looks anything but angry.

Rebecca smiles back at his smile and funny look.

"You had a visit?" she repeats her question.

He doesn't look up.

"Black Lincoln? Navigator?" Rebecca continues, not giving up.

Jeremy Creek puts the potatoes in the oven and takes a long look at his granddaughter.

"An old model, but well preserved? I met it about twenty minutes ago."

"Yes? What about it?"

"Who was that?"

"The Atkinses."

"The Atkinses and? Surely you know something else about them?"

Another smile flashes over Jeremy Creek's face, then disappears. He's trying to be serious.

"They're our new neighbors," he answers casually.

"Your *new* neighbors? You didn't tell me anything about having new neighbors."

"There was nothing to tell. They only moved in two months ago."

"Where are they from?" She grabs a raw carrot from the huge table in the middle of the kitchen and bites into it. The taste of the food, even raw, reminds her how hungry she is.

"From Texas. At least, that's what they told us."

"Don't you *know*?"

"My child, it is not polite to stick your nose where it does not belong. Plus, I don't care where they're from as long as they're okay and mind their own business."

Rebecca swallows the rest of the carrot and gives him her best disarming smile.

"Is it rude to ask what they wanted?"

"*That* is not rude." He struggles to remain serious. "They came to ask if we could sell them some vegetables to replenish the vegetable garden. The frost has destroyed everything."

"I see. And you, of course, sold them vegetables."

"I did, but I also *gave* them some. Otherwise, they would take nothing."

"Where's Grandma?" Rebecca changes the subject.

"I think she's in the greenhouse . . ."

"Good. I was going there anyway. I should pick some flowers for dinner."

"Uh-huh, yes. That'd be nice."

"Grandpa, why didn't you invite them to stay for dinner?" Rebecca asks him from the door. "Just to get to know each other better?"

She then disappears without waiting for his answer.

* * *

Warmth. Dampness. Scents. Colors. Attacking Rebecca's senses with full force as she enters the greenhouse. *A transparent, crescent moon*, as she likes to call it.

She left her jacket in the house and her grandmother, of course, doesn't miss it. She reprimands her for being so careless and softens only when Rebecca hugs her and places a wet *I-love-you-Granny* kiss on her slightly wrinkled cheek. As much as she tried, Elisabeth Creek wasn't immune to her granddaughter's charm.

Walking among the flower beds, Rebecca tries to come up with a logical explanation of what she had forcibly pulled out of her grandmother before she disappeared from the greenhouse. What ought to be logical is sagging under the weight of the il-logical and eventually mixes in one sound burst of colors, voices, scents, and beliefs.

Rebecca closes her eyes before the sudden onset of dizziness. When she opens them again, she sees a yellow rose bush in front of her.

(She succumbed again. She gave in again. She couldn't resist them again—her beautiful yellow roses.)

Yellow like the summer. Yellow like the sun.

Picking up the flowers and putting them in the basket, she feels anger build up in her. Anger begins to flow in her like the tide of a cold ocean she doesn't know how to stop.

That surprises her. She doesn't have the slightest reason to be angry because she doesn't know the Atkinses. Yet she cannot handle it. *(This is not science fiction like the* Star Wars Trilogy, *which, in anticipation of the premiere screening of the first episode* The Phantom Menace, *is once again filling up New York theaters.)* She has to find out the truth. And there is only one way to do this.

The roses are picked and their intoxicating scent fills Rebecca's lungs. It is the scent of love, and it makes Rebecca cry from it.

Inside her, a void opens which grows more and more. Lamenting for lost words and erased civilizations, people she misses so much.

Those who are gone forever. *(Mother!)*

Those who threaten to disappear. *(Michael! Father!)*

She hurries out of the transparent, crescent moon toward the house, toward the computer that monitors Creek's estate, her only connection to New York.

Chapter

2nd: . . . the front truck to its front end. Bend your knees. Extend your back leg. Pop the tail down. Drag your front foot toward the nose. The outer or top side of your shoe slides over the grip tape. Straighten your legs out. Bend down to soften the landing when your wheels hit the ground. The . . .

ANGELA KENNETH IS IN HER BED, half awake—half asleep, her eyes expressionless. Unnoticeable heartbeats bounce below her aged and wrinkled neck. Her surprisingly smooth face captures the glare of a pale glimmer of light from the hallway.

The curtains on the balcony door are drawn, the lights in the room are off. Except for that night-light on the shelf above the head of her bed.

The sound of a flushing toilet comes from the bathroom. After relieving themselves, someone is washing their hands. The door slides open and closes even more silently behind the shadow that enters the room and sits on Angela Kenneth's bed.

"Nana?"

Tired eye movement. (Recognition sign?)

"Nana, can you hear me?"

Barely noticeable, "I hear you."

"I have to go now. See you tomorrow. All right?"

"You're already going . . . ?"

His face in the dark is foreign and unfathomable, as if it is hidden behind a mask. But the voice behind that dark mask is full of love. Angela Kenneth feels its strength and warmth, though, disoriented, she cannot recognize the source of where it is coming from.

"I have to. It's getting dark."

"When will you come again, Craig?"

"It's not Craig, Nana. It's me. Your grandson, Victor."

"Victor?"

"Yes."

"Oh, it is youuu . . ."

"Yes, Nana. But now I have to go. You get some sleep, okay?"

"I'll go with you—"

Victor's strong yet gentle hands prevent her weak attempt to get out of bed.

"No, Nana. You can't come with me. You're too weak. You don't want something to happen to you, do you? I'll see you again tomorrow."

"You promise?" Her voice slowly sinks into sleep.

"I promise. See you tomorrow for lunch."

Victor pushes himself up from the bed, leans over Angela Kenneth, and kisses her warm forehead. He whispers a soft *bye* to her ear.

He pauses for a moment at the door in the half-light, glancing at three, poor, wrinkled creatures who melt into silhouettes on the last floor of the nursing home, at the last resting place before arriving at the place where everything ends and ceases to exist.

He sighs and pulls the skateboard from under the bed without a sound. He turns off the lamp above his grandmother's bed and closes the door of room 508.

On the way to the elevator, he meets the duty nurse and exchanges smiles with her. What else shall they say to each other after ten months of acquaintance?

Everyone already knows Victor here. *The best grandson in town*—they call him fondly. *The best grandson.* The head nurse especially loves him, because few today, particularly young, find time to visit their weak and incapacitated grandparents every day. Very few.

Victor would always remain silent on her praises. For him, his visits to his nana are a normal thing. He doesn't perceive them as a sense of obligation or duty, or perhaps guilty conscience. It is nothing *special* to him.

The elevator door slides open and he enters the cabin. He pushes the ground floor button, leaving behind a stationary corridor filled with silence, solitude, the pungent odor of disinfectant mixed with the smell of urine and the distant faint slamming of rubber soles across the washed linoleum floor.

Several times the head nurse told him she would like to publish an article about him in the newspaper. Victor was shocked by the idea because he was no celebrity. He's just an ordinary guy, no better and no worse than the rest.

On the other hand, he *is* a hell of a skateboarder with a degree from the School of Applied Arts and an award-winning *writer*. His drawings and graffiti adorn many nightclubs, discos, music stores, and street walls throughout the East Coast. Victor is one of the most talented and sought-after, young artists with sprays.

When his grandfather died sixteen years ago, Victor stayed with his grandmother. In addition to drawing, skateboarding, and girlfriend Nancy, Victor adores his grandmother, the only living being with whom he has a blood relationship. He has no memories of his parents, who were killed in a chain-reaction, car accident. Victor, then a nine-month-old baby, miraculously survived by falling out of the car with the car seat when the collision occurred. In the chaos of screams, crushed metal, shattered glass, smoke, and blood, over thirty of the injured were waiting to be rescued that night. Some of them lived until the paramedics came, others didn't. Victor's parents were among those who failed to reach salvation.

Victor walks past the young porter who is watching the evening news with little interest on a portable television and goes out into the street. It is fresh outside, so he buttons himself up.

Ignoring the *NO SKATEBOARDING* sign, he jumps on the board and rolls through

an apparent night.

In the collision with the bright lights of the city, the darkness melts into an artificial day. All kinds of vehicles are sliding across the streets, and the sky is filled with zeppelins and balloons lit by light cannons. The night is bright, and this is the most expensive, but also the most popular way to advertise during calm and nice weather. The helicopters of many companies perform a celestial dance, roaring loudly and being annoying.

Victor exits the no-skateboarding zone without being stopped by any of New York's Finest. The NYPD is busy as every evening at this hour, when, at about seven o'clock, the action against drug dealers begins—a comprehensive, nightly witch hunt.

This is a devil of a time for everyone looking for some drugs. Not even a single pill could pass. Druggies who have no gold reserves at hand fall into a coma, while dope peddlers go crazy because their business collapsed as if stuck in gridlock.

But that is a happy time for skateboarders. With the night sinking deeper, their time is coming. As cops rush in other directions, the freedom of the night belongs to them.

* * *

The first thing that catches his eye is the noise. A commotion. Laughter. Unusual liveliness.

Michael is in the spotlight. He stands on one of the benches in the park and yells.

Gesticulating, in poor French he reads Rimbaud's lyrics from the poem "Sensation," eliciting a roaring laughter, all sorts of remarks, and whistling.

"Didn't this guy learn English at school?" Fernando, a Latin American, remarks.

"A real *sensation*, man!" Andy says. "Sensational nonsense!"

Eruption of laughter.

"Okay, okay," Michael says in self-defense. "You asked for it, so now hear the English version, too."

Victor greets his buddies as the air fills with a loud *booooo!*

"Ken." They shake hands and then grip only their fingers.

"Andy." Victor slaps him a high-five.

He nods to Stu, Ian, and Alex, and parks himself next to Justin.

"What happened to him?" he asks Justin, pointing his head

to Michael.

"You're asking me?" the thirteen-year-old skater from Harlem says. "He's been this way since he came. Putting on the loony, harebrained act!"

Michael's voice turns into a cry, demanding their attention.

"Enough babbling, get that translation already!" someone calls out to him. Maybe Ken? Victor is not sure.

"And don't take too long! You are getting boring," Alex adds, picking up the applause of the male auditorium. "Yes, baby! Way to go! Just be harsh with him, girl!"

Michael begins to translate, that is, to read the translation, pretending that he is translating himself.

"Wash your head, wash! And cool off, dude," the skaters interrupt him, not caring about passersby and an inline skater sneaking past them as though walking through a minefield.

"*YEEESS!* With a *woman*!" Cheers and applause greet his last words, except Victor and Alex. "Where's your woman, Mikey? Lost her on the way?"

Laughing again.

Ignoring them, Michael jumps off the bench.

Someone growls, "Hail Rimbaud! We want more!"

But Michael shoves his book in his backpack and catches Victor's gaze, as if he has just spotted him.

He slowly walks toward him. A few steps from him, he grimaces and catapults himself into his arms, wrapping his legs around his waist. Taken by surprise, Victor stumbles, and they almost knock down Justin.

"Hey!" Justin protests.

"He ain't your woman, man! Leave him alone!" Stu starts a new eruption of laughter.

Michael digs his fingers out of the bleached strands of

Victor's carefully arranged, just-got-out-of-bed hairdo and Victor lets him slip out of his embrace. Disappointed, skaters return to other topics.

"What happened to your face?" Victor asks him.

"How did you like the poem?" Michael evades the answer to Victor's question.

"You don't think you are degrading Rimbaud and the very concept of art by reading him to that bunch of banana-heads?" He points at skaters draining Budweiser cans.

"Good point." Michael rubs his chin. "You're smart."

"Who did you run into?" Victor returns to a question that is still waiting for an answer.

"But not *too* smart." Michael wags his forefinger. "Or you'd have known that."

"Have you been drinking?"

"Nope. Do I look drunk?" he asks, boyishly innocent.

"A little. Maybe."

"I didn't even smell the booze. But that doesn't mean I won't get drunk by the end of the evening."

"Here comes Alien!" Justin cries from the depths of his lungs.

"Alien! Alien!" other skaters start chanting.

"Oh, the new jacket! *Survival apparel!* Are we planning any snowboarding?"

"You're helping Lenny keep his store above the water again?"

"Boys, get off me!" Alien tells them.

The skaters circle Alien, completely enclosing him.

"Alien Workshop!" Fernando crosses his middle finger over his ring finger.

"I told you, take a walk! What do I have to do with you at

all?" Alien pushes himself through them, jumps on the board, and grinds the stairs.

"It's a wide universe, Alien!" they shout after him and jump on their boards.

Washington Square thunders under the wheels of cheerful skateboarders. The benches groan from sliding, the stairs squeal from grinding. And that is just the beginning.

"Let's sit down, my friend." Victor gestures to the bench and Michael sits next to him.

"You want some water?" Michael offers.

"No, thanks. Are you OK?"

"Why do you insist on irrelevant things? You are making a mountain out of a molehill. Shit happens, okay?"

"And this show of yours is also irrelevant?"

"I got served on the rail, okay?" His gaze is piercing. "Why do you care so much? *You* were the one who broke a leg. Do you remember?"

"I also remember that you used to visit me all the time when I was in the cast. But forget it. You don't have to talk about it if you don't want to. Forget I asked."

Michael's tension eases. He changes the subject. "How's your grandma?"

"Same old story. She didn't recognize me again today. She thought I was her husband. It took me a while to explain to her who I was."

"It's hard. She's lucky to have you."

"Yes, you're right." Victor sighs. But he doesn't tell him of the depression and frustration he is going through because he is powerless to do anything, but watch the person he loves fade away day by day. If Nancy wasn't helping him, he probably wouldn't have been able to endure it.

"Do you want us to visit her tomorrow?" Michael offers. Unexpectedly.

Pleasantly surprised, Victor nods.

"I'm at Nana's for lunch. Nancy will come in the evening. Will that work for you?"

"No problem."

"Agreed, then." They shake hands by gripping their fingers.

"Thanks, Mike. Have you seen Nancy? I told her we would be at the park."

"No, I'm afraid not. Maybe the guys know something? They would surely tell you she was looking for you."

"I have to call her later. She's probably stuck in the hospital. They had some fuss about changing the shifts. Are you in for some skurfing?"

"Seriously! Did you forget about the contest? I *have* to skate."

* * *

"Boy, life can be beautiful!" Alien shouts and grinds the stairs, which Stu sets on fire by pouring gas over them.

His wheels get caught by the flames, but Alien extinguishes them as he continues to skate.

Stu follows him, and then Andy, and Ian. Ian's Fourstar pants get burned a little at the bottom of the legs.

With the expert eye of Steven Spielberg, Lenny, owner of Division Pro Skate Shop, continues to shoot the film for his new video.

The camera lens focuses on Victor and Michael slapping the high ten and wishing each other *Break a leg!* for luck before they hop on their skateboards as one.

Without a problem they jump over the stairs and the flames that lick up from them. Safely landing, they roll away.

Elation erupts among the skateboarders, now over twenty of them. A growing crowd of tourists, evening strollers, and young couples are watching their stunts with interest.

Justin and Sven—the two smallest and youngest skaters—crouch down and protect their heads with their hands, waiting for Michael and Victor to jump over them.

Victor and Michael grin at each other, shoot forward and fly over Justin and Sven, without even touching them.

With thunderous shouts, they continue riding. They perform a *backside 180* and a forty-yard-long *manual*, combining a *nose manual* and a *tail manual*. At the end, Michael does a *kickflip* and Victor pops a *heelflip*. They successfully complete an agreed *line* that Lenny, with a happy grin on his face, shoots equally successfully.

Out of the blue, someone yells, "PENNIES!" Backpacks are quickly grabbed, and skateboarders disappear at the speed of Bode Miller as he winds his way down the slopes of Beaver Creek.

Splitting into smaller groups, they leave behind Washington Square Park full of empty cans and the smell of burned gas that the fire devours before it extinguishes itself.

"Damn popos!" Alien mutters, escaping the patrol of three young men and a girl who storm at them on their rollerblades like bats out of hell, armed with pads and helmets with the NYPD abbreviation for New York Police Department. Or New York Pork, Penny, and Pussy Department, as skaters like to call them. "Hey, shitheads, take off those pussy pads! Let's see how tough you are without them!"

"You won't live long enough to see that," Victor comforts

him, catching his breath. "They do that, and they're out of the Pussy Department before you say Jack Robinson!"

"Come on, guys," Michael hurries them. "Let's get out of here. I'm working up an appetite from all this excitement."

* * *

A little later, at the end of the meal at The Empire Diner parked at 210 10th Avenue.

"I don't know how you can drink that," Alien says to Michael with disgust. "Peach juice!"

"Why? What's wrong with it?"

"What's wrong with it?! That's what the girls drink, smartass!"

"I'm sorry to disappoint you, but my stomach turns into a nuclear bomb when in contact with anything carbonated."

"You could have had iced tea then. Or water! Good old plain water."

"Gotta go, guys," Victor says, his voice hoarse with boredom and impatience. "Can't wait any longer. I need to see what's going on with Nancy."

He gets up and rolls his skateboard with his foot, which is under the table.

"See you tomorrow," Michael confirms their agreement.

"Sure."

"What? You are up to something without me?" Alien protests.

"Of course not! I'll go with Victor to his grandmother's tomorrow," Michael explains. "Are you coming with us?"

"No. I'm sorry," a sound of relief in his voice. Alien hates institutions and places that remind him of his own mortality.

"I'm delivering pizza. Maybe I'll see you in the evening?"

"Anything is possible," Victor replies, and waves them goodbye.

"Coming to my place?" Alien invites Michael after losing sight of their friend.

"I'd love to, but I must go home. My old man's waiting for me."

"Come on. School's out, if you forgot!"

"I know. Still, I can't."

"Come on, do yourself a favor and come with me. You won't regret it. Call your old-timer and tell him you are sleeping at my place."

"If it were that simple. Dad *expects* me to be home tonight."

Alien gives him a serious look.

"Don't look at me like that. I know as much as you do. He is the one who wants to talk to me."

Alien scowls even more.

Sensing what his friend is up to, Michael relents. "To hell with everything! Think I'm gonna call him. Just don't give me that look again."

Attaboy! Alien grins and turns into pure kindness.

* * *

"Take this. Put it on your face." Alien hands him ice wrapped in a kitchen cloth. "That should help you."

"Isn't it a little late for that now?"

"If nothing else, it will refresh you."

"Thanks, buddy."

"Don't give me that crap."

"I don't just mean ice. I mean the whole evening."

"In that case, you are welcome." Alien smiles, pleased. He presses the PAUSE button and restarts the video. Luke Skywalker is back in the battle with the enemy fighters of the Empire.

The sound is muted all the way. Instead, soft music is playing. Dream-dance. Future Breeze, Vertigo, H2O, Robert Miles, Chicane.

Cheesy, European music that usually irritates Michael. No *real* skater would listen to such music. But surprisingly, his refined musical ear isn't offended by it now. He surrenders to its hypnotizing rhythm, forgiving Alien for that stain in his otherwise Joe Perfect record.

He closes his eyes in semidarkness and drifts away. The hands on the clock turn back in time and the lyrics stream down his lips once more like bad wine down a drunkard's beard. He doesn't understand what got into him. And only recently he was messed up until he met his pals. What a change of personality!

(How did this happen?

(Did he forget so quickly about his father he felt resentful and angry about, his deceased mother whose death he could not reconcile with, and his baby sister he misses almost desperately?

(And what about her yellow roses? So real in his fleeting vision. . . .)

Despite the emotional turbulence that Michael went through today, he finds peace in the hospitable haven of Alien's interplanetary lair.

And he is glad Hank didn't answer the phone when he called. Michael doesn't think about him anymore tonight. He'll think of him tomorrow. Darvocet pills kick in, and Michael is tired and stunned. Terribly tired. As if he carries the future of the world on his shoulders, with the Death Star in front of him. And he is armed only with his skateboard, good intentions, and the vision of a happier future.

He opens his eyes. Alien is watching him.

"I didn't fall sleep," he says. "I've been thinking about something."

"So did I. I wouldn't be at all surprised if one day someone fell hard for your eyes. And that could hurt!"

Like a battery-powered toy, Michael leaps to his feet, crosses the room in two long jumps, and kisses Alien on the cheek.

"Phooey!" Alien wipes Michael's saliva from his face. "I didn't mean myself, you idiot. And be quiet! You'll wake up Mom."

Still choking with laughter, Michael walks to the door.

"Where do you think you're going?" Alien insists, not looking away from the movie he has seen a hundred times before.

"You just have to know every damn thing about my plans, dreams, intentions, and needs?"

Their eyes meet. "As long as you're in my galaxy, I do! I don't want any disturbance of the Force in this part of the universe."

"Then raise your ass if you will watch me while I take a leak. Can't hold it any longer."

"Nah, thanks. I'll wait for you here."

Torn with laughter, Michael disappears in the bathroom.

When he is done, he looks at the reflection of his face in the mirror (sprayed with water droplets and a little too pale in contrast to his reddish lips) and then into his eyes. Despite a shiner, they are beautiful.

(What if Alien is right? Aren't those eyes the source of all his troubles and injuries, both those visible to the naked eye and those that cannot be seen? And they hurt the same. If not even more . . .)

Not expecting the mirror to answer those questions, Michael switches the light off and tiptoes out of the bathroom.

Alien is already sleeping with his clothes on when Michael returns to the room. *The Empire Strikes Back* is still on, and Michael turns off the video recorder. Then he switches off the music and slides into his improvised bed—Alien's sleeping bag.

Alien mutters something in his sleep.

His steady breathing is like a lullaby, and it lulls Michael to sleep.

Chapter

3rd: . . . *backside 180 ollie* start similar to the *ollie*. Turn your shoulders and upper body in the opposite direction you are going. Straighten your legs. Turn your upper body in your 180 direction. Pop the tail like you are doing the *ollie* motion. Slide your front foot toward the nose. Push forward. Your nose . . .

THERE IS NO TRACE OF HIS FATHER in the apartment when he comes home.

His bed is unused, the kitchen clean and untouched. It's all like Hank left before he went to work last morning.

There are two messages in Sergio Unit's mailbox for Michael, and he clicks them open. The first is Rebecca. Rebecca replied to his message, sending him Grandpa's and Grandma's love. The second message is from Hank. Michael relaxes when he reads it. Yes, Hank is worried that Michael wasn't home when he called, but he doesn't raise a special fuss about it. He sent him an email to let him know that he won't be home tonight (now last night) because he is in the middle of an experiment that can last until the morning. He will come over the next morning to change clothes and take a shower before re-turning to work. Hank's message ends with the words: *Take the money for Juanita out of the safe and leave it on the kitchen table for her. Today is her day off, but she'll stop by to pick up her pay. Make sure you lock the door on the way out three times. Love, Dad.*

Michael hates the patronizing tone with which Hank speaks to him—as if he were some stupid ten-year-old—but this time he lets it go without comment. He is too excited and too happy to bother with it because *everything is A-OK. His father skipped over him being AWOL last night. His trepidations were exaggerated.* Just in case, he doesn't delete his message from the Sergio Unit memory. One never knows when it may come in handy, in case Hank raises the issue again.

He turns up the heating and starts undressing, leaving scattered pieces of clothing on the way to the bathroom. He runs a bath and turns on the jetted tub, adding plenty of bath salt and foamy shampoo into the hot water to relax. Having no clothes on, he returns to the computer and makes a call to Sebastian's. He orders fried pancakes stuffed with mushrooms and tartar sauce to be delivered in half an hour to forty minutes. That is how long he needs to get out of the tub clean, relaxed, massaged, reborn, and perfumed.

A brand new man.

Then he takes out the money for Juanita from the safe and puts it in an envelope on which he scribbles *For Señorita Juanita*, unable to resist temptation to tease her.

Before locking himself in the bathroom (his old habit that he hadn't given up even when he was alone at home), he removes the key from the inside of the apartment door and unlatches the security chain in case Juanita arrives while he is still in the tub.

Señorita Juanita, the mother of five children and the grandmother of a bunch of grandchildren, the only person outside the family who has the keys to the apartment, is now free to come in.

* * *

Through the mist of steam and the scents of intoxicating salts and the bathing shampoo, he thinks he hears the doorbell. He turns off the jetted tub and listens. The doorbell doesn't ring a second time. Maybe he imagined it.

He gets out of the tub and wraps himself around the waist with a thick terry towel. He consults his wristwatch: he stayed in the tub for twenty-two minutes. It is still too early for Sebastian's delivery.

He rubs himself dry with rapid moves and combs his wet hair. He doesn't dry it with a hair dryer, thanks for asking. Michael never dries his hair with a hair dryer, no matter the season or the weather. The possibility of catching a cold is one of his last concerns.

He drains water from the tub and places the towel on the toilet bowl lid. He stares at his nakedness in mirrored walls. He pulls in his washboard abs, then relaxes them to retract them and relax them once more. Satisfied with his appearance, he reaches for the door handle on the bathroom door.

Before he pulls the door open, a tingling sensation runs through his body. *Something's not right.*

Without waiting for another warning sign, Michael opens the door wide.

Steam rushes out of the bathroom and cold air flows into

it. Michael freezes in motion, as if attacked by the stinging drops of cold rain.

"I think this is yours."

With a terrified look, he stares at a figure that appears out of nowhere: a familiar face overgrown with a fast-graying beard, sleepless and bloodshot eyes, a smile filled with fatigue. Big fatigue, but still kind of lively, and with something else alarming that Michael doesn't want to remember.

Hank's eyes explore Michael's face for a moment, then his gaze slides down his son's naked body before looking into his eyes again.

Hank raises the hand in which he holds Michael's shorts and shoves them into his face.

In a split second, Michael realizes his mistake: his fully exposed nudity.

"Dad," he mutters in a muffled voice and grabs his boxers. He covers his privates, too upset to put them on.

Through a thin vapor dissolving around him, Hank stares at Michael. Tired eyes look alive. Smiling in a way Michael doesn't like.

"I didn't hear you coming . . ." Michael can hardly find the words. "I was in the jetted tub. I was tired," he is babbling, but he cannot help himself. The words now flow by themselves, unstoppable like a torrent. "Have you been here long? Need the bathroom?"

Hank makes a move with his hand and Michael steps back.

"I'm sorry about this, Michael." He touches the bruise on Michael's face.

Michael, this time, tolerates his touch without flinching.

"I didn't mean to hurt you. I'd like you to believe me. But you pissed me off . . ."

"Everything's fine, Dad. Really. You see? Soon it will be gone. And it doesn't hurt anymore."

"We always cooperated, you and me. Always." He continues to caress him as if he wants to remove the pain and restore the beauty of his son's face. "And all was good. Why did you defy me? Why were you *disobedient*?"

Nothing was good, if Michael was asked. Nothing. That's why he acted like that. That's why he stood up to him.

Trying to let him know that this will have to stop. (Another futile attempt.)

Trying to let him know that something will have to *change*. (Nothing has changed.)

Or things will go from bad to worse.

Hank will have to realize that Michael can no longer bear it. *(Perhaps this is the right time to explain it to him? His great opportunity to talk to his father as adults talk?)*

But Hank, as if reading his thoughts, says, "Can you imagine if Rebecca were home? What would it look like to *her*? What would she think of it? What would she think of *you*? Do you think she would understand?"

A good moment is gone. Like the jackpot in a card game, turned to dust.

Another opportunity disappears forever. Another attempt is useless, doomed. Michael's determination dissipates like steam outside the protective warmth of the bathroom.

Michael's shoulders sink and his indifference returns.

"Of course not," Hank continues uncompromisingly. "That's why we won't let such a situation happen again."

"No," Michael utters with effort.

Hank cups his face with both hands. "We'll cooperate again, won't we?"

"Yes . . ."

"Yes, what?"

"We will cooperate," Michael says submissively.

A smile lights up Hank's face.

"Did I ever tell you, Michael, that you have beautiful eyes? Did I ever tell you how much you look like your mother? Your mother was a beautiful woman. *Exceptionally* beautiful. Too beautiful and too delicate for this world. And too good. Just like you.

"Unfortunately, she didn't make it. She wasn't strong enough. But that won't happen to you. That won't happen to *us*. You and I, we will *survive*. We have to because of Rebecca. And because of your mother. She was the only woman I truly loved in my life. I don't want to let go of that love just like that. Neither should you. Because I love you like I used to love your mother. . . ."

He kisses him.

Michael doesn't move away from him, nor does he return the kiss.

"Get dressed before you catch a cold. Go now. I need to take a shower before I get back to work."

Michael steps aside from the bathroom door and lets him in.

He jumps into his boxers and gathers the remaining clothes.

"Michael?"

"Yes, Dad?" He turns around. Hank is standing in the same place where Michael had stood a few moments ago, stark naked, too.

"Your pancakes are in the microwave. I put them there to keep them warm for you."

"Thanks, Dad."

"You're welcome."

The bathroom door closes.

Seconds later, a song comes from behind them.

* * *

"He went?"

"He's just leaving." Michael waves goodbye to Hank on his way back to work.

"Tonight," Hank forms a word with his lips, and Michael nods absently. He leaves fifteen minutes after Juanita, leaving Michael alone in the company of Rebecca, who watches him on the screen from distant Denver, and Sergio Unit—a confidential witness to their conversation.

"Daddy's all right?" she asks him, as if she doesn't trust her father's sweet words and fresh, but tired looks.

"He is. Mostly. He works a lot."

"He looks *drained* to me."

"He didn't sleep a wink last night. He spent all night in the lab."

"It's crazy! I don't like it. How are you?"

"Me? I'm fine," he tells a lie. "I was skating, and I made a total fool of myself. You should have seen me! I spent the night at Alien's. All in all, I can't complain."

"What's on your face? I don't remember you having it the last time we spoke."

"That's nothing. *Just a scratch*, as Mercutio would say. I slipped while grinding a *50-50* on the rail. It's much better now."

"You're bats, Michael! You will kill yourself one day. I

don't understand how Dad lets you skate after this?"

"Like he can stop me! You know he can't. I would still skate, no matter what he said. At least I don't have to explain to you how much skating means to me."

"I thought I understood you. I'm not sure about that anymore."

"You don't understand me because you are not a skater. That's the thing."

"Thank God for that! If I have to look like you do now, then I'd rather miss the pleasure."

"You didn't understand me. I'm not ashamed of the bruises. They come in a package. There is no *progress* without them. If you don't get hurt here and there, you can't be good enough. Injuries are not for *posers*! And I'm not a poser. If I have to pay the price to skate well, that's okay. I can live with that. I can accept that. So one day, when I'm too old to skate, I can look myself in the eye. Got it?"

"Do you really believe in what you said now?"

Michael sighs. Rebecca is a tough one. *(Just like him, sometimes.)* He tries a different approach.

"Why do you like to ride?"

"That's not the same!" she protests. "You can't compare that! Riding is *healthy*. It benefits the body. You're in fresh air."

"And skateboarding is not? When you skate, you are not in the fresh air?"

"If the smog and various vapors are fresh air for you, with cops chasing you around every corner, then yes, you're in the fresh air."

Michael smiles.

"I'm not afraid of those flatfeet. Cops on inline skates? Where do you see such a thing in the normal world?"

"Where? Everywhere, dear brother. Everywhere. From New York to Amsterdam and Melbourne. As if you don't know yourself!"

"That's *sick*. Any skateboarder who holds his reputation dear will tell you the same."

"Admit it! It's inline skates that bothers you, not that they chase you from everywhere."

"And what if that's true? If they're such tough guys, why don't they keep order on skateboards? Inline skaters don't exist. They're all skateboarders in their heart, they just don't have the guts to skate the board."

"You're impossible!"

"I'm your brother."

"Please, don't remind me!"

"I love you, too, sis."

"Asshole!" Rebecca laughs. "You know, you're not that bad, after all."

"What do you mean?" Michael laughs too.

"In fact, some people think you're pretty cool with those pants down so you can see what kind of boxer shorts you're wearing."

"What people?" Michael gapes in disbelief.

"Girls in my class. They go crazy when you walk past them. They say they would like to lick you."

"Really?" he exclaims. "Which ones? I want their names!"

"No way!"

"What else did they say?"

"Forget it! But I have to admit to them they are right." She moves closer to the screen.

"Sis, you don't have the hots for me, do you?" He does the same, putting his fingers on the screen.

"Of course not, you silly!"

The touch of their fingers, an invisible connection between them. And static electricity.

"It's a shame."

"Pervert!"

"I am not!"

"Yes, you are!"

"I'm not." His gaze is absent, a deep focus on his face.

"Michael, is something wrong?"

"Uh-huh?"

"Michael, are you okay?"

"Yeah. It's just . . . I think I feel something."

"What are you talking about?"

"I feel the expectation about you. The challenge of the unknown. Something happened— Something is happening. You met someone or you will meet someone. I see an encounter . . ."

Rebecca's smile is gone. She stops breathing for a moment. She holds her breath for so long that she thinks she will suffocate.

(Is he playing games with her? How could he know? Grandma and Grandpa didn't tell him anything, she's sure. Michael didn't talk to them. It's all weird. Very weird.)

Then, "What are you talking about?" *(How much does he really know?)*

Michael's face changes again. It is completely relaxed. *Now his eyes have a different glow*, Rebecca notices.

Nervously, "Michael!"

"Baked apples . . . I smell the baked apples."

Rebecca whips around in her chair and almost falls.

In the kitchen, behind her back, Jeremy Creek is baking

apples.

She stares back at her brother's smiling face, her eyes wide in disbelief.

He had to see Grandpa wandering around in the kitchen, she concludes. *There's a reasonable explanation for this.*

"What is funny?"

"You, Rebecca. You're funny. You look like you saw a ghost."

"Well . . . I'll see one soon if you don't start looking after yourself."

"I'll be careful. Don't *worry*." He knows the conversation is coming to its end. "Are you going for a ride?"

"Yes."

"I won't hold you back then. I'll talk to you again, okay?"

"Tomorrow. Call me again tomorrow."

"I will. Can I talk to Grandfather and Grandmother now? I'd like to say hello."

"Sure. They'll be glad to see you. They were sad when you didn't come. They still hope."

"I told you. You know how it is—"

"Yes, I know. Not enough asphalt to skate. But given that they predict a cold wave from the north with a chance of snow, you will have no excuse this time."

"Snow is coming? In *August?*"

"The latest news. It's already snowing in Canada."

"Sounds interesting. Summer on the snowboard," he teases her.

"You're a real asshole, I have to admit. Really."

"I was kidding! Besides, I can board in Colorado, just like anywhere else."

"You only think of yourself! I hate you!" She sticks her

tongue out at him and calls her grandfather. She leaves him waiting in front of a blank screen.

She puts on her boots and slips into her jacket. She takes her riding hat and pauses for a moment, thinking. *Maybe a beanie would be more appropriate given the weather forecast?*

Michael's voice beckons to her, and she returns to the computer to greet his grinning face.

"It would be nice to change the water of the roses before you go out. The yellow roses you picked today are really beautiful."

Rebecca gasps with astonishment. Blood rushes to her head. (Her cheeks turn the color of red roses.) She tries to say something, but cries out in a high-pitched voice, "Grandpa! Get yourself over here already! Michael's waiting for you!"

A little too loud.

A little too hysterical.

She runs out of the house, forgetting to change the water of the roses.

Chapter

4th: . . . is at 90 degrees. Lift your back leg up. Level out. Swing the tail the rest of the way with the toes of your back foot. Ride in the direction you want to go. This goes for the *regular-footed* riders—skateboarders who ride with their left foot forward on their board. Those who ride with their . . .

THE ATKINSES' ESTATE IS SOME FIVE MILES east of the Creeks' estate. Rebecca, like a fury, gallops to the west. *Not caring* what her grandmother will tell her when she returns.

She's too upset to think about it. Everything is boiling in her and she needs someone (or something) to vent.

Rebecca is *mad* at Michael. He used to play his silly games with her, but this time he crossed every line. *(Yellow roses!)*

She could buy the thing with the apples. There is a *logical* explanation for that. He saw Grandpa, so he knew. But he *couldn't* see the yellow roses. And yet he knew.

He knew.

Disoriented and faster than an atom splitting, she loses track of time. Her gaze clouds from the sharp, biting wind so she can see almost nothing. Just outlines. Only blurs.

But she doesn't stop. Nor does she slow down.

She keeps on riding.

Not caring.

She remembers Michael told her something about an encounter. True, she had the encounter yesterday. But *how* could he know about that?!

She has no idea what to think about it or how to interpret Michael's . . . *visions*. Yes, *visions*!

She pulls the reins and almost flips over the mare's neck when she halts in her track. The kiss of death misses her by a fraction, but Rebecca seems unaware of it. Overcome with a surge of new emotions, her thoughts are elsewhere, with Michael.

"Oh, Michael, you fool!" she whispers with fear, and lopes Vanity back toward the ranch.

* * *

Thousands of miles to the east, Alien is speeding through the streets of New Queens, jamming his bicycle pedals to deliver his last pizza on time before taking a break. He is making his way through the traffic, which crawls in comparison to him. About eight minutes ago, he got rid of two persistent cops who chased him a full, four blocks on their rollerblades, because of his suicidal ride, before they gave up. It was not until the end of the fourth block that they conceded defeat and Alien then triumphantly flew forward at the speed of light, disappearing from their sight.

This little NYPD adventure steals his precious time, so he will have to make up for the delay in delivery any way he knows and can: either out of his own pocket or once again to decide on a crazy and perilous ride, in which case he might get arrested so it will be out of his pocket again.

Deciding to take a chance, Alien chooses the second option and delivers the pizza on time.

And, more importantly, he doesn't have to reach into his pocket.

Radiating with complacency, he thanks the customer for the tip with a wide smile and takes a well-deserved rest. The return to Little Italy for tired Alien seems terribly long, too great a challenge for his strained muscles. He curses the client for which he has traveled over half of the city to deliver him a pizza. But the balding fatso has been their best customer so far, and according to the frequency of calls from a new neighborhood east of the East River, where he recently moved, he intends to keep that status. Although he is burning with a low, blue flame when the *fatso with his fat tips* opens the door wearing a silk, burgundy robe, Alien's face glows with a broad smile that earns him the fattest tip so far. Nevertheless, it is a bloody deal, and Alien won't mind if he doesn't get such a *special* delivery in the next few millennia. Across the East River, New Manhattan is still unreachable, like the sun obscured by the heavy clouds and the grayness of the day.

(What a change compared to last night's clear night sky!)

So much for summer. The thought flies through the void in his head.

Then he unzips his overalls covered in Pizza Martinelli stickers to his belt and turns the baseball cap with the same name sewn on it backwards. He turns on a brand-new, silver, Sony Discman and the music mutates to a roar in his ears. An absent look in his eyes, he listens to it for a while, and then he jerks like a suddenly awakened zombie. He zips himself up and, without turning the music down, mounts his bicycle and heads toward Vernon Boulevard.

The incident, which then occurs in one of the side streets, forces Alien to forget how tired he is and how far his destination is—New Manhattan.

The two, surviving members of the almost extinct punkers tribe are knocking about two kid skateboarders. They take their skateboards, trying to ride them on their own, but it is a very short ride. As soon as they put both of their feet on them, they crash hard, with a repertoire of obscene curses that Alien's ears have never heard of before.

On their feet again, they take out their anger on the boards. They kick them with their heavy worker's shoes and hurl the boards at the walls of the houses, trying to break them.

Stiff with fear, the little skateboarders stand aside while saying goodbye to their expensive skateboards. And when they already saw them busted and broken into pieces, something yellow flashes past them and swoops down on the punkers. Like a pogrom. Like *Armageddon*.

"Hey, kiddos, *help* me out a little?! These are your boogie-boards."

Both boys jump as if on command and close ranks with an enraged Alien, who is frantically throwing blows everywhere.

The closer kid jumps onto the back of the first punker, allowing Alien to thwack the second bully. Both the punker and the little skater lose their balance and fall on their backs. The punker grabs the skater who is tugging at him by his Iroquois haircut, but his friend comes to his rescue. Mightily and expertly he smashes the punker with the skateboard over the head. Only the *THUD*. With a brief, force-cut half-sigh, the punker disappears into the land of dreams.

At the same time, Alien is working on his buddy. With a few, well-placed punches to his ribs, he forces him to eat some dust from the dirty asphalt and leaves him there only when he is sure he is no longer a threat to anyone. The three skaters take a quick flight, followed by howls for help from a punker who is waking up from fainting.

"Ugh! Thank you, man. You saved us," the boy with the ruffled blond hair says to Alien. "I thought they would *finish* us."

"It probably would be like that, once they're done with your boogie-boards," Alien says without false modesty. He lights a cigarette and offers it to the tousle-headed boy, who accepts it before Alien changes his mind.

The other skater refuses. With a big smile on his face, he eyes Alien from head to toe, and says importantly, "But Pizza Martinelli showed them who's the boss here."

"Cheers to Pizza Martinelli!" they both shout.

"I'm sorry I couldn't save your boogie-board too," Alien says to the non-smoker. He takes the skateboard from him and looks at it closely. "The axles have not been damaged, and the wheels are still in good condition. But if you want my advice, the next time you buy a deck, take AWS with a bigger concave. You'll love the way it rotates when you pop it."

"You skate?" The blond kid is surprised. He blows out a puff of smoke and graces Alien's bike with a suspicious look.

"I skate," Alien replies to him. "You want me to show you?"

"Yeah, *sure*. Just try not to crack my board," he says a little mockingly. "I haven't had it for two weeks. It's *new*."

"Don't worry, it will stay *new*." Alien flicks a cigarette and crushes it out with his DVS shoe. "I'll be *gentle*."

He grabs the board, rolls away and does the *nollie*, the *inward varial heelflip*, and the *feeble grind* on the curb. He rolls back to them.

"I can do that!" the blond mophead complains, not too impressed. *Big deal!*

"Oh yeah?" Alien frowns at the challenge. "And can you do this?"

It happens very fast. Alien is spinning and jumping like a deer on the run. Supple and technically flawless. This time he starts the *line* with the *frontside kickflip to fakie 50-50*, and continues it with the *switch-stance 360 kickflip*, the *smith grind*, and the *Turk* he performs over the bike.

He screeches the wheels to a halt in front of the bewildered kids.

"Wow!" exclaims the skater with the broken deck. "*This* is what I call skateboarding! Awesome! Where did you learn that? Are you a *pro*?"

"Nah, I'm not a professional," Alien replies. "I'm not interested in that."

He returns the board to the mophead and pulls the visor of the baseball cap over the kid's eyes.

He mounts the bike.

"What's your name?" the blond skater asks cautiously, unable to conceal the glow in the corners of his eyes that give off how impressed he is. He turns the board in his hands, eying it. *He did it on my board?*

"Alien. Guys, why don't you drop by at Union Square or Washington Park sometimes? I'll be happy to show you more tricks."

"Alien? Is that your *name*?" the boy with ruffled hair asks suspiciously.

"Now that you mention it, I might just legalize it." Alien grins and disappears.

Quickly and suddenly, just as he entered their lives less than forty minutes ago.

* * *

The sky is building up to a storm. Rare drops combine to form a light rain that quickly thickens and turns into a downpour. Now it is raining cats and dogs. The gusts of wind are ruthless, the strong wind ice-cold.

She stands in a clearing, soaked wet and chilled to the bones (the same goes for her mare), her eyes fixed on a small ranch behind which the evergreen forest rises. A crystal-clear streamlet creeps next to it, and not far from it lies a frost-covered vegetable garden.

Slightly askance to the south and separated from the main building with a big yard, is the barn.

And the Lincoln Navigator, parked in front of it.

So, this is the place where the Atkinses live, Rebecca thinks. *Newcomers from the south who don't allow their children to attend school and deny them the education necessary for survival in this world.*

This is where people who have chosen isolation live, hiding from the rest of the world as if it is infected by a deadly virus. Like members of some crazy sect.

This is the place where she finds herself riding, in the worst weather, forced to seek refuge with *these* people.

Someone shows up at the back door. An unrecognizable silhouette, head to toe wrapped in a raincoat, runs across the yard and into the barn.

Thunder rumbles the sky, and Vanity rears up. Whispering soothing words in her ear, Rebecca hurries to the barn. She gets the creeps from the thought she will have to ask these people for help. If she were alone, she would have made it somehow to her grandparents' ranch. But she isn't alone, she has to think about Vanity.

She reaches the barn entrance and slides out of the saddle. She calls out, "Hello? Is anyone there? Good afternoon?"

Mooing of a cow answers from the dark inside, accompanied by some rustling.

Rebecca takes a step, two, and stops. She waits for her eyes to adjust to the darkness, focusing her gaze on something that resembles a human shadow.

She repeats, "Good afternoon? Excuse me. My mare and I got lost. We were riding when the storm came."

The shadow moves and Rebecca startles. Her eyes wide with fear, she muffles a scream and staggers back.

"For God's sake, Miss, get out of that rain!" the shadow says, and grabs the reins of her mare. Unlike Rebecca, Vanity shows no fear of the stranger, but allows him to take her into the shelter of the barn.

"Sorry if I scared you. It was not my intention," the stranger apologizes, unsaddling Vanity. "You have a beautiful thoroughbred mare, if I may notice. How old is she, two years? What's her name?"

"Vanity," Rebecca finally finds words to respond. "She's a two-year-and-two-month-old Dutch Thoroughbred. How did you know?"

The stranger laughs warmly.

"I love horses," he answers simply. "I love horses a lot. Miss, if I may, why don't you take shelter in the house? You can have my raincoat. I'll take care of your horse. There is no point in freezing here. You will be much more comfortable in the house."

Rebecca wants to object, but the mention of the house, the warmth, and perhaps the large fireplace from which the nice smell of burning wood is spreading reminds her how wet and cold she is. "Thank you. You are very kind. I can wait for you."

"Nonsense! You go ahead. Tell Mom, I'm sending you."

Then he comes out of the shadows and approaches her. And only after a series of flashes of lightning Rebecca gets a clear picture of the stranger's appearance. Young face, fair skin, very young face, curly hair, and dark-blue eyes.

The boy in front of her cannot be older than her brother Michael.

The boy introduces himself, "My name is Red Sunshine. My folks call me Sunny. They say, whenever it's hard or they're sad, they only need to look for a smile on my face and the world is a much better place for them." He shrugs and gives her the smile he was just talking about.

It is a special smile. Big smile. A warm and genuine smile that reminds Rebecca of the summer sun, enchanting her. She just can't resist it.

She returns the smile—Red Sunshine's smile—and says, "I'm Rebecca. And I'm pleased to meet you." She shakes hands with him, but refuses to take his raincoat. "You keep it. I'm soaked wet. It will hardly be of any use to me."

"As you wish. See you later in the house." His smile is glowing in the darkness of the barn.

"Yes," Rebecca gleefully acknowledges and runs in big strides across the yard.

(I see an encounter ... The challenge of the unknown ...)

Lightning strikes somewhere in the woods. The wind brings the smell of the burned moist earth.

Rebecca skips a puddle of water at the foot of the stairs and jumps onto the porch. She turns back and looks at the barn once more before she knocks at the door and enters without waiting for an invitation.

Just like in her own house.

* * *

They are in the living room. Rebecca swings gently in the rocking chair in front of the fireplace; next to her on the thick carpet is Gentle Wind—Sunny's youngest brother. He is seven years old. In the two-seater opposite them are Louise and Ted Atkins, and Sunny and blond and blue-eyed Blue Sky Atkins occupy the only two armchairs in the house. Blue Sky is ten, and he is five years younger than his older brother, Red Sunshine.

Looking at these three remarkable boys, Rebecca has to admit how well these unusual names, given to them by their calm, withdrawn, and above all kind parents, match them. It is as if they had always known what their children would be like once they grew up.

Red Sunshine: a redhead, young man with rich curls and an angelic smile; Blue Sky: a beautiful child with azure eyes and almost completely white hair is the sharpest and most curious of all brothers; and Gentle Wind: gentle like the breeze and refreshingly sweet and cuddly.

At the end of dinner, while everyone else was sitting at the table, he left his chair and climbed into Rebecca's lap. This unexpected act of intimacy made Rebecca blush and the rest of the Atkins family laugh. But Rebecca kept the boy in her lap when Louise Atkins wanted to send him back to his seat.

An hour later, Gentle Wind is again purring like a kitten beside Rebecca's feet, waiting for the right moment to crawl again into her lap. Rebecca smiles at him and that is enough. The boy is all over her, stroking her neck with his little hands and playing with the curls of her hair.

Her prejudices melt like ice cubes grilled in the scorching sun. From sentence to sentence, every new thought expressed, Rebecca is being won over. Her sharpness, sarcasm, and willingness to quarrel with her hosts in defense of justice are completely numbed. She is ashamed of herself. And of human nature. So ready for condemnation and excommunication, so unwilling to show understanding.

As if she is part of the family, these *outcasts, fanatics,* and *weirdos* have welcomed Rebecca into their home, with all her convictions and beliefs. The guilty feeling tears her apart, and the pine smells so fine. . . .

Caressing the boy's brown hair in response to his gentle touches, Rebecca's gaze meets Red Sunshine's gaze. The young man's eyes adore her. His hair is like a torch, lit by the fire of the hearth and oil lamps. The air is filled with the smell of firewood and resin bleeding from the walls lined with wood. In this atmosphere he looks like the embodiment of a deity from Native American legends.

She wants to give his clothes back on leaving, his pants and shirt, a little too big for her, but pleasantly warm. He refuses to take them; her clothes aren't dry yet. "Next time," he says. "I'll see you again, won't I?" *Of course he'll see her*, she doesn't doubt it at all. Not in the least.

It is hard for her to get out of the car when they reach her home. So hard to say goodbye, even only for a short while.

It is not easy to accept reality again.

She still knows little about the Atkinses. Many questions are still waiting to be answered. Many unknowns remain hidden behind this encounter. Only one thing is certain.

Rebecca loves the Atkinses. There is no doubt about that. And that is all she cares about, no matter what others say or think.

"Thank you for the ride. And everything," Rebecca thanks Ted Atkins.

"Thank you, Rebecca, for enriching this day for all of us."

She blushes. She is glad it is getting dark, albeit a little too quickly—if someone asked her. She has so much more to tell them.

"You are always welcome in our home," he encourages her. "Whenever you want, come by."

"And you don't have to wait for the rain to catch you again while riding," Sunny says, unable to take his eyes off her eyes. "The blessing of the sun can have even more beautiful charms."

"I have no doubt at all. May this blessing be with you this night." She feels so different, so *poetic* and spiritual in his presence.

"Thank you, Rebecca." Red Sunshine takes a bow. "Say hello to your grandparents. I hope they didn't worry too much. Will you excuse us for holding you so much?"

"If anyone held anyone, then it was me. I enjoyed your company. I'll be glad to see you again."

Sunshine's eyes give her one last shine in the descending night. "Me too."

"Give a hug to Wind for me."

"I will."

She wants to say more, but unties Vanity from the trailer

hook and heads for the house. Why spoil the night and ruin this moment of magic with superfluous words?

The windows are illuminated, waiting for her. She greets them with a tired smile, leading Vanity on the reins of memories, visions, and unspoken hopes.

(She must first tell her grandparents she has arrived, and that nothing has happened to her.)

The Lincoln drives into the night.

(Then she'll take care of her mare.)

Its lights are gone.

(And then she will call her father and tell him all about the blessings and beauties of life, but also about the seeds of the curse from which they sprang.)

She hopes it isn't too late.

Chapter

5th: . . . right foot forward (like me) are *goofy-footed* riders. There are also *mongo* riders—who push their board with the front leg. If you pop the nose instead of the tail of the board with your *front* foot, you *nollie*. What do you need to grind? Just pop on and grind with your trucks along any . . .

MICHAEL IS CONFUSED. HE KNOWS how much Rebecca loves roses. He knows she loves them a *lot*, as did her mother. Of all the flowers, Melanie Hope loved roses the most. To her, all the roses were precious. She enjoyed each species with the same passion and equal fervor. But not Rebecca. Rebecca loves yellow roses the most. To her, yellow roses are *especially* endearing.

Knowing how much Rebecca loves them, he told her not to forget to put them in fresh water. He didn't need to be a super genius to put two and two together. He used his noggin and came to an easy conclusion: sooner or later his sister would decorate a table with them, if she hadn't done so by now.

An inner voice warned him to remind her about the

flowers, because Rebecca seemed somewhat distracted. Not so much to arouse suspicion, but she was more distracted than usual.

And yes, he wanted to tease her a little—he admits. He thinks he didn't go too far despite her reaction.

(He hurt her, he hurt her a lot.)

(He was a real bastard!)

At first, nothing was clear to him. He wanted to apologize to her, but she scrammed so fast. He didn't call her later; it was stupid to call her just to say he was sorry. The more he ponders it, the less clear Rebecca's reaction is. In the end, he decides that she is the one who overreacted. *She* didn't get the joke.

Truth to be told, Michael didn't want to be mean to her. They had been in similar situations before, and everything turned out well. Good God, they were in much worse situations than this and Rebecca wasn't so angry. *(What happened this time? What got into her?)* There must be something else.

(She must have been keyed up because of something. Maybe she was thinking about Mom's death again? Maybe there was too much past, too many fond memories in Denver?)

He misses their mother too. Although he is an older child, he loved his mother too. And he also lost her. He could hardly accept the abyss of the void that had taken her place.

And changed Rebecca's and his life. Both had to face a new reality, with or without help from the side.

Michael didn't ask for help. But he was ready to help Rebecca whenever he needed to.

And he was helping her. As much as he could and the best he knew.

And he will help her in the future. To the best of his ability and as much as Rebecca will allow him.

But he won't apologize for something that isn't his fault. His mother's death isn't his fault. Melanie Hope died because she was ill. Although there are moments when he is no longer sure of that. There are times when everything seems artificial and different to him. Like a distorted picture of reality.

(Why is Rebecca so angry with him?)

* * *

Victor is waiting for him at the agreed location at the agreed time. Seeing the expression on his friend's face, Michael concludes they are the perfect couple. Both of them sullen and with anxiety at heart.

Michael can guess what Victor is going through now. Although he doesn't have a grandmother in the nursing home, Michael understands his situation.

They get caught in the pell-mell at the infirmary at St. Mary's Heart nursing home. The nursing isn't done yet. The hastiness (or rather, the slowness) all over the place.

Fortunately, room 508 in which Victor's grandmother lies is ready.

(Or not?)

Angela Kenneth's diaper is full, so a volunteer is required to change them. Again.

"Nana, do you need to go to the toilet?" Victor asks her, even though she already had an accident. He knows what to do; it is not his first time.

"I could," she replies in a shy whisper.

Expecting such an answer, Victor gets to work. He pulls his grandmother out of bed, takes a new diaper from her closet, and walks her to the bathroom.

"Do you need help?" Michael offers.

"No, but thank you. We'll be back in a minute."

"You're his friend?" an old lady lying in bed by the balcony door asks Michael.

"I am," Michael replies, with one ear listening to Victor having trouble with his grandmother.

"He is a fine young man. He comes every day."

"Yes, I know."

"A very nice young man," the old lady repeats. "Excuse me, if you do not mind, would you be so kind as to give me my pills? I can't reach them," she says in a low voice that chokes with self-pity.

"Of course," Michael says enthusiastically, happy to be of some use. He feels stupid standing idly while Victor is stuck sweating in the bathroom. "Did you mean these?"

"Yes, yes, please."

"You want me to get them out of your bottle?"

"No need, thanks. I can do that myself." She reaches for the bottle, fishes two pills from it, and swallows them with freshly squeezed orange juice.

Michael returns the bottle to its place. "Do you need anything else?"

"Ah," the old woman sighs. A faint glow in her eyes behind the blurry gaze. "I wouldn't want to bother you, but my pillows are not good. The nurses again messed them all up. They are so snappish; you don't dare to ask them anything. If you don't mind, would you lift them up a little?"

"Like this?" Michael says obligingly.

"A little more, please."

"Better now?"

"Much better. Thank you. You are very kind."

"No trouble at all," Michael gives her a smile of understanding.

The bathroom door opens, and Victor comes out, supporting his grandmother from behind under her arms. He takes her to the bed and changes her into a dressing gown.

"Good girl," he praises her. "Shall we take a walk now?"

Michael isn't sure if he is referring to him as well, but he follows them anyway.

"I see you've been busy," Victor comments. "Mrs. Hilde jumped at the opportunity."

"Oh, that? That was nothing. I just gave her some pills and helped her with her pillows."

"Come here more often and then you'll tell me."

"She seems nice to me."

"I didn't say she isn't nice, don't get me wrong. It's just, there are days I'm sick 'n tired of everything. Today, for example, I'm not in the mood for anybody's crap. If you know what I want to say."

Michael nods in understanding.

"Victor, can we slow down? My legs hurt."

"Nana, you know who I am!" Victor cheers up.

"Why wouldn't I know?" Angela Kenneth is amazed.

Victor slows down almost to a stop. "What am I to you? Come on, don't disappoint me now!"

"You know that quite well yourself!" she replies cunningly.

Michael almost laughs, but he gets a grip on himself.

"You're right. *I* know," Victor isn't giving up either, "but I want to hear that from *you*."

"You are my *graaandson*. You thought I was senile, you rascal!"

This is too much for Michael, so he bursts out laughing.

His laughter is contagious and in no time Victor and his grandmother are laughing along with him.

There are moments like this in this sad place. As strange as it may seem, laughter still hasn't died here, no matter how shy and rare it is.

* * *

Victor finishes talking to Sylvia, a young nurse in her early twenties from Jersey City. Sylvia thought about finding a new job as soon as she graduated. She doesn't see her future in a nursing home ruled by honey-mouthed but resolute nuns. Victor understands her. But he is still sorry she is leaving.

Candid Camera is on TV, Victor's grandmother and Michael, together with several other old men, are having a good time. Victor slides into the armchair next to his friend and whispers in his ear, "They changed her therapy. With these new drugs she should be more lucid."

Michael nods.

"Sylvia says that Nana has been depressed lately. She constantly complains of pain. Unfortunately, this is common in her age."

"What about depression?" Michael asks.

Victor shrugs. "It's all connected."

"And they can't do anything about it?"

"I'm afraid not—"

"Whee-m-I?"

"What the . . . ?!" Startled, Michael turns to the stench that bursts into his face. Unconsciously, he protects his nose with his hand, concealing a grimace of disgust.

"Whee-m-I?" The almost bald woman bends over him and

smacks her lips dangerously close to Michael's face. Her thin, wrinkled hands full of age spots clench her rumpled wig.

"You're in the nursing home, ma'am!" Michael squeaks, desperately controlling the bile arising from the bad breath coming out of her mouth. It is a disgusting stench of rot and decay, strong enough to kill even the dead, and Michael has nowhere to go.

"Whee?"

"In the nursing home!" he snaps at her, trying to shoo her off. To no avail. Until Victor saves him from falling victim to bad breath suffocation. Not only his friend saves his dear life, he saves his reputation as well.

In a cool manner, he satisfies the confused curiosity of the lost woman.

"In five hundred nine. You are in room five hundred nine," he repeats to make sure she understands him. "Down the hall on the left." He glances at Michael. The old woman moves away, and Michael is free to breathe again.

"In five hundred nine?" she asks, still a little confused.

"Yes. In five hundred nine," Victor repeats patiently.

"Thank you very much." She bows slightly and steps aside. She puts the wig askew on her head and takes under the arm the other old woman, who claps her hands nervously. Slipping her arm under hers, she reports, "Five hundred nine." Without fixing her wig.

"Five hundred nine," echoes her girlfriend and claps her hands twice.

"Five hundred nine," they repeat together just in case, lest they forget the number until they get there.

"I admire your nerves," Michael says, gathering himself.

Victor smiles absently at him. "There's nothing to admire,

dude. It's easier this way. Trying to ignore them is even worse. You answer them, and they leave you alone. At least for a while."

"Yeah, they can be a real nuisance. Not that it's their fault. They are not aware how much they can irritate a person."

"Fortunately for them! That's why we can't blame them. I just hope it doesn't happen to me when I'm old. I don't want to reach that age. I don't want to *go around the bend* one day, Michael. I'd rather die young and sane."

"I see eye to eye with you about this," Michael replies with a serious look.

* * *

It's lunchtime, and Michael and Victor take Angela Kenneth to her room. They sit her on the bed and Victor puts a napkin under her chin so she won't get her nightgown dirty while feeding her. Just in time, he gives her some juice as lunch arrives.

And new problems with it.

"Nana, open your mouth, please. You have to eat."

"You eat!" Angela Kenneth says resolutely, not relenting.

"I'll eat later. Michael and I will have lunch after I feed you. Come on, open your mouth . . ."

Angela Kenneth cracks her mouth open like a little bird and snaps it closed. "I don't like it! It has no taste."

"It's not true! The soup smells nice. You like to eat soup. Look how savory it is." He brings the spoon to her mouth.

"Then eat it if you like it so much!"

Michael roars with laughter at her remark. "Do you want me to try?" he asks Victor. "Maybe she'll listen to me."

"Do you think you can?"

"I can try."

"Ah, never mind. I'll do it." Victor shakes his head. "Come on, Nana. Be a good girl and open your mouth. That's it."

Another spoon gets in. It's time for the next one.

"Mrs. Kenneth," Michael says in good faith, "you must eat. Otherwise, you'll weaken and get sick. You won't be able to get out of bed at all."

"So what?" she brushes him off curtly. Her tongue is like a blade, and Michael is speechless. He gives up further attempts to reason with her.

Unlike him, Victor doesn't think about surrendering. He makes a serious face and commands, "Open your mouth, please. More!"

He runs out of patience; it can be felt in his voice, which has no tolerance for complaints.

Angela Kenneth opens her mouth, frowning. She doesn't like Victor's tone. She doesn't like lunch either. But she listens to him anyway.

Victor feeds her a spoonful of soup with a piece of crumbled and soaked bread swimming in it, waiting already with a new spoon as she slowly chews and swallows.

"If we could at least distract her from food," Michael thinks aloud.

Victor muses for a moment, and then it strikes him. "Do you have Rimbaud?"

"I do. Why?"

"Read it!"

Michael gapes in protest. "But it's in French!"

"I know French, *cher ami*." An old woman in the bed next to the door wakes up from her world. Michael and Victor look at the poor creature. For six years she had been lying like that without getting out of bed. Her back is covered with open wounds, which nurses treat every morning. It is painful, but Mrs. Lipton isn't aware of it. Rare are the moments when she flees the land of the senile to a world of the sane, like now.

"That's terrific," Victor praises her. "The more reason Michael reads us something. But since the rest of us don't know French, we will ask him to read us an English translation."

Michael looks at him in surprise. *How did you know?!*

I'm not a total ignorant, Victor's eyes answer.

"Well, if you insist." He reaches into his backpack and sighs. He flips through Rimbaud's *Collected Poems* and begins reading "The Bridges."

As the melody of Rimbaud's poem fills the room, Angela Kenneth's resistance weakens. She looks at Michael as enchanted, munching French potato salad and mechanically opening and closing her mouth.

Finishing the poem, Michael flips the pages in reverse and picks a new one. Encouraged by silence of approval, he pauses on page 105 and slowly, clearly, and with lots of emotion reads his favorite poem "The Sleeper in the Valley."

After a few verses, Angela Kenneth nods to the rhythm of his voice, experiencing the poem and accepting the fate of the soldier with the seriousness of a fully conscious person.

The poem is short, and when Michael finishes reading it, Angela Kenneth calms down. However, she keeps watching him, as in expectation.

"Very nice, my friend," Victor thanks him and peels the pear—his grandmother's dessert.

"Wonderful, young man," agrees Mrs. Hilde. "You have a gift for poetry."

"Did you really like it?" Michael is bursting with pride.

"Absolutely." Victor grins broadly at him. "We liked it so much, you'll have to read another one so Nana can finish her dessert."

"I'd be glad to, but my head is starting to hurt—"

"One more," Angela Kenneth makes herself heard, and everyone stares at her. "One more," she repeats, her eyes fixed on Michael.

"I don't think I will be able to refuse this request," Michael says, sighs, and opens the book at random.

He barely glances at the text before reciting it. He knows this poem by heart.

> *"I defy you, winds!*
> *Color the sky with voluptuous sounds of trumpets*
> *the day I die and become one of you!*
> *Pave heaven with laughter and tears*
> *so the morning that dawns, dawns with clarity and joy*
> *Of precious memories that I've left behind to walk into*
> *A new day."*

Silence fills room 508 when Michael completes his recital. All are moved to tears.

Victor is the first to say something. "Powerful and deep. I like it."

Then he turns to his grandmother. "Do you need me to take you to the toilet before I go?"

"I don't need to," she replies, still staring at Michael. "Will you come tomorrow?" she asks.

Michael is surprised. "Of course. I'd be happy to come."

"We'll come together." Victor winks at him.

I owe you one. His eyes fill with gratitude.

* * *

"That wasn't fair of you, bro. That wasn't fair at all."

"Why?" Michael says, troubled. "You think they noticed something?"

"They? I don't think so. But that's not what I meant. It's not fair you made them cry."

"Oh, that. They are too sensitive." He waves his hand.

"*They* are too sensitive? What about you, then?"

"You knew right away, didn't you?" Michael's smile flashes.

"Yeah, I knew it right away. It wasn't difficult to figure out it wasn't Rimbaud at the end."

"I didn't know the poem was so different."

"That's not the point. A little too *accidentally* you came across such an impressive poem."

"That means you liked it?"

"Of course I liked it. Didn't I say so?"

"Well, let's say you did, but not directly. Thank you. It means a lot to me."

"Just don't get too excited over it or you'll be watching my back all the way to Battery Park." He jumps on his skateboard and rolls down the street, with Michael five pushes of the board trailing behind.

They chase each other down Pacific Street, Boerum Place, and Borough Hall. They slow down on the Old Brooklyn Bridge, but still cause commotion and frighten the wits out of pedestrians walking over the East River. They continue riding along South Street Seaport and all the way to Battery Park at the tip of New Manhattan, only to run into Ian, Stu, and Andy at Police Plaza.

Ian is catching his breath, panting. "The cops were on our heels until five minutes ago! We gave them the slip by a hair's breadth."

"You should've seen Andy! He played with one cop until he crashed into a limo!" Stu says, gesturing wildly.

"Well," Victor says with regret, "you cannot always be Johnny-on-the-spot."

"So, where were the two of you?" Andy asks. "I doubt you were picking flowers."

"You got that right." Victor glances at Michael. "We had a little fun on the other side of the river." He points to New Brooklyn. "Watch the evening news, guys. Maybe they'll say something about the tornado hitting the Old Brooklyn Bridge."

"My men!" Stu slips them five. "What are you up to now?"

"Nothing special," Michael says. "We were thinking of maybe cruising around Downtown."

"How about we all go to Grand Central? We can check on Andy's inline skater on our way." Stu's eyes glow.

"That son of a bitch isn't *my* inline skater!"

"I'm afraid he is now. Until he puts a collar around your neck and tames you." Stu bursts out laughing. "But have no fear. We're with you, buddy."

"Yeah, right! You're with me because I invited you to a party. Some friends!"

"And because you have the cutest dreadlocks in town." Ian ruffles his hair, teasing him. "You have the best look among skaters. Pretty stylish."

"Kiss my ass!" Andy brushes him off, then says to Victor and Michael, "Think you two can come?"

"If the admission is free and provided there is something to rock the night away, then it's a must," Victor says.

"You'll have all night to rock if you bring Nancy." Ian is unequivocal. "Actually, that's the only requirement. To bring a chick with you."

"Leave that up to me."

"And you, Mike?" Andy asks. "What about you? Are you coming?"

"Perhaps." A chorus of whistles interrupts him. "If I find a date," he corrects himself.

"What do you mean, if you find a date?" Stu interferes. "What happened to sweet little Irma?"

"We are not together anymore."

"What, did she dump you!? Yes, that's it! She dumped you, didn't she!" Stu is straightforward and tactless, as usual.

"No. We split up. We reached an agreement."

"Shit, man! You sound like some of our congressmen! *We reached an agreement?!* Don't give me that crap! Speak loud and clear. Was it sex or what?"

"Knock it off, Stu," Victor makes a stand. "It's none of your business."

"Hell, no! If he isn't banging her anymore, then it is my business."

"You can really be disgusting," this time Victor doesn't bother to be tactful. "Michael is coming with me, period. Is that so?" He looks at Michael for confirmation.

Michael shrugs his shoulders. *(If you don't mind, I don't either.)*

Ian, Stu, and Andy fake astonishment. "Boooo! We didn't know you had such *tendencies.*"

"Lick my deck!" Victor cannot be embarrassed.

"You lick mine," Stu returns him in kind.

Andy takes control of the situation. He says, "Okay, guys, we've made a deal then? Ian and Stu, you are coming with whoever you want, and Michael comes with Victor and Nancy. You don't have to bring the booze, I got it in gallons. Special wishes aren't included, though. You have to take care of that by yourself. Fair enough?"

All skateboarders agree. "Fair enough."

"Well?" Andy urges them on. "Shall we hit the road, or are we going to spend the rest of the day chitchatting here?"

"It will snow," Michael whispers.

"Excuse me?" Andy doesn't understand what he's talking about. He sniffs the air.

"It's snowing," this time he repeats louder so everyone hears it. He looks at his friends in amazement. *(Didn't I tell you?)*

"Where? In your head?" Ian tilts his head back and looks up at the sky. Something falls in his eye. Something cold and wet. "Ouch!" He rubs it.

The first snowflake.

"Hey! Look!" Victor spreads his arms in excitement, welcoming the gifts of the prodigal sky.

"Let's go, guys, before it gets slippery!" Stu hops on his skateboard. "Let's contribute to the oncoming traffic chaos!"

Four skateboarders follow his example, pushing their boards through the traffic jam and the first snow to catch on dry asphalt. In a line, one after the other, protected from cold and snow by ultra-lightweight, breathable, snowboarding jackets that keep the body warm without letting the cold in. And who can do anything to them when almost everything stands still?

Everything except summer approaching its end.

Fall is slowly arriving, heralded by the falling snow.

Chapter

6th: . . . narrow object like copings, benches, (hand)rails, curbs, ledges, etc. If you prefer to slide, do the same, but sideways on your deck or on the wheels. There are several types of *grinds* like: *50-50 on the rail* (both trucks are grinding the rail); *5-0* (just the back truck is grinding); *f/s* and *b/s* smith (the . . .

NEIL BERESFORD LOVES THREE THINGS above all: money, fame, and pleasure. None of these he lacks.

A leading expert in biochemistry and a donator and benefactor with a degree in psychology, he is always gladly seen at the fundraisers organized by New York's cream every now and then. He has many published articles on the effects of drugs and narcotics on the behavior and psyche of the individual and society as a whole, while a book about his latest research shall be published early next year.

Neil Beresford is also one of the pillars of the Roosevelt Island Research Institute (RIRI), which, like some futuristic fortress from the virtual world and guarded by scientific visionaries, anchors on an island of the same name in the heart of the city. This modern complex is erected on the ruins of the former hospitals, correctional and mental, as well as the former penitentiary there. Now, this entire area is managed and owned by RIRI, including a multi-story system of underground canals and premises equipped with dozens of laboratories and chambers where a variety of research is conducted. The entire Institute is transformed into an untouchable cocoon, protected by state-of-the-art security systems.

Neil Beresford knows that public opinion does not look too favorably upon this *oasis of the future* in which he has spent most of his research life. On several occasions, it came under sharp criticism from the public, with all kinds of rumors circulating. The truth is, RIRI is part of Washington, DC that sprang up on NYC soil. Thus, the experiments and research conducted there are directly supervised and approved by the White House, while their true nature is kept a secret from anyone outside the Institute.

Another closely guarded secret, though not directly related to RIRI, is Neil Beresford's personal secret. Should *this* secret be uncovered, Beresford's position at the Institute would be questionable, regardless of his expertise, connections, and social status. And that Beresford just cannot afford.

He loves money too much. And the feeling of power that comes with it, as well as the accolades that have come to him from all sides. He is too full of himself to give up all this.

The real knack is to reconcile his passion for money with another, no less significant and equally mysterious passion, as is the research he conducts for the RIRI. It became a real challenge, especially after his wife left him. Ruth is no longer around to hold him back, and he himself is not determined enough to give up his old weakness.

Thus, his "pleasure trips" became more frequent than when he was still married, and therefore riskier. *That* is the problem Neil Beresford has not yet solved. That is where the only danger to his career lies. Ruth is no longer a problem for him, as long as he is financially able to pay for her silence. And that silence costs him dearly. A damn awful lot.

But that, too, will change soon. Soon, everything will change.

His good friend and colleague will help him with that. Beresford will enjoy life again without fear of consequences. A promise has been given to him.

He made him a promise. As a reward for a favor. A small one.

A real trifle for him.

* * *

The evening is fresh, the air is purified by snow. Pleasant for breathing and desirable, sugared with the light tones of Vivaldi that fill the inside of the white Volvo with tinted windows. A classic, almost a museum specimen. Rare and sickly expensive.

But not too expensive for Neil Beresford. In fact, anything cheaper than a Volvo that quietly purrs through the night isn't his style. Everything else is inappropriate to his status. As it is inappropriate to see cars like this on the streets offering and buying love for less than thirty bucks an hour.

The car crawls on the trodden and not too deep snow, leaving the impression of a lost soul in search for paradise. The impression is, naturally, wrong. This car is looking for something else, knowing full well what.

The Volvo crawls to a stop at the dark entrance to the

staircase. There is no streetlight here. Everything looks cold, dead.

The window on the passenger door rolls down, Vivaldi leaks into the night.

"Isn't it a little too cold for a walk in this weather?" The male voice speaks to a silhouette shaking with cold. "Need a ride?"

The silhouette takes a step toward the car.

A very young African-American, maybe twelve years old. Chilled to the bones, his moves are stiff and slow.

The boy opens the door and climbs into the car. Accepts the ride. The smell of snow melts with Vivaldi's "Spring."

"Where to?" Beresford asks him.

"Doesn't matter. As long as it's warm."

Beresford smiles. "Today is your lucky day. I know the perfect place to warm you up."

The boy believes him. It is really cold outside.

* * *

When Justin spots the car approaching him, he quivers with hope. He is already freezing, his nose is running, and his ears are icy as if they are glued to his head. He can't feel his fingers; they may as well be cut off. But all this is nothing compared to the thought he would have to return home with empty pockets.

The car speeds up a bit and approaches him even closer. A Volvo. White, polished, and expensive. As he walks down the street, the car follows him by the length of several cars. Justin turns around the corner of 42nd Street, and so does the Volvo. Justin comes about halfway up the street from the next intersection and stops under the dead streetlight. He waits in the dark, his face turning into a smile. The car stops right in front of him and Justin's face brightens.

(There will be work tonight, after all. Luck smiles at him with a quick job and good earnings, just as he is about to go home. Something like that doesn't happen every day.)

He scans the car, thinking about the price. *Tonight he can charge more than usual. The guy obviously isn't short of money. A buck more or less won't make a difference to him.* But it will make a lot of difference to Justin. He can use every dollar. *He urgently needs a new jacket. The one he wears is leaking cold like a sieve. This summer caught him unprepared.*

He harbors hope Lenny will keep his promise and save him the jacket for two weeks as agreed. After that, it is for sale again.

But with tonight's developments, he won't have to wait that long. If he is successful in negotiating, he may have it already tomorrow! And maybe even tonight.

The apartment to which the stranger takes him, Justin doesn't commit to his memory. Except that it is expensive and meticulously furnished.

The man offers to make him tea and Justin says okay, calculating a new price in his head.

Tea is great, though somehow oddly sweet. Justin is dizzy from it. His disposition improves. *(The guy isn't a niggard; that's the f-a-c-t. He pays attention to the smallest detail. First tea, then a nice chat.)* Justin's only regret is that he won't make it to the skate shop for his jacket tonight. But tomorrow it will be his.

A five-minute fellatio in the warmth of the car turns into a two-hour intimate companionship in the man's apartment. During their love game, Justin never reveals his real name, even though the man asks him several times about it. Nas, Justin lies to him, praying to God that the guy isn't a fan of hip-hop.

But the guy is curious, too curious. He wants to know everything about Justin. He wants to find out about his family and his friends. Justin doesn't tell him anything. He doesn't tell the moneybags that his mother is a dancer in a nightclub in New Bronx so she can support a family of six since his father lost his job because of hitting the bottle. Every now and then, Justin also helps her by making money, because it is not easy to feed her four underage children and her drunkard husband, and pay rent for a basement apartment near the ultra-modern and arrogantly luxurious Harlem Desire—a grand five-star hotel that greedily sprawls its golden tentacles across Madison Avenue to Marcus Garvey Park. He also doesn't tell him about his skateboarder friends, who would have something to say when they heard how he is earning his pocket money.

So he makes up the whole story—tired, intoxicated, relaxed, and a little irritated by the long conversation. He gives his best to make his story as credible as possible and not to contradict himself. He is losing concentration, and that makes him even more nervous.

The man then leads him to the bedroom and states his wishes. Justin tells him his price. He accepts, not wanting to spoil their companionship with such conversations. The night is too beautiful to bargain. Too romantic. The sky is dotted with invisible stars, and the streets are still in the intimate embrace of icy snow. The sheets on the bed are perfectly white and freshly ironed. And they are insatiable in making love.

They lie side by side, in the respite and stillness of the moment. Sleepy, as the minutes tick away.

It's time for Justin to go home. He needs to be back before his mom worries. But the guy tells him to stay a bit longer.

He fills the tub and asks Justin to repeat everything in the water once again. Justin tells him it will cost him extra, but he just smiles and lifts him in his arms.

Tonight is his night. A night of pleasures and taking risks. Night of payment.

Tonight he will reward his little friend.

The following nights will also be his. And days. And the pleasures. Only there will be no more risk.

Someone else will take the risk. And paying. It's about time Neil Beresford collects his reward. It will be a rich reward.

He is pleased with himself and he doesn't have to fake a smile when a boy named Nas dives underwater.

* * *

Dad isn't too concerned, Rebecca has the feeling. As . . . as if he doesn't care. No . . . *as if he expected something like that.*

That surprises her. She expected a different reaction from him: a thoughtful face, a wrinkled forehead, eyes covered with a veil of worry. Instead, Hank seemed glad to hear the news. Rebecca is so confused that she is no longer sure if it is her imagination or not. Because, already the next moment, Hank's face expresses pure disbelief. (And insecurity?)

"Rebecca, are you sure? How can you be so *convinced?*"

"I'm sure, Daddy. I saw him. He looked like he was on something. He's been acting strange lately." She wants to say, *since Mother's death,* but thinks better of it.

Her father is silent for a moment, as if reading Rebecca's thoughts, and she feels so exposed, vulnerable, and fragile that she almost screams at him. *Will he also play games with her?*

"Rebecca, honey. Michael is stressed, as are all of us. It's difficult to deal with the situation. It's not easy for him. He spends a lot of time with his friends, which is good. I'm sorry I'm so busy so I don't have more time for him. I'd like to help him, but we barely get to see each other. I know it's *my* fault, but I can't do anything right now. Give him some time and you'll see he will be better. I promise you. Give *us* some time."

"I didn't mean to blame you, Dad. I'm just afraid that Michael will get himself into something. That he already *did*."

"I'll talk to him. I can promise you that much. Open. Like a man to a man. But I assure you, I didn't see any signs that Michael was taking drugs. What I have noticed is post-traumatic stress from which he is recovering. And that's good."

"Does he still visit Mom's grave every day?"

"To be honest, I don't know. I don't follow his whereabouts. Michael was always too standoffish and independent. Distant and inaccessible. He just cannot stand that someone cares for him. I wish it wasn't so."

"I wish that too. It will destroy him." Rebecca sighs, concerned for her brother and feeling guilty for her deceased mother. *(When was the last time she visited her? When was the last time she visited her grave?)*

Unlike Michael, Rebecca doesn't have the courage to visit her mother. Or what's left of her. Her mother, the real Melanie Hope, still lives in her heart as if she had not died. And that's where she'll stay, forever.

But still she cannot bring herself to go to the cemetery, no. She doesn't see it as her mother's place now. That is not *her* reality.

"Daddy," she says with a tentative voice. "Have you considered finding help for Michael?"

Mild tension and interest in Hank Daniels's gaze.

"I mean, professional help? Maybe it would help him?"

A brief flash in his eyes. A twitch on his face.

"Psychiatric help? Do you think it's that serious?"

"No, but I'm worried. I don't want something to happen to him too. I don't know if I could . . ."

His reassuring smile.

"Rebecca, I don't think Michael needs that kind of help. He never did. But for your sake, I'll ask a friend of mine to talk to him. Remember Dr. Beresford?"

"Sure. He treated Mom after returning from Bolivia. He was very nice."

"And he gave you nice jigsaw puzzles with horses," he reprimands her forgetfulness with a smile.

"I didn't forget," she returns a smile. "I still have them somewhere. Although I would prefer that he gave me a live horse. I'm too old for jigsaw puzzles, and riding a real horse is a lot more fun."

They are joking again, because everything will be fine.

"Thanks, Dad, for talking to me. And don't forget to call your friend."

"I won't. Thank you for caring about what I should. I love you so much, Daughter."

"I love you too, Daddy."

That is how their conversation ends. But now, as she rides to the Atkinses' estate, a new unrest awakens in her. New doubts arise.

It all seemed *too* simple.

And until recently it was *so* complicated.

Yellow roses trouble her more than anything else. She only mentioned them to her father, and she wanted to talk about them most.

(How could she forget them and let it go just like that? What's going

on with her?

(What's going on with Michael?!)

She rides up to the Atkinses' house, now fully convinced that a visit to a psychiatrist isn't the best solution for Michael. The conversation cannot harm anybody, but words are not the solution to Michael's problem. At least Rebecca thinks so.

Pushing Michael out of her mind, she dismounts and shouts aloud, "Good afternoon, everyone!"

* * *

"I'm glad you came by."

"I told you I'd see you again. Thanks again for lending me your things."

"Do you want me to admit something to you?" The sun is shining on his face, coating the fields covered with snow with the glitter. "I didn't think it would be so soon."

"I hope you're not disappointed."

"No, not at all! On the contrary." He takes her hands in his, absorbing the moment. "I was hoping for that. Ever since you left. From the moment I *saw* you."

Rebecca says nothing. She lets him take her into the woods. Where the sun is not so warm, strong and blinding, where it is more tame and gentler for human eyes.

"Yours were angry."

"They were," she admits. "Grandma was beside herself. Grandpa said I could at least call so they wouldn't worry."

"But you couldn't!"

"I know," she says, smiling.

"Did you tell them why?"

"I did."

And? the question in his eyes.

"They just looked at each other. They probably thought I was teasing them!"

"Poor grandmother! Poor grandfather!" Red Sunshine laughs.

"I was inconsiderate and selfish. I thought only of myself. Something like that must never happen again." A sudden change in her face. Not even Sunshine's smile softens it.

"I'm sorry if you feel that way."

"I do. But I don't blame you for that."

"But I *am* to blame for that. Me and my folks *are* guilty of not having a phone!"

"Sunny, can I ask you something? Honestly?"

"Of course. Whatever you want. My heart is an open book to you."

The play of shadows on her face hides the feelings caused by his words. Rebecca relaxes.

"How can you live like that . . . isolated?"

"Without a phone, you mean?"

"That, but other things too. You know, you're not going out anywhere, you don't hang out with other people—"

"I'm sorry to interrupt you," a soft grip of his hand as a confirmation of his words, "but we *hang out* with other people."

Her laughter is like a song of elves in a sleeping forest.

"You do because I came to you. I didn't notice you socializing with other people. Except when you have to get something."

"Maybe it's because no one invites us?" He absorbs her eyes.

"That's not true," she corrects him. "You've just been invited."

He loosens his grip.

"Thank you, Rebecca, for feeling that way. But your grandparents—"

She silences him. Her fingers innocently on his lips.

"My grandparents invited you. I just have to arrange when."

"Yours are . . . very kind . . ."

"Well, mostly they are. But they have their moments too. They can be a real pain when they want to."

"I don't believe that."

"You don't *want* to believe. *I* know that, and that's the difference. Just wait when they see you holding my hand and then you'll believe me."

Red Sunshine lets go of her as if burned.

Rebecca breaks up laughing and slips her hand under his arm.

"Don't be afraid. We won't tell them. It will be our secret."

"Just this one?" he asks, after regaining his breath.

"I can't recall anything else." She frowns in a futile attempt to remember. "Give me a hint?"

"If I tell you, it will no longer be a secret."

"You have secrets from me?" She pretends to be offended.

"No, but I have secrets *with you*. It's up to you whether we tell anyone that we love each other."

Rebecca's mouth drops open. She blushes from her toes to the golden tips of her hair. Her whole skin is burning with flames.

"Young man, I must tell you you're too much puffed up!"

"I love you, Rebecca. And I know you love me too. What's so bad about that?"

"What's *so bad* about that?! Except that we know nothing about each other, everything else is fine!"

"So what? Does it have to be an obstacle to our love? The reason we don't love each other?"

"But, Red . . . Sunny . . . You cannot be serious! You *are* serious, aren't you?"

"No less than you." He is ruthless in his honesty. Leaving her breathless, still without mercy.

"I'd like to kiss you now." He makes a move as if he will do that. "Here. In this wood, under the spell of the snow. Where the sun doesn't penetrate every corner, but leaves enough room for hiddenness to keep its magic. But I won't!"

He steps away from her. His breath is lost in the coldness of the day.

"Why . . . ?" Rebecca whispers in a hoarse voice.

"It's not gentlemanly to kiss a girl when she isn't ready." He shrugs, as if it is a normal thing.

Once again Rebecca is thrown off track of her understanding of the world. Breathless and without an opportunity to do what she wants to do with all her heart: to grab his red tufts and press her lips onto his. Until they turn sun red.

Gentlemanly! she snorts to herself, disappointed and furious. But also determined.

(We'll have the pleasure of talking again, Mr. Nice Guy. Only then will someone else decide when we will kiss! You better believe it.)

"We'd better go back," she says to the young man who keeps smiling. Although she is humiliated, she still thinks his smile is irresistible.

"We should better go back," he repeats.

"Gentle Wind and Blue Sky are waiting for us."

"Yes, they are waiting for us."

"We promised to help them build a castle in the snow."

"Yes, we promised to help them build a castle in the snow."

"Are you teasing me?"

"Am I teasing you? No."

"You ass!" she throws an insult at him and flees.

He heehaws from the top of his lungs and runs after her.

The woods are laughing.

* * *

While skateboarders mostly curse the summer, except for a few who decide to take advantage of the situation, Lenny rubs his hands as happy as a clam while cashing in on low temperatures and bad weather. This morning he sells the remaining two jackets (the last one to Justin, while Nathan sells the other one to some guy who isn't a skater). He also sells three pairs of shoes, replacements for the worn-out and ragged DC, ES and Axion skateboarding shoes with holes in their soles, five, long-sleeve, cotton T-shirts, two pairs of Burton gloves, and one snowboard. And it is just past noon.

They are more than enough reasons for satisfaction on Lenny's and Nathan's faces. The Division Pro Skate Shop is still *full*. Although not all customers buy something, Lenny knows some of them will return later. And then buy. And send others too. Who will also buy something.

Lenny has no complaints about this summer. As far as he is concerned, he won't mind if it lasts a little longer.

In a small room upstairs, he checks the supplies to make sure he has everything in stock before he runs short of some items. A fire burns in two steel drums, one on each side of the store entrance, while the fierce beats of the song "Violence" by the white rap band D-Mand fire up the mood of the skateboarders in the store.

Nathan swings to the rhythm; Ken dubs the music for the video for tonight's premiere at Andy's place. Newest stunts, latest tricks. *Cruel Summer, Part II.*

Alex is trying on a new pair of Alphanumeric pants in the toilet.

Alien does the same, except in the crowd of the store, shamelessly exposing his boxers and butt to anyone interested in inspecting it. All are welcome!

Ian cuddles with his girlfriend, who giggles in his lap, as Stu studies the latest issue of *Transworld Skateboarding* magazine.

Everyone expects Victor and Michael, and even more Fernando, the one in charge for the weed for tonight. There is a special demand for Mary Jane in New York City these days and it is almost impossible to get it, but despite that everyone's spirits are high.

They are eager for the night to fall, when the *real* life will begin.

Chapter

7th: . . . back truck is grinding, the front of your body facing the edge/away from the edge and toe-side/heel-side rail grinding); *b/s feeble* (the back truck is grinding, *b/s*, the toe-side rail grinding/sliding the edge, the front truck over the deck); and *crooked* or *k* (the *nosegrind* with the nose . . .

"MOTHER, I KNOW YOU CAN'T HEAR ME, but I must talk to you.

"I need to talk to someone. Anyone. About things I would never say if you were alive. About things I didn't want you to know because they would hurt you. This way I will say them, and you won't hear them. This way it will be much easier for me to pour my heart out to you . . .

"Mama, I'm not happy. Nothing's been good since you've been gone. I'm lost in a world I do not understand, and I am trying to find myself. I despise so many things, and there is so little worth living for. Worth suffering for. So little.

"You were one of them. You were one of my reasons to keep fighting. As I was one of your reasons you loved to live. I know that, Mother. I know that very well. Although sometimes you used to drive me crazy with your excessive care. With too much attention. You have to understand—I was no longer a child. And you still cared for me.

"Somehow I miss all that now. I need something to keep me going. To guide me. I need someone to give me a reason to try.

"I miss our talks the most. Our plans. There's nothing left. Everything became meaningless. Pointless. Everything is so *hard*.

"It's cold. It's snowing. But you don't feel it. Time has stopped for you. It's waiting for a better moment.

"I shouldn't be telling you this, but I'm thinking of quitting school. Father would kill me if he knew. That's why I won't tell him. At least not for now. It would kill you to hear me say that. But I have to tell you, Mama. I have to tell *someone*. I have to confide in someone.

"I see no point in going to school anymore. And I don't feel like going to school, to be honest. I'll dedicate myself to skateboarding and try to make a living out of it for a while. My first contest will be soon, Mama! Lenny already offered to sponsor me. He'll give me as many free shoes and boards as I need. I just have to hang around the city every day and skate, it's my obligation to him. Cool, right? Other skateboarding companies haven't called me yet, but I am expecting their reply any day now. Their sponsorship would mean a lot to me. Not only financially, but also as moral encouragement. It is very important for skaters with the ambition to someday become pro to have someone with a name behind them. Someone who *believes* in you.

"It means a lot to me, Mama. Skateboarding is my life.

Don't be angry about that. I *think* about my future and that's why I decided to take that step. I think I'm good enough to accomplish something. I think I'm well prepared to win that contest. I could make some money, Mama. Could have already made it, had I not been so hesitant, indecisive, and stupid! Everyone tells me I'm crazy for not competing. I didn't take them seriously; I didn't believe them, and I made a mistake. I must not repeat the same mistake again. At least this time I will give it a try. I have a good feeling I won't disappoint us, Ma. In the end, I'm doing this partly because of you. For you and our shared dream. Which will never become reality because you're gone. But I didn't give up on it. It's just that I must live it myself now.

"Rebecca and Pa have no interest in sharing it with me. They don't have our adventurous spirit. They are happy with what they have. Nothing drives them to move on, to visit places they have not seen yet. Nothing can *trigger* them. Maybe because they didn't listen well? Or they listened but didn't hear what you were telling us? You were a great storyteller, Mother. And I was your best student. Thanks to you, I learned to love places I didn't know or see with my own eyes. Thanks to you, I wanted to travel. And one day I'll do it, I promise you. Soon enough. Thanks to my first contest.

"I want to follow your footsteps, Ma, and go from here. One step at a time, from contest to contest, if there's no other way. From Sattel in Switzerland to God knows where. I just want to travel. This is a unique opportunity for me to see the Old Continent. I know I won't see all those places you've been to, but I'll be much closer to Paris than I am now. And next time I will visit the medieval castles and swim in the crystal-blue waters of the Republic of Croatia. After all, one cannot expect to see everything in one's first trip overseas. Rome wasn't built in a day.

"That's my goal, and I won't give up on it. I've already wasted too much time. If it only weren't so hard to leave my friends! They are like family to me now. I belong to them. Don't worry, Mama, I haven't forgotten my promise! I'm looking out for my sister. It's just that she seems a lot stronger than I am.

"It's better for her to be so strong. She's doing fine. She is tough, unbreakable, and stubborn as always. She's in Denver with your folks. Enjoying her vacation. I wish I could say that for myself. But this stupid summer drives me nuts."

He is oblivious to the world, alone with his sorrow, thoughts, and dreams. Surrounded by the whiteness of the snow. The silence of the beautiful graves and the memories that cannot keep him warm.

He stands alone at the end of the world, at his mother's grave. Evoking the days that will never come, the comfort that no longer lives at the same address. Wanting to bring back again:

Days of joy,

His mother,

Happiness of the past (it was a long time ago; he was still just a little boy when he was truly happy last time),

His girlfriend he left because he couldn't do otherwise. And she begged him not to. She begged for another chance to let her try for both of them. He didn't give her that chance. Like others didn't give it to him.

Not one shitty chance.

"I got into a fight with Dad. That's why I wasn't in the mood to talk last time. He broke my lip and gave me a shiner. He didn't get a scratch. I'm better now. It doesn't hurt, and I don't care about the looks.

"You know, Ma, I still don't understand how you could have married such a man. I don't want to interfere with your life, but something keeps bothering me. . . . Beneath his pleasant looks, beneath his kindness and generosity, I think Hank is a bad person. Rotten. Forgive me for saying that, but how can you know for sure if he is good or not? And how good was he for *you*?

"You'll think I don't love him, and you're right. I don't love him. I don't love him because for the most part I'm afraid of him. I'm scared when I'm alone with him, but I'm even more scared when he's not around and I don't know what he's up to. I hate not knowing what's on his mind! That's why I'm out a lot. Thank God Rebecca is at our grandparents' so I don't have to be home. If only she stayed there for a while. And what would she do in New York in this weather?

"That way he has less opportunity to hurt me. I never told you that, Ma, but Hank used to hurt me. He still does sometimes. I don't know how long I will endure it. I'm losing patience. I'm losing my self-control. That's why I kicked him back. We had a fight until one of us was bleeding. Until *I* was bleeding.

"You might wonder why I put up with him? I put up with him because of Rebecca. I'm afraid he may get after her if I'm not around. I can't let that happen. I can't let him hurt Rebecca. And I'm doing it for you. Out of respect for you, I suffer that shit. And I will bite the bullet again and suffer . . . until I kill him one day. Or until he kills me. . . ."

Tears stream down Michael's face. Washing away the bitterness and pain of a ruined childhood.

"Later . . . after hurting me . . . he would be good. He would be considerate and gentle and give me painkillers. He would stuff me with all kinds of pills and vitamins until I was *healed* again.

"I hated these pills, but still took them. I was afraid *not to take* them. They made me sleepy. But that was their purpose, right? He watched me taking them. Especially the vitamin pills. He was worried for my immune system; all sorts of viruses going around and causing epidemics and that kind of shit. I could catch the *flu*. Like I've never had the flu before! What can I say . . . ? But there was another reason I listened to him and took them. I discovered something.

"The pills helped me. After taking them, I would skate better, I was more aggressive in riding and insanely daring. I feared nothing. I got hurt a lot, like a savage, but the guys were *impressed*. I rocked the universe! Without false modesty, Ma, I think I'm as good as Victor or Alien. If only I could get rid of these occasional short circuits in my memory—as I call them. There are moments when I black out. It's like I find myself somewhere else, in some different place. As if I'm not in my body, and yet I'm here. At first it was a creepy feeling. I thought I was hallucinating or something. I didn't tell Dad about that, because he would stuff me with more pills. And that's the last thing I need! But if my condition doesn't im-prove, I reckon I will have to tell him. What if he poisons me in the end?!

"You don't mind me telling you all this, Mama? I had to tell someone. I had to pour out my heart. Who would I tell if not my mom? My friends? Yeah, sure! They'd think I'm nuts! *Mad as a hatter*. I don't need that. My life is complicated enough already.

"I love you, Mama. I'll come again. But I don't know if I will be so chatty then. I really needed to *talk* today.

"Now I'm going to see Victor's grandma. Nancy is with her for lunch, but I have a feeling Vic might be there too. I need company, Mama. I need *his* company. So I don't think so much about myself, now that I can't skate. The streets are not cleaned yet. And I should skate . . ."

* * *

Nancy doesn't even try to hide her surprise when she sees Michael. She greets him with a wide smile, excited to see him there.

"Mikey, what are you doing here?"

"I came to visit Victor's grandma. Good afternoon."

He smiles back at her as she continues indulging Victor's grandmother with the last tablespoons of fruit yogurt she brings her daily.

"Victor, is that you?" the old woman asks, not seeing well, and confusing Michael for Victor.

"It's not Victor, Grandma," Nancy corrects her. "It's Michael. Victor's friend. He came to see how you are."

"Michael?" Mrs. Kenneth remembers now. "Of course! The sweet young man who reads poems. Hello there, Michael."

"Hello."

"The sweet young man who reads poems?" Nancy wonders and tosses the empty plastic cup into the wastebasket.

Michael shrugs. "When I was with Vic here yesterday, his grandma didn't want to eat, so Vic came up with the idea that I read something to get her attention off the food. Rimbaud hit the bull's-eye."

"Interesting," Nancy says. "Victor didn't tell me anything about it. I guess he forgot."

"There wasn't much to tell."

"No? I wouldn't totally agree with you. Put yourself in my shoes. This little piece of information might come in handy. Isn't that right, Granny?" She tickles Angela Kenneth under her chin.

Angela Kenneth jerks her head away. *(Don't!)* It is one of those rare moments when Mrs. Kenneth refuses Nancy's patient hand. She addresses Michael as if Nancy isn't there. "Did you bring your poems with you today, Michael? Will you read to us again?"

"See what I mean?" Nancy winks at him, already forgetting the old woman's rude reaction.

Michael flashes her a smile with the discomfort of becoming the object of Angela Kenneth's undivided attention.

"I will, ma'am, but not right now. A bit later."

"That's right," Nancy regains control of the situation. "Now, the two of us will take a nice walk to the bathroom, and Michael will wait for us at the television."

"Are you sure? You won't go away?" Angela Kenneth looks him in the eyes, overwhelmed with fear.

"I won't go away, I promise. I just got here! See you in a few minutes."

He steps out into the corridor and closes the door. As soon as he turns around, a heavy-stinking breath fills his nose.

"When is lunch?"

"Excuse me?" He stares in astonishment at the old woman who gave him a hard time the day before, letting out her stinky breath in his face. Her breath is no fresher today. Michael regrets that he forgot to fill his pockets with chewing gum before leaving the house.

"When is lunch?"

"I have no idea. I guess soon."

"In half an hour?"

"Maybe. I don't know that. I don't work here. Why don't you ask a nurse?"

He moves on, but the old woman follows him like a puppy.

"What do you want from me?" he loses his temper. "I already told you I didn't know. Maybe in half an hour, maybe in an hour. You better find the nurse and ask her! She will tell you."

"Lunch is in an hour," a familiar voice startles Michael from behind and Victor's arm leans in a relaxed manner on his shoulder. "At one o'clock, to be more precise."

The old woman thanks him and retreats.

"I have to rescue you again, my friend. What's the matter with you? And what brings you here at this hour?"

"I've been waiting for you."

"You've been waiting for me? What made you think I'd be here?"

"Fox Mulder."

"I beg your pardon?"

"Never mind. Speaking of which, what's your excuse?"

"I came to see Nana, if you forgot."

"And your nana invited me, like yesterday, in case *you* forgot?"

"I didn't forget."

"Then you thought I wasn't coming. That I said that out of courtesy."

"Well . . ."

"Thank you, I think I've heard enough."

"Good dog!" Victor ruffles his hair. "I'm joking. Don't be such a child. Come on, let's see what's Nana doing."

"We can't."

"What do you mean, *we can't*? Why?"

"Nancy took her to the toilet. She told me to wait by the boob tube."

"And who wouldn't love her?" Victor heads for the room despite Michael's warning.

Michael halts him. "I think I've made myself clear. She said to wait *there*!" He pushes him in the opposite direction.

"She said that to *you*, not me! But since the lady who fancies you so much is on her love crusade again," he nods toward Miss-Bad-Breath approaching them with astonishing speed, "I'll stay with you for a while and babysit you."

"Oh dear." Michael breathes in a lungful of air so suddenly and audibly that Victor cracks up and doubles over with laughter.

* * *

Stu is a real bastard! Victor cannot forgive him for being so cocky to bring Irma to Andy's party.

Victor would have beaten the hell out of him on the spot because of that, but he doesn't want to ruin the party for others. It is already ruined for him, anyway.

And for Michael.

Victor finds him cooling himself on the balcony, while recovering from shock. Alien is also with him, making sure he won't throw himself into the abyss below. Michael doesn't look good.

Victor wishes to kick Stu.

"Michael, Nancy and I are leaving. You can come with us if you want."

"Come on, man! Don't be a party pooper," Alien tries to

make him change his mind. "Don't give him that pleasure."

"I better go. I might kill him if I stay. Stupid, selfish bastard! I would only spoil the evening for you guys."

"Let's at least watch the video together. You can leave after if you still feel that way."

"I'm afraid it won't work, buddy. It's either me or him. I better leave."

"I think I'll stay a little longer. I'll be with Alien," Michael decides.

"Are you sure?"

"Yes. Thanks for your concern. Alien can take me home if I don't feel well."

"That's what friends are for." Alien loops his arm around Michael's neck.

"Fine, if that's your choice. Just don't do something stupid *you* might regret later."

"Don't worry." Alien is confident. "He's in good hands." He pats Michael on the back.

"Thanks, Vic, for bringing me with you."

"Anytime, kid. Have a good time. I mean it."

"I know. See ya later?"

"See ya later," Victor confirms.

He finds Nancy and says goodbye to the rest of the guys. He doesn't even look at Stu and Irma.

Andy sees them off to the door.

"I'm sorry, Victor. Forgive me, Nancy. But what could I do? Not let them in?"

"It's not your fault, Andy. It turned out the way it turned out. No one could've foreseen something like that would happen. Just don't let him ruin the rest of the evening."

"Sure."

"Look after Michael, will you?"

"I'll carry him like a drop of water in the palm of my hand. No need to worry."

"Thanks."

"Thank you for coming. I wish things turned out differently . . ."

One hour later. Exhausted with making love, Nancy stretches her full length on a damp sheet next to Victor's sweaty body. He takes her in his arms and kisses her on the lips. "I love you."

She smiles at him. And remains lying like that for a little while, before she slips out of his embrace and sits up in bed. Pulling the sheet up to her chin, she looks at her boyfriend, who is watching her bleary-eyed.

"We need to talk, Victor," she says without preamble.

"Now? About what?"

"I know it's not the right moment. Especially after what happened today. But for some things there is never a good moment, so . . . I have to tell you something."

Victor sits up beside her. His eyes are clear. He runs his fingers through her hair. "What's the matter, hon?"

She hugs her knees as he continues stroking her hair.

"It's about your grandmother. She is not well." She can't look him in the eyes.

"What do you mean?"

"Your grandmother's health is deteriorating. It's deteriorating very fast. I don't know if she will live to see this winter."

She hates herself for telling him this. Chewing on her lower lip, she blinks the tears away.

"Is it that serious?" he asks.

"I'm afraid it is. Have you noticed anything?"

"No, but Sylvia told me they had prescribed her a new therapy because Nana was complaining about pain. She's a little better now and even responds to my jokes."

"That's because she reconciled. It's always like that before . . . the end," she tells him in the voice she used as she comforted her little, frightened patients. Because her boyfriend is now as frightened and no less worried.

"Your nana knows she's dying, darling. She knows she won't be with us much longer. That's why . . . that's why she tries so hard . . ." Her voice betrays her.

"She's doing that for *me*? To make it easier for me?" He grabs her by the shoulders and turns her to face him. "Nancy, look at me, damn it!" He steals her gaze despite her attempts not to meet his eyes. Too much pain in them.

"Victor, don't . . ."

"Tell me! Tell me and look me in the eyes! Tell me so I can believe."

It's blurred. His loving image in her eyes.

"She wants you to keep her in good memory. This is not unusual. Everyone who leaves us feels the same. . . . It's the least they can do for us."

"Nana is concerned about leaving an impression?! She's concerned what I will think of her? That's what you are trying to tell me?"

"You have to understand her—"

"But I *love* her, Nancy. No matter what! I will love her no matter what happens! Nothing will change that. . . . Nothing."

"Will you also love her when the pain becomes intolerable, so that even the medicines won't ease her cries and screams? When she will no longer know about herself or you, or anything that happens in this godforsaken world because cancer eats her inside? And then nothing will change?"

She is appalled by her own fierceness. And with the shock that turns out the light in Victor's eyes.

She feels miserable enough.

The spasm stiffens his face in incredulity, and he collapses into bed, powerless.

"Victor, darling, it's the only thing left for her," she says in a gentle voice. "A little satisfaction she can still give us on the brink of dignity. Before the fall happens, from which no one will get her back."

She snuggles against him, caressing his face. Kisses him.

"We must be strong, stronger than ever. Your nana will need us. She'll need everything we can give her."

Victor opens his mouth. He says something. Nancy is not sure what; it is softer than a whisper.

She kisses his neck, his shoulders, his chest. He remains motionless and calm. Only tears continue to run down his face, disappearing in her hair.

She tries to bring him to life. To awake him with the power of her love.

He keeps crying.

It is the first and only time Nancy has seen him crying. The first and the last time in a year and a half since being together.

And she doesn't know how to help him.

When Victor speaks again, his words are clearer and Nancy can hear them.

"I wish she could see the sun one more time. Nana loves the sun so much . . ."

"Oh, baby, of course she will. She will see it many times. I'm sure of that."

But Victor isn't so sure. Although he wants that more than

anything.

This time he doesn't resist. He embraces her with his body, absorbing her warmth. So powerful and pleasant, it melts the icebergs of his heart and illuminates the night that spreads its wings over the whole town.

New York City also doesn't sleep.

Chapter

8th: . . . sliding at the same time). To *noseslide* ride parallel to an obstacle. Do an *ollie*. Turn the board and your body 90 degrees. Land on the ledge with the nose of the board sliding on top of it. Lock up the front truck against the edge. Slide until you are ready to come off or to the end of the ledge.

THE FOUR SEASONS IS PACKED. Elegant clientele. Rich dinner. An expensive menu.

Exquisite guests who don't care about the thickness of their wallets when they walk out into the windy night.

The table at which Hank Daniels and Neil Beresford sit is in the farthest corner of the restaurant. Their faces serious, the subject too important and sensitive not to be discussed in hushed voices.

"So, Michael isn't well, you say?"

"Rebecca pointed it out to me today. It's just not clear to me. I didn't notice anything."

"Is there anything else you haven't noticed?"

Hank Daniels ignores the irony in his friend's voice.

"I've been busy. You know that."

"Things like that happen when you run with the hare and ride with the hounds. Do you think you can do this? Think you can control the situation?"

"If you have doubts, say it now. I want to know what the stakes are."

Beresford watches him like a predator lurking on its prey. "The stakes are big. The risk is even bigger. I don't know . . ."

"And big bucks that are smiling at you if you stay in the project are no longer enough to take some risk?"

In the project, the words echo with cynicism in Beresford's head. He says to Daniels, "If things get complicated, we will have to reconsider our agreement."

"*Nothing* will get complicated if we stick to our plan and do our part of the job."

"That's settled, then." Beresford licks his fingers before wiping them on the napkin.

"Was there any doubt about that?" Daniels gnashes his teeth. His friend's constant mention of money gets on his nerves.

"Very well. When will you send me the kid?"

"I haven't talked to him yet. In a day or two. I'll try to get it done tonight."

"Try?" Beresford sneers. "So much for authority."

"This is not about authority. The thing is, Michael doesn't like to talk about it. He thinks he doesn't need help. He shows temper each time I raise a subject. There might be little problems, but I'll handle it."

"Really? May I ask how you'll handle it? As I see this, when you say frog he doesn't really jump," he says with a tinge of disdain.

"He will obey when I explain to him that Neil Beresford is a very nice and elegant gentleman waiting for him with a jar full of colorful candies. I'm sure he won't be able to resist the sweet candy party."

Beresford knows he crossed a line. He had gone too far by teasing and belittling his friend, and the boomerang is now coming back at him, bouncing off Daniels's thick skin.

"This is amusing to you, isn't it? I wonder where my mind was when I let you get me into your nonsense."

"Then let me refresh your memory: on serious money. You were greedy, pal!"

It all comes back to him. Daniels strikes back, telling Beresford what he thinks of him. Beresford wonders how the two of them are friends at all, so different, and mostly annoying each other? The only reasonable answer is—their passion and weakness for money. This keeps them together, forcing them to cooperate and to understand one another.

It is in the interest of that passion that Beresford waits until he calms down, because Daniels isn't one to settle a dispute between the two of them. He is like a ticking time bomb that can explode at any moment.

"I apologize if I was rude. This wine must have gone to my head. It's excellent." He takes a sip to confirm his words.

"It is. Let's have another round? This one's on me," Daniels accepts Beresford's peace offer.

"Thanks, but tomorrow I need a clear head. And you will need it, too, if you want to achieve anything with Michael tonight."

"Don't worry about him. He may seem tough, but even the toughest have a weak spot."

Beresford raises his eyebrows, expecting clarification, but

Daniels's grin tells him he won't get any.

"No, no, my friend! That's your job. Make your money!"

Beresford grins back and they touch glasses.

They are friends again.

* * *

From the balcony of Whaler's apartment stretches a magnificent view of Strawberry Fields and The Lake in Central Park. On a nice day, it would be breathtaking with its vivid colors and vibrancy, but now, covered in snow and silence, it is more like the hostile planet Hoth from the second part—*Episode V*—of the *Star Wars Trilogy*. Alien doesn't forget to mention it to Michael.

"You can feel its coldness penetrating all the way up here. Want to get inside?"

"No, thanks. I'm fine."

"If you're fine, then I'm fine," Alien agrees.

They continue to look at the skyscrapers across the park. Despite the strong gusts of wind, several airships sail the sky.

"Guys, can I get you something?" Andy appears at the door, shaking with cold.

"Thanks for the offer, pal," Alien replies. "We are okay."

"But there is something you can do for me." Alex materializes next to Andy and smooches him on the mouth. "Come inside. Let's find a quieter place. It's too crowded for my taste here."

Andy grins at Alien and Michael and lets Alex lead the way.

They move slowly, avoiding stepping on the bottles scattered on the floor and half-drunk and pepped-up couples who occupy every corner of Andy's apartment.

Someone vomited in the bathroom, but they continue to Andy's parents' room without stopping.

The double bed is large, empty, and irresistibly inviting. Its owners in the distant Yucatan, celebrating another anniversary of marital happiness and love.

Alex plops down on the bed and pulls Andy after her.

"You have a Trojan?" she whispers in his ear.

"Mmm, yeah." He bites her neck.

"Give it to me." She peels his shirt off as he digs through his pockets.

Their bodies come together in a rush of wild, untamable passion, not caring if anyone bursts in.

It is love for one night. Never before and never after. They're lovers tonight. Tonight they are taking and giving. Tomorrow they will be friends again. And everything will be the same.

Alex screams.

For a moment Andy stays lying on top of her, and then he rolls over onto the bed.

They start dressing. Alex first . . .

* * *

Michael cannot stop thinking about the moment Irma approached him. He signaled Alien to leave them alone. Alien hesitated a little and then withdrew.

They are in the kitchen, just the two of them among the food leftovers and a heap of empty bottles, a barbecue soaking in the sink. The smell of alcohol hangs in the air.

Irma speaks first. The usual, *How are you?*

He shrugs his shoulders. *Good, I guess. And you?*

She's fine too.

But something still makes her uneasy.

"Michael, I want you to know something. Regardless of what you think and what kind of image you have about it, I didn't come here because of Stu. True, he invited me, but I didn't come to spite you or to make a scene. I still love you, no matter how much you try to change that. Besides, these are my friends as much as yours. Even though the two of us are no longer together."

Michael stares at her in silence.

"I just wanted to tell you that. So you know why I'm here and how I feel about you. We had a great time together and I would like to believe it's not over. But, I'm afraid, it's no longer in my hands."

"I'm afraid you're right," is all he tells her. "It's no longer in your hands."

That's all he says to the girl he loves so much, he cannot be with her. He cannot make her happy, because with happiness the pain will come too. And suffering. Too much suffering. Michael cannot do that. As he is incapable of loving devotedly and without holding back.

Because they destroyed him. Because they deprived him from every opportunity to love and be loved.

"Well, I'll be going now. Stu will take me home."

"Okay. Take care."

A glimmer of hope? Too long a moment of anticipation. And,

"Good night, Michael."

"Good night, Irma."

Alien shows up and stops his train of thoughts by elbowing him under his ribs.

A fire is in the sky. The Valjek Cosmetics airship catches fire and explodes. Burning debris falls toward the Hudson River.

"Man, this is madness! Did you see it!?"

He disappears inside to share the news, but no one shows interest. The others do not share his excitement. *Burning zeppelin, so what? Big deal! Who cares?*

Dispirited, Alien returns to the balcony.

"Let's take a closer look?" he tries to persuade Michael. Everyone else is too doped or dead drunk.

"Sorry, I'm not in the mood."

"Come on! Don't be such a wimp!"

His adrenaline rises from the sirens of firefighters and paramedics.

"I'm really not in the mood, Alien. Go if you want to. I'll be going home."

"Home? You are certainly not! You promised to stay overnight at my place."

"I said *maybe*. I have to ask Hank first."

"So call him! Give him a buzz and tell him we're going to my place."

"It's too late. He must be sleeping already."

"Then don't call him and let's go to my place right now! You'll call him in the morning."

"I can't. It's not that simple."

"It would be simple if you didn't complicate things so much."

Michael gives him a look. (How many times have they had a conversation like this before?)

Alien draws in his horns.

"Okay. Fine. I'll call a cab. We are going to your place. *Both of us.*"

"*Both of us?*"

"Yes. We will wake up your old man, tell him we are going to another party at my place, send him back to the land of Nod, and get ourselves lost while the going's good."

"You're out of your mind!"

* * *

They don't need to wake up Hank because he still isn't sleeping when they arrive at Michael's home, making a hell of a racket.

But they fall silent in front of his scrutinizing gaze.

"Dad! You're awake," Michael says.

"You observe well," Alien whispers in his ear and giggles.

Michael suppresses laughter.

"I see you had a good time, boys." Hank Daniels puts down his glass of cognac on the table. "Hi, Roy."

"Good evening, Mr. Daniels. Or good morning. I don't know if it's evening or morning. It's still damn dark outside!" Alien babbles.

"It's morning, Roy. Two hours after midnight. Sleep time, if I'm right?"

"You are absolutely right! In fact, we were just going to bed. Isn't that so, my friend?" He pinches Michael's butt.

"Yes, yes! Sure. Dad, I came to ask you something. Can I stay overnight at Alien's?"

"Tonight? I'm sorry." He shakes his head no. "I don't see the point. It's only a few hours before dawn. Plus, I need to have a word with you."

"But Dad—"

"Mr. Daniels, don't be angry, but—"

"Enough, boys. It's not going to happen. You and I, Michael, we need to talk. And you, Roy, you can stay here overnight. I will not throw you in the street. That would not be wise, considering your condition. But you'll have to wait until Michael and I are done."

"No problem, Mr. Daniels. It's fine with me. Whatever you say. As long as I have somewhere to sleep. It will be just fine here, since Andy's is overcrowded."

"What do we have to talk about?" Michael is impatient. He doesn't like the idea of a two-in-the-morning conversation. "I'd like to go to bed. I'm tired."

"Excuse me, I have to go to the bathroom, if I am allowed. You can have a private talk then," Alien says, hiccupping.

"On second thought, I'd ask you to stay, Roy," Michael's father says. "I would love to hear your opinion. As Michael's friend."

"What opinion?" Michael insists, losing his patience by the minute.

"How about we take a s-e-a-t?" Alien pushes him down onto the couch and sits next to him.

"About you, Michael," Hank tells him. "And your health. I'm worried about it."

"Thanks for your concern, but I'm fine," Michael says defensively. "You have nothing to worry about."

"Do you think so, Roy?"

"Well, yes . . . of course! I mean, mostly."

"What do you mean, *mostly*?" Michael gives him a stern look.

"You know. You are fine until you get wild!" He giggles. Hiccups again. "Oops, sorry!"

"Would you mind explaining that?" Hank keeps a serious

face.

"You see . . . I meant nothing bad with that. One moment he is quiet, calm and withdrawn, and then he is a freaking wild cat on his boogie-board!" He slaps Michael on his back. "You should see him, Mr. Daniels. He's phenomenal, simply *the best*! Nothing can stop him. Nothing can get in his way."

"Nothing but a broken neck. That's what I was afraid of. My suspicions were well founded."

"Suspicions? What suspicions?! What is this about? Will someone finally tell me?!" Michael is more and more desperate, losing patience.

"It's about your recent behavior, Son. You have become a danger to yourself and other people. That's why I asked Dr. Beresford to talk to you. You have an appointment with him tomorrow."

The news strikes like lightning. Into a nuclear reactor.

Alien's mouth drops open, not understanding.

Michael turns pale, losing his breath. Chokes. He squeezes out, "Excuse me?"

"You heard me. Meet Neil Beresford tomorrow and have a nice chat with him. It is in your best interest."

"A bunch of crap! I have nothing to talk to him until you explain to me what this is all about!"

"You see? That's what I'm talking about. The last time you spoke with Rebecca, you scared her to death."

Alien is quiet like a grave. He almost forgets to breathe.

"Rebecca called? You talked to her? What did she say?"

"She opened my eyes, Michael. She's worried about you. Try to understand that. She's afraid for you. You scare her."

"And she asked me to go to a psychiatrist?"

Hank Daniels nods.

Michael is dejected. He withdraws into himself. A reflection of complete disappointment. And conciliation—with the inevitable.

(Rebecca . . . My Rebecca.)

Daniels seizes the moment.

"It will be fine, don't worry about anything. Everyone is seeing a psychiatrist nowadays. It's kind of *the in thing*." He smiles.

Michael is silent. Completely broken.

"All right, boys, time for bed now. Everything's going to look much better tomorrow, I assure you. Let's sleep on it. Talking to Dr. Beresford will only help you. You'll see that I was right."

Michael uses his hands to push himself up on his feet and heads for his room.

Alien falls in behind him. Still in disbelief, surprised, and totally confused.

(Did he drink so much or is this really happening?)

* * *

In bed, Michael isn't the least talkative. He is completely alienated, like a stranger. Alien cannot cheer him up at all.

The darkness is around them; the darkness is between them; the darkness is in Michael. Cold and unpleasant.

And then, for the first time in his life, Alien doubts. *What if Hank was telling the truth? What if he is right? What if Michael needs professional help?*

The days to come will answer these questions, Alien is sure. But not even in his wildest dreams can he imagine what that answer will be.

Chapter

9th: Opposite to the *noseslide* is the *tailslide*. The *tailslide* is when you turn 90 degrees and the tail of the board lands and slides on the edge of the ledge or rail. The *lipslide* you can do either by *b/s* or *f/s 180 ollie* or faking into it, whether *fakie* or just lifting up your tail over the obstacle. Let's move on to *kickflips*.

IT SMELLS OF LEMON AND DISINFECTANTS.

Impeccable cleanliness. As if someone swept all the dust right now. Not a speck of impurity remains. Not a trace of dirt.

Just a shine.

Shine.

Shine.

Michael takes a sip of orange juice from the sterilized glass. Moderately cooled, so as not to catch a sore throat.

He clears his throat and says, "I don't know what to say to you. Except that I don't see the purpose of all this."

"Your father doesn't think so." A gentle tone full of understanding and confidence. *Hey, kiddo. No sweat. You can rely on me. Discretion guaranteed.*

A moment of silence. Then another one.

"How about you ask me what interests you?" Michael suggests. "I don't know what you want to hear."

"Will you answer me if I ask you?" No urging in his voice. No *pressure*. Just a friendly chat.

"Maybe."

"And I can ask you anything? Anything I want?"

Shorter hesitation. Then, "Yes."

"And you will answer me?"

"You won't tell anyone about this?"

"This is a confidential conversation, Michael. Everything you say is between you, me, and the lamppost."

"Not even Dad will know about it?"

"Not even him. Unless you want otherwise."

"No, that's okay. Go on, ask."

Neil Beresford shifts himself and crosses his legs. The leather armchair creaks under him.

Awkward sound, Michael thinks. *Strange.*

"Where did you get the bruise?"

Michael looks away. At the painting of undefined content, a set of intertwined colors with no order and meaning, hanging on the wall behind Neil Beresford. Michael isn't impressed by it.

"Do you like it?" Beresford asks, following his gaze.

"Excuse me?" He is back from the world he had wandered into for a moment.

"The painting. What do you think of it?"

He takes another look at it. He shrugs.

"I don't know. I don't think about it. I have no opinion."

Neil Beresford smiles, saying nothing, but his gaze is louder than any words. *I think you have, my friend. I think you have some-*

thing to tell me. I'm almost certain of that.

"You'll say now that not having an opinion is also an opinion. It's okay if you think so. I don't care."

"I didn't say anything, Michael. If that's what *you* think, I'll agree with you."

"The painting sucks, if you want to know." He becomes nervous. Suddenly he has a strong urge to defend himself. As if someone, or something, is attacking him. As if invisible shadows are closing in on him, carrying with them evil intentions.

"This is the work of a loony," he says after a while. "Who painted it?" he asks.

"Unknown artist," Beresford says calmly.

"How did you get it?"

"A gift from a patient."

"That's all?"

"I helped her deal with her childhood traumas."

"And she gave you this painting. I believe she settled her account as well."

Beresford smiles innocently.

"Sometimes we do something for someone that no money can pay. It means so much to them. If I hadn't taken this painting, I would have offended the woman."

"How did you help her?"

"I didn't perform any miracle, if that's what you mean. I talked to her. I talked to her until she was ready to face her traumas. And to face herself."

"Did you use hypnosis? You hypnotized her?"

"Yes, I also used hypnosis. Why, are you interested in that?"

Michael reaches out for the glass of juice, but does not drink from it.

He looks at the painting again. Dreamily.

"No reason. Just asking. You're paid to talk to me."

"But I'm not paid to steal from your father."

"Of course. First, you need to see if it all makes sense before you send him a bill. You want to see the *results* first."

There is a smile on Beresford's face Michael cannot interpret.

"You asked me what I thought of the painting." Michael redirects the conversation. "I think it's a cry for help."

Beresford knits his brows. He leans forward.

"What makes you think that?"

"Because it's too damn mixed up. Pure chaos. Makes you feel uneasy."

"Does it make *you* uneasy?"

"Yes."

He watches it in a trance. Something is happening to him. Something is going on *in* him. As if the painting has come to life, is opening itself, and pulls him in. As if the colors are moving apart, forming a small opening for him to creep through. Only if he has the *courage* to do it and plunge into the world beyond.

"What else do you feel?" Beresford encourages him. "What else do you *see* in it?"

"Nightmare? I think I see a nightmare or something. I see a torrent, or a whirlpool . . . Lots of passion. I feel passion in every stroke of his hand."

"Whose hand?"

"His. I feel passion for what he has lost."

"You mean the creator of the painting?"

"Yes."

"What did he lose? Can you see that, Michael?"

"I'm not sure . . . I only feel his strokes. But I can't see anything. Like I am blind . . . The strokes of his hand are random. But with lots of love, with lots of passion. Full of longing . . . for the things he had lost." He is getting more and more ecstatic and unreachable. Too distant. Then he winces. Looks away from the painting. The hand in which he holds the glass shakes. He brings it to his mouth and drains it.

"You all right, Michael?"

"Yeah." He nods. He looks Beresford in the eye. "Who painted that picture?"

"The son of the woman who gave it to me."

"You said earlier that the artist was unknown."

"I didn't say *the artist* was unknown. I meant that he was unknown in the art world."

"What else do you know about him?"

"Not much more than you do. He was sixteen when he painted it. It was after he had a car crash."

"In which he lost his sight?"

"Yes." The content smile on Beresford's face.

"He painted it blind?"

Beresford confirms with a slow nod of his head. "It was his cry for help. But you already know that. A kind of lament for lost sight."

"I see."

He is shaking. All of a sudden, he is cold. As if someone had opened wide all the windows and let the rush of cold air from the street in.

"Do you want more juice, Michael?"

"Yes, please. Could you also turn up the heating?"

Beresford pauses in a half move.

"Heating is almost at maximum. Are you cold? We can

move to the bedroom. It's warmer there."

"No. No need for that, thanks."

"As you wish. I'll get you a blanket, then. Would you prefer hot tea to juice?"

"If it's not a problem for you."

"Coming in a few minutes."

* * *

The aroma is rich and intoxicating, and it easily finds its way through Michael's body. Restoring him with strength and warmth, confidence and courage.

"Thank you. Tea is great."

"My own recipe. My small contribution to the well-being of mankind."

Michael smiles. For the first time since he got here.

"How are you feeling, Michael? What do you think about this conversation? Did it benefit you?"

"I don't know, to be honest. I was kinda hoping you would tell me that."

"But it hasn't done you any harm, has it?"

"No." Michael returns his smile.

Intimacy between the two of them is slowly establishing itself. (Possible friendship?) Beresford is gaining Michael's trust.

He asks him, "Is there anything you want to tell me before we finish for today?"

"Are we done?" Michael is surprised.

"I wouldn't want to go too hard on our first meeting. Unless you have something to add."

Michael shakes his head.

"Very well, then. I would like to meet you the same time

tomorrow, if that suits you. Do you have any other plans?"

"Nothing I couldn't postpone."

"Good. That'll be all for now. Depending on our progress, we'll see whether to change your therapy."

"You mean hypnosis? Do you think it might be necessary?"

"Perhaps. Michael, tell me honestly, are you afraid of hypnosis?"

"No, it's not that. I'm rather interested in it."

"Excellent!" They shake hands. "See you tomorrow."

"Oh, there is one other thing," Michael remembers. "You won't prescribe me anything?"

"I don't see the need for that now. Your father told me you are taking multivitamin tablets and occasionally antidepressants. We'll stick to that for now. Just don't go overboard with them, okay?"

"You think talking is better than pills, right?"

"Always," Beresford confirms.

"I'll see you, then."

"Michael?" Beresford stops him at the door. "I know it's not my business, but I'm glad your eye is getting better. It would be a shame that such an ugly bruise disfigures your pretty eyes."

"Uh, thank you," Michael says modestly, almost rushing into the spiritual arms that Beresford opens wide for him, promising serenity, happiness, and absolution if he confides in him all his secrets and innermost thoughts.

After all, they are still strangers, though Neil Beresford turns out to be more likable and normal than Michael remembered him.

Although he seems to be a man no one should be afraid of.

* * *

Family is important.

Family is the most important.

Everything else is impermanent and temporary. That is the life philosophy of the Atkinses.

The Atkinses don't advocate asceticism. They practice it even less, far from it. But they also shy away from the spirit of materialism and the servitude to electronic devices. Galloping progress and an exaggerated escape to the future are not their concern.

They live a quiet life in their house,

On their land,

Within their family.

Defending themselves against intruders who try to disturb their peace, destroy family harmony, and burden them with unnecessary debts.

They subordinated everything to their family, unlike those who subordinated their family to the computerized lifestyle.

Whether the Creeks have an understanding for such a philosophy is hard to tell. At least they are so polite that they listen to their whole story, trying to be open-minded to their ideas— as far as possible. After the abundant dinner, with both families involved in making and serving the food, it seems that their first neighbors aren't as weird and difficult to understand as the Creeks thought they would be.

Elisabeth Creek and Louise Atkins are chatting happily in the kitchen, exchanging recipes and admiring the delicious food they prepared. While Elisabeth Creek praised with only the nicest words her computerized kitchen, Louise Atkins reminds her of the pleasure of manually preparing food.

Dinner is quite enjoyable, except for the initial silence

interrupted only by the tinkling of the dishes and the laughs of Gentle Wind and Blue Sky Atkins.

The only crisis occurs when Elisabeth Creek tries to bring up the schooling issue. In her opinion, the Atkinses' children are at a loss for not going to school, and she makes it clear to their parents.

If Red Sunshine, apart from having an irresistible smile and gorgeous ginger hair, were not incredibly smart and a little tricky, she probably would have succeeded in giving them a lesson.

But he spoils her plan by asking Rebecca, "Rebecca, did you know that the sun radiates an energy of three point eighty-six times ten to the thirty-third ergs per second, but we receive only a fraction of the potential solar energy?"

He ignores the Creek people who stop eating corn pudding from the southern states, made and brought by his mother. Their forks halt halfway to their mouths, he notices from the corner of his eye.

"I'm telling you this to see what power it is. Only the effective surface of the sun has a heat of something under six thousand kelvins."

"You don't say!" Rebecca suppresses laughter, knowing where Sunny is heading.

"That's right. Can you imagine what would happen to us if we were not one astronomical unit away from it?"

"One astronomical unit?" Rebecca fakes amazement.

"Forgive me for being thoughtless. That's ninety-two point ninety-nine million miles or one hundred forty-nine point six million kilometers, if you prefer it that way. Now, what would happen to us if the distance between the sun and our planet instead of roughly ninety-three million miles or one hundred fifty million kilometers were ninety-three thousand miles or one hundred fifty thousand kilometers? Can you imagine that?"

"I can," Jeremy Creek jumps in, seeing through their game. "We would be overdone!"

The sidesplitting laughter at the table.

"But we wouldn't be as tasty as this duck in pineapple sauce," Louise Atkins corrects him. "Mrs. Creek, my compliments to your cooking," says the lumpish woman with an affectionate smile.

But the way she looks at her eldest son isn't so affectionate. Although proud of him, her gaze doesn't promise a pleasant conversation when they return home.

"Thank you very much, but the credit goes to my husband," Elisabeth Creek recovers from the shock. "And please, call me Elisabeth . . ."

Louise Atkins gives her another warm smile.

"If we were closer to the sun, we wouldn't be so cold now," Gentle Wind protests in his innocence. "We wouldn't have to heat in the middle of summer! And we would still have our garden. And I could grow dahlias, wisterias, hibiscuses, and tulips."

"Gentle Wind adores flowers," his mother says modestly, quieting down the laughter. "He planted all the flowers we have around the house. He has a green thumb."

"Really?" Rebecca enthuses. "Then you must come to us again and I will show you our greenhouse. It's full of flowers! I'm sure you'll like it."

Elisabeth and James Creek exchange silent glances.

"Can I? Super! What is your favorite flower, Rebecca?"

"Her favorite are the yellow roses," Red Sunshine is quicker to respond.

"I love yellow roses," Rebecca confirms, blushing.

"Ah." Gentle Wind is disappointed. *(So common. So unimaginative.)*

"Dad?" Blue Sky lets himself be heard, unable to stay the only one unnoticed.

"Yes, Son? What is it?"

"Can we listen again to the Third Piano Concerto in D minor by Rachmaninoff on the record player before bedtime tonight?"

Rebecca spits the milk back into her glass. "Excuse me." She wipes her mouth clean with the heel of her hand and flees into the kitchen.

Red Sunshine buries his head in his chest, shaking with laughter.

Goggle-eyed, Elisabeth Creek is racked by a cough. She doesn't stop coughing until Jeremy Creek comes to her aid with a glass of water.

Louise Atkins is whispering something to her youngest son, or pretending to do so, desperately trying to stay serious.

Ted Atkins scolds his son, who doesn't know what he had done wrong.

"But, Dad!" Blue Sky exclaims, not understanding.

"That's not how gentlemen behave at the table," his father says sternly.

"But I didn't spill the milk! Rebecca spilled it!"

Rebecca, who has just returned, escapes back to the kitchen. Overwhelmed by the loud burst of laughter.

"Not a word anymore, young fellow!" Ted Atkins is resolute. "Apologize to Mrs. and Mr. Creek at once. You'll get yours when we get home, you better be ready for that."

"Come on," Jeremy Creek speaks in defense of the blue-eyed boy. "We were all children. Blue Sky meant nothing wrong. Isn't that right, child?" He beams at the boy, who doesn't dare to move. Blue Sky's eyes are fixed on Rebecca's grandmother, who almost choked a few minutes ago. Thanks to him!

That is how the chapter on education is permanently closed.

At least as far as the Creeks are concerned.

***

"You were great!" Rebecca doesn't hide her delight. "That's what I call fast thinking. Not even I would have done it better!"

"You only think so," Sunny replies, glancing down from the night sky at her eyes, also strewn with stars. "It was instinct. The impulse that helps us survive. A touch of nature. You would have also thought of something if you had to."

"Maybe you're right. But it was still you who saved the evening."

"Which, by the way, was wonderful."

"If only there were more of them . . ." Sorrow in Rebecca's voice.

"There will be. I don't see why it wouldn't be so."

"Ah," her sigh. "School starts soon."

Red Sunshine watches her silently.

"And the magic will be gone," she adds with true regret.

"It doesn't have to go away if you don't want it."

"You mean, I shouldn't go to school?" she checks him.

"What would you miss?"

She cannot find an answer to his question. Not after today.

"I would teach you everything. And if you couldn't stand it without books and real professors, Denver is much closer than

New York."

"I can't, Sunny. You know that. It's not that I don't want to. I just can't."

"Because of your brother? Because of your father?"

"Yes. Because of them."

Red Sunshine is reasonable enough not to push any further. At least not tonight. But he doesn't give up either.

(School will start soon, yes. But not that soon to not allow him to carry out his plan to the end.)

He wants to tell her something else—a word of encouragement, perhaps, but he doesn't get to do that.

His folks come out of the house, followed by the Creeks. It's time to go home. Time to say goodbye.

No matter how much his heart longs to stay a little longer, decency requires otherwise.

"Rebecca . . ."

He doesn't finish his thought. It happens so fast and unexpectedly. Like a bolt out of the blue.

Rebecca kisses him. Spontaneously and without thinking.

(A touch of nature.)

It happens in a flash, but it lasts long enough for his knees to buckle. To regret even more that the day is dying.

"Rebecca . . ."

Too late.

She walks toward the cheerful voices, leaving him alone. Elongated shadow on the whiteness of the snow.

The moon is shining.

Chapter

10th: The *kickflip* is in its initial stage similar to the *ollie*. Bend your knees. Pop the tail. Drag your front foot up toward the nose and to the left. Kick it forward off the nose. Your foot off the grip tape, flip the board with your toes. Lift your back foot up. Prevent the board from flipping over.

IT'S NOT EASY TO FOCUS ON SOMETHING when chaos is everywhere around you: noise that irritates, screams with curses that are a little too much for your nerves and, on top of everything, you are on a tight schedule that breathes down your neck.

Time is merciless. Tomorrow night is the opening, and no one will care if everything is okay with you or not.

Time is money, and it doesn't give a damn for its victims.

A few more minutes and the wall is finished. That is all Victor needs. A few more minutes and he is out of this nuthouse. Once and for all.

He received a check this morning. Several hundred bucks. A decent amount, though hard-earned. Very clean money.

One last look at his work and Victor's mouth stretches to a smile.

California in New York. As it was—not so long ago. The sea, the beach, the surfers. A girl on roller skates with a Discman in her hand, undressed in a size and a half too small and too tight yellow bikini. Oh, baby!

Heavy clouds pressing from above. Stormy, apocalyptic, advancing fast. A warning sign of things to come. A stark contrast to the sunny summer day in which the scene takes place. A little too strong for Victor's taste, but it is the owner's wish.

Heavy clouds and stormy sky—an invisible bridge between the idyllic past and the ominous vision of the future—the new image of Der Soundgarten nightclub. Iron nets, steel chains, and cyborgs.

Lots of cyborgs, Victor is lost in thoughts, not noticing the ladder worker who walks past him and bumps his head with a ladder.

Victor curses and gets back to work.

(Just a little longer, dude, hold on just a little longer. Just a few more touches of spray. You can be patient that much, can't you? Then they can all lick your deck, good dogs!)

He is patient that much and finishes it.

He picks up his stuff, throws the rest of the usable spray cans in his backpack, and fixes the skateboard under his backpack.

Leaving behind The Verve and "Bitter Sweet Symphony," he disappears in the direction of the subway.

Back to New Manhattan, please.

Speeding somewhere under the bed of the East River, he wanders from the daylight of oblivion into the darkness of last night's memories, fighting an emotional battle with brutal reality.

Accepting it, but not accepting it.

Knowing it, but not understanding it.

His nana is dying. Cancer devours her. It's been two years, and he found out only yesterday.

Last night!

A few hours ago!

Only because it couldn't be hidden anymore!

(Where have his eyes been? All these years?)

In two years from now she will be one hundred years, but she won't live that long to see one hundred summers.

Ninety-eight years of giving, caring, loving, and understanding.

Fears. Rejoicing. Forgiveness.

Selflessness. Sacrifice. Loyalty.

SELF-SACRIFICE.

Why? What for?

(Thank You, Lord, for Thy mercy.)

Getting to New Brooklyn, he climbs out of the subway, two stairs at a time.

On the way out he spots a blind, homeless man praising God and begging Man for alms. A cardboard sign hangs around his neck:

> I AM HOMELESS AND HUNGRY,
> ANYTHING WILL HELP!

Victor reaches into his back pants pocket and pulls out a ten-dollar bill. Gives it to the old man, who almost kisses his hand in gratitude.

So much for mercy, Victor thinks to himself

and continues to his destination. Toward the "almshouse" for deserted and abandoned old people who have no one to look after them. Except for a few enthusiasts who have Mercy where their heart should be.

"Cold is the world we are living in and mornings do not warm us. Dawns are stale . . ." Victor mutters to himself. "If you only know, Michael, how right you are . . ."

He pulls out a skateboard under his backpack and throws it on the frozen sidewalk. This is his challenge, both to God and to man.

Full of irony and accumulated anger, he jumps on it, inviting danger. Having one wish only—to fall and break his neck. But this, also, is too much to ask from God, Victor knows this well.

He rolls his board all the way to his grandmother's nursing home in one piece and jumps off it. Not breaking his neck.

(Wasn't he right?)

* * *

"How are you, Nana?"

Looking into her eyes, Victor's throat tightens.

"I'm in pain . . ."

"Did you take the medicine?"

"The nurse gave it to me."

"It will be better, then. Hold on until it starts to work."

(Where does he get the strength to lie to her, mask the truth behind a nonexistent hope? Who gave him the right? If life has meaning, where is it now? Has it evaporated like droplets of dew in the morning sun? Was it so thin? So frail, weak, and inconstant?)

"She ate poorly. She barely touched her dinner last night.

Nothing this morning."

Victor turns to Mrs. Hilde. The old woman is covered up to her neck, only her right hand peeks from under the layers of blankets and a sheet.

"What do I hear, Nana? Why didn't you eat?"

"Don't blame her. It's not her fault, poor thing," Mrs. Hilde shows compassion.

(Does she also know that Nana is dying? Did everyone know that be-fore him?)

It doesn't get to his head that Nancy could have kept this from him. He didn't tell her about it, but Nancy felt the coldness and the change that happened in him. He is like New York's summer. Cold and cruel.

Although he cannot understand it, he wishes Nancy were here now. He wishes he could hug her, kiss her, and bring a little love into this death home.

In this room of death.

Room 508.

(True. This isn't Nana's fault. She didn't choose when she would be born, she couldn't choose the day she would die.)

Victor takes the banana from the nightstand and peels it.

"Have some of it."

"I'm not hungry." She shakes her head wearily. "I can't."

"How can you not be hungry? Mrs. Hilde says you didn't eat anything."

"I am not hungry."

"Come on, Angela, eat some," her roommate encourages her. "You must eat."

"I can't . . ."

"Nana, please. Don't make me angry. If you don't open your mouth, I'll go."

Her gaze full of begging, she opens her mouth. Too weak to resist.

"That's right," Victor praises her.

"Is she eating?" Mrs. Hilde asks, not seeing from her bed.

"She is." Victor sighs. "I just don't know who's eating who. Whether she eats banana or banana her."

He wishes Michael were here to read them poems. To help him by just *being* here. But he isn't here. Not even him.

Minutes pass before Angela Kenneth eats half of the banana. Victor then pulls her out of bed and takes her to the toilet. His every touch is filled with pain.

He tries to make her walk, but to no avail. She has deteriorated a lot, and she is in great pain. Her strength quickly abandons her.

Reality hits Victor. It hits him hard.

He leans over her, straining to hear what she wants to say.

"What did you say?"

"I want to go home."

"But you are home, Nana. *This* is your home now."

"Home. I want to go home . . . to my mom . . ."

Then Victor realizes. The home his grandmother wants to return to is no longer there. Just like her parents are gone too. The childhood she now lives in has long since died. Buried in the past, no traces left behind. Only fragments of memories remain.

He chokes back the tears in his throat that are opening new wounds. Fresh scars start to bleed, flowing into the sea of death, toward a house on the coast from Angela Kenneth's childhood memories.

With a cold, trembling hand, she touches her grandson's hand. Victor takes it, afraid to crush it.

"Will you take me home, Victor? Please . . ."

Tears stream down his face, overgrown with a rare, long stubble and stained with traces of dried color. Silently disappearing, never to return . . .

* * *

It's cold. Fast-paced and well-camouflaged and sheltered under layers of warm winter clothes, passersby walk to their destinations. But not James Stowe. He has no problem with the biting cold. Good-looking, slim, tall, with radiating, blue eyes and dark hair, he is the image of a model on a catwalk. Only James Stowe is not a model, despite his handsome *appearance*. And his well-built body and harmonious moves are the result of many years of playing volleyball—since his boyhood days.

Walking up Broadway to the north and further toward Riverside Park, his twenty-four-hours-a-day busy eyes capture every detail in search of inspiration. For something fresh that will bring him money, prestige, and fame. But more than anything, satisfaction with a job done successfully.

At twenty-three, James Stowe is a very ambitious young man. And very gifted, though he left the academy, where he studied art photography, without getting his degree. For Stowe's gift is far ahead of time for the taste of his professors, *old fogies*, and *senile moths*, as he calls them, who are too old to understand the evolution of contemporary photography.

During his studies, he was always at odds with them, so he soon became a burden and a nuisance to them. That's why they did nothing to keep the Academy's most promising student. That is the price Stowe had to pay for being ahead of his time.

His career didn't suffer much because of that, though. He

didn't give up, nor did it discourage him. He completes his education and earns his degree in the streets of New York, among *real* people. On his feet, instead of sitting on a school bench, always on the move, with his expensive camera slung over his shoulder. Taking photos of street life and cashing them. Shooting things the others would not even notice and turning them into success.

At this point in his career, Stowe has something big in prospect. Something *huge*. Dennis Kay showed an interest in his work. This fashion designer of men's underwear and clothing from the Garden State is a hit on the New York fashion scene this season. He is also looking for equally talented, ambitious and promising young people with whom to start a whole new trend to outrun his competition. Among just a few, selected and chosen, young talents, Dennis Kay takes his chances with James Stowe as well. After closely reviewing his work, they make a contract. Stowe will help him ascend the fashion throne, and in return will have a free hand to follow his instinct. Kay has only one request: the material he brings before him must be first-rate quality and ice-refreshing. Stowe has no problem with that.

And what Stowe now sees is exactly that.

He takes the camera out of his bag and takes some shots.

Then he looks for a spot to get a better shot of the desolation of a skatepark and a single skater, stubborn in performing tricks on chain-linked objects in New York's last skatepark.

If that isn't ice-refreshing and provocative enough, then I'm giving up, Stowe thinks.

The skater lifts his T-shirt and wipes his face with it. He has nothing under it. His bare chest, bathed in sweat, collides with the challenge of snow and frost. It is more than easy for Stowe to picture himself a Dennis Kay trademark on the young man's boxer shorts wet from sweat, peeking over his provocatively low-slung pants.

He shoots another picture. His hand shakes. Then he shoots three more.

The kid is good. The kid is *hot*. The warmth of his body creates a cloudlet around him, following his every move as if dancing around him.

Then the skater jumps on the skateboard again and Stowe, as spellbound, starts toward him. He cannot resist it anymore. That is already too much for him.

Although burning with excitement, he continues to approach his new muse, parading gracefully and elegantly as if on a catwalk.

* * *

Alien is confused. By the looks on their faces, he sees that not everything is clear to Stu, Ian, and Nathan too. They are not sure whether to believe him or make a complete mockery of him. Lenny puts an end to all doubts, saying, "If you mean to do it, don't forget to mention that you are getting the rest of your clothes in my store. You advertise me, I give you a discount," he concludes and disappears upstairs to show the new boards to some kids.

"Listen, dude, are you serious about this? You're not putting us on or anything?" Ian is careful not to jump to any conclusions.

"I'm telling you!" He waves Stowe's business card in front of their noses.

"And he runs into nobody else, but a loser like you!" Stu is more inclined to make a good joke out of the whole thing.

"Maybe it's because I'm the only loser still skating. While other losers keep their asses warm."

"Or maybe they are preparing for snowboarding," Stu corrects him. "Are you sure the guy is interested in shooting pictures of you only? What if he's some pervert who wants your ass under the pretense of this underwear ad story?"

"You are disgusting."

"Stop it, Stu," Nathan cuts him off. Turns to Alien. "Tell us again what happened. It all sounds unbelievable."

"I guess it does," Alien agrees and starts over.

"I was in a skatepark, on the vert, when I noticed this guy hanging around with a camera. I didn't pay attention to him at first. But then he approached me while I was taking a break and asked me if I had a moment."

"I thought the park was closed in this weather," Ian marvels.

"The park is *always* open to those who want to skate," Alien answers without much explanation. "So, the guy tells me who he works for and asks me straight up if I am interested in being his model. He gave me his phone number to call him when I make up my mind."

"Will you accept it?" Ian is curious.

"I might. Probably."

"And how much will you get for it?" Ian says.

Alien scratches behind his ear. "I forgot to ask him."

"Loser!" Stu fires. "What am I telling you all the time? And what happens to our boarding? That means we can't count on you anymore?"

"In that case, the plans will have to change, yes."

Stu curses.

Ian takes a deep breath.

Nathan remains silent.

"I'm really sorry, guys. I wanted to go with you, but—"

"But you got a better offer," Stu finishes instead. "Beware, though! Maybe this stud pays in kind! Anyhow, I wish you a fun time. I hope you learn something new from him." He is angry. Jealous and malicious, and he doesn't bother to conceal it at all.

"Will you leave him alone, already?" Nathan intervenes again. "If he doesn't want to come with us, we'll go without him. We'll take someone else. Nando mentioned that he would like to go, but his board is damaged."

"That can be resolved," Alien says in a conciliatory tone. "If Nando wants to go with you, I'll lend him my board. Provided I get it back without a scratch."

"You have my word," Stu calms down, too, tamed by Alien's generosity. "Just make sure you stay clear of scratch until we get back."

"Don't you worry about me." Alien cracks a smile. "Maybe I'm young, but I'm not *that* inexperienced."

A few jokes about Alien's inexperience.

"I hope you are not angry that I spoiled your plans. But if I went with you, it would be like a one-night stand. And this could last a little longer if everything turns out right."

(Why does everything he say sound ambiguous?)

That also doesn't go unnoticed by his friends, who once again throw ambiguous jokes at him.

"And don't forget to charge him plenty. Let him show the money," Stu comments instead of goodbye.

Alien gives him the finger and out he goes. Pizzas are waiting for delivery.

* * *

The next day, Michael rings with more confidence at Beresford's door in Hamilton Heights. Partly because he is impressed by Beresford's living space. He likes the futuristic look of his apartment a lot. Okay, maybe he exaggerates a little, but that doesn't change anything. Beresford's place is *high class*.

He has been exaggerating lots of things lately. One minute he is resentful of his father, and the next moment he is resigned and uninterested in anything.

He is disappointed in his sister to the point that he lost confidence in her. He knows that she only wishes him well, but he is still angry with her.

At first, Michael felt an aversion to Neil Beresford and therefore kept his distance. But that is now on the verge of growing into something else. Especially when Beresford greets him with hot tea and a big smile on his face. It seems to Michael as if they had parted ways just moments ago, and not that it was yesterday.

He still feels lost and confused every time he thinks of his mother's death. The pain of the loss is still sharp and, therefore, Michael continues to visit her at the cemetery almost every day. He will talk to her there, cleaning his emotional wounds and pretending to be happy.

On top of everything, he began to doubt himself. He became eccentric, touchy, and liable to different moods and oscillations. Mentally unaccountable, as his father would say. A danger to himself and other people. Fortunately, he is not completely left to himself. He still has Alien and Victor he can rely on when the going gets tough, and now there's Dr. Beresford.

He will help him deal with his problems. He will help him regain control of his life again.

"How are you today, Michael?" Beresford asks him.

"Good. I think."

"Glad to hear that. How did you spend your day?"

"I was at home. I slept late into the morning and when I woke up, I called Victor—he's a friend of mine. I couldn't get him, so I had a slow and long brunch, after which I planned to go skateboarding. But I changed my mind. I wasn't in the mood to skate alone in this weather. I stayed at home and wrote some poems. Just when I finished the new poem, it was time to go to see you, and here I am."

"That's very good, Michael. Writing is often a good vent for our frustrations. I know this from my own experience."

"Yeah."

"Michael, I believe you know that I talked to your mother in the same way I talk to you now?"

Michael nods.

"I talked to her about many things, including a lot about you too. Your mother sang your praises. She told me you had a gift for poetry. I must say with regret that I have never read any of your poems."

"My mother talked to you about me?" Michael asks.

"I've heard only positive things about you. That you are a great student, that you love Rimbaud very much, and that it is your dream to visit the places where he lived and worked. You still want that?"

"Mom and I needed to do this together . . ." He falls silent.

It is hard for him to talk about his mother. He doesn't even talk to Hank and Rebecca about her. But now, his psychiatrist, his mom's therapist, leads him to talk about her against his will. And Michael does nothing to stop him. He subordinates to him, believing in the positive outcome of this session and hoping to see the light at the end of the tunnel of his life.

"I'm sorry it didn't work out as you planned. I'm sure your mom, if she were alive, would love to see your dream come true," Beresford says.

"I know. I still haven't given up on it."

Michael digs into his pants pocket and produces a crumpled piece of paper. Gives it to Beresford. A gesture that the conversation about his mother is over.

"I finished it on my way here, as I went to see you. It's a little crumpled," he apologizes.

"Thank you for your trust, Michael." Beresford takes the paper from him and begins to read.

Michael shrugs his shoulders. *(Why not?)*

A little later, when he finishes reading, he stares at Michael for a long moment.

Michael holds his gaze. *(Why not?)*

Then Beresford reads his poem a second time and hands it back to him.

"Exceptionally good. I have to admit I'm surprised."

Michael grins. Thinks, *What therapy will I get now? Maybe it's time for hypnosis?* He doesn't care, actually.

"The peace you seek, is it so unreachable?" Beresford's voice is gentle and soothing, like the surf of the sea along the southern tip of New Manhattan.

"Sometimes I think I found it," Michael says. "When I'm calm, relaxed, and satisfied. But for the most part, I'm hyperactive. Not literally."

"Can you, please, clarify this a little?"

"I can try. I sleep poorly at nights. I dream a lot. Sometimes I think I dream with my eyes open. I'm not even sure if those were dreams. These are the *pictures*. Extremely real and present images. Are you following me?"

"Describe one."

"They're usually blurred and fuzzy. And they dissipate fast. But when I focus hard, they become clearer. They are almost crystal-clear.

"I don't know if that has anything to do with being a brother and a sister, but I see images with Rebecca. It's like I'm following what she's doing from a great distance. I see her picking flowers, riding in a car, things like that. As if I can see her thoughts. Weird, isn't it?"

He looks Beresford straight in the eye, and Beresford encourages him with a slight nod to continue.

"Then that started happening to me and others too. These images were not as clear as those with Rebecca, but I had them anyway. First it happened with Pa and then with Victor. I didn't see anything in these two cases, but I knew it happened. My premonitions didn't deceive me, though I was blind, so to speak. I was like a TV with the sound and no picture." He plays with a piece of paper. He says nothing about the image, the scene of his father drowning in a thick whirlpool of objects and confusing events. Michael had that vision only once, though it was powerful. The whole experience was too disturbing, which is reason enough for Michael to try not to think about it. The spasm on Hank's face was so intense that it distorted his face, and the blood splashed across his eyes, like a waterfall between his eyelids. Not a single drop was spilled. None were wasted. That was sick, *way* sick!

"The images you are talking about, how real are they? How credible? Do you have any confirmation something like that happened?"

"I have. I know it happened when I visited Victor's

grandma in a nursing home. It wasn't planned or anything. We didn't expect to meet there. Well, Victor didn't expect to see *me* there, but I had a hunch that he might be there."

"And Victor was there?"

"No, but he came later. About ten minutes after me. What's interesting to me is that he didn't plan to stop by, and he was as much surprised as I was when I saw him, and it turned out that I had a good feeling."

"Is there anything else similar that happened to you?"

"There is. But I don't know how credible that is. When I spoke to Rebecca on the computer, I warned her not to forget to change the water in the vase with yellow roses. She got upset about that. Like I said the truth. Like I guessed it right, and she really forgot to change the water to the flowers."

"Rebecca is in Denver now?"

"Yes. She's coming back in two weeks."

"And you made contact with her at such a distance, so to speak?"

"If you want to call it that. But that probably happened only because she is my sister. We know each other very well. I don't think I could do that with someone else."

Beresford falls silent, analyzing Michael's words.

"Doctor, does this have anything to do with telepathy? Or clairvoyance? I've read some books on the subject, so I know a little about it."

"I don't know, Michael. Perhaps it does. I can't answer that question right now. You caught me off guard a little. And also got me worried, to be frank with you."

"You don't have to worry about that. This is nothing terrible. Sometimes it can even be fun. The problem is that I have been feeling weaker and more exhausted since it started. Pa's vitamins do not help me as before. I mean, I feel better when I take them. Like I'm *high* or something. As if I could carry the globe in the palm of my hand. And then their effects weaken. And I'm tired and languid again. I want to sleep, but I can't. Lots of things are going through my mind, and then I see those images."

Neil Beresford's face expresses deep concern. He resembles a wise man who through meditation tries to figure out a formula for a cure that will save humanity. Although his humanity in this case is reduced to only one seventeen-year-old boy.

"Michael, have you talked to your father about that?"

"No, I haven't."

"Did you tell *anyone* anything about it? Tell me honestly."

"I didn't. I didn't tell a soul. I swear."

"I would ask you to stay that way. Let's keep this between the two of us. Until I see what we will do."

"You think you can help me?"

"I have something in mind, I just don't know if you're ready for it."

"You mean hypnosis? I'm in. I've already considered that possibility."

"You seem to be one step ahead of me, young man." Beresford allows himself a smile. "Yes, I meant that. But there is also something else."

"I'm sorry to interrupt you, but I would like to agree with you about something first."

"Go ahead. I'm listening."

"If you hypnotize me, I want you to promise me that you will not enter areas of my life that have nothing to do with this problem. Once I'm under your control, my privacy will be in your hands. Some things I would like to keep to myself. Since I won't be able to influence it then, your promise now is the only guarantee I have left that you will honor my wish."

"It's all right, Michael." His gaze is full of confidence. "You have my word that it will be the way you want it. You don't have to worry about that."

"Thank you. What was the other thing you mentioned?"

Beresford sighs. As if having second thoughts about that.

(Always present doubts?)

Then he gets up and motions to Michael to follow him.

"Come with me. I want to show you something."

Michael listens to him. But before that, he pockets an almost completely crumpled piece of paper in his pants.

> *In the end, I will die anyway.*
> *So why keep worries that embitter our lives*
> *and deepen our pain,*
> *yelling and screams erupted with the passion*
> *of drugged emotions?*
> *What is the point, when the only thing I wish*
> *is to reach the bottom and—vanish?*
> *(I have no pride anymore.)*
> *The heights are too distant and I don't crave for them.*
> *(I only seek peace.)*
> *And liberation of the morning—*
> *in the night too distant, unreachable like a dream.*
> *So I seek, but I cannot find.*
> *(What?)*
> *It is a dream, it is death,*
> *or maybe it is both of it.*

Chapter

11th: Put your front foot on the board. Land. If you want to do the *heelflip*, it's an opposite to the *kickflip*. Your front foot is in the middle of the board, your back foot is on the tail. Use your heel to flip the board while you drag your front foot toward the nose and slightly to the right. As already said, . . .

THE FIRST CALL THAT EVENING comes the moment he opens the door. Still impressed by the conversation and what Neil Beresford later showed him, Michael has to do his best to enjoy the delight with which Alien radiates. Considering that after his meeting with Beresford, he also visited his mother's grave, where he stayed a good twenty minutes, it is not so difficult to understand his restraint.

Alien showers him with information about his new, super job. Before calling him, Alien had just finished talking to a guy who will pay him two hundred bucks for two to three hours of shooting pictures of him. Alien is beside himself because of this deal. He refuses to give Michael more details over the phone because he wants to see him. He persuades him to come to the pizzeria, luring him with the promise of a free dinner.

"Alien, I'm not in the mood." Michael cannot shake off his low spirits. "But since you insist, I'll come. Just don't blame me later if you don't like my company. I warned you."

"Don't talk nonsense! Why should I blame you? Just take your boogie-board and get your ass over here."

"My boogie-board? Are you planning on skating?"

"Why not? Johnny-be-goods are too busy chasing junkies and pushers. It's their curfew, which leaves enough space for you and me."

"What about your pizzas? Someone else will deliver for you?"

"Of course not, dumbass! I'll do my own deliveries. But that doesn't mean I can't do a *grind* here or a *slide* there in between deliveries."

"You're nuts! You'll get fired!"

"Who cares! Now I have another job. A *better* job, sugar. I wasn't planning on doing pizzas forever. But, enough of that. Are you coming or not?"

"Like I have a choice!"

"Cool! See you, then. And don't forget your boogie-board."

Michael hangs up and sprints toward the bathroom, dying to take a shower. Alien pulled him out of the shower at the last minute. Now he will have to wait if he wants to see him. Luckily, his shift has just begun.

It is strange, but since he began to confide in Neil Beresford, Michael has a growing need for water. He showers more often, sometimes twice or even three times a day, and he is more thorough with his personal hygiene. As if he wants to hasten his *purification*, remove the spiritual dirt that came out of him during his sessions with his psychiatrist.

With his psychiatrist.

Eventually, he admitted he now has a psychiatrist. His personal shrink. He needs help. There is no point in denying it, living in a world of illusions. He ended up just like his mother. Only his problem is far more serious.

His mother had no premonitions. His mother didn't see the images. In that aspect she was better.

He is thinking, what if his illness runs in the family? What will happen to Rebecca if it's in their genes? Will she get ill too? Will she also end up with a psychiatrist?

As he thinks about it, the phone rings a second time. Half-naked and a few steps to the bathroom (some habits never die), he pulls a sweater over his head so as not to catch a cold and hurries to the computer. It's closer to him than the cell phone he left in his room while talking to Alien.

Alien, shit! Michael remembers, now sure he will be late.

Sergio Unit's screen switches on and Michael holds his breath.

"What's the matter? Something wrong?" Her worried eyes scrutinize him from the other side of the link. No hello, no introduction. As if she had just come home from school on an ordinary day.

"No, everything's *fine*. I just thought about you and you called."

"Really? I'm glad to hear you think of me, since you don't want to call."

"I'm sorry. I just didn't get to it. I'm too busy."

"Too busy? Doing what?"

"I am. And if you are interested, the therapies are going well." He is sarcastic. Dangerously sarcastic. He is like poison.

He cannot forgive her, not yet. Although she did the right thing when she called her father—he does not deny it. But he could not stand that she invaded his privacy without first asking him. He cannot forgive her *that*.

That's why he is like that. Direct and ruthless. He wants to hurt her, at least a little, so let her think. Let her be in his shoes. Besides, he still has to take a shower. *He's in a hurry to go out.*

He can only guess if he had hurt her, but he sees that she is surprised.

"You are seeing a therapist?"

"Dr. Beresford is a nice man. I didn't have much of an opinion of him before. We talk openly and, I must tell you, it helps. I no longer have to carry my burden alone. It is an indescribable relief. You could visit him, too, when you have problems."

"What is that supposed to mean?"

He confuses her, makes her lose her temper. *Good!*

"Why should *I* visit him?"

"Don't take it so personally. We all sometimes have problems. I worry about you, sis, so I want to recommend someone to you in advance. Have it handy when you need it."

The shock in her eyes. Disbelief. And wonderment.

In his eyes triumph, superiority, and arrogance.

"Do you have to be such trash?"

"What do you mean?"

"You have to ruin this conversation? That's not why I called you."

"Then why did you call me? What damned *reason* did you have to call me? Don't you have a good time without me? Or do you just have to be you and stick your little nose into everything?"

"I have a phenomenal time here! Better than you in stinky New York with your stupid skateboarders!"

"Leave them out of this. I warn you," his voice is icy. "Or you might regret it."

"Already did! I already regret it! For being stupid enough to worry about you . . ."

"Nobody asked you to. I was fine until you interfered. Until *you* ruined everything."

"And most of all, I regret YOU ARE MY BROTHER!"

"I'm sorry, but I can't help you with that."

Rebecca dabs at her eyes. She wipes her nose on her sleeve, struggling to find words.

"How can you be like that?"

"How can I be what?"

"That . . . coldhearted. Selfish. And so mean."

"Forgive me, but I am not responsible for my actions. I am *sick*. I need *help*. You have to understand what situation I'm in. I am *potentially dangerous* to everyone. You have to be careful with me. Or I could EXPLODE."

"You . . . you are angry with me. Because I talked to Dad."

He doesn't answer her.

"I didn't mean any harm, Michael. I didn't mean to hurt you. I wished you well. Please believe me!"

"You did the right thing. I needed help. But not like this. *I* would ask for it when the time came."

"I'm sorry."

He is quiet. A static image of her brother.

"Michael, what happened to us? Will things be like before between us? Can they? Can we just turn back time and forget everything?"

"I don't know, Rebecca. A lot has happened. All I know is

that we need time. . . ."

Tears on her face again. Eyes full of begging and lost hope.

"I have to go, Rebecca. Alien is waiting for me."

"I should have known. Why does it still surprise me?" she snaps and goes offline.

The screen in front of Michael blackens. The connection breaks. No warning, no goodbye.

He stares at it with an empty head and wandering thoughts. As if the emptiness in front of him sucks him in and then spits him into his sister's room. Where she will throw herself on the bed and weep her heart out. And then curse him and call him names with all sorts of epithets, but loving him, nonetheless.

Deep down in this world of blackness and flashing images, a sense of serenity descends on him. He realizes that his sister has found comfort. Someone is with her, someone is helping her get through this crisis.

"Forgive me, Rebecca," he whispers into the darkness. Then he stands up zombie-like and, unaware of his actions, goes into the shower.

He fails to answer the next call when the phone rings a third time. He slips on the wet bathroom floor and almost bangs his head against the door frame. When the phone rings again, Michael is already showered and on the way out.

"Dr. Beresford, good evening! I didn't expect your call."

"Hello, Michael. What are you doing? I haven't seen you in ages."

"Yeah, a whole two and a half hours?" Michael accepts his joke.

"It must be my poor memory serves me less and less. You sound out of breath. Going somewhere?"

"Actually, yes. I'm going to meet a friend."

"Splendid. Have a good time."

"Thanks."

"Your father is home? I need him a little."

"He isn't. Why? Do you mean to discredit the confidentiality of information I gave you?"

"No, Michael. *I do not mean to discredit the confidentiality of information you gave me.* That's what we agreed, didn't we? I'm calling for another reason."

"I know. I'm kidding. Sorry."

"No damage done. I was kidding too."

"Pa isn't home yet. Think he should be here any minute."

"Can you leave him a message to call me right away? Unless I get him first."

"No problem. Anything else?"

"That would be all, thank you. Say hello to your friend and I'll see you tomorrow."

"It's a deal."

The mere thought of what should happen tomorrow sends shivers up and down Michael's spine, but he won't let anything affect his mood tonight. Therefore, he says nothing about that to Alien. He fills him in about how the therapy had gone. Alien doesn't ask any questions; instead he talks at great length about the young photographer he met and who will shoot pictures of him for Dennis Kay men's underwear billboard ads.

Alien could become famous. His face might appear nationwide. He could become the new Marky Mark, Joel West, or one of the Brewer Twins. It all depends on James Stowe, in whose hands his future is now.

"He wants to take pictures of me naked from the waist up!" Alien exclaims, mouth full, chewing a slice of pizza.

"And you agreed to that?"

"For the money he offered me, I would pose for him only in my shorts!"

"And when you catch pneumonia? Have you thought about that?"

"Nooo . . . you got me wrong. I won't be half-naked all the time! I'll have my clothes on until I work up a sweat."

"I still think it's risky. And weird."

"Well, that's the point, wise guy! It should be *risky*. It needs to be weird. That's what he wants! I think it's a brilliant idea."

"And where are you going to shoot?"

"The first series of photos we shoot in the skatepark. I don't know about another one. We haven't come up with another location yet. I reckon we'll do one series per day. Otherwise, I could get something I hadn't planned."

"It's great that the money didn't go to your head yet. There's still hope for you."

"Sure, sport, whatever you say." He blows him a kiss across the table. "So tell me. Do you envy me at least a little bit?"

Michael grins, swallowing a larger piece of pizza.

"Admit you envy me!"

"Hell, not in the least." He washes it down with a few gulps of orange juice. "Just the opposite. I'm proud of you."

Alien would kiss him this time if Michael hadn't backed up in time.

Having finished their dinner, they set out together to do Alien's deliveries. One in Midtown New Manhattan; the other one in the Upper East Side. Michael follows Alien's bicycle on his skateboard. When they are done, Alien unchains his skateboard off the bicycle, and they thunder the streets. Grinding the stairs and tossing each other in the piles of snow at the curbs of cleaned sidewalks. They run away from the howls of the

FDNY sirens, thinking the cops are after them. Sorry, guys, false alarm.

They part around midnight. Michael returns home, while Alien hurries to get some new pizzas. The beeper on his bicycle had been screaming at him for fifteen minutes already.

* * *

(No one has hurt her like that so far, no one. No one has caused her so much pain. No one has been so unfair to her.

(What for? Why? Because she meant well? Because she wanted to help?

(How can people be so cruel? How can they be so unfair?

(How can Michael be so unfair!?)

Rebecca is sobbing, her face buried deep into the pillow, so Grandpa and Grandma won't hear her cry. And then ask questions she doesn't want to answer.

They will only worry if they see her like that. What will she tell them? That she had a quarrel with Michael? That's old news—brothers and sisters lock horns all the time! How will she explain to them that this is no *ordinary* feud? Deep inside, Rebecca feels that something between her and Michael has gone forever. That a part of them has become a distant part of the past.

That hurts her the most.

From the ground floor, she hears voices. She rushes to the mirror and stops, horrified.

With quick moves she tries to fix what Michael has damaged, but it is difficult to conceal her true feelings. She is *torn* by the pain.

Dear God, if she could only die! If she could disappear only for a moment. Until all this passes. Until the last light burns itself out and the last breath comes to rest.

She responds to the calls and walks down the stairs. Levitating above them like a ghost.

Sunny's smile gives her courage. She grasps his hand, giving him a pale smile.

(How did that turn out? Did he notice anything?)

His entire appearance is radiating, his face lit up with a sunny smile. Jeremy Creek and Elisabeth Creek are also smiling. All around her happiness and smiling faces.

She wants to cry.

"Don't bring her home too late," Elisabeth Creek says on their leaving.

"And drive carefully," Jeremy Creek remarks.

Sunny says goodbye to them and holds the passenger's door for Rebecca until she climbs in her seat.

Then he starts the engine and shifts into gear.

"Are you sure you know how to drive this?"

She is looking straight ahead.

"I came this far, didn't I?"

"I didn't know you drove."

"I drive occasionally. When Dad lets me. I don't have a driver's license yet."

He drives off into the night.

"Why didn't your dad come?"

"You will see when the time comes. Besides, he likes to give me small pleasures."

They drive for a few minutes in silence, and then Sunshine veers off the road, stops, kills the engine.

"Why did we stop?" Rebecca's voice is nervous and it cracks.

Red Sunshine fishes a clean handkerchief out of his pocket and hands it to Rebecca.

"You can cry if it will be easier for you. I'll wait."

She just waited for that. For his right words that will let her cry.

She is crying and sobbing, watering his handkerchief. Clutching it in her hand, holding on to it like a drowning man clutching at the string of salvation.

"I'm sorry for this. I didn't mean to spoil your evening."

"Tears can't spoil the evening. Tears are healing."

She blows her nose. "Healing? If that were true, I would be the healthiest person in the world."

"I won't ask you what happened. You will tell me when you're ready. Just tell me how you feel now? Can we continue, or is it wiser that I take you back?"

"It's wiser to take me back, but I want to keep going."

"I thought you would say that."

He restarts the car. His hand is already on the steering wheel when Rebecca covers his hand with hers.

"Sunny?" she asks in a serious voice. "Suppose someone hurt you, someone very close to you, for no good reason, because they misunderstood or interpreted it differently; suppose someone you love very much hurt you, and that person now thinks about you all the worst . . . What would you do, what would you say to that person who was close to you and whom you still love very much?"

"Was?" His gaze is too serious for his age. "Not close to you anymore?"

"What would you do if someone you love hurt you? If Blue Sky or Gentle Wind did something after which you wouldn't want to see them nor hear from them?"

He ponders it motionless while the engine is humming, and that is the only sound in the quiet empire of the night.

Then he laughs.

He says, "If something like that happened to me, I'd beat the living daylights out of them! But that's not the answer you were looking for."

Caught by his sincerity, Rebecca starts laughing too.

"I would beat them, so it never crossed their minds again. But I wouldn't leave them in doubt thinking I did it because I love them less for what they did. Or that I punished them out of anger or because I was furious, and not out of love. They should know that I kicked their asses because I love them and that I will always be there for them no matter what."

He caresses her face.

She surrenders her cheek to his palm.

Then he kisses her, and she returns the kiss, rests her head on his chest. Listening to his heartbeat.

(Footsteps of time on a lonely road.)

"We can go," she whispers.

He steps on the gas pedal, holding her head in his arm.

* * *

The sounds of the violin remove the last traces of restlessness, worry, and sorrow. Relaxing the soul and waking the sleep. Reminding of the warmth of life and the beauty of existence. Indestructible and eternal.

They fall silent, followed by a loud applause. When Rebecca hears them again, the impeccable harmony of Ted Atkins's gorgeous voice accompanies them. Watching her with love in his eyes, he sings in harmony with his wife, who plays the violin.

The notes are bleeding from beauty.

A touch of nature, a thought flashes in Rebecca's head like a shooting star.

A touch of the most beautiful thing she has ever heard.

A touch of intimacy. A touch of family.

Tears moisten her eyes. So impatient, so eager to escape . . .

This evening Rebecca witnesses something special. Although she is a stranger, she, too, now becomes part of something special.

A new beginning is marked this evening. Her new beginning, greeted by the sounds of the violin running through the wilderness—messengers of happier days.

(The notes are bleeding.)

She wishes them a long and happy journey.

She wishes them to get all the way to the shores of New York, where someone special will hear them.

Chapter

12th: . . . *backside* (*bs* or *b/s*) is a body turn or the rotation of the board in the direction your toes are pointed so that your back is facing the outside of the arc. Opposite to *bs* is *frontside* (*fs* or *f/s*). It is a body turn or the rotation of the board in the direction your heel is pointed, so that your front is facing . . .

AN UNUSUAL AND HEAVY SILENCE DESCENDS on Lenox Hill Hospital at 100 East 97th Street, after the sobs of little Norma stop. Her big, walnut-colored eyes, purified with tears, are wide with horror. From somewhere inside her, the attacker will strike again. Silent and in anticipation of shaking her weak body with a new dose of pain. But this time the dose will be stronger and will again start the Great River of Tears.

The attacker is insatiable, heartless. It had already taken her beautiful, curly hair, and that isn't enough. It will only be satisfied when she is completely bald and ugly. When no boy will want to look at her again. Even if chemotherapy helps her by some miracle, which she doubts, she will never be as pretty as she was before the cancer started spreading through her veins.

That's her reality. Without a window to look into the future, trapped behind the heavy door of pain, suffering, shame, drugs, and tears. Nothing new to her—she had been down that road, hadn't she?

For an hour already Nancy sits in a chair by her bedside, telling her stories and humming her favorite tunes. Talking to her in half voice so as not to wake two other little girls with whom Norma shares a room.

Her big, moist eyes focus on Nancy's lips in an unbreakable plea, while her thin, almost translucent fingers clamp Nancy's hand tightly, surprisingly strong for a child suffering from cancer. Nancy's wrist is chalky white, but she doesn't pull her hand free from the child's grip.

She continues to absorb Norma's pain through this touch, and with the power of her positive thoughts exorcises evil spirits and irradiates the malignant cells that ravage Norma's body.

Slowly, trusting her, Norma's grip loosens.

Moments later, she is already asleep. For a few short hours she will be protected from the pain and suffering of this world.

Marking the page with her finger, Nancy puts *The Celestine Prophecy* on her lap. She cannot concentrate on reading tonight. Her thoughts are all over the place. Not even a good book can relax her.

Her eyes lock with the lifeless expression of the wall clock. Half an hour after midnight, the minute hand winks at her without stopping on its lazy journey through eternity. Tonight's shift will be long. Very long.

She closes her eyes for a moment. She doesn't plan to fall asleep or something; she just needs a few minutes to rest her eyes. That's all.

A few precious minutes.

In her mind she hears the clock ticking; feels the seconds rushing faster on their run. And her eyes are so heavy . . .

At that moment she hears the footsteps and opens her eyes. She sees her own reflection in the mirror. Through the open door that leads into Victor's room, she catches sight of his naked body under the crumpled sheets, inviting her.

She reaches out to touch his image in the mirror, but she jumps, scared by the dull sound.

The book slides from her lap and slams to the floor.

The image in the mirror vanishes and Nancy's eyes spot a pair of legs standing in the doorway.

"Are you okay?" a faint, little voice asks.

Thank God, Nancy thinks with relief, *it's just Dean.*

"What are you doing here, Nancy's little sparrow?" She addresses the little, five-year-old boy who is watching her from the door frame. There is no reproach in her voice. Only remnants of surprise mixed with undisguised sympathy. Because Dean is her favorite. Her secret love. Dean is her little weakness. "Shouldn't you be in bed?"

"I can't sleep." He rubs his sleepy eyes. "I had a bad dream."

"Nooo," she fakes surprise. "Come to me and tell me what you dreamed, Nancy's little sparrow."

He clatters in oversized slippers and climbs into her lap.

That is *his* hidden sympathy.

Nancy is holding a frightened boy in her lap as he tells her about a big bug with huge claws who chased him in the dream, threatening to gouge his eyes out and cut off his tongue and little peter. Although the bug was moving backwards, it was too fast for Dean and *grew* more and more night after night. One day it will outgrow him, and Dean will no longer be able to escape it. "If it kills me in a dream, will I see you again?" he asks Nancy in a trembling, little voice.

"Of course, you'll see me again," Nancy replies. "But this won't happen, I promise you." Still, there is too much symbolism in his dream.

Too many bad signs.

She comforts the boy, and his small body comforts her. Mutual exchange of affection and sympathies.

Nancy suddenly remembers diapers. She must buy them tomorrow before she drops by to see Angela Kenneth. She used the last one today.

Thinking of diapers, she remembers one other child she will have to comfort too. That boy also has nightmares. And he also lives in fear for someone threatened by a horrible bug.

But she won't be rocking him in her lap like she's rocking Dean now, she's sure of it. She has other plans for him.

* * *

The night is late and calm for most New Yorkers who, distracted by artificial light, are trying to find their way to a haven of dreams, before the dawn of a new day. That isn't the case with Hank Daniels, though. True, he needs rest badly, but a gay couple under his window is too loud for the dead hour of the night.

Hank Daniels pours another glass of bourbon, waiting for the horny couple to walk away to their next kissing stop.

"Here's to you, Michael," he makes a toast and smacks his lips. This is his fifth drink tonight, and he's already half-drunk.

He doesn't care if he gets drunk tonight. Usually he quickly sobers up, so tomorrow at work no one will suspect his early-morning vices. No one will be able to prove anything and ask him to explain himself. That's none of their business, anyway! Like he doesn't have enough reasons to get drunk!

Neil Beresford has ruffled his feathers. Again he reproached him and accused him of negligence. Daniels can't tolerate it anymore.

Who does he think he is to tell him he pays too little attention to Michael? Who is he to accuse him that the boy has run out of control?! None of this is true, so he needs to shed some light to him on how things are.

"That's why you're here. It is your job to control his actions and thoughts. Why do you think I hired you?"

"I know very well what my job is. You don't have to remind me. But I'm afraid you still underestimated Michael a little. He is an extremely bright and sharp-witted guy. Sometimes I wonder if you are aware of *how* sharp-witted he is?"

"I am, my friend," a sudden change in Daniels's voice. "Believe me, I'm well aware." The torrent of feelings that burst from the mouth of a man with an iron heart takes Beresford by surprise. "Michael is a wonderful boy. Clever, obedient, patient; I love him unconditionally. I cannot tell how sorry I am that he is not my flesh and blood."

No doubt, Daniels's melancholy and regret are genuine. Beresford almost physically feels them across the computer screen.

"That's why you need to be more careful. We can't afford another mistake. It must not happen again that I learn something from Michael before you tell me about it. Do you understand what I'm trying to tell you?"

"Of course," he acknowledges. "I understand what you are saying, Neil."

"Michael will keep his promise and keep quiet about what

we are talking about. I have no doubt about that," Beresford continues. "But what if he spills the beans by *accident*? What then?"

"Do you think that can happen?"

"Hank, tell me honestly. Did the possibility of failure ever cross your mind? That we won't make it?"

"No, it didn't. I planned it all well. Everything is under control."

"*We* are under control! You and me. But what about Michael? How much is he under control? How *well* do you know him?"

"Better than you think. I know him a lot better than you think. Michael won't be a problem. He will understand that it is for his own good once he realizes the value of the *gift* you and I will give him. He deserves it. He deserves to be someone special."

"I'm not sure if that's what *he* wants. Will he accept your gift? Michael is happy with his life, as far as I can conclude from what he told me. He is a brilliant student, naturally gifted, and really enjoys skateboarding, though I don't see the pleasure in it. I just don't know if he would want to trade it for some-thing new and foreign to him."

"He won't have to change anything! He'll just be even more satisfied. He would be *foolish* not to grab this opportunity with both hands."

"All right, I'll take care of that," Beresford says. "The boy will be fine. Everything will be fine. But you and I will have to work more closely. I'm telling you this for everybody's sake."

"Sure. At least that is not in question."

Then why is he restless, and why had he emptied half a bottle of bourbon already? Why does he feel so *lonely*? Lonelier than ever since Melanie Hope passed away? His wife, his light, and her beautiful body that he still adored with his every memory. It gave him many pleasant moments and unforgettable nights. And two beautiful fruits to stay with him now that she is gone.

His Rebecca and his Michael.

He doesn't move when he hears the apartment door unlock. His eyes are glued to the thin trace of light peeking out from under the door of his room. He keeps eavesdropping silent and considerate footsteps, the splashing of water in the bathroom.

When silence creeps into every corner of the apartment again, he puts his empty glass on the nightstand and leaves the room.

Michael's bed is dimly lit by the pale streetlight dripping through his window and, with the lazy moves of a tired artist, drawing a figure lying on it: white T-shirt, an uncovered leg, his back facing the door when Hank walks into the room and sits on the bed next to him.

Hank's hungry hand strokes the soft skin on Michael's leg. Up and down, squeezing and releasing it until it crawls to a stop before the Independent tattoo with the sign of a cross on his calf—a trademark of Michael's favorite skateboarding company.

The hand claws its fingers into a smooth and strong muscle. One day, that same leg will make him proud, when Michael wins something more than a skateboarding contest.

To get as close as possible to him, Hank Daniels did his best to understand skateboarders. Among other things, he learned from Michael that every year rivers of money flew into this sport and entertainment, fighting for new investment projects—daring and bold teenage boys like Michael.

Like Michael's expensive leg with the Independent tattoo inked on it. It is all his now. Only his. It rests in his hand, not backing away.

So graceful and still . . .

So tamed . . .

"Michael, I'm so lonely." He exhales a slow and muffled whisper. The smell of alcohol fills Michael's room. "And you are so *handsome* . . . And I love you . . ."

Michael turns to him. He isn't sleeping. He doesn't pretend to be asleep.

His breathing is slow and barely noticeable.

"I love you so much, it hurts me. . . ." he whispers again. Gets closer. "Do you love me too?"

The hulking shape becomes even bigger, towering over him. Bare chest with thick hair, broad and built shoulders. The face scarred with problems, worries, and dedicated work, but still handsome and somehow fresh. Parted lips from which the smell of bourbon intoxicates him.

He is completely passive while those big and strong hands skin off his T-shirt. He is aware of his nakedness in the cold embrace of the night and the shadow looming over him. And what he actually sees are hordes of demons. Legions of them, far beyond this space and his understanding of time.

Michael doesn't see their faces, because his sight is blurred with only one face. But their voices are wicked and evil, so familiar. Mocking screams and horny moans . . .

This is your night, Michael. A night to remember. Enjoy the gift we seeeeent you . . .

The bed dances under him while Tony Hawk's poster above the head of his bed spins around faster and faster. More violent, more brutal. Everywhere he looks, there are demons.

(Stronger, faster, more violent.)

Jumping, playing, dancing.

L A U G H I N G.

One of them lets out an inhuman cry that scatters them to nothingness. The world stops turning, and Michael is hurt.

The tears on his face are silent and ashamed while his father is leaving his room. When he closes the door behind him, they grow into a torrent of despair.

* * *

A few hundred miles north, the night is pitch-black in the Federal State of Vermont. The road sleeps under virgin snow, and new snow continues to fall. An ambience that gives one the creeps. Solitude, desolation, and isolation again. A rare car coming from the opposite direction, hidden behind headlights that would flash through the snow wall.

That's all they see. No one behind them, no one in front of them, no one to overtake them regardless of Andy's slow and careful driving.

The winter road maintenance services failed, surprised and unprepared. It is *summer*, for God's sake! Who would expect snow at this time of year? Who would expect that much snow?!

The forecast warned possible precipitation. *Possible* precipitation! Instead, heavy snow covers everything. Too much snow even for Andy's taste.

Was this a wise move? It rather looks like a reckless decision driven by a wish to brag. *(We skied in August! And last year we were sweating and couldn't find a shadow to hide!)*

Andy is sweating even now, if he was asked. He swelters

from the ghosts that lurk in the night and the heat that is turned up to the max. All the windows are steamy, and it is almost impossible for him to drive. He is in his shirt, and he wants to take it off.

"You want a chocolate bar? It will keep you awake." Fernando unwraps the chocolate bar for him and Andy pops it into his mouth.

"Thanks."

He likes the taste. Besides being concerned, he is also hungry.

Fernando opens another for himself and eats it. He doesn't offer Stu or Nathan. They are sound asleep in the backseat.

"Spooky," he says just to say something, afraid that Andy may nod off and swerve into a ditch. Who will haul them out given the traffic density? They could freeze before the first vehicle arrives!

He doesn't like how their trip started. First, Alien abandoned them because of some gay photographer, as Stu explained to him. Then, Ian canceled because he didn't like the way Stu talked about Alien. Alien gave no reason for that. So Andy took his place in the last minute. He, too, had his doubts and second thoughts, but then he agreed to come and took his Jeep. And now he threatens to fall asleep at the wheel!

Fernando sends a prayer to all the saints he can think of, asking them to help them finish their trip in one piece. From the very beginning, everything has a bad sign. They should have canceled this trip, but no one saw it back then. No one.

"What are you doing?" he asks Andy, his voice tense with fear.

"I'm taking my shirt off. What do you think I'm doing? I'm hot."

"Watch out! We'll run off the road. We'll smash into the snow! Or hit a tree . . . !"

"Don't panic, Nando." Andy wriggles his arm out of his shirt, holding the steering wheel with his other hand. He repeats the whole process with his left arm, asking Fernando to take over the steering wheel.

"Why?" Panic in Fernando's eyes.

"Because I'm going to take off my undershirt as well."

"You're nuts! It's bitching cold outside! You are not thinking of driving naked, are you?!"

"I'm nuts for taking this trip in the first place. And yes, I'll drive naked if you don't mind!"

He lets go of the steering wheel that Fernando grabs, having no choice.

The Jeep zigzags while Andy wrestles to work free his dreadlocks. When he is done, he takes over the wheel from Fernando.

"I have to admit you're really crazy," Fernando says, recovering from the shock. "I haven't noticed it before."

Andy grins, much more pleased now.

Fernando continues his monologue. "But I have news for you too. I bet you didn't know I was even crazier!" he exclaims, and starts taking his clothes off.

Andy guffaws.

His crazy laughter wakes up Stu, who, still half-asleep, squints one eye. Seeing the two skateboarders naked from the waist up, he mutters through his lips, "Fucking jerks." Then he goes back to sleep, covering himself with his jacket over his head.

* * *

Loneliness suits him most. He may be in the mood for company a little later, but now he doesn't want anyone around. He wants to be alone.

He wants to *skate* alone.

He meets several skateboarders on the Brooklyn side of the Old Brooklyn Bridge. Together they do a few tricks on the curb under the bridge. Above them, a feverish rumble of traffic.

They don't talk much (Victor isn't in the mood for socializing). He says a few words only when spoken to and then rides off in the direction of Furman Street. At the River Café, he quenches his thirst and feeds his hunger, thinking all the while about the skateboarders he had just met. He recalls what he was like at their age, when he admired anyone who did the simplest trick. Back then, he looked upon them as "gods on wheels." He was so young and inexperienced that he didn't even dare to think he would soon do the same tricks himself. It took him some time to master it, to get this far. And a lot of effort, practice, persistence, and perseverance. Above all—skateboarding. He spent almost half of his adolescent life on a skateboard until he perfected his skating, whether by day or night, rain or sun. All this to become "one of the gods," which some new kids now view with admiration and awe.

The kids under the Old Brooklyn Bridge.

He smiles at them friendly when they approach him to tell him how awesome his skating is and ask him what they have to do to learn to skate so elegantly and softly, and at the same time aggressively. You don't need to do anything special, he tells them, just keep doing what you're already doing. Watch other guys do tricks, learn from them, and *skate all the time*. That's all it is; there's no magic there. Then they ask him if he is skating in contests, and he tells them he used to, but not anymore. Before they can ask him anything else, Victor says goodbye to them, making them sad.

Cruising the streets again, he returns in his thoughts to his first, official contest in Canada. An unknown kid from New York City, with only one sponsor behind him, came without a lot of fuss and won the contest. Although it was in the amateur category, his approach and his skating were in the ranks of the greatest pros. The skateboarding world became interested in him overnight.

Already at the next contest, in Mexico, his name is mentioned as one of the favorites. This time he came with three sponsors and won again.

He also won his first professional contest in Washington, DC, after which Victor was already a star and sponsors started to fight for him.

Victor took his new role most seriously. He devoted himself to skateboarding to the point that he neglected his school. He neglected it completely so he could continue to score well in contests. That came to fruition in Brazil and Marseilles—his first triumph on the not-too-friendly, European soil.

And then Philadelphia happened. And something that the skateboarding world has not yet fully understood even today. Although it has been six years since then.

Why did Victor Kenneth give up the title? Why did he ruin his career?

These are the questions which still arouse curiosity and torment many heads who live for skateboarding and from skateboarding.

Victor belongs to the first category, to those who live *for* skateboarding. Money was never his priority. That's why he did what he did—handed the title to a boy from Munich, who, in

Victor's opinion, was better than him. But the jury didn't share Victor's opinion.

Victor, however, is not alone in his belief. He had heard from more people that Magnus was better; even some judges thought so *off the record*. But only unofficially. Those were the times when a European boy could not be allowed to win a contest on American soil. Relations between the States and the European Union were still, politically, quite tense, and even contests like this represented something more than just a sporting event.

That's why the scandal that Victor caused, because he wanted to play fair, echoed with such a bang. The reporters were on his heels asking him to *explain* himself WHY HE DID IT. They didn't want to believe the simple truth. They did not want to believe him when he claimed that Magnus was better than him. *They couldn't accept it.*

(By what right does he question the credibility of the judges' judgements? Isn't he paid to skate and not to decide who is the best? Who qualified him to make such decisions . . . ?)

Victor responds to the challenge, "The streets have qualified me. The streets I've spent most of my life on. I was bleeding on them and I learned to be a skateboarder. The streets are where you will find true skateboarders! All this . . ." he said, as he gestured to the skatepark and the thinning crowd, "this is money. This is *business*!"

While other reporters yawned in shock, a local journalist takes advantage of their confusion and asks him, "Victor, how do you see your future after today? I don't think it's pretentious to say that some of your sponsors will likely show you distrust."

"That's a good question," he agrees with her, "but I'm

afraid I cannot answer it now. I do know one thing, though. I'll go back to school and graduate. It's not too late for that."

"First, I must congratulate you on your actions," a French journalist could not hide his delight. He does not pay heed to his angry, American counterparts, but continues in good faith, "One must have courage to do such a thing. I have only one question for you. Can we hope to have the pleasure of seeing you in two months in Paris? The French people would be proud to host such a great person."

Silence descended among all gathered. There was no person who was unaware of what the French journalist had just done. Expressing his admiration for an American, he also restored dignity to his country and offered it a hand of reconciliation.

"Why, thank you, sir, for thinking so. I appreciate it and thank you very much for the invitation, but I regret to say that Paris is not likely to see me. At least not as one of the contestants. If I come to Paris, it will be in a private arrangement. I'll be among the skateboarders of Paris, and if you want to see me skate the board, it's best to look for me on the streets of Paris. I'm sure there are a lot of good kids out there who will never get to contest. Not because they are not *good* enough, but because they know better than me and you what the real meaning of skateboarding is."

With these words he finished the interview. More questions remained hanging unanswered in the air, but Victor said what he had to say.

That day Victor withdrew himself not only from the eyes of the cameras and the ears of the microphones, but also from professional skateboarding. Up to the present day, he has skated no contests.

As the young, female journalist predicted, all his sponsors left him but one. Only Blackout stayed with him, his first sponsor who believed in him while he was still an unknown, but a very promising boy from the hood. It still carries Victor Kenneth's name on its products, and Victor Kenneth Blackout skateboards are still selling like hot cakes.

The irony is that Victor Kenneth never skated on his boards again, but he allowed Blackout to use his name until they are bored with it.

It is a small compensation for the faith Blackout showed in him at his hardest of times. When he was all alone and ready to conquer the world.

* * *

It's been hours since the night came down from the sky, and Victor decides he has enough of skateboarding for today. He is tired and will need a clear head tomorrow. Tomorrow, he will think about everything, which requires a rested body and a fresh mind.

He is already in his mind in the long, hot shower, when he brakes to a stop, missing a familiar face by two lengths of a skateboard.

He goes back a few steps and wonders aloud, "What are you doing here?"

"Uh, nothing. I'm just going home," Justin tries to dodge his question.

"At this hour? Here, alone?"

"I was at my friend's. We chatted with some guys online and forgot about the time."

"Have you been to Sven's?"

"Nope, Sven lives on the West Side. You don't know him."

"I see . . ."

Justin looks at the thin layer of ice that shines on the asphalt.

"Just, is something wrong?"

"No. All is well. Really."

"Come on." Victor locks his skateboard under his arm. "I'll walk you home. You can tell me on the way."

Justin doesn't know what to think. He is doubly confused. It is confusing enough that Victor expects him to tell him something, but even more confusing is Victor's offer to walk him home.

He blinks in disbelief.

"You'll walk me home?"

"Yes, why not? It's too late for you to go alone. I don't want to have you on my conscience."

Justin smiles. "Vic, do you have some time before we go? You in a great hurry?"

"Not so much that I couldn't find a minute to spare. What's up?"

"I'd like to show you something."

A few buildings later, and then a few more, they are in front of an old warehouse.

Without trouble, Justin picks a poorly secured lock and slips in with Victor on his heels.

The warehouse is covered with dust, the air in it stale and dry. And so are two ramps, a bank and a fun-box, of which a small skatepark is made, illuminated by the dim streetlight coming through dirty and broken windows.

"How did you find this place?"

"I've been following some kids." Justin shrugs. "Been

watching them come in and out, locking the door behind them. Once I sneaked to the door and listened to what they were doing. That's it."

"That's it, you say? They saw you spying on them? They know you know about this place?"

"No." He shrinks into himself. He didn't expect reproach from Victor.

"Then this is breaking and entering. Illegal trespass on someone else's property."

"They didn't see me," he explains, "but they know I know about their hiding place."

A question in Victor's eyes.

"I met one boy. I faked that I happened to be there just when he was leaving the warehouse. He was embarrassed that I caught him, so he tried to sell me a lie. But he changed his mind and showed me inside, giving me permission to skate provided I didn't tell anyone about this place."

"It means you broke your promise. That's not right, my friend. Not right at all."

"I know." Justin is contrite. He hoped his idol would be at least a little more grateful for sharing this secret with him. "I'm sorry, but I had to do it. Just this time. It won't happen again. I will not tell others about the warehouse."

Victor's eyes do not leave Justin's face for a second. "You told me, but you won't tell others? Isn't that even more unfair?"

Justin sinks deeper into despondency. No excuse for what he did. The damage is done. Double damage.

"Why?" Victor wants to know.

"I thought you'd be glad. Thought you might be interested."

On Victor's face still the question: *Why me?*

"And because I thought, I hoped, that you would show me how you won the contest," he speaks what is on his mind. Seconds of hesitation, then seconds of silence and consideration. Too long, in Justin's opinion. Way too long.

Then the question, "What made you think I'd do that? That was a long time ago. I put that all behind me."

"Maybe for you, but not for me!" Justin says too much. He bites his tongue, but it is already too late.

His eyes glow in the dark. The older skater looks for the truth in their light.

"I want to be like you," Justin tells him. "I'd like to be a pro . . ."

(Some things never change, no matter the cost. Not even when remorse comes after ideals collapse. When naivety stumbles before reality. . . . Why is that so?)

Studying Justin, Victor sets his brain cells in motion. He faces an uncomfortable decision: to break a promise he made to himself long ago or to disappoint a boy who wants to be like him?

Victor used to be the same. And now Michael and Justin also want to follow in his footsteps.

But things are different for Victor now. He turned his back on professional skateboarding.

Michael, in contrast, is a different story. He is good enough to put everything at stake, and even to drop out of school to pursue his dream like Victor once did. And now Justin wants the same, nurturing the same hopes, wild dreams, and unconcealed ambitions. History repeats itself again.

The kid is good. Victor has been watching him for some time. But will he be persistent enough to develop into the skater others will pay to have fun? So many want to take this road, and only a small fraction of them succeed. Is he one of them?

If there were only enough room for all of them in the world, Victor thinks and sighs.

"I know I ain't good enough," Justin continues, "but I'm ready to work. I'm ready to sacrifice. I'm ready to learn. But I need a teacher. Do you want to be my teacher, Victor?"

What is he supposed to do? What else can he do, but to break a ten-year-old promise?

He flips the skateboard in his hand and without a word walks up to the ramp.

(I'll be your teacher.)

He pumps up high and over the ramp, and the sound of the wheels echoes in the stillness of the warehouse.

(Beautiful sound of rolling wheels.)

He does the first trick; the same one he did in his best days—never before and never after he skated as good as he did then—and yet it wasn't good enough. Someone was better than him.

Magnus Müller.

And Victor was the only one to openly admit it.

It was the end of his professional career, when he was in his prime and the years before him were ripe with promises.

He does *mctwist* and dances in the clouds of dust.

The rapture in the air, the rapture in Justin's eyes bursts with the glow of the supernova.

That is his idol. And he is still *the best*.

Chapter

13th: . . . the outside of the arc. The next trick is the *frontside kickflip to fakie 50-50*. You start this trick on the flat by doing the *kickflip*. Rotate both your body and your board 180 degrees simultaneously (the *frontside kickflip*). Land on top of the obstacle. Lock your wheels up against the edge or grind . . .

HE IS MORE SCARED THAN HE IS WILLING to admit. He isn't ready to enter the chamber, not at all. No way.

In the light of last night's event, it looks different to him than when he first saw it. The sarcophagus-like oblong chamber has a small window on the lid, so the observer on the outside can see the face of the person in the chamber, but not vice versa. Sealed in an ultra-modern uterus of some kind, or protected like a baby in its mother's womb, the person inside is cut off from the rest of the world and everything happening outside the chamber.

The chamber Michael is supposed to enter is called the *Womb*. But this "womb," unlike the real, biological one, is daunting to him, all Beresford's reassurances and explanations aside. Michael is still influenced by what had happened to him this early morning, when the day was just beginning to be born. He is still in awe of the demons and still in pain. How hurt would he be if he had resisted Hank? He remembers well how it ended last time. If he had stood up to him, Hank would have first beaten the hell out of him and *then* raped him so he wouldn't be able to make a single move. This way at least he didn't beat him, though he has trouble walking. Michael is afraid to enter the chamber because he might bleed again. And that's the last thing he wants his doctor to know. He is ashamed and humiliated and will rather see himself dead than let anyone know what his father is doing to him. That Hank Daniels is not his biological father is a very small comfort to Michael, because Michael treats him like his own father. How can he explain this to anyone? Who will understand him, let alone empathize with him?

He would be labeled a pervert who deserves nothing else. Because he didn't stand up to him. But does he have any choice at all? *And who says he didn't try to stop him?!*

Where do those scars on his face come from, then? Right, he fell off the rail. He got served skateboarding—that's what he told everyone. *That* is their truth. That's what happened, period.

He sighs deeply and slowly, as if pressed by thousands of atmospheres.

Never mind. He wasn't present when Hank took his body against his will. He wasn't *there*, and he certainly didn't enjoy it. Yet who will believe him?

Therefore, he must stay silent. That's why he can't say anything to Neil Beresford. As he could say nothing to his mother who left this world without knowing what was happening to her son. If she had known, she would have somehow prevented it. She would find a way to stop Hank. She would have the guts Michael didn't have. Only who would tell her? Who would tell her the *truth*? Hank? Michael??

(Who is fooling who here!)

And what will Neil Beresford say if he finds out his secret? Michael wondered. What will he say from his psychiatric point of view? He will send him to recovery in a loony bin where male nurses will subject him to new therapies of rape and fornication. They will rent his body for money, because ONLY THE *FLESH* WILL REMAIN.

Who to trust, then? In whose hands to trust your life when you are no longer capable of controlling it yourself?

Neil Beresford seems sincere and well-meaning. Hank Daniels had to pay him well for trying so hard around Michael. That looks wrong in Michael's eyes. He smells a rat.

Hank Daniels is hurting him, Hank Daniels is destroying him, and Hank Daniels is taking *care* of him. He loves him and he wants to help him heal.

Which Hank Daniels to trust, then? How will he know when the good one is there and when it's time for running—because Mr. Hyde's clone in Hank's body has returned home? Michael cannot fathom that.

As he cannot understand his sudden need to indulge Dr. Beresford. True, he isn't exactly dying for that, but he opened up a crack for him to access.

Beresford's voice is convincing, his endeavors sincere. He wants to help Michael. They are friends! There is something more than a doctor-patient relationship between them. Trust is between them. Beresford understands Michael. Beresford wants to help him as his *friend*.

"Michael, the sooner you face your problems, the sooner

you will solve them. That must end. You have to take that burden off yourself. Unburden yourself or you'll snap. Believe me, I saw it with my own eyes. I have helped many, and I will also help you understand those images that haunt you and learn to deal with them."

"I didn't say they haunt me," Michael corrects him. "I just don't think it's something that happens so often."

"My point exactly! That's why I'm here, Michael. That's why you and I will come to the truth together. It's always easier for two than one."

"I reckon you're right, doc," Michael agrees.

But he doesn't tell him that his problem *is* finding out the truth. Michael is afraid of facing the truth. The only thing he is more afraid of knowing the truth is that someone else finds out about it.

"I'm glad we agreed. Michael, you will undress now and lie down in the *Womb*. I'll be with you all the time and I'll watch you through the computer from the next room. If something goes wrong, I will notice it and end the therapy. You don't have to worry about anything."

"If I get in . . . inside," he still wasn't fancying the *Womb* much, "will you respect our agreement?"

"Of course. I promised you we would not shy away from the problem that is bothering you. Get undressed now, please. I'll be back in a minute." He disappears into the observation room, closing the door behind him with a *swoosh*, hermetically sealing the room. He gives Michael enough time to undress and resolve his doubts in peace, if he still has any.

Michael neatly folds his clothes and puts them on the single chair in the room beside the *Womb*. He plops into a knee-deep liquid before he changes his mind. Right foot forward, left behind. The liquid is clean and pleasantly warmed water. Not too hot, and not too cold.

Michael squats down just as Beresford appears with another *swoosh*.

"Everything okay?" he encourages him with a smile.

"Yes," Michael replies.

"I will close the lid now. In a few seconds, you will hear me through the loudspeaker. You can talk to me through a microphone, so answer me when I speak to you."

"All right."

Michael stretches out, and the water closes over him. Then the lid of the chamber closes, too, with a strange, hissing sound.

A sudden feeling of being suffocated sweeps through him, and Michael panics. His chest contracts. He gets cabin fever and his body convulses. He thinks he is on a sinking shipwreck that sinks deeper and deeper. Deeper and deeper. Into darkness, into death itself. What a bizarre thought!

"Michael, can you hear me?" A gentle voice shatters the world of darkness.

He answers with a barely audible yes.

"Relax, Michael. Relax your thoughts and forget about everything around you. Try to feel the silence that surrounds you."

"I'm relaxed." Michael regains his voice as the panic attack in him wanes.

His head tilted back, he is half-floating on the water, his hands two alien objects drifting beside him.

"Relax, Michael. You have to relax completely."

"Yes."

"Tell me how you feel now."

"I'm wet . . . I feel wet."

"Again, how are you feeling?"

"Good."

"How are you *feeling*, Michael?"

"RELAXED?"

"You're relaxed, Michael. You're safe. And you're in a safe place. Nothing can happen to you. You are in a world without pain. Now, focus on something and tell me what it is."

Dead silence.

"Michael?"

"I'm trying. But I can't think of anything. I talk to you, I hear your voice, and that's it."

"Wrong, Michael. You talk to *yourself*. Can you remember that? You talk to yourself."

"I'm talking to myself."

"Very good. What are you thinking now?"

A moment of hesitation, then,

"I don't know . . ."

"You're thinking about water, Michael. You're thinking about *water*."

"I'm thinking about water?"

"Yes. Water is everywhere around you. What do you feel? How do you feel about the water?"

"I'm thinking . . ."

"Don't think! Say the first thing that comes to your mind. Feel it. So, how do you feel about the water?"

"I feel gratitude!"

"Good, Michael. Very good. Why do you feel gratitude for water?"

"It's everywhere around me. It guards me. It protects me."

"Water is everywhere around you. It guards you. It protects you. What does it protect you from, Michael?"

"From pain!"

"Water still protects you. You are in a place where nothing can hurt you. You are in a world without pain because water protects you from pain. Can you tell me what kind of pain it protects you from?"

"From great pain . . ."

Signals in the next room. Increased amplitudes. Water transfers them to the computer. Nothing remains hidden.

"Don't be afraid, Michael. No one will hurt you. The pain you feel is only in your head. Only in your thoughts. It doesn't exist. Do you understand me? *The pain doesn't exist.* You are in a world without pain."

"Yes . . . The pain doesn't exist. Not in this world . . ."

"Not in this world, Michael. Not in this world. I want you to do something for me now. Do you think you can do that, Michael?"

"Yes."

"Fine. Think of something nice now. It can be an item, some event, or a flavor. Anything. Imagine it and tell me what it is."

"It's a she-wolf . . . I imagined a she-wolf. And Romulus and Remus."

"You have imagined an item? The she-wolf that feeds Romulus and Remus?"

"Yes."

"Describe this item to me, please."

"It's a paperweight. It's made of bronze. My mom brought it to me when she returned from the Congress of Archaeologists and Naturalists in Rome."

"When was that, Michael?"

"Long ago. I think I was eight years old."

"You are in your childhood now, Michael. You're eight

years old. Your mother came back from the congress in Rome. She brought you a she-wolf with Romulus and Remus. What else can you tell me about this item? Did you like it?"

"It was beautiful."

"The item was beautiful. But you didn't like it?"

"I liked it. But I expected Mom to bring me something else."

"Something more appropriate for an eight-year-old boy?"

"Yes . . . Something more appropriate."

"What happened to the she-wolf suckling Romulus and Remus?"

"It ended up in my dad's room. He used it as a paperweight on his desk."

"You gave your she-wolf to your dad? Very selfless of you."

"I didn't know what to do with it, so I thought it might be more useful to my dad. That's why I gave it to him."

"What did your mom say when you gave the she-wolf to your dad?"

"She was sad," he admits after a little hesitation.

"Your mom was sad that you gave away the she-wolf she brought you. Did she tell you that herself?"

"No, she didn't tell me that. I saw it on her . . . I knew she was sorry, I knew that I had hurt her. But I didn't want to. I didn't mean to hurt her!"

"It's okay, Michael. That was nine years ago. Your mother has certainly forgiven you that. Everything is fine now."

"Everything is fine now . . ."

"That's right. Everything is okay. Tell me, what happened to the she-wolf? Is it still in your dad's room?"

Silence in the chamber. Silence in the loudspeaker behind

the plexiglass.

"Michael?"

"It's gone . . ."

"Do you know what happened to it? What happened to the she-wolf your mother gave you?"

Silence again.

"Michael, what happened to your mom's present?"

Then, "We're home alone. Rebecca and I. Mom works. She's in the Museum of Natural History. Dad's out, probably shopping. Rebecca is in the bathroom. She has had stomach problems for two days and often vomits. I think Dad went to get her medicine. . . . I'm sneaking out of the house. The she-wolf is with me. . . .

"The street is empty. Dad's car is parked right in front of the house. . . . The she-wolf in my hand is getting heavier . . ."

The amplitudes go wild. Powerful signals are transmitted through the liquid.

In another room, Neil Beresford is deeply thoughtful.

"Carry on, Michael. What happened next? The she-wolf in your hand is getting heavier . . ."

"I smashed the window on my dad's car. I smashed the windshield . . . to pieces."

He relaxes again. Smaller amplitudes on the computer.

"It's okay, Michael. That's not happening now. It's all a thing of the past. No one will blame you for that. No one will know. What happened to the she-wolf later?"

"I threw it away. I ran to the trash can and disposed of it. I returned home before Dad arrived. Rebecca was still in the bathroom . . ."

"Has anyone seen you do this?"

"No."

"Your dad knows you did it? Did he ever find out?"
"No."
"What about your mom?"
"Neither did she."
"Did they try to find out what happened to the she-wolf?"
"They did. They questioned me. But I didn't tell them anything. I didn't tell them I threw it away."
"They believed you didn't know anything about what happened to the she-wolf?"
"They didn't. They knew I had done something with it, but they didn't pressure me."
"They knew you wouldn't tell them anyway?"
"Yes."
"Michael, *why* did you do that?"

The water stirs up. Quiet sobs in the speakers.

"Michael, what happened to you that you did that to the she-wolf? WHY DID YOU THROW IT AWAY?"
"BECAUSE HE HURT ME!"

Michael is crying. The computer seems to be out of control.

"Who hurt you?"
"I'm in pain! It hurts me a lot!"
"Michael, what did your dad do to you? Tell me!"
"No! NO! NOOOOO!"

The water is splashing, stirred by hurricanes of the past.

The chamber lid opens and Michael opens his eyes.

"Let me go! Don't touch me! Get away from me!"

He breaks free from Neil Beresford's embrace and backs off. The water drips from his naked and wet body all over the floor.

"Don't you ever touch me again! NEVER! *Do you understand me?!*"

"But, Michael, I did nothing! All I did was help you get out!"

Michael's gaze is full of hatred. He is looking at Neil Beresford, and he is seeing somebody else. Someone who isn't there.

"Just don't touch me," he repeats again.

"No problem." Beresford raises his hands as if in surrender. "As you wish."

Michael is shaking.

"Don't worry, Michael," he tries to calm him down. "Everything will be fine."

"Oh yeah? You think so? Do you *really* think everything will be fine?"

Beresford doesn't answer him. He muses, his face an expression of a man who had just lost his fortune by playing the wrong card.

"Where are my clothes? I'm cold."

"I'll get them for you. Hold on."

The grim look he hides from Michael is gone. He mutters to himself, "I'll make you pay for this, Daniels. You'll pay for this *dearly*!"

* * *

James Stowe doesn't hide his true feelings from Laurie. Hiding them would make no sense, given that she knows him like the back of her hand—he never forgot it. Especially since they broke up after an unsuccessful attempt to build a normal relationship. It was Laurie who broke up and had enough determination to confront James with himself. She had the courage to say what she told him, and it was not easy for her. She loved him.

But James wasn't in love with her. It's not that he didn't bother, but James just loved her. He still loved her as a friend, but not the way a man loves a woman. It was hard for her, but she couldn't change James, no matter how hard she tried.

So, the only solution was—to break up. Laurie knew that James would never love a woman the way a woman wanted to be loved. James will never love *her* the way *she* wants to be loved. She said it straight to his face. He was not comfortable to hear it, but he was relieved to share the burden of truth with someone. And end the failed self-delusions and futile attempts.

After that happened, he felt like he was starting a new life. Laurie isn't sure if James had a lover after her or not. His intimate life is no longer her concern. But she is glad he is happier now. And that they are still friends.

That expression is on his face again. A familiar expression of happiness, the joy of a lover awakened by the arrival of spring. Laurie recognizes it. In his every look, in his every move.

"James, are you sure this is a business meeting?" she teases him. "Am I not superfluous, *one too many* here?"

"My dearest Laurie. You could *never* be superfluous. And yes, this *is* a business meeting. And yes, again, I need you here."

"Your eyes tell me differently."

"How different?" He whistles an old melody Laurie cannot recognize.

"*Different.* I was hoping so much that I would be the reason for your happiness one day, but it didn't happen."

James Stowe laughs out loud and heartily.

He is so handsome, Laurie thinks. *God, that's not fair!*

"No one is to blame for your impatience. You quickly gave up on me."

"Not again as fast as I should have." She sticks her tongue out at him and asks, "What's he like?"

"Who?"

"That skater of yours."

"I'm not an expert in skateboarding, but I think he's good."

"That's not what I meant! Is he *hot*?"

"*Voila!* So here we are. We are impatient, huh? Wait till you see." He turns his back on her and ducks his upper body in her car to retrieve his camera.

"Go soak your head! And you're supposed to be a friend. I don't know why I'm helping you?"

"Not out of love, darling. We are both professionals. We're here for the money."

"Is that so? It seems to me that you have something else in mind besides money."

He laughs again. "Are you jealous? You should be. *I* would be if I were you."

"So, he is hot!" she exclaims triumphantly.

"What does that have to do with *you*? If you forgot, *I* hired him."

"I hope to God, James Stowe, that that skater has better taste than you! That would make my day!" Her gaze halts and remains fixed at the guy speeding toward them on a skateboard.

James stops fumbling around the camera and looks in the direction Laurie is looking. A smile lights up his face.

"That's him," he says.

"Not so bad," Laurie mutters, and jumps when the skater stops in front of her with the squeak of the wheels.

"Hey. Sorry I'm late. Traffic problems."

"What?" Laurie says provocatively, angry at him for scaring her. "You had a flat?"

"Forgive me, Alien, let me introduce you. This cynical person is Laurie. My dear friend and assistant."

"Pleased to meet you, Laurie." Alien nods, but doesn't offer to shake hands. "I'm Alien."

"Really? From which episode?" She is still spiteful. Realizing that she is exaggerating, she apologizes, "Sorry. I crossed the line a little. Let's get to work?"

"Sure. I'm going to warm up," Alien says, and disappears.

"You were way out of line!" James reproaches her. "What got into you?"

"I have no idea! It was stronger than me," she says, confused by her mixed emotions. Watching Alien's strange jumps, she asks James in disbelief, "You are going to shoot this?"

"Yes! I am going to shoot this. Do you mind?"

"No, I don't. Just asking."

James looks at her questioningly. "Laurie, if we want to be frank with each other, I don't like *your* look either."

"What look?"

"You can do better than that. You know very well what I mean."

Laurie chortles.

"Did you think you were just going to get him? You better prepare for war!"

"I knew you would like him! I just knew!"

James can't stop laughing at her bewildered expression.

"I'm ready." Alien surprises them both, materializing suddenly. He asks, "What are you laughing at?"

"Laurie just declared war on me," James says, still laughing.

"Why?"

"Let her tell you that." James doubles over from a new burst of laughter.

Laurie frowns at him, and then laughs too.

Alien shakes his head. *(These artists!)*

"Sorry, buddy, it isn't much," James points at Laurie's vehicle, "but I hope you'll have enough room to change."

"Thanks, but that won't be necessary. You have the shorts?" Alien asks him.

"I do," James says cautiously.

"Give them to me!"

Laurie's eyes bulge. She cannot trust her own eyes as she watches Alien unbutton his belt, take off his shoes, and then his pants.

"Can you hold them for me, please?" He hands her his pants, and she takes them as though they are infectious.

He pulls on the boxer shorts, James gave him, over his undies and then slips back into his pants.

"Here, done!" he says, satisfied. "How do I look?"

"Perfect. You look perfect." James recovers from the surprise Alien prepared for them.

"Awesome! Can we start now?" Alien flashes content smiles from James to Laurie and back.

"I'm ready if you're ready. And you, Laurie?"

"Oh, yes. I am. I'm ready too . . ."

At least she thinks so.

She barely finishes the thought, and Alien throws her out of orbit again. He strips off all his clothes, including his baseball cap, until he is naked to the waist, and hands it over to Laurie for safekeeping. *(Holly shit, James didn't mention anything to her about that part of the shooting!)*

"Give me another minute to work up a sweat and we'll get started. Okay?"

"Whatever you say, boss!" James waves his hand in a relaxed manner.

Alien nods and bounces away on the skateboard.

"This one is completely crazy. Where did you find him?" Laurie is flabbergasted.

"I told you the kid was a bomb."

"The kid? Are you sure he is a kid? How old is he?"

"I don't know. I didn't ask him. Seventeen, eighteen maybe."

"You could be right, considering how fast he takes off his pants. I wonder if he is so quick with his underpants as well?"

"That's a question I would also like to know the answer to."

Laurie gapes at him.

Then, "Only in your dreams!" She smacks him on the shoulder with Alien's cap.

James dodges another attack and heads for the skatepark. Alien is calling them to join him.

It would be stupid to let him wait and catch pneumonia while the two of them bicker.

* * *

He finally cools down. He is sorry for the outburst and for blaming Beresford. But the vision of rape was *so real*. Terrifyingly real and painful. Michael is almost certain he will never get rid of those nightmares. Not even state-of-the-art therapy will help him.

So he makes the decision to thank Neil Beresford for his hard work and efforts, and to end the sessions. At least the ones in the *Womb*. But first, he must apologize to him.

"Dr. Beresford," he is struggling to find the right words,

"I'm very sorry for what happened. Please, accept my apology. I didn't mean what I said. I was scared. I lost control."

"I know you didn't mean that. Things like that happen," Beresford's response is polite, but again somehow different from when they had spoken before the incident. "You still don't want to tell me what happened in there? If you want me to help you, I need to know what scared you so much."

"I don't remember exactly what happened," Michael says a small lie. "It happened so fast that I didn't even get to know what it was. Plus, I don't think it had anything to do with why I'm here."

"I wouldn't totally agree with you. If that something upset you so much that you don't even remember what it was, I think it has a lot to do with why you're here. There's something in your past. Something dark and disturbing. Something that must be *expelled* before things get complicated. I hope you realize that."

"You mean the images I see? The presentiments of events I have?"

"This is an area we have not yet been able to reach, but yes, possibly."

"How could something that happened so long ago affect me today? I don't see the logic in that."

"I must correct you here. This is, in fact, very likely. Stress or emotional pressure can awaken the sleeping demons of our subconscious. This has happened before, and it could happen again."

"Correct! That's exactly what I'm telling you. *Demons* can awaken. But this is not about demons."

"Forgive me, but I don't think I'm following you. Can you be more specific?"

"The images I get, the images I experience are *not* unpleasant! They are not scary, either," except for the vision of his father he keeps to himself again. "They do not affect me in any way, though I am a witness to their existence. It's like I'm an observer watching everything from a safe distance. It's like I have an insight into a reality that doesn't affect me."

"I think I understand what you're talking about."

"You do?"

"The images or visions that come to you are like a *gift*. Or something like that. Something you didn't know you possessed."

Michael blinks his eyes.

"They do not scare you; moreover, they slightly amuse you. But you still want to know where they came from. How they got in your head. What is their purpose, and will they ever disappear? What will happen to you if they disappear . . . ? How close am I to the truth?"

"You're absolutely right. You are at the very epicenter of truth."

Beresford smiles. For the first time since the incident in the *Womb*.

"How can we find out the answers to these questions?" Michael wonders. "I never had them before, and now, every now and then something happens to me."

"It may sound a little strange to you, but you may have *always* been able to see them, but you were not aware of their existence. Maybe you carry it with you from birth. Maybe your parents passed it on to you."

"I don't believe that. No, I'm sure it's not that. Neither Mom nor Dad experienced anything like this." He broods over it for a moment. "Actually, I don't know about my dad. I know very little about him . . ."

"You see! Maybe your father passed on something genetically to you he didn't even know he possessed. And you, unlike him, became aware of your abilities. You learned to control them."

Michael snaps alert from thinking. He looks at him with piercing eyes. "What did you say? I don't remember mentioning anything about control."

"Well, that was my conclusion. That was a logical assumption."

Like an X-ray, Michael penetrates Beresford's thoughts, scanning them with his Michael-X-rays.

(Something is wrong there. Something is in them, but he isn't sure what. He sees a disease, some form of tumor that should be removed at once before it becomes malignant . . .)

Beresford's voice startles him and he blinks a few times, as if it awakens him from a deep sleep.

"If you didn't have control over these images," Beresford's voice continues to explain, while Michael strains to follow him, "you would lose sense of what is reality and what is illusion. And that's not happening to you. You have control over the images so you don't let them affect your life.

"Michael, have you heard about cases of people who survived a lightning strike? These are just isolated cases, but some of those who survived the lightning strike were no longer the same as before. What do I mean by that? Suddenly, they become aware of new abilities or powers or whatever you want to call them. Some of them have become clairvoyant, with developed telepathic abilities that they have used to help sick people diagnose what they are suffering from and recommend the best treatment for their illness. In some cases, they even healed someone."

"You are kidding me! And they could never do that before?"

"Not to my knowledge. It was the result of a lightning strike. Their brain cells *reconstructed* under the strong energy shock. As if someone had switched off the switch and then restarted the power. Only, instead of light, their new abilities shone."

"I don't remember being struck by lightning," Michael says.

"I didn't say that." Beresford grins. "I just wanted to show you how complex and fascinating our body is. And how little we know about it. How little we know about ourselves. One woman struck by lightning claims we all have those abilities. In each of us lies that potential. No one knows why we are not capable of developing and using them."

Michael says nothing to this. He is engaged deep in his thoughts, surprised by the reversal of the situation and the information he absorbs like a sponge.

(So, he's not alone. There are others with abilities. There are others with images, visions, and telepathic abilities. Whether it was a gift or a curse, he still couldn't tell.)

He is confused. Frightened. Joyful.

Excited by this discovery and wanting to share it with others, especially his friends. But he's not sure how smart that is.

They could get scared of him and run away from him. He would be *marked* and everyone would avoid him. He would no longer belong to their company; he would no longer be part of their world.

He decides to wait a little longer until he sees what happens to his images. *(They may disappear on their own, and that's the end of the whole story.)*

"Michael, can you imagine what a blessing it would be for humanity to find out how to discover and *use* our abilities?" Beresford says, fascinated, staring at Michael like a dreamer. "It would be the dawn of our civilization, the renaissance of a human race that didn't happen since Genesis!"

Michael stretches his face into a broad smile, imagining himself communicating with Rebecca through their thoughts, emotions, and images. All technology would become unnecessary, computers would turn into waste. Post offices would be closed, annoying cell phones would be extinct, fax machines would be surplus. Because all they needed would be THOUGHTS.

The only thing people would need would be themselves. Human technology.

"Yeah, that would be mighty cool. It's just that we're still so far from that."

"That's right. But with each new day we are getting closer. With every new step we take in this direction, every successful research. But most of all, thanks to people like you."

Michael looks at him, puzzled.

"Yes, Michael. If we could find out why some of us have these abilities and, unlike the rest of humanity, they know how to control them, we could find a formula to help others to develop their abilities too. In short, we need people like you to help us learn about ourselves."

"I don't know how I could help you with that," Michael says, his heart pounding with excitement like after a long and exhausting race.

"You should do nothing more than what we have already started."

"Oh, no! No, no, no. That is out of the question! I'm not going into that machine again."

"Did you feel so bad in it? The *Womb* is not designed to be a torture device. No one has characterized it like that so far."

"I'm sure it's true, but I'm not getting into it anyway."

"What are you afraid of, Michael? Yourself? The past? But it's dead, it cannot hurt you."

"But it affects my actions *today*. You said it yourself. I don't want to bother with something I forgot long ago. I'm happy with my life as it is, and I don't want to change it."

"I can understand your anxieties. I don't blame you. But think again when you get home. Think it over in peace and try to imagine how much you could help yourself and others with your gift. You will tell me what you have decided the next time we meet. Deal?"

"That is all? That's all you want from me? To think it over and nothing more?"

"Yes, that is all I want from you. Try to imagine a world where wars and killings would cease, in which there would be no more misery. Wouldn't you like to live in such a world?"

"Of course I would. Everybody would love it! But I do not believe that will ever happen. And if that happens, what if some lunatic abuses those powers against the rest of the world? It wouldn't be the first time." He contemplates everything for a while, then agrees. "All right. I'll listen to you and think about it. I promise nothing more than that."

"Thank you. I'd like to ask you something else before you leave."

Michael motions him to go ahead.

"While you were in the *Womb*, I asked you to think of something nice. Why did you think of the she-wolf that fed

Romulus and Remus?"

"I don't have the foggiest idea. I did as you told me, and it came first to my mind."

"And that's it? There is no other explanation other than that?"

"I don't know. Maybe there is. Maybe it symbolized something I lost a long time ago. Just like I lost the she-wolf in the end."

After he bids farewell to Beresford, Michael spends the next half hour at his mother's grave.

The clouds clear, and the sun is dancing in the crystal-blue sky. It is still too cold for this time of the year. A warmer wave is expected—the satellites have forecasted. The weather should improve.

Summer is coming to its end. Or is it just beginning?

* * *

It takes James less than thirty minutes (not including Alien's warming up) to shoot all the pictures, and now he is eager to develop them and show them to his boss.

The shooting itself went fine, except for one fall when Alien landed hard and got served yo-yo before scraping his forearm. As painful as it was for Alien, it's been a godsend for James. He isn't a ruthless bastard, but a shot of Alien who looks like he could spend all day on a skateboard with his bleeding wound couldn't better match the slogan accompanying his photos.

YOU DON'T NEED ANY PROTECTION—EXCEPT FOR DENNIS KAY MEN'S UNDERWEAR

After the shooting is over, Laurie washes Alien's wound with water and then uses the first-aid kit.

"Pull up your sleeve so I can wash your wound," she instructs him.

"You don't have to. It's no big deal."

"It's no big deal, but it could get infected. I don't think you want that."

Alien doesn't even bat an eyelid as she cleans his wound, powders it, then puts a bandage over it.

"How old are you?" she asks him, closing the first-aid kit box.

"Why do you want to know?" Alien checks the tightness of the bandage and looks at her.

"I like you and I want to sleep with you. I wonder if you're old enough."

"I'm twenty!" Alien fires as if launching a rocket.

"You're lying! You are not twenty years old."

"It's not polite to tell a lady she's lying, but you're not telling the truth either. You don't want to *sleep* with me."

She smiles at him. Flashing her pearly-white teeth.

"You're right. I don't want to sleep with you. But I'm curious how old you are."

"Nineteen. I'm still a teenager, as you can see. Why do you insist on this if not for the reason mentioned before?"

"Because I want to know if I shall worry about you or you can take care of yourself if James wants to sleep with you."

Alien's mouth drops open. A quick glance at James lighting a cigarette, then fixing his gaze back at Laurie.

"You are kidding me! So he is gay, after all?!"

"What do you mean, *after all?*"

"Forget it. I'm thinking out loud."

"Did you suspect something?"

"No! My friends teased me he was gay, and I assured them he wasn't. They will eat me alive if they find out I stood up for a fag! Man, what a mess!"

"Look, no offense, but I'd appreciate it if you didn't use that word in front of James. James is quite an *okay* guy, and I wouldn't want him hurt."

"Hey, no sweat. I have no prejudice against other people. It's his life! He can do whatever he wants with it, as long as he doesn't try anything with me."

"So, you are a little afraid?"

"Me? I'm not afraid of anything, so why should I be afraid of a fa . . . I mean, him? Besides, I don't think he would hit on a sixteen-year-old. He isn't that desperate!"

"And here comes the truth! You're *only* sixteen!"

"So what! I'm not ashamed of that." He pauses for a moment, then asks for a cigarette.

"Want to prove your manhood?"

"No. I don't have to prove anything. I just want a *smoke*. Do you have a cigarette or not?"

"I don't smoke. But James probably has one. Why don't you ask him?"

"It's okay, I can live without it."

"Don't be ridiculous! He's coming here anyway, so ask him."

"What do you want to ask me?" A glimpse of an intriguing smile on his face when he looks into Alien's eyes.

"Nothing." Alien is vague, pushing his skateboard back and forth with his foot in a casual manner and looking for any signs of oddity on James.

"Alien wanted to ask you for a cigarette, but he is ashamed," Laurie steps in to make Alien's life even more miserable.

"It's not true that I'm ashamed!" He is a bit too loud.

"You smoke? I didn't get that impression."

"No! Uh, yeah. Sometimes."

"I'm sorry. If you had told me before, I would have saved you one. This is my last one." He offers him a half-smoked cigarette. "You can have it if you want to."

(A sign of an offer. Testing him? *Will you sleep with me?*)

He looks at Laurie. A common expression on her face, only slightly altered by aroused interest and a shy smile. Not a trace of ridicule.

He looks at James, who also seems normal. The question in his eyes, *So, you want a drag or not?*

"Why not?" He takes the cigarette, has a puff. "Thanks."

"You're welcome. You two, are you in the mood for a snack? My treat."

"Good idea!" Laurie says merrily. "I'm almost chilled to the bones. Hope that's okay with you?" she asks Alien.

"Sure. I'd love to."

"Super. I'm waiting for you in the car," James says. Adds to Alien, "Sorry, but you'll have to finish it here. Laurie doesn't allow vices in her wheels."

"Laurie?" Alien stops her before she follows James. "You think . . . Do you think he likes me?"

"Absolutely!" She laughs at his expression. "But not *that* way. He thinks you're cute. That's all."

"Are you sure?"

"You're out of luck, my poor thing. You're not his type."

"How do you know that?"

"A guess? Female intuition? You tell me. If he were interested in you as his future boyfriend, he wouldn't have brought me along."

"I don't get it." Alien looks confused.

"Don't worry your head about it. You are in no danger from him, if that worries you."

"Well, it's comforting to hear. And what about you? Am I in danger from *you*?"

"You forget you're sixteen."

"But today's kids are *advanced*!" he protests but makes no impression on Laurie. He flicks the rest of the cigarette and hurries after her.

Thinking, *If she hasn't realized this by now, this is her unique opportunity. He will not miss his opportunity to show it and prove it to her!*

Chapter

14th: . . . (to *fakie 50-50*). The *switch-stance 360 kickflip* you are doing with the stance that isn't "normal" for you. If you are *goofy-footed* you are doing it regular, and vice versa. This is a hard trick (like riding a bicycle only backward) and therefore you get more points if you do it in a contest. Now . . .

NOTHING IS GOING ACCORDING TO PLAN, as though bewitched. As though it is guided by some invisible hand that cast a curse on them. If he believed in voodoo, Andy would have thought this was the work of a bocor who, using black magic, had been playing with them since they set out for a summer vacation in the snow. This summer vacation itself is incredible enough and abstract—like the incomprehensible painting of one of the contemporary artists—even without the witchcraft.

They barely survived a trip to Killington. Because of bad weather, it stretched two hours longer than planned. At one point they nearly crashed when a deer jumped out in front of them, running across the road. Andy's reflexes were fast, but not fast enough; he felt the consequences of the arduous journey.

He hit the deer. In the collision, he smashes the left headlight, and damages the bumper and the edge of the hood. Blood droplets soon froze on them. The deer stumbled and fell from the impact, but within seconds got on his feet and fled into the forest.

Andy and Fernando watched in shock as the forest closed behind him. Somewhat better were Nathan and Stu, who the impact woke from their sleep. They were wide awake when it was over and the deer deep in the forest. Then reality hits Fernando, and he flips out. They couldn't calm him down, so Nathan switches seats with him and crawls into the passenger seat. He gives Stu an almost impossible mission to convince Fernando to take a nap. After about fifteen minutes of arguing, Fernando relents and turns his back to Stu. Before long, he forgets about the whole incident.

This is not the case with Andy. He relaxes only when they arrive in Killington and when he dives into the hot bath. During this time, his buddies seek refreshment at the hotel bar. About an hour later, Andy joins them.

The next day dawns for Fernando, Andy, and Nathan with another surprise. Stu leaves their company for a young Canadian who speaks only French, which didn't bother Stu too much. After abducting her from her friends, he spends all day with her, and only in the early hours of the morning he sneaks back into the room he shares with Andy. He stays in bed until noon, while his friends had been in the snow for hours. This scenario repeats itself the next day and the day after.

Despite everything, Nathan and Fernando are enjoying every minute of the boarding under the innocently blue sky, not allowing Stu to spoil their enjoyment. Andy does not lag far behind them, at least with snowboarding. He does an impressive *frontside 540° spin*, grabbing the board and triumphantly shoots his hands high in the air, rewarded by Fernando's and Nathan's euphoric cheers.

Unlike these two, he can't put Stu out of his head. Stu isn't fair to them. He is even less fair to Irma, whom he had won while she was still recovering from her relationship with Michael. Andy can't grasp why Michael did it; everybody's opinion is that they were a nice couple. But it is crystal clear to him that Michael doesn't give a damn what others think of his relationships. He always did what he wanted.

At first, Andy sympathizes with Michael and Irma, but then he stops thinking about them. They are history and that's where the story ends. That is the case at least until Stu brings the whole thing to life again.

This time Andy can't stand aside; Irma doesn't deserve that. The problem is, he doesn't know what to do. Should he talk to Stu? Unreasonable and stubborn as hell, Stu isn't easy to talk to. Plus, he is a big-time operator. Andy can only hope that Irma will realize that before she gets *too* involved with him and things get even more complicated for her.

The fallen trunk juts out of the snow and Andy directs the snowboard toward it. He launches himself by combining a *boardslide* with a *tail grab*, once again thinks of Stu, who is probably sleeping like a log, and ends up upside down in the snow. The snow is soft and deep, and Andy sinks. He tries to push himself out, but swallows more snow and sinks even deeper. The only thing left for him is to save his strength and wait until Fernando and Nathan come to his rescue.

The seconds stretch into minutes, and there is still no

sound of them. Andy worries. His brain begins to swell and drum, and he recognizes the first signs of nausea. Soon he will puke, unless these two smartasses show up first. He is running out of air too fast, so he makes another desperate attempt to dig himself out of the icy embrace. Again, without success. And again, he sinks a little deeper.

Again, he swallows some snow.

And again, he runs out of air.

(Air! Air! I need air . . . Nando, Nathan . . . where the hell are you? What are you waiting for?!)

Strength is leaving him so fast, and once more he tries to reach a cell phone from the inner pocket of his jacket. His fingers are thick, clumsy and like a stone. He feels nothing in them. Soon the rest of his body disobeys too.

It rings in his head. He can hear the faint squeaking of his cell phone, but darkness surrounds him more and more and he drifts away. Disappearing under the snow and mountains of Vermont.

In the split second before he faints, sunlight shines through.

"Trying to kill yourself?" Nathan wipes the snow from his face while Fernando frees his boots from the bindings on his Burton Motion snowboard.

Andy wants to say something, but his stomach churns.

"Easy," Nathan calms him down. "Take it easy, buddy. Throw it out."

"Phooey! He shat himself all over! Just look at the snow!" Fernando doesn't hide his disgust as he watches Andy sitting in the snow, covered with his breakfast.

"How are you?" Nathan ignores him. "Can you breathe?"

Andy confirms with a lazy nod of his head, still too weak

to speak.

"You were lucky. You slipped into the air pocket. It took us a while to spot your board and pluck you out before hypothermia cuts into you. Luckily, you had a cell with you, so we heard it when Nando called you."

"I didn't know," Andy coughs, "that it was an air pocket. I saw nothing, but that trunk."

"Can you get up?" Nando asks, and Nathan offers him his shoulder as support.

"I can try." Holding on to his friends, Andy stands up and stumbles. His whole body is shaking, his knees swaying.

"You go look for Stu," Nathan instructs Fernando and grabs Andy tighter under his arm. "I'll bring him back to the hotel."

"Fuhgeddaboudit, man! To hell with Stu! I'm going with you." He takes off his jacket and wraps it around Andy. "Here. Put it on yourself."

"Thanks. And you?"

"Don't worry about me. It is warm enough for me even in the short sleeves."

It's almost noon. The sun is rushing to its zenith. The sky is clear and wide, the air pleasantly fresh.

Snow is shining everywhere.

The avalanches of air down the mountain are getting warmer as they stumble toward the hotel; some big hand turned on the hair dryer and pointed it down the slope. Somewhere, if someone listened a little better, a quiet murmur of melted snow can be heard.

* * *

Changes are also happening in the distant vastness of Colorado. The sky is high and blue, with no clouds. The sun sails undisturbed over the blue infinity.

The day is very nice, but cold. Temperatures are still low, *too* low for August.

But not for Rebecca and Red Sunshine resting in the saddles of their obedient and loyal friends, after a long and exhausting race.

"What should I do to give me your thoughts?" Red Sunshine asks her.

"Nothing." She softens her reply with a smile. "You've already done enough for me."

"What did I do for you?"

"Well, you went with me for a ride. It means a lot. Thank you."

"You thought I'd let you go alone? After what Michael did to you?"

"Please, let's not talk about it now." A pensive expression on her face. It makes her ten years older, and Sunny instantly dislikes it. But not the vision of the woman he sees for a moment. She is so beautiful to him, much prettier than the girl he is now looking at. "Today I would like to talk about nice things. Today I want to rejoice. I want to *enjoy* life. It's so beautiful here."

The moment seems right. He didn't plan anything. He just speaks what is on his heart.

"Why don't you stay, then? You belong *here*, Rebecca. Don't you feel it?"

Silence takes away his words. Then,

"I cannot. You know that . . . I've already explained it to you."

"I know. I remember."

"Then why do you ask again?" She turns to him and looks into his eyes.

"Because I love you. And because I want to be with you."

"We can't have everything, Sunny. Most often we cannot have what we love most."

"I don't want *everything*, Rebecca. I want you."

"But you have me!" *(How can he not understand that?)* "You will have me when I return to New York and when I'll be here for the next vacations. You're my best friend. You're the best friend I've ever had."

"A *friend*? Is that all I mean to you?"

She absorbs the sorrow of his gaze, drowned in the lakes of disappointment.

"You mean much more to me than just a friend. You mean so much to me that—"

"Don't!" she interrupts him, before he can say anything else. "Let it stay as it is, and it will be easier for us."

"Easier? I don't want it to be *easier*! I want truth. I want you. I want you to stay here and give birth to my children. I want to have triplets with you, *three times* triplets!"

Her eyes are wide, beautiful and big with surprise. Then she blinks and tears flow into a new life, accompanied by her laughter.

"Something funny about what I said?" Red Sunshine asks, seeking an explanation.

"Sunny, you are just amazing! Three times triplets? Isn't that too much even for you?"

"Well, we can discuss that later, if you say yes." He strokes Darkfall's neck.

"If I say yes to what?"

Her laughter fades.

"To be my wife, of course."

Darkfall snorts. A heavy, unnatural silence descends on them.

Sunny is sorry that he misses seeing Rebecca's expression before she runs away from him at full gallop.

He ponders for a second or two, then spurs his horse. He turns into a blur that soon disappears with already melting snow.

* * *

The light pulses in colors. Like a kaleidoscope. The waves alternate one after another: green, blue, yellow, purple. The water is dark, calm, and deep. There is no bottom under him. No bottom at all.

Something is dragging him down there, into the mysterious depths. Something is trying to sink him, and yet he is still floating. On a cold and flat surface of water that reminds him of a finely machined metal surface.

No reflection around him, only the walls of the *Womb* radiate colors. Flashing in his eyes as if in a mirror.

No sound. The complete absence of any sound.

"I'm in a skatepark. I don't know exactly where. I've never been here before. Just a moment . . .

"This is Staten Island. I'm at the skatepark in Staten Island. Wooden structures are dilapidated and just about to collapse.

"I see other skateboarders. Chris, Luke, and Thomas. And some other guys I don't know.

"I don't know any of them. I've never seen them. But I know their names. Don't know how it's possible, but I know their names. I just *know* them. They don't know me. In fact, they don't even notice me. It's like I'm not there.

"Luke is good, very good. The others aren't bad, either, but Luke somehow impressed me the most. Their skateboarding style is a little strange. It's not like mine or like that of the guys riding today . . .

"I don't know. In which. Time. I am. If time. Exists. Here. At all.

"Luke catapults himself from the launch ramp just before it disappears under him. Just like that, the earth opened, and it was gone. Jesus!

"Luke looks back, trying to find Thomas, who disappears with the bank. Chris yells something to Luke in a panic. The park begins to collapse, and they flee to save their lives. I'm running too.

"The earth opens and swallows everything in front of it. The whole island is collapsing, sinking into the sea. Water pours over it without noise and waves. It covers it, still like oil.

"Boards float on its surface—abandoned skateboards looking for their owners. No sign of them. They're not aboard the ship I jump onto in the last minute. Only boards remained.

"Lots of boards. Tens of them . . . Hundreds . . .

"Floating toward the open sea.

"The Staten Island Ferry docks along the shore of Washington Square Park. I am the only passenger.

"There are lots of people in Washington Square Park, including skateboarders Bruno, Jim, Harry, Jeremy, and Aaron. They're all here. And many more. I know everything about them even though I have never met them. But they know nothing about me.

"Jim and Eric and Spencer are also here, and more are

coming.

"The East River and the Hudson River are rising from their beds and the water is pouring into the square. Nothing can stop it!

"The surrounding buildings disappear, sinking into the water, collapsing into the abyss. New York University, Asch Building . . .

"Sixth Avenue and Washington Place are disappearing. And with them the terrified skateboarders.

"About thirty of them flee pell-mell in all directions before the overflowing water. Looking for a way out . . .

"I collide with someone, beside myself with fear. *Where shall I go?* Panic and madness everywhere. People disappear, buildings collapse, the earth swallows whole blocks.

"Someone's wheels rattle so close that they almost run over me. In panic, I turn after them.

"*Victor!* He doesn't hear me, but I still shout after him. *Victor, wait!*

"I follow him on a skateboard down Broadway toward SoHo, and further south. But he's too fast for me, and I'm falling behind.

"A thick cloud of dust comes down from the sky and swallows him whole. The last thing I recognize are his Pig wheels, and then I hear them disappear. I *hear* them disappear.

"I lost him somewhere between the ruins of West Broadway, Hudson Street, and Leonard Street. The water is up to my knees, and still rising.

"Then the whole island shakes. Hilly Land trembles, dancing to the wails of Algonquian people. The air smells of song and lamentation. The air burns with colors: green, blue, yellow, purple, red, falling from the sky. The flashes of metal from above, the angry roar of water from below.

"I hover above it all and I ascend upward, weightless. My board floats on the turbulent water, calling after me. It doesn't want me to leave it, it needs me, but some invisible force is pulling me up. Toward and into the luminous, hovering, metal object.

"One side of the spacecraft splits open and the brightest light I've ever seen pours over me and shines all over, even the streets of New York—already deep under the sea. And him, my friend Victor, who is struggling with one big whirlpool with the last remnant of his strength.

"*Victooor!* I reach out to him, but he's too far. Far too far.

"He reaches out to me, but I'm too far. Far too far too far.

"VICTOOOR!!

"I'm lying on a gurney. Two pairs of slippery hands keep me from rising and touch my naked body.

"I want to resist them, but I can't. They take my strength, they suck the life out of me, killing my will to resist them. I can't see their shapeless faces, translucent as luminous crystals. But I know *who* they are and *what* they want.

"The creature to my left caresses my forehead. *I am so lonely, Michael. And I want you so much. . . . Make me happy . . .*

"The creature to my right holds a huge syringe in its hand. *Imagine, Michael, a world without wars and killings, and give us some of your gift. . . . Be our leader, be a pioneer of the New Age and show us the way to know ourselves . . .*

"Each of them longs for me and each of them loves me in their own way as I scream for help, tearing my lungs out until finally someone hears me. I know someone has heard me because the world of their love explodes in colors and dies out like fireworks."

He hugs her tightly and without shame, pressing his crying face against her cheek and pushing his body, soaked in the cold sweat of fear, into the warmth of her embrace.

"Young Daniels, it's okay. Everything it's okay. That just a bad dream. A very bad dream."

"Juanita, you are a sight for sore eyes. You are a comfort to my soul. I'm so glad to see you! Don't leave me, please. Don't ever leave me!"

He kisses her cheek, crawling back into her wide embrace.

Juanita Dolores gently pushes him away.

"You kiss young girls. I too old for that. I too old for you."

Michael gives her a smile wet with sweat and tears.

"You're in the prime of your life, Juanita. You will experience much more joy."

"Listen him!" She gets up from his bed and wags her finger at him in a warning. "How impudent he!" She tries to reprimand him, though she is flattered by his words. "What your father say if he hear young Daniels speak like that? Kids today impossible! Impossible!"

Michael wrinkles his nose at the mention of his father. He runs his fingers through his damp hair. He thinks he could use a haircut.

"What smells so good?" he changes the subject, trying to appease Juanita again. "I'm starving."

"No wonder when you sleep all day. Where you been last night?"

"I was cruising around with my friends."

"So late? Young Daniels get hurt bad one day." An expression of genuine concern on her face.

"We didn't go too far. We skated mostly around Central Park."

"Central Park!" Juanita Dolores crosses herself on the mention of the hated place.

Michael titters.

"Young Daniels looking for devil! One day he find him."

She wags her finger at him once more and crosses herself before she waddles off to the kitchen.

Michael stays in bed until he completely recovers from the dream in which he was in a therapy session with Neil Beresford, lying in the *Womb* and experiencing that horrific and so *real*, so frighteningly real dream. He turns on the stereo and pumps the volume all the way up. Not waiting for Down Low to finish their "Moonlight," he rolls over the bed and heads to the kitchen, guided by the alluring smell and Juanita's singing.

* * *

Michael knows full well where to find him, so he goes there. Following his blessing, guided by his *gift*. The same gift that could soon become a stumbling block for someone once he announces he is quitting the sessions. He doesn't want to hurt anybody, especially not Dr. Beresford, with whom he has just begun a friendly relationship, but he already made up his mind. Last night's dream was crucial.

He is rushing to the docks of the Old Brooklyn Bridge as if everything, even his pathetic life, depends on when he will get there. A few minutes later, he is convinced in the reliability of his gift.

"How did you find me? How did you know I'd be here?" Victor gives him five, surprised to see him.

"I heard the sound of your wheels. I followed them all the way here." He gives him a slight shove with his shoulder.

"Good doggy!" Victor fails to *hardflip* because of him.

Michael shows him how to do it and waits for Victor to reach for the next trick.

It is *180°* over the backpack.

Michael distracts him again and Victor falls while landing.

"What the hell is wrong with you!" He grabs him by his jacket. "Want to lick my deck?"

Michael sticks out his tongue at him. "I'm ready. How about you?"

Victor pushes him away. He kicks him in the butt with his Emerica skateboard shoe, goes to get his skateboard and stumbles again when Michael rides him by jumping on his back.

Victor has had enough. He grabs his friend and wrestles him off himself, booting him in the process.

"Is this enough or you want more?"

"Thanks, but you filled your quota for today." He dusts off his pants.

"The therapies seem of little help to you." Victor eyes him questioningly.

"On the contrary! I never felt better. I feel so good that I'm done with them starting from today!"

"That is clear. You are chilling like a good dog."

Michael shows his teeth and walks toward him, growling. "Woof!"

"Get lost!" Victor grins and shoves him away. "Told you to beat it!"

Michael is suddenly serious.

"Okay, I'm going." He jumps on the skateboard and rolls away. Victor catches up with him.

"Where are you going?"

"Nowhere in particular. Do you have a suggestion?"

"Is that an invitation?"

"If it sounded like that . . ."

"I gladly accept the invitation, but I have to see Nana."

"How's your grandma?"

"Bad, I'm afraid. She has cancer. I found out yesterday."

"Jesus. I'm sorry! I had no idea."

"Neither did I."

They pass a few buildings in silence. Then Michael says, "The good thing is that it slowly progresses in old people."

"I suppose so," Victor confirms. "But in the end it gets them. Sooner or later."

"Maybe it's better that way. They don't have much of a life anyway," Michael adds, too worried to notice Victor's glance.

"Exactly."

"Vic, what does your grandma like to eat the most?"

"Why do you ask?"

"We could buy her something before we visit her."

Victor almost gives in to his feelings, but still keeps self-control. He only indulges to one little betraying smile—a sign of appreciation he gives to his friend.

Chapter

15th: . . . something about the *shove-it flip*, the *hardflip*, and the *inward varial heelflip*. Pop the *shove-it* by rotating your board 180 degrees (not your body!). The *shove-it flip* is when your board also spins 180 degrees. The nose rotates in the direction opposite to the side of the board on which . . .

ELIJAH PETERSON CURSES. HOW ON EARTH could he forget it after he kept it in plain sight all day to prevent just that, and yet it happens to him?!

He spent yesterday afternoon browsing the boutiques, jewelry stores, and antiques in Midtown New Manhattan until he found what he was looking for—a tiny, glass dolphin with diamond eyes that shimmers in all the colors of the rainbow, when light refracts through it. A gift to his girlfriend and soon-to-be fiancée, he plans to surprise her at one of the fancy and expensive restaurants on the Upper East Side, during a quiet dinner after visiting the Guggenheim Museum. He will take her to the new American-French restaurant, Sign of the Dove, and if that restaurant isn't to her liking, his second choice will be the ultra-expensive Daniel. On second thought, Daniel may be a better choice, since Ursula adores French cuisine.

Peterson is just hoping she will forgive him for being late and waiting for him. Given that she doesn't carry a cell phone or a pager when she is off duty, because as a translator at the UN she has very little free time that she can devote entirely to herself, she is now unavailable for Peterson to let her know that he will be late. She is probably already on her way to the Guggenheim, which makes him angry with himself.

And he is furious for another reason—the dolphin—the true cause of his troubles. The only thing missing is that after this dinner, his fiancée decides she won't wait for him. That would be the crown of everything. That would be the end of this carefully planned evening; the end of his life!

Luckily for him, Pérez is on duty at the reception today, who, as usual, doesn't bother him with formalities. The nice fifty-year-old has looked favorably upon him since day one since Peterson came to work in the Institute. It was only a month ago when Peterson asked him where he needed to report, too impressed and nervous to find his way in those cold and clean corridors, monitored by the latest technology. There are only a few places in RIRI where one can be *alone* and to himself. Very few or almost none. RIRI isn't designed to give anyone privacy. Its purpose is completely different.

Peterson's quick steps echo through the ominously deserted main building of the Institute, and the pressure of secrecy lurks behind every locked lab door.

Had Peterson not been so preoccupied with his thoughts about the date he was late for because of his forgetfulness, he might have noticed that the Institute is not *so* deserted and that he isn't *the only one* there. He would see the light burning in one lab and then he would think twice before bursting through the door. His life would have taken a different course and perhaps all that would not happen to him later.

But Peterson *goes* into the laboratory.

As his hand grips the door handle, he feels something is wrong—the door isn't locked. And when he jerks it open and sees two men staring at him with hostility in their eyes, his legs turn into jelly. Realizing that he interrupted something he had better not witnessed, he gets the crazy idea of slamming the door shut and running away as fast as his legs can carry him.

He does none of that.

He remains standing in place, motionless and frozen before the scrutinizing gaze of his mortally pale mentor. His eyes glow with raw anger. The other man is leaning casually on the table, but with an air of something dangerous around him. Something Peterson had not noticed in him before, nor in his photographs published with his articles in various publications.

Hank Daniels addresses him in an icy voice and Peterson stiffens even more. He somehow squeezes out a timid apology and forces his paralyzed legs to go that extra mile to his desk, where a beautifully wrapped dolphin box is waiting for him.

Out of the corner of his eye, he spots a crumpled piece of paper in his mentor's hand before offering to Daniels and Beresford a fake smile instead of saying goodbye and hurrying out.

He will remember that event later, after many questions and digging through his memory, which he had buried in the meantime so he would never have to remember it again.

* * *

There are times in life when everything seems perfect. When a person feels serene and satisfied and confidently walks through it, at peace with himself and everybody around him—master of his future. So is Michael Daniels now: the true, One and Only Lord of his Future, the Captain at the Helm of his Life, in possession of the precious gift God Himself so generously honored him with.

Unfortunately for others, he has no wish to share this gift with the rest of the world. Maybe it's selfish, and maybe it's not (maybe he's just careful). Maybe he did the right thing, and maybe he didn't; time will tell. He has his own turmoil and doubts about whether he should tell anyone else about it besides Neil Beresford, but he gives up.

After their last conversation, Michael feels peace he had not experienced since his mother's death. He continues to visit her grave; he still misses his mother. They had a special relationship, and Michael is sure none of his friends has such a good relationship with their parents. Victor, for example, loves his grandmother very much, but Angela Kenneth is not his parent. She's not his *mom*.

Michael still visits Melanie Hope in his sorrow and emptiness. But his emotional scars, scars of injustice, started to heal, mostly thanks to Neil Beresford. There are moments when Michael still needs his mother, but he has learned to cope and live with that loss.

When she couldn't be with him to help him, understand and comfort him, Neil Beresford appeared. Their mutual doctor and family friend discovered his special gift he didn't know he possessed. But with that gift also came something Michael isn't exactly dying to experience: his dreams. Sometimes these are ugly dreams, real nightmares, and the images in them are like a bad omen, like a window to the world of dark occurrences, an unmistakable insight into the power of evil forces.

He is still haunted by the traumatic vision of his father, his eyes bleeding while he struggles to break free from a supernaturally powerful vortex tearing off pieces of flesh and skin from his body. Another image bothers Michael even more than this one. It is a dream in which Victor repeatedly disappears into a dark and gloomy cloud of unknown origin.

Michael says nothing to Beresford about those dreams. He feels bad enough that Beresford had taken his decision to stop therapies personally. So he writes him a short letter of appreciation explaining everything to him.

As for the gift we talked about, I don't think it's something I should share with others. It's nothing personal, I just feel that way. If God wanted it otherwise, He would do that and make others aware of their gifts. He obviously had something else in mind.

I'm not ungrateful. I know full well what you did for me. I know I owe you a lot and I am grateful for everything. But I can't become a "laboratory rat," I just can't. Please, try to understand that. If I could change things, I would do it right away. But I'm not the Messiah. I'm only Michael.

If I could help someone, I would've done it already—with or without a gift. I just wanted you to know that.

Sincerely yours,
Michael

* * *

"Selfish little bastard!" Hank Daniels hisses after reading Michael's letter for the third time.

Elijah Peterson is already far away, hurrying with the

dolphin to his belated date.

"I'll beat the hell out of him when I see him," he adds in anger. "Not even his own mother would recognize him if she were alive after I finished with him."

"Don't blame the boy for everything, Hank," Beresford tries to reason with his friend. "You would have done otherwise if you had been in his place?"

Daniels gives him a stern look. Out of helplessness and anger, he continues chewing on his lower lip.

"Try to understand him. The boy is beyond delighted. He will calm down when elation passes, when he loses his powers. Then he will turn to me again for help."

"He'll be delighted when I get him!"

"I don't think you are making wise judgments. Leave Michael to me. I'll talk to him—"

"To you?! *You?* What have you done so far?! What have you done for our *cause*? Nothing! You just sit and talk to him. Wag your tongue! You are capable of nothing! You're zero, my friend! Zilch! Even worse, you can't even blow it! I bet you didn't even get to stick your useless tools into his butt!"

His voice is ice-cold, poisonous. Spoken wickedness and malice of the world.

Beresford jerks as if being hit in the middle of his face. He turns red with anger, but is too shocked to say anything. Daniels's words came to full effect because Beresford is so surprised and helpless that he has nothing to say in his defense.

"It's time to take matters into my own hands and deal with the situation before it's too late." He hates Beresford for his infirmity. "I don't believe he will turn *me* down. And neither will he send me queer letters in apology."

He shoves the crumpled letter into his white, overcoat

pocket and dashes out, slamming the door shut in Beresford's face.

* * *

The only pity is that such moments never last longer.

His board cracks at the height of preparations for Sattel. And even the weather improves and works for him.

Michael can't believe his bad luck. He cannot get over it, *To crack his board doing the simplest thing in the world—an* ollie! *Okay, he was also jumping over the stairs, but still . . . Damn, he didn't even have it ten days! Now, he will have to ask his old man for money if he wants to see the contest. He has some savings, but those wouldn't cover his travel expenses. Lenny promised to give him a new deck, maybe even a spare one, but he would still need lots of cash, so his father is again the only way out.*

He lets off steam and curses his fill. And then with the boys, according to good, old, skateboarding custom, finishes the deck until they have completely crushed it. They save the trucks and wheels, and only pieces of wood are left of his deck. It was its funeral, the last farewell to its skateboarding life.

Victor wasn't present then. His grandmother got sick and her condition is critical. Her life is hanging by a thread and it is a question of days how long she will live. Victor isn't leaving her bedside. Michael offered to stay with him and keep him company, but Victor refuses. There's no need for both of them to watch her agony. Michael takes his advice without complaining too much.

He has enough of his own problems. And if he didn't have them by now, he certainly will soon.

He can see it on Hank's face, waiting for his answer

whether or not he will lend him money.

"I hope that's not a problem. I will return everything to you after the contest. I'll even get a job if I don't win, but I don't believe that will happen. I have a very good feeling about it. Either way, I'll pay you back."

Hank's question surprises him.

"Why did you stop your therapies?"

An alarm goes off in Michael's head. Chaos of thoughts on the highway of comprehension.

"What do you mean . . . ? How do you *know*?"

"Beresford told me today."

"He *told* you?! I thought it was confidential!"

"And I thought I at least deserved to hear it from you. Why didn't you tell me?"

"I thought . . . I'm sorry." He is putting in a huge effort to gather himself. "I wanted to tell you, but I was waiting for the right moment."

"And when was the right moment for you?"

Michael shrugs his shoulders nervously.

"Soon, I guess. Maybe today. I don't know. I'm really sorry . . ." His gaze meets his father's: a look of remorse with the look of accusation. "What else did he tell you?"

"Why are you interested in that? You don't trust your doctor?"

"I do, but . . ." He lowers his gaze. "Never mind."

"He didn't tell me anything. He said nothing about what you talked about."

Michael wants to believe him, but he is suspicious of something, even though he doesn't know what it is. *(If only he could remember . . .)*

"Michael," Hank continues, "I promised Neil that you

would rethink your decision and continue the therapies. I trust you will not embarrass me."

"But, Pa! I—"

"If you don't listen to me, I don't know if I can help you with your new board."

"But I don't need therapy . . ."

"Perhaps in this case Europe won't happen either."

"Everything is fine with me!"

"If you don't do some serious thinking about it . . ."

"Don't you hear what I'm trying to tell you? *I don't need treatment!*"

"*. . . you can say goodbye to the contest.* Because you are grounded. Did you hear me?"

They both fall silent at the same time as they began to speak.

Michael frowns as if he hadn't heard it well, as if he had misinterpreted Hank's words.

But he heard it well. His father is clear, *He can say goodbye to the contest.*

(He can't do this to him, no. He can't! Michael's not a child. He can't command him! He can't blackmail him. HE CAN'T DO THIS TO HIM!)

"You can't do this to me!"

"You think so?"

"You can't blackmail me!"

"Watch me."

With his arms folded across his chest, he fixes his gaze on Michael, who is looking at him in disbelief.

(This isn't happening. This is just a bad dream! I'll wake up soon and everything will go away. Everything will be fine, if I just last a little longer.)

"As long as I feed you and dress you, you will listen to what I tell you."

The minutes roll. The dream is nearing its end. And with it, Michael's patience.

The tamed hurricanes of suffered days rise in great rebellion: the world will soon disappear; the world is about to collapse and will never be the same.

"As long as I am your father and you live under my roof, you will go to Dr. Beresford until *I* say enough."

But it is enough already! Michael almost screams. He cannot stand it anymore. Hank pushed him against the wall, and he snaps.

"BUT YOU ARE NOT MY FATHER!"

The storm strikes with hammer and tongs. The wild gale comes in full swing. Michael's eyes flood with tears.

"You're not my father . . ." He is sobbing.

And calling after his real dad,

Dad? Dad, where are you? I need you . . . Why don't you answer me? Why didn't you come back? We were waiting for you, Mom and I. I'm still waiting for you. Come back, Dad . . . Come home, please . . .

Shattered memories of a familiar TV screen image: the desolate surface of Mars with no signs of life. Spacecraft only—abandoned remains of terrestrial civilization hidden in red sand. Not a trace of the Roswell crew. Only the footprints of colonizers, disappearing in the distance. Never to return.

Minutes of waiting.

Hours of anticipation.

Years of hope.

All in vain.

Michael's father never returned from the depths of space.

"If you think so, you can pack yourself and go. Right now."

Michael's rage turns rocket-fast into an apocalyptic storm, ready to wipe out whatever is in its way. Instead of a complete devastation of the environment, it remains focused on one pair of eyes that Michael cannot stop staring at.

"I hate you."

Even more rage and even more destruction that is about to happen.

And again, "I hate you."

At the last moment Michael looks away from Hank and at the spider-shaped floor lamp next to the armchair in which Hank sits. The light bulbs on the spider's feet explode one after the other.

One.

Two.

Three.

Blown up.

The floor lamp shakes under the power of an invisible human force at work.

Four. Five. Six.

Poof! Poof! Poof!

The shards of glass fly all over the room. Hank covers his face and eyes with his hands, trying to protect them from dangerous debris.

What happens next, Michael doesn't know. He storms out of the apartment and into uncertainty, becoming a street child and an outcast with no vision of the future.

With no idea of what is waiting for him out there and with a vague understanding of what had just happened.

Chapter

16th: . . . you flip the board. Riding in the same direction is the *hardflip*. The same goes for the *heelflip*. *Ollie* the board. Your front foot is on the toe side of the board. Pop the board. Flip. Land. The nose is flicking the opposite side. If you are *regular-footed* and you flip the board by rotating it . . .

YES, IT HAPPENS. NO ONE WANTS IT, no one likes it, and everyone feels weird about it, but it happens anyway. The time comes for Victor to say goodbye to his grandmother forever. There will no longer be a strong and acrid odor of urine for him, no more odor of disinfectants and aging. The shrill sound of the radio from the next room is turned off for him, and he will no longer have to talk in the incomprehensible language of the old people he doesn't understand. This is his last walk down the hall under the ceiling of *Rhaphidophora*. His last, "The lunch is at one o'clock, ma'am. Wait for it in your room, five hundred nine, remember? It's the number of your room."

It all ceases to exist, the moment Angela Kenneth dies. *All.* Nancy is shaken; wiping tears with a tissue, waiting for the elevator door to open. She cannot stand the curious glances from everyone around her, *Why are you crying, girl? Not feeling well, honey?*

No, I'm fine. Only, someone I loved very much died . . . That's all.

After years of waiting, the elevator door slides open and she disappears into the cabin. Burying her face in Victor's shoulder, she surrenders to tears.

Victor doesn't cry; a strange calm envelops him. But what is really happening in him, no one knows. No one, except maybe God.

Nancy can't think of God now. Now, she does not care about Him. She is desperate, confused, she is grieving, and the only thing that can comfort her are Victor's strong arms, his warm embrace. She will later turn to her Heavenly Father in humble prayer, but not now. It's too early for that. She's tired, doesn't understand anything, she's on the brink of exhaustion and, if Victor didn't support her, she'd collapse.

(God, why do I miss her so much?!)

Her thoughts are dedicated to Angela Kenneth, the old lady she loved with all her heart as if she were her own grandmother. Nancy never had a grandmother; she had never known the truth of her origin, nor had she felt the power of true motherly love. The love she received at the boarding school could not be compared to the love Angela Kenneth had given her back for everything Nancy had done for her. *My child, my dear child,* the old woman would tell her.

And I was yours, Nana. I was, Nancy whispers and cries again.

"She was a wonderful person," Victor mutters to her ear and kisses her soft and freshly washed, lemon-scented hair. "She loved you very much."

From the warmth of Victor's chest, Nancy digs up her

lovely but sorrow-devastated Julia Ormond face and stares into the coldness of his eyes. Those deep, distant, and beautiful eyes shine with the purity of the polar sun.

"I will miss her very much," she whispers again, as if afraid that someone might hear her. With her thumb, she catches the tear in the corner of his eye.

And then she kisses his lips, salty from her own tears.

Looking in his eyes again, she plunges into the memories that project in them like a movie.

It was last night. The sun is setting, its light shining on Angela Kenneth's bed, bathing her in the warmth of its rays.

Victor returned from the bathroom, holding a glass of orange juice. He hands it to Angela Kenneth and kisses her forehead goodnight. She tells him how much she loves him, and he tells her, *I love you too, Nana*. These are the last words exchanged between two people who love each other. *I love you too, Nana. I love you a lot.*

And then she opens her eyes once more and stares at the sun that had shone on her before it went down—forever.

The elevator stops downstairs and Victor wraps his hand under Nancy's arm. Making their way out of the cabin through a group of old people who are just waiting to swarm into it, they pass the reception and Victor takes her out into the street. Into the motion of life and the world of living.

He looks into the distance, trying to glimpse what the future will bring him, but he sees nothing.

The sun is too strong, and it blinds him.

* * *

He slows down his steps and reduces the pace, gasping for

breath and trying to calm the insane beating of his heart. His lungs will burst, and his head will explode from so much drumming.

He is on the corner of Greenwich Avenue and Perry Street, thinking where he will go, with no faint idea which di-rection to take.

Most New Yorkers rush on their daily routes, and the traffic comes to life again thanks to the nicer weather. The traces of snow have almost disappeared: only a few, dirty, brown piles remain that have not yet melted—a reminder of this summer's whimsy.

Michael slips his hands into his pants and searches his pockets. The whole content comes down to 9.75 dollars, two tissues, and the keys to the apartment he left there by some miracle. That's all he has on him except the clothes he wears. An old, long-sleeved, hooded, Blind T-shirt, a T-shirt, chocolate-brown Droors pants, and worn DC shoes.

After a few moments he spends thinking and in doubt, he sets off again following his instinct, the same impulse that drove him to flight after the lamp had exploded.

He still doesn't know what had happened in the apartment, he is sure he isn't the only one scared of it. Hank was scared too. That was *obvious*. And he has a reason to be afraid. Because if Michael hadn't stopped himself at the last moment, Hank would have been blown to pieces with this awakened force, and the whole room would have been bathed in his blood. An expensive Persian carpet would be destroyed by the torn remains of his brain, heart, lungs, and other internal organs.

His father was defeated; he was on his knees facing death. Yet, there was a brief flash of triumph in his eyes Michael glimpsed before running from the mess he made without touching anything.

How is that possible? Was he not afraid of him? Wasn't he afraid of what Michael had done? Isn't he afraid of what Michael *might do*?!

Either way, Michael isn't thinking of going home until Hank thinks about everything. And when he gets home, things will be different. *Everything* will be different. Hank will no longer have a monopoly on him. Hank will no longer blackmail him or tell him what to do and what not to do. HE WILL NEVER TOUCH HIM AGAIN!

These are his terms. If Hanks wants to see him again, then he's better off agreeing to it. Michael will give him two, three days to think it over, and that's it. What happens next, Michael doesn't know. Except that this time he will run the show. He is no longer scared. He isn't the same kid anymore. The *power* is with him now.

Next time, Michael won't relent. Next time, Michael won't suffer.

Next time, he'll strike back, hard. For e-v-e-r-y-t-h-i-n-g.

He is finally free. Hank can't hurt him anymore. And if he only tries to touch Rebecca, he better watch his back. He isn't so naïve anymore. He will no longer buy any of the stories about his baby sister who will get hurt because of his disobedience.

A good thing is that Rebecca is out of town. Michael has enough time to sort things out within the family. When Rebecca returns from Denver, there will be no more danger for her. There will be no more danger for *them*. The power will be on their side and it will keep Hank's horny hands away from them both.

The day is so beautiful, Michael thinks. *How has he not noticed that so far?*

He is swimming through the bloodstream of the Theater District, glancing at the colorful store windows and listening to the muffled music of its plays through the channel of time. Experiencing his city with different eyes, he absorbs every de-tail he missed when thundering these same streets at breakneck speed on a skateboard.

The vastness of Broadway, dazzled by sunbeams bouncing off thousands of windows, blows him away. How come he hadn't noticed this beauty before? How could he be so *blind*?

He makes a big circle and turns from Broadway to Washington Mews. Washington Square Park is just around the corner.

He mixes with the group of people at the foot of the marble triumphal arch and stretches his neck to see what's going on.

Washington Square swarms with the cops who surround a small group of skateboarders and cram them into an irregular circle. The raid is over and, before being released by police, Michael recognizes a few faces from Division Pro Skate Shop and some kids from New Bronx and New Brooklyn.

A heavy hand lands on Michael's shoulder from behind him and he jumps startled, barely holding back a cry.

He wheels around and finds himself face-to-face with Alien.

"Holy cow, you scared me out of my wits! Thought you were a cop. What was that?"

"The raid, what do you think it was? I almost got busted, too, but I got away with a few more. They caught us off guard, but we escaped them anyway."

"Escaped?" Michael looks at his friend quizzically.

Alien sighs. "You don't know, do you? They were looking for Nando and his gang. It's all about the drugs."

"No way! But he wasn't here, was he?"

"No, but that doesn't mean we didn't expect him. Someone must have told him to stay away from old Washington."

"Sorry, you are losing me. How about you explain it to me in English?" Michael tries to digest this bit of information.

"You're really behind everything." Alien rolls his eyes and continues, "Some dudes started moseying around here two days ago. They were reportedly interested in skateboarding, so they asked us if we could show them a few tricks and such. We told them there was no problem, but they had to get the boards first. And that's what they did. Three of them came back with a brand new Toy Machine board! Once we recovered from the surprise, Rich, Marc, and a few other guys took turns in showing them tricks. The dudes tried to repeat them as we showed them, but all they did was make us laugh. Man, you should've seen them busting their asses! But they didn't give up. I have to give them credit for that—if nothing else, they have been persistent.

"Then the Chad dude, who probably works out twenty hours a day in the gym, approached Justin, Sven, and me on the bench and offered us some weed. All three of us passed, so Chad smoked it himself and then joined the other two who were already so exhausted and bruised that they could barely stand on their feet, let alone skate. He fumbled with the board for another twenty minutes or so, and it hurt my eyes watching him destroy such a good deck.

"They also showed up the next day while we were here, but this time they didn't just ask for a skateboarding lesson. They were friendly to us and wanted to know each of us by name.

They were even interested in where we live and such. We decided to get rid of them by moving to Union Square until the air was clear again. Everybody's opinion was that they were cops who worked undercover to get Nando. I guess they thought one of us would snitch him if they clicked with us, but they were wrong."

"Oh great! That's just what we needed. Now we will have even less space to skate with them hanging around."

"And why does that bother you so much? As far as I can see, you still have nothing to ride. So, how could that harm you?"

Alien says it seriously, but Michael sees through him.

"And as things are now, it might take a while."

"Don't shit with me! Your old man didn't give you the money?"

"I have to correct you a little. My old man kicked me out of the house," Michael announces and bursts into a mad laughter. When he regains his composure again, he tells Alien almost everything from A to Z.

"I thought I'd ask you if you could take me with you, at your place, for a couple of days," he continues. "I wouldn't stay long."

"Strange things happen," Alien says in disbelief. "This summer has kind of struck everyone in the head, as it seems to me."

"Yes, it probably is. I wouldn't bother you much, you know. I just need a day or two to work things out with my old man."

"Don't be stupid. You can stay as long as you want. I'm sure Mom will be glad to have you with us."

Alien could say that with certainty because he knew his

mom still remembers what it feels like to be thrown out on the street with a four-year-old child. Even today, she remembers well that summer day, twelve years ago, a day that was so hot that her tears dried and she couldn't shed them, no matter how much she cried. If she didn't have friends who helped her find a job and took care of her with her baby, Alien could only speculate on what their lives would look like now. He would probably never have met Michael, his mom would never become one of the editors of NYKR radio, and Alien would be anything but a well-cared-for kid who has enough free time to skate the streets of New York with his friends.

"Are you hungry?" he asks Michael. "How much money do you have on you?"

"Just under ten bucks. That should do until I work things out at home."

"Ten bucks? It must have been a real hassle when you took to your heels with ten bucks in your pocket!"

"Actually, it was." He grins, remembering the light bulbs whose delicate but sharp pieces flew all over the room. He says nothing about that to Alien yet, because then he will have to tell him also about his gift, and he is not ready for that yet.

Alien puts his arm around his friend's shoulder and says, "Let's go. You deserve a treat. I didn't think you had the guts to do something like that! What would you like to eat? You can have anything you want, and you can eat until you burst. So, what's your choice?"

"Thanks, but I'm not hungry right now. Maybe later."

"You are not hungry? You are kidding me! I could eat a horse if I were you! But since *I* am hungry, we have a little problem. You'll have to join me, whether you like it or not. Or I withdraw the offer and you will have to pay what I order. And believe me, your ten bucks will not be enough in that case."

"Okay, okay, it's your treat," Michael agrees before Alien leaves him flat broke.

"So? Where are we going?"

"I don't care. Everything suits me as long as it isn't called *Martinelli*."

* * *

He's drunk, Juanita tells him. He sat on the couch all night and emptied bottles. He went to work like that. Juanita is amazed that he could work in such a condition, how they *let him* work in that condition. This is, to say the least, dangerous!

Juanita Dolores is pleased to hear that Michael is okay and had stayed at his friend's place. She asks him if he needs anything, but he assures her he is fine. Truth be told, having some extra money wouldn't hurt him, but he doesn't tell her that. He'll be home soon anyway, and that puts her mind at rest.

Juanita is sure that Hank will be sober by then. Hank misses him, even though he tries to hide it, and he will be glad to hear that Michael is planning to return home.

After they had finished talking, Michael goes to the kitchen and pours himself a glass of water. He returns to Alien's room and finds Alien at the computer, engrossed in the game *Jedi Knight-Dark Forces 2*, for the umpteenth time breaking his own record.

Michael sprawls out on the bed and stares blankly out the window.

It is raining outside. New York City is dressed in gray. There aren't many things a person can do in such weather. Such a sad day, and so sleepy.

Strange things are happening this summer.

Fifteen minutes ago, Alien told him about Victor's grandmother. Victor must have looked for him at home to tell him in person, except Michael is no longer there. Michael called him as soon as he heard the news, but there was no one at Victor's place when he called. There was no one to answer the phone, neither he nor Nancy. They miss each other again.

Strange, Michael thinks, *really strange.*

As neither of them have cell phones and since there is no other way to get in touch with him, he tries to locate him with his gift, but again to no avail. He can't focus enough to find out where his friend is. He just can't.

He knows that Victor needs him; he *can* feel it. It is pure intuition, with no trace of the paranormal. Nothing special, nothing unusual, and nothing supernatural.

Nothing strange.

Michael wonders why Victor doesn't look for him at Alien's. He's been here for three days and Victor should know that.

He is watching the rain fall, and his eyes grow heavier with every raindrop that cries on the window. Lulled by the silent hum of Alien's computer, he dozes off. But before he is unaware of the world around him, he sees Victor disappear into the black cloud.

The moment consciousness gives way to subconscious, an idea is born in his head. What if there is a connection between that cloud and the death of Victor's grandmother? What if that is the sign Michael should recognize and do something about it?

(But what?)

And if that has to do with Angela Kenneth's death, why is

that cloud still here? Why is it still swallowing Victor?

Michael doesn't get to find the answers to these questions. He falls asleep.

A minute later, he opens his eyes, awakened by a noise. It is Alien.

"Sorry, dude. I didn't want to wake you up," Alien apologizes. "I forgot something in the room."

"Never mind. What time is it?"

"It's almost eight."

"Already?!" Michael jerks upright in bed. "I slept so much?"

"Precisely three hours, fifty-two minutes, and sixteen seconds," Alien consults his stopwatch.

"I cannot believe it! Why didn't you wake me up?"

"You slept badly last night. You needed rest."

"How do you know that? Oh boy, you didn't sleep because of me either."

"No worries. I am made of stone. I'll catch up on it."

"Sorry about that. I really am."

"Hey, I told you, no sweat! I don't sleep much, anyway."

Michael stretches and swings his legs over the edge of the bed.

"Anything new?"

"Not much. I'm making dinner for us and . . . Oh, yes. Victor called."

"No way!" he protests again, and his voice cracks.

"Yes, I wanted to wake you up, but he insisted on letting you sleep. He said he would call again later. He went to arrange things for the burial."

"That's something we should have taken care of, Alien! We should have helped him with that."

"And we did. I made some calls while you were sleeping."

Michael is boiling inside. He is so cross with himself that Alien has a real challenge to calm him down.

"Relax, okay? You were literally worn out, your body needed rest, so you rested. Stop eating your heart out. You'll catch up with everything else."

"Yeah! And my dad will get a nice pair of wings and become a seraphim."

"That would surprise you?"

Michael doesn't know what is funnier: Alien's expression when he said it, the way he said it, or the image of Hank Daniels flapping his wings in the choir of angels and singing to the glory of God.

Tears go to his eyes as he rolls across the floor of Alien's room, dying from laughter.

Through a blurred veil of tears, he sees Alien drop to his knees. Screaming with laughter, Alien crawls over to him and gives him a friendly hug. They are patting each other on the back and shaking under the assaults of unstoppable laughter, unable to delete the image of angel Hank from their heads.

Chapter

17th: . . . clockwise while your body rotates 180 degrees, you are doing the *180 kickflip*. If you also *heelflip* in the same direction, that is the *inward varial heelflip* (not the *heelflip 180*).

Something completely different is the *Turk* (that is how skaters in Croatia call this trick). Push the board under the . . .

REBECCA HAS NO LUCK WITH MEMBERS of the opposite sex. That is an irrefutable fact.

The more she loves them, the more pain they inflict on her. She is only fourteen, for God's sake, and there are days when she feels like an old woman.

In a series of emotional blows, the last comes from Michael. Her dear brother hurt her when she least expected it, and she only called him to hear how he was. He told her things he shouldn't have and probably doesn't mean. Rebecca is aware of that, but what is her consolation? What does she have from it now? The words of condemnation fell, and nothing happened since then. Nothing.

And then Sunny comes and inflicts new pain upon her by

proposing to her. Rebecca didn't know what to answer, and now she also doesn't know what to say to him. She hides behind the wall she built between them and doesn't see him again.

She spends most of her time on the farm helping her grandmother canning food for winter and making cakes, visiting the greenhouse and talking to flowers, caring for horses, and bothering her grandfather.

The Creeks use every trick in the book to get her off the ranch and persuade her to visit her friends the Atkinses, but in vain. Suspecting that something is wrong and realizing that Rebecca will not open her heart to them, they reconcile with their granddaughter's new whim and leave things to work on their own.

Still looking for a way to deal with Sunny's courtship, Rebecca turns her attention to New York. At the risk of another crisis with her brother, she calls home every few hours. All her attempts result in conversations with the Sergio Unit, which is not the talk she had hoped for, and once, she gets Juanita on the phone. There is still no sign of Michael and her father.

Juanita is all sweetness, emotional and gleeful when she hears Rebecca's voice, but when Rebecca asks her how things are back home, or more precisely how her dad and her brother are, she avoids answers, which is unusual for her.

"Young Daniels skating all days, until he breaks his neck. Your father on work. Both good."

Rebecca gets this much out of her: that Michael is skateboarding with his friends, which she could have guessed, and that her father is working around the clock, as if it is some news. There is only one way to find out what is going at home and why Juanita is so secretive about everything.

Rebecca ignores her father's instruction to call him at work only in an emergency because this is an emergency for her.

Miraculously, her father answers the phone on the first ring.

Hank is surprised to hear her, but to Rebecca's amazement, he doesn't reprimand her for calling him at the Institute. But when answering her questions, his answers are similar to Juanita's!

"Michael is fine. He is mostly out. I work a lot. That's why you can't get anyone."

"Are you *always* out? Dad! I called you at all times and only found Juanita at home! Not a sound from you or Michael. It's like the earth swallowed you!"

"Did you talk to Juanita?"

"Yes, I talked to her, and we had this conversation already. You didn't tell me anything I didn't know already. *Michael is skating, Dad is working.* Blah, blah, blah. Do you do anything other than *research* and *skateboard*? For heaven's sake, Dad, what's *going on* there?"

"What would be going on, Rebecca? Nothing is happening. Everything is as usual. How are you?"

"Me? I'm great, thanks for asking. I'm an obedient girl for Grandma and Grandpa, I play *Star Wars Monopoly* with them every night, and when I get tired of it, I play tic tac toe with Gentle Wind and Blue Sky. When the weather is nice, I ride with Sunny, and that's about it. Everything is as usual."

Ah, yes, Daddy, she adds to herself, *I almost forgot. Did you know I will get married soon? No, I'm not kidding you. Sunny proposed to me. I haven't answered him yet, but I think I'll say yes. Sunny is a very nice boy and he would like to play moms and dads a little for a change. Frankly, I think I need a little change too. I am getting bored and, if that continues, I might wish to return to New York. Only, what would I do there? Considering all the options, marriage at fifteen seems like a much more interesting possibility.*

Grandma and Grandpa are fine too, thanks for not asking. They're still alive, if you haven't noticed. They send you their love and tell you you could call sometimes . . .

"I'm glad you are having a good time. Please, say hello to Elisabeth and Jeremy for me and Michael. Will you do this for me, baby?"

Rebecca bites her tongue, but still cannot get rid of the sarcasm.

"I will, Daddy. I'd be happy to do that. Do you want anything else? Do you have something else to tell them?"

(Do you have anything else to tell me!?)

"Nothing, sweetie. That would be all. Don't be angry, but we better end the conversation now. This is an official line."

"Of course, Dad. How could I forget that? We don't want to block an *important* call."

A moment of hesitation on the other side.

Then, "Baby, are you sure everything is okay?"

"Everything's perfect, Dad." She is indignant at herself for not being able to tell him the truth. "You have nothing to worry about."

"I'm sorry I neglected you lately. I'll make it up to you when you get back. I promise."

"Yes, Dad." *(If I get back.)*

Then she asks him for something else.

"Dad?"

"Yes, sweetheart?"

She feels he is nervous and would want to get rid of her, but he doesn't know how to do it without hurting her.

Rebecca couldn't care less about that. She will not make it

any easier for him.

"Tell Michael to call me when he stops by the phone. I need to talk to him."

In the handset, deep breathing mixed with silence.

"Daddy, did you hear me?"

"I heard you," he says, almost in a whisper. "I'll tell him as soon as I see him. That you want to talk to him."

"Take care of yourself, Dad. I love you."

"I love you too, Daughter. You don't know how much I love you."

Why did he have to tell her that? As if she doesn't have enough to worry about without it! First Michael, then Sunny, and now her father. Three people: her three worries and her three failures.

Tears of misunderstanding sting her in the eyes. *(What did she do wrong? Why is this happening to her?)*

She takes a deep breath, blots her eyes with the back of her sleeve, and puts on a fake smile.

Now she is ready for complete defeat, another failure.

(Grandpa? Grandpa, where are you?) She looks for the fourth man she loves as much as the ones who let her down so far. *(I need you . . .)*

He recognizes the desperation in her silent plea and doesn't let her down.

* * *

His life turns into an avalanche. At first, a slight sliding of snow because of imperceptible warming, and then everything goes unstoppably downhill. The foot is still far away, but destruction is on the pier. The avalanche is crushing everything in its path.

The tremor of the earth and rumbles alert him to the impending disaster.

Neil Beresford decides to be ready when it comes. He prepares for the worst.

He takes precautions to, if nothing else, save face if something goes wrong. And things *will* go wrong. He can feel it in the air.

What he realized a moment ago doesn't surprise him much. Yes, Hank Daniels lost control of the situation. But he expected something like that to happen. What surprises him was his own indifference to it.

It is more news to Hank that Michael is out of control than to him.

Hank, as expected, didn't admit it, but Beresford hears it in his voice.

My friend, I screwed up. Michael is tougher than I thought. I need your help. I don't know what to do with him!

Why doesn't that horrify him? Does he feel relieved that everything will be over? That Daniels is finally giving up?

Beresford doesn't dare to rejoice too soon.

He knows the boy is dangerous; with newly discovered abilities even more. The suspension of the sessions is only temporary, and Beresford will soon have to deal with him again.

Yet, in some strange and perverse way, he is looking forward to it. And he is both excited and terrified by the challenge.

If things go awry, he won't be the only one to bear the consequences. Daniels will suffer, too, in that case. The very thought spreads a grin over Beresford's face.

Maybe Daniels will eventually get what he deserves, Beresford thinks. *His name would be embossed with gold letters in human history, but not in the way he had hoped. The world will remember him as a lunatic and a monster, which is what he is. A lunatic who almost destroyed one kid's life.*

The more he thinks about it, the less it is clear to him how in the first place he got involved in dealing with such a man. How could he accept him as a friend? Was Daniels right to say he had only money in his mind? Did the promise of new wealth so mess him up that he could no longer think rationally?

Or did he do it for some other reason? Maybe he did it because of Melanie Hope, who he fell in love with the moment she stepped into his office?

Yes, that's his sin. He loved his friend's wife and all he wanted was to be around her. Every moment, every minute, always. He wanted to listen to the light walk of her heels; he wanted to inhale the perfume she left behind wherever she went (violets just drove him crazy that year); he wanted to listen to her thoughts as she spoke so intelligently. He couldn't listen to her enough, and he couldn't stand for long without touching her. It felt so good as he traced the fine line of her chin with his rough thumb. . . . No one knows how much he missed it. No one knows how much he suffers because she is gone.

He adored a woman who belonged to another man and is not ashamed of it. Because his friendship with Hank is a friendship out of interest only, and that's true of both of them.

Everything was perfect: lying in her arms, making love to her, breathing in her breath. Until one day they came to a river that only one of them would cross, leaving the other behind. The virus she got was new and mutated so quickly that she was gone in just a few days. It was fast, but painful, and there was nothing he could do to prevent it. There were no therapies to help her and stop the life from running out of her.

Losing Melanie Hope and living without her, for Beresford,

seemed almost impossible. But it is no less painful to watch her beauty on the face of her child, so young, so handsome and so desirable.

Beresford loves Michael the way he loved his mother. It is kind of family friendly: his love and their beauty. Beresford fell in love with Michael two years after falling in love with his mother.

It is because of that love that he hesitated to do what Hank Daniels offered him. He doesn't take Michael's body at the first opportunity that appears to him.

Beresford and Daniels aren't alike at all. Although they both have a great need and passion for someone's love—which almost turns into obsession—Beresford, unlike Daniels, never took anything by force. He is disgusted with forcing someone to do something.

Daniels will never understand this because he is a liar, a scoundrel, and a cheater, and only money, with his magnificent brain that frightens people most, makes him an honorable citizen. Beresford, again, never doubted the veracity of true motives of the "great mind."

It's true, Daniels never cared too much for his children. He doesn't want to make *them* special, but *himself* to become special and superior, The One with the Keys that unlock All the Secrets of the Universe. Michael is just his guinea pig, a means to an end.

But there is someone who dared to obstruct his grand plan. Someone whom Beresford is supposed to receive *as wages for sin*. Instead, Michael Daniels befriends Beresford and thus turns into Daniels's enemy.

Michael has no idea what was going on around him: about the great battle that is fought for his body and his mind, which might be best for him. On several occasions, Beresford was very close to admitting and telling him everything, but he balked every time. Neither of them is ready for that kind of revelation yet. But they will soon have to be, as the situation faster and faster escapes control.

The situation is dangerously out of control.

Daniels is just about to move on to *Plan B*.

Either way, Michael Daniels will soon become the New Michael Daniels or Michael Daniels will be the Dead Michael Daniels. God knows what would happen to Rebecca then. Beresford doesn't know if her father is planning the same fate for her, but he can pretty well guess so. With one difference: Hank Daniels won't eliminate her immediately if something goes wrong, which cannot be said for Michael.

Michael isn't his blood, Michael isn't a *real* Daniels, so he's just as good as dead if he won't serve the purpose. He is just an ordinary mortal, though an above-average, handsome mortal for whom it would be too great a pity to be dead.

And besides, he's a friend of Beresford's. It's a little hurdle that Daniels didn't count on because he doesn't believe something like that could ever happen.

Beresford does not yet have a plan for how to help his teenage friend. But when dinner with Daniels at The Rose Room of the Algonquin Hotel ends, Beresford pioneers a completely different mission. His new mission is to save Michael, not just to clear his name. He has a few ideas how to do it, but none of them are ideal. In each one, someone gets hurt: either he or Michael or both of them. In the best-case scenario, Michael develops his gift and becomes another man. But what about them then? Hank Daniels is sure to end their friendship, which is something Beresford cannot accept. Other options are even more unacceptable, and that is why Beresford is in a great dilemma.

Come what may, he must no longer wait. He *has* to do something.

So he sits in front of his computer and opens a new file. A clean, blank, white document appears in front of him, but he is already looking somewhere else, far away.

(Dear Lord, will they understand him? Will anybody understand that he is just a man who gave in to temptation and who repents for everything . . . ? The only thing he wants now is to help Michael; no one can do it but him. Will he understand that he was the one who saved him . . . ?)

He closes the untouched document and shuts down the computer.

(That's not in his power, though, is it? He almost gives way to his feelings again. Too sentimental, too passionate.)

But it *is* in his power to walk to the kitchen and take two aspirins from the drawer. His head is ringing, his brain is not functioning, and he has to do something about it urgently.

* * *

Michael changes his mind. He postpones the date of his return home. He isn't ready yet. Not that he is afraid of returning home; it is not the right time for that. He has such a premonition—as when people sometimes have premonitions they cannot explain.

Just the same, Michael couldn't explain his reluctance to meet his father. He knows that he cannot stay with Alien forever at the expense of his mother and will have to agree with himself fast if he doesn't want to replace Alien's cozy home with the cold streets of New York. Maybe he gets lucky and sneaks into some dark and warm corner of the subway or gets hooked with a group of junkies their parents kicked out of their homes or fled on their own will.

If none of this works out, he will be forced to seek shelter at Victor's. Victor is not in the mood for a companion, but if he has no other way out . . .

To tell the truth, it is partly because of him that Michael delays his return home. He worries about his friend and empathizes with what Victor is going through, so he doesn't have the strength or the will for a serious talk with Hank.

The farewell to Angela Kenneth was short, modest, and without much fuss. But it nonetheless leaves a striking mark on all of them. Everything is over when her ashes are scattered from the Statue of Liberty Island into the sea. Those few who come to say their goodbyes to Angela Kenneth were already going to their homes.

Nancy cried the most. She sheds enough tears for everyone gathered at that sad moment.

Victor and Alien didn't cry, though Alien struggled to hold back tears most of the time. Michael also didn't cry, but he sympathized.

(With whom?

(With Victor's grandmother, or her remains now sailing on white crests of the waves toward the open sea, carried by a light sea breeze?

(Or Victor, who with the death of his nana lost his last anchorage with his past and missing childhood?

(Or was he sympathetic to himself and what awaited him in the nearest future?)

So many questions, and he is so confused . . . So lost.

After the funeral, four of them went to Victor's apartment.

Michael, Alien, and Victor pull out of a bottle of Scottish Ballantine's, while Nancy excuses herself and retreats to the bedroom. Within minutes, Victor follows her. Waiting for him to return, Alien and Michael toss around a tin box in which a bottle of whiskey is packed and sold. This is the year Finest Scotch Whisky sponsors the International Snowboarding Federation's World Pro Tour.

Victor comes back much paler than when he left, and Michael and Alien decide he ran out of fuel. They offer him a bottle from which he takes a long pull. Not long after, he is drunk. Michael and Alien follow his example, and they get wasted too. It's lucky the boys didn't have their skateboards with them, for on their way back to Alien's house in Patchin Place they would end up with a fracture.

That is why Michael still can't talk to his father. But as much as he sympathizes with Victor, he cannot fill his friend's emptiness because he himself is empty inside. In any case, these are the days when their friendship is stronger and better than ever.

Nevertheless, something *has* changed. Victor is no longer the same, from the day he found out about his grandmother's death. Michael cannot explain *how* different Victor is because this change can't be seen with the naked eye. It is something else, like when everything looks fine, but it isn't, and you know it, but can't explain it.

Two more days had passed since Angela Kenneth's memorial, and Michael finally decides to call his father. He achieves nothing more by delaying; he already made his point that he means it seriously. Now it is time to act upon it.

First, he accompanies Alien, who is going to watch *Scream 2*, taking Laurie. Alien apologizes to him for not inviting him, but he has plans he wants to carry out alone with Laurie, so he asks for his understanding. He'd wanted to do that since they made another Dennis Kay underwear ad together; the big boss already accepted the first. Alien learned of this a few weeks later, when he spots his photo on billboards across New Manhattan hovering over a skateboard in a high jump, his pants lowered enough so that Dennis Kay can be seen on his boxers. His bare chest is shiny with sweat, and a stream of blood runs down his forearm. Large gray artificial clouds float in the background.

You don't need any protection—except for Dennis Kay men's underwear.

The same slogan will go with the new ad featuring Alien and Laurie kissing in the middle of Fifth Avenue during a gridlock. That kiss is the main reason Alien is taking her to the movies today. Intentional or not—Alien still doesn't know it—Laurie reached between his legs as she kissed him. He was instantly aroused, although angry drivers honked all around them, some of them cussing and some grinning and winking at them. So embarrassing! His otherwise too large pants were now too tight, and Alien thought he would explode. At the last minute, James announced that the shooting is over, saving him from further humiliation.

Alien didn't forget that. He is preparing for revenge, when *his* hand will wander under Laurie's miniskirt, accidentally or not.

He says goodbye to Michael and leaves him his boogie-board to redeem for the movie. Michael takes it and, without grudges, sets off. He cruises the city at a wild pace for two hours before returning to Patchin Place.

Alien's mother has a night off, so she warms up his dinner

while he showers. They talk while he eats, and she gives him some advice on how to stand up to his father—she has experience in this. Michael listens intently to her even though he already knows what he is going to do. He worked out a plan for how to get what he wants.

The moment has come, and he will do it now—or never.

Chapter

18th: . . . obstacle. Jump *over* it. Land on your board and roll away (like Alien did over his bike). A *line* is if you do a few tricks in a row and add the *manual* (also called the *wheelie*), whether it is the *nose manual* (you ride your board on the front wheels and your nose is not touching the asphalt) or the . . .

HANK DANIELS ALSO KNOWS WHAT HE WANTS and has a clear idea how to accomplish it. His confidence comes back completely when Michael calls him, after hearing nothing from him for days. It is a good sign—that he called. That means he is ready to cooperate and wants to settle things out. And where there is a will, there are also opportunities for water to be diverted to your own mill—Hank thinks.

He is in good spirits, and he intends to stay that way. He won't let him slip from his hands again. A seventeen-year-old will not outsmart him twice, whether or not he has a *gift*! He should be grateful to him, not act like that.

Hank was angry that Michael had escaped. He should be punished for that and, if necessary, Hank is ready to spend the whole night teaching him good manners. He has his ways and means; methods that Michael despises. But they are effective, and each time the lesson is over, Michael is again meek and obedient like a lamb.

Although raging because of Michael's escape, Hank was delighted to see his son's *power* at work. It is the first time he had seen what Michael is capable of doing after learning from Beresford that Michael had become aware that he is *different.*

At first, Michael scared him when he demonstrated his strength, but he quickly recovers. He is bursting with admiration, satisfaction, and excitement. His effort paid off! He can't stop wondering where Michael's boundaries are. How strong is his power?

Hank knows that it is his fault that Michael escaped. He himself is guilty of still waiting for answers to questions that interest him. Waiting for Michael to call him and tell him he is coming home, he is killing time with a few glasses of drink.

After a few days away from home, Michael calls him, and Hank's bluff works. He plays the role of a good and worried father ready to forgive everything. He doesn't rebuke him because such things happen in families.

He does his best to convince him that everything is fine and that he has no reason not to return home. If they need to talk about anything, no problem, they'll talk man to man.

Hank Daniels is all sweetness and light while talking to Michael over the phone. Even his voice quivers when he tells him he is missing Michael and that he wants him to come home. He doesn't ask him where he is or what he is doing; just plain come home, please.

Michael promises him he will be back, and Hank is so glad to hear that he promises to buy him a new board. And not just any board, he'll buy him *the best* board Michael can find.

Michael tells him that there is no such thing as *the best* board. It's a matter of personal choice. Some like narrower boards, while others prefer boards with bigger concave. There is also the question of wheels and the like. There are several things to consider when buying a good skateboard. Not *the best*, but the best one for *someone*. For a skater with a different riding style, that same skateboard might be *the worst* one.

Hank doesn't get confused by Michael's efforts to introduce him to the skateboarding world and promises him he will get a board which will help him be brilliant at the contest. And if by any chance he doesn't win, it won't be the end of the world. There will be other contests and plenty of opportunity to prove himself.

Yes, there will be other contests, Michael agrees skeptically, giving Hank the sign he is waiting for. Slowly but steadily, he begins to pressure Michael.

Why should they talk about it on the phone when they can meet and discuss everything face-to-face? This way they cannot even see each other, let alone have a serious conversation. Couldn't they talk normally—like father to son?

Hank regrets things he has said to him. It was thoughtless, his tongue was quicker than his brain, and he hopes that Michael has forgiven him. He is sorry that Michael has taken so seriously what he said in the heat of angry blood. Hank still loves him, and he wants to prove that to him. He is begging Michael for another chance.

Michael does not doubt his sincere motives (at least he tells him so) and Hank shivers with excitement when he feels Michael's resistance weaken. He is melting in his hands as he melted at nights when he lay in his embrace. His face turns into a grimace and spreads to a big grin, warning Michael to stay alert. Michael can't see it, Hank knows it. Had Michael seen it, it would have all been over, turned into the ruins of the lost world of Atlantis.

Michael agrees to come home to continue the conversation, sharing Hank's opinion that it's not the best solution to talk about it over the phone.

Hank is more than pleased with himself. Michael's assent is a fresh start, in his mind. An opportunity to correct his mistakes and never repeat them again.

Then why the serious expression on his face as he watches Beresford speak to a ten-year-old boy named Bryan on the second floor of the Institute beneath the ground level? Bryan's room is floor-to-ceiling all painted blue and serves as both a private and workroom. Next to the wall to the left of the door is his desk with a computer. Above it are three shelves full of floppy disks, CD-ROMs, and magazines from all areas. A television and a VCR are in the corner opposite to it, while the adjacent wall is occupied with an army cot. There is some space in the room for a closet with his personal belongings and two sizable armchairs for visitors.

The whole room looks like a cell in one of the better-equipped prisons (except it has no toilet and no running water tap) and is all Bryan's living space. This is not a prison, though, and his room is not a prison cell, since Bryan is free to get out of it whenever he feels the need to use the restroom or when he goes to the dining room for daily meals. Bryan visits three times a day with his classmates in a small classroom for twelve students, equipped with state-of-the-art teaching equipment. Here, children with extremely high IQs gain knowledge and education under the highest standards of the American educational system.

Bryan's head is covered with a helmet. All his senses (except hearing) are deep in the world of virtual reality. He listens to the instructions Beresford gives him, absorbing his every word and nodding in agreement.

Beresford touches his arm and Bryan takes off the helmet, with a beautiful smile he offers to his tutor. Years later, that beautiful smile will contribute to the well-being of the world when, at thirty-two, Bryan will prevail in the new US presidential election. With his appearance and good looks, his abilities, his knowledge, and his *gift*, he will win the hearts of Americans and lead them, along with the rest of the world, into a more peaceful, happier, and safer future.

Before saying goodbye to him, Neil Beresford exchanges another word with the boy. Once he is alone again, Bryan gets to work to bring his new skills to perfection. He sits down at the computer and starts to memorize information from the screen. Enormous amounts of information about all US presidents scroll up and down before his eyes and Bryan will remember them all. When finished, he will connect himself to another data bank. The United States of America is just a drop in the sea. There are so many other countries and statesmen to study, so much more to see and learn, and time is running out.

That doesn't discourage Bryan. He is a diligent and dedicated boy who loves to learn. He has no playing time; there will be plenty of time for that later—when he gets a well-deserved award. A very dear, respectable, and well-to-do family who cannot have children of their own will adopt him. Then he will play as much as he wants. Then he will play in the *sun* and under the *stars*, and if he is a good boy for his new parents, they might even let him swim in the pool with warm water under the big, yellow moon shining above his head. Bryan wants it so much as a boy of his age could only want something, and Neil Beresford skillfully fuels his imagination with such promises.

But until that moment comes, he will still have a lot to learn, just like the other above-average, intelligent children from the Institute. Bryan has no idea what institute he is at—no one had ever explained it to him. All he knows is that it is a place for *very special children*. And Neil Beresford and his other adult friends did their best to make Bryan feel like someone very special. Especially Neil Beresford, who says goodbye to him so he can visit Katrina, a pretty, little girl with curly hair, Bryan's first neighbor and his best friend.

The walls of Katrina's room are painted in her favorite color, orange, and adorned with cut-out photographs of fashion creations from various magazines from all around the world such as the one Katrina just flips through with a hungry look in her lively eyes. Her desk drawers are loaded with her own drawings and fashion creations, quite challenging and daring for a girl of such a young age.

Although Katrina has the potential to one day become a world-renowned fashion designer, her career will take a different direction. In 2018, she will win the title of Miss World when she, with her beauty, charm, her *gift*, and her abilities, will win the hearts of the jury and the sympathies from viewers across all the continents, and break the heart of a future President of the United States. Amid his political activities, young, handsome, and ambitious Bryan will fall in love with beautiful Katrina. It will be their first encounter since they lost contact when he left the Institute for an adoption sixteen years ago. Katrina and Bryan will thus become the most beautiful and beloved presidential couple the White House ever had.

Hank Daniels turns his gaze away from little Katrina, who had stopped flipping through the latest issue of *Vogue* to greet her visitor with a lovely smile.

Familiar with his friend's daily route, he leaves the room where monitors follow each of the Institute's protégé children and heads for the elevator.

While the central computer is checking his identity, Hank thinks about Michael and Rebecca. His children will also become *special* and thus contribute to the well-being of mankind. But the importance of their contribution will be much greater than that of Bryan and Katrina, because much more effort, risks, and patience will be invested in Michael and Rebecca. Much more *love* and feelings.

Resurfacing from the underground floors, Hank Daniels is almost convinced that nothing will go wrong this time. He will do everything in his power to keep Michael and Rebecca obedient like Bryan, Katrina, and other children, and not to turn against their benefactors.

Michael had tried it once, but he achieved almost nothing with it. Now he is crawling back, regretting and begging for forgiveness.

And what about Rebecca? Will she follow her brother's example and rebel? No, she won't do it. And neither will Michael again. That will be their end, Hank Daniels has no doubt. Because his love has limits, after all.

* * *

It is nice of Alien to offer to go with him. Michael appreciates it, but he can't accept it. Also, he can't agree to Alien waiting for him in front of the house until he is sure he is okay. What would it look like in front of his dad if he finds out he came with backup? That would mean Michael doesn't trust him. How would he explain it to him?

As for Victor, he didn't suggest such a thing because he looks at the whole situation differently. Victor knows Michael has to do it *himself*. But just in case things don't go as Michael plans, Victor's door will be always open to him. Nancy won't mind either. In fact, Nancy has been in agreement with everything Victor would suggest.

This is a great encouragement for Michael when he sets out to face his father. There is no one in the apartment when he walks in, his father hasn't arrived yet, and Michael is glad he is the first. He is also pleased that Hank, in his zeal and determination to drive him out, had not changed the locks on the apartment door. Michael takes that as a good omen. This is proof that Hank wants to smooth things out so everything can be like before.

Well, not quite *everything*.

He changes into clean clothes and takes his dirty clothes he had on to the bathroom; Juanita will take care of them tomorrow. Then he returns to his room.

He takes a backpack from the floor and tosses Rimbaud's *Collected Poems* into it. Holding the book in his hand, he wonders how much it means to him just to hold it again. Then the turn comes for the trucks and the wheels, which he had removed from his skateboard, to put them in his backpack.

The shelves that covered one side of the wall bent under the weight of several-year-old magazines like *Transworld Skateboarding*, *Transworld Snowboarding*, *Crasher*, *Thrasher*, *411VM*, and *Slap*, as well as several encyclopedias and a bunch of fiction in the *Dark Secrets of the Heart* by Ethan McCoy genre. Michael reaches out to the second shelf from the top and pulls out *Fear of Dreaming: The Selected Poems of Jim Carroll*. He opens the book and finds five ten-dollar bills in it. He folds them and stores them in his hip pocket. Returning the book to its place, he realizes something.

Michael is packing. Michael is preparing to leave.

(Is it the faint voice of his subconsciousness that whispers to him not to expect much from the negotiations with his father?) Anyhow, he only takes what he loves most, and there isn't much of it. (Michael is not used to being attached to things. Things are only things. Today you have them, and tomorrow you are without them because you give them to someone, or someone steals them from you.)

When he's done packing, he rolls onto the bed. Before long, he hears the front door open. Father's here.

Michael pushes himself out of bed and stands by the window. He won't go to say hello. He will wait for his father to take the first step.

He's ready.

* * *

Hank Daniels's eyes gleam as the door opens after the first turn of the key. That means Michael is already here, waiting for him.

The nostalgia and melancholy, with which he watched Bryan, Katrina, and five other *Predestined*, *Chosen*, and *Special* children half an hour ago, fade from his gaze. Because one of *his own* kids is waiting for him in the comfort of his home to make him special. Although a little more stubborn and unpredictable, Michael will still not pose a problem for Hank. Hank loves challenges, and his stepson being tougher and stronger than before will give that challenge an extra boost. Once he is done with him, the pleasure will be great, to unimaginable limits.

Hand to heart, Michael has no chances. By the time he figures out what is happening to him, he will already depend on Hank's mercy. It's a pity that Hank is not known as being a very merciful person. If Michael wants to fare well— Heck! If Michael wants to skate tomorrow, he'll have to agree to everything without objection.

He opens the door to his room and rests his eyes on Michael, who is leaning against his desk. Attractive, handsome and *desirable* as ever.

"Hello . . . Pa."

His eyes, his beautiful, dreamy eyes, fear nothing. They radiate only strength, firmness, and determination.

"Hi, Michael," Hank greets him with a smile.

But for how long? How long will he be so sure of himself, glorious in his defiance? Hank ponders. *He thinks he can oppose him? He thinks he can win this battle? Poor, naïve boy. He doesn't understand that he will knuckle under, like he always does. Sooner or later, only a matter of time.*

"I'm glad to see you. Are you okay?"

"Yeah, I'm fine."

He thought he could do without him? That he can survive without his help in this cruel world? No, darling, Hank addresses him in his thoughts. *It doesn't work that way. You'll find out soon enough. Very soon . . .*

"Are you hungry? You want us to go somewhere and have a snack?"

He invites him to dinner, Michael thinks. *He wants to take him out. He is afraid of him, so he wants to go among the people where he cannot use his powers against him!*

"No, thanks. I'm not hungry. I had a bite at Alien's before heading here."

"So, you've been with him all these days?"

See how easy it is? Hank speaks to him in his thoughts again. *You trust me with everything that interests me without even asking you anything! I'm glad you, too, feel the need to be close with your dad again. You couldn't have been without me for a long time, right, kiddo?*

I'm part of you, Michael, you just don't know it yet. I am in you: in your thoughts, in your feelings, and in your dreams. You are mine and I am yours, forever. Don't reject me; just take what's yours. Take what belongs to you.

"Why don't you call that boy by his real name? I mean, what's wrong with *Roy*?"

Am I nuts or what? Michael asks himself. *I was careless only for a moment and I already blabbed! Why did I have to say something I wasn't asked? Now I can forget about staying at Alien's if something goes wrong! Bravo, Michael! That's where Hank will look for me first. And if he doesn't find me there, he'll walk up to East 78th Street and knock on Victor's door.* Victor lives near the Ukrainian Institute of America and Hank knows this because Michael once told him. *Good job, buddy, really good job.*

Hank's question is rhetorical, so Michael doesn't answer him. *(I don't know. We just call him that.)* He just shrugs his shoulders.

"Shall we move into the living room?" Hank suggests. "If you don't mind?"

"No. I have nothing against it."

I thought so. I know you, Michael Daniels. I know you better than you will ever know yourself. Are you aware of this? Are you aware that you are mine and that you will be mine and only mine forever? You cannot escape me, Michael. Never.

They sink into the armchairs, one opposite the other. Between them is a glass table, supported by thin brass legs. The heavy and expensive ashtray, bought by Melanie Hope when she was in the Czech enclave, and a porcelain vase of inestimable value of Asian origin, maintain a balance on each side of the glossy surface.

"Want something to drink? I need a beer."

"Not now, thanks. Maybe later."

"You won't mind if I drink while we talk?"

"No, just help yourself."

He sips his beer straight from the bottle, not bothering to get a glass dirty. This is more delicious.

"So, Michael, I'm listening to you. What's bugging you? What did you want to talk to me about?"

Michael takes a deep breath and then another one.

"First of all, I'm sorry about what happened and for not calling you afterward. I was wrong, my feelings carried me away and I acted rashly. I want to tell you I'm sorry about that."

If I hadn't already told you myself, I might be surprised to hear it from you, Hank says to himself in triumph. *But that's what I told you, didn't I? You are getting it fast, Son, and soon you will understand the rest too. Parents deserve to be respected. If it wasn't for them, there would never have been you. They gave you a home, they gave you their love, and everything you could want. You lacked nothing. You had everything you wanted, Michael, and you'll still have plenty of it.*

Then why did you act like that? Because you were about to get even more? Because you were supposed to become a child superior to the others? Only the few who are naturally conceived have what you will soon receive, and only a few such as you will be able to cope with generations of the future—some of whom are already among us. You should be grateful for that, Michael. And you'll be grateful, I'm sure, when you find out what your father has prepared for you and your sister. You'll be grateful, Michael . . . You'll be grateful . . .

"I'm pleasantly surprised you feel that way, Michael. But I don't blame you for what happened. What I want to say is that we were both hasty that evening. We both acted without thinking, carried away by our emotions. You felt threatened, you thought I was putting pressure on you and insisting on something against your interests. But I only wished you well and that's why I acted like that. I couldn't understand your refusal of the help Beresford and I were providing, and I still don't understand it now."

"I do not refuse your help, Pa. I explained everything to Dr. Beresford, and I wanted to explain it to you, too, but I didn't get to. You know why."

Hank takes another sip of his beer and thinks to himself, *Sure, I know, but will it happen again? Has Michael learned his lesson, or does he need extra training?*

"That's behind us now, isn't it? I'm sure it won't happen again."

"That means—you aren't mad at me? You forgive me?"

"Son, if I were mad at you, I wouldn't sit here talking to you. Yes, I forgive you if you forgive *me* for what I said to *you*."

There is the first glimpse of the sun in Michael's pupils obscured by clouds and doubt. The first rays herald the beginning of a new day and their new relationship.

That's right, Michael. That's my boy. Relax and put your life in my hands. Trust me! Everything I've done wrong to you is history now. From now on, you and I are starting anew. Soon the entire world will be ours. And then Rebecca will join us. Our little Rebecca . . .

"Thank you."

"Thank *you*, Michael. That you understand and that you are

back home."

Michael couldn't believe that everything would be resolved so easily. Has Hank changed that much, or is he up to something again?

Hank smiles at him and Michael chooses to believe that his stepfather has really changed. So he smiles back at him.

"Is there anything else that bothers you, Michael, or did you just want to apologize?"

Michael's smile fades. He knows *it* is coming now. The *main* thing that bothers him and what he needs to talk about the most since he was eight or something, but so far he has not had the courage to do so.

This time it's different, though.

This time is the time. Once. And for all. To put. An end. To this.

"Actually, there is," he replies, not knowing how Hank will take it.

Michael doubts he would respond as favorably as he did to his apology.

* * *

Stu is furious, *The police were at his door this morning, shoving a search warrant in his face, demanding his cooperation and asking him a ton of questions.* He howls at no one in particular—blaming everyone.

Someone snitched on him. Someone snitched on *everybody*.

Division Pro Skate Shop is no longer a safe place to hang around. Almost every one of them is suspected of dealing or drug possession.

They squeezed someone after the Washington Square raid and that one tattled, Stu is almost certain. He suspects everyone, but Victor and Michael, who are clean all the time, Alien who escaped the raid, and Fernando, who is dealing drugs but didn't find himself there.

When it dawns on him that he, too, is under suspicion, Lenny goes ballistic and shoos them all out of the store.

"Wait until they come to your door!" Stu tells him, leaving.

Alien had left fifteen minutes ago because he could no longer listen to them arguing. But he agrees with Stu about one thing.

No one can sleep peacefully anymore because someone has buckled under. Someone relented under pressure and sang.

Alien doesn't care who. He is in bigger trouble than all of them together. He's in deep shit—caught between the New York Police Department and Skateboarding Unified Forces of New York City. And no one knows what is worse.

Or from where the greater danger is coming.

* * *

Something bothers Michael, Hank can see that. Something will float to the surface, carried by unknown forces of nature, with rumble and strong vibrations. As if a geyser will boil, or a volcano erupt.

There is something dangerous about that—he smells it, all right—but not so dangerous again that he can't handle it. He did well while bursting bulbs flew with pieces of glass around him. Hank is bothered by only one thing: the force he had created had been used against him.

That's what hurts him.

(Not the shards.)

That's what humiliates him.

(Not the two tiny cuts—one on his right cheek, the other just above his left eyebrow—which are already almost healed.)

This will never happen again, Hank knows, as he knows that Michael's powers are weakening and will continue to weaken until he undergoes therapies again. The process needs to be completed, so the gift becomes his permanent property. It takes so little more to make Michael someone *special*. Now he is someone *common*, an ordinary boy, or close enough. With the power leaving him, Michael is harmless, and it will not be a problem for Hank to overpower him.

"Pa, I'll be frank with you. I don't want to beat around the bush, for we won't get anywhere."

Pa. How nice it sounds from his mouth, Hank thinks with melancholy. *How nice to hear that he still feel that way about him. Pa. Pa. Papa.*

"I want to make a deal with you about something if I come home."

"*If?* Michael, I thought you were back! What is this nonsense now?"

(Nonsense? What will he say about what's yet to come if this is nonsense?)

"I am back. But if I mean to stay, we must agree on something. You and I."

Then he spills it out. No stopping, without shame. Like a torrent.

"If I stay, some things will have to change."

"Things? What things? I don't understand."

"I won't sleep with you again. Under no circumstances! That's *over*."

"But—"

Michael interrupts him before he is interrupted. He isn't

finished yet.

"So don't try to blackmail me anymore. Don't threaten to hurt Rebecca, because something bad could happen."

"For chrissake, when did I say I would hurt her?! Michael, what's wrong? What's wrong with you? Where do you get those ideas from?"

"Furthermore, I didn't have to tell you this—I could lie to you—but I want to be honest with you. I'm leaving school. I will devote myself to skateboarding for a year or two, depending on how good I am. I've already decided that, and there's no point in trying to talk me out of it."

Hank Daniels is looking at his son in utter disbelief and doesn't know what to say to him.

"We cannot negotiate about that, Pa. Also, we cannot negotiate about the following: I will no longer go to *any* therapies. I will not go only because you want it or somebody else thinks it's best for me. I don't *need* them!"

"Somebody else?? Michael . . ."

"I'm old enough to think with my head. I know what's best for me. That's not some great wisdom, you know? I'm sorry if your expectations don't match mine, but that's my life. I know what I want to do with it, and I also know what I *don't want* to do with it. I don't want to disappoint you, but what I want is more important now because it's about my life I'll have to live even when you're gone."

He stops to take a breath, half-expecting Hank to seize the moment, but Hank remains silent.

It might have worried Michael if he had time to think about it, but he has to carry on. He has a goal in front of him, he has to stick to his plan, and nothing must divert him from that.

"Sorry I had to say it, but it's true. That was the only way for you to understand how serious I am. Pa, *this is my life* and no one has the right to take it away or tell me how to live it. No one. Do you understand me?"

"What do you want? What do you want from life, Michael?" Hank asks in a low voice, his expression a disfigured mask.

Michael isn't expecting that, it's clear. Least of all he expected from his father to show interest in what *he* wants. So far, it has meant nothing to him. *(Where did this sudden change come from?)*

"What do I want?" Michael repeats, surprised. "Well, for one, I want Rebecca to know nothing about this conversation. I don't want her to know that it happened, and I don't want her to know *why* it happened. And I want her to know nothing about you and me. I want you to promise me that. I want you to promise me you won't tell her anything, and the case is closed for me."

"Good, I promise you. Satisfied?"

Michael is confused again. He stares puzzled, eyes wide open.

"I'm afraid I wasn't clear enough," Hank says as he grins at him, "so I'll say it again. I promise you Rebecca won't know anything about us, so you can forget the whole thing. That's what you wanted, wasn't it?"

"Well, yes." He is still bewildered, and his father is so fast, too fast for him.

"I have indulged your wish, haven't I? But what about you? Did *you* decide what you want from your life? You haven't answered me yet."

"What do you mean? I told you . . ."

"You don't mean it seriously, do you? Are you going to

spend your whole life skating on some stupid board? Forgive me, but I had a much better opinion of you."

"I don't mean to spend my whole life skating on some stupid board!" Michael says angrily. "I was talking about *years*. About a year or two. While I'm still young and my bones are soft and flexible enough to withstand falls. I didn't mean forever!"

"But you sounded like that. What about your education if you drop out of school now? Have you thought about *that*?"

"Yes, I have! I'll finish it later!"

"Will you, Michael? Will you indeed?"

"Yes!"

"Such potential. Such intelligence! Thrown away! Ruined. I don't believe that you will finish school, if you quit now. I don't believe it, because I know you."

Michael is silent for a reason. He cannot think of anything smart to say to that.

"It will be beneath you, Michael. You will be embarrassed and ashamed. Because you'll know you can do better, but you didn't do it. It will haunt you for the rest of your life."

"You're wrong. That is not true!"

"I'm right, Michael, and that's the truth. And you know what? This may be a surprise to you, but I will understand because you deserve so much more in life, because you are someone very special and exceptional. Someone rare."

They look at each other. Michael at Hank with incredulity and hesitation, while Hank looks at Michael calmly and patiently, knowing what he means and wants to achieve.

He says to him, "You are special, Michael. Why throw it away? For what?"

"I think . . . I don't think I understand you."

He is all at sea about what Hank is talking about, having no idea that Hank thinks so highly of him. He is clutching at the last straws of reason slipping through his fingers.

"I think you understand me. And I think this lamp, whose bulbs I had to change, also understands." He points at the spider-shaped lamp behind Michael's back.

At that moment, Michael realizes what his father meant when he told him he is someone special and rare; a forgotten revelation.

And then an alarm sounds in him.

(How much does Hank really know? How much does he know about his gift? And how? How much did Neil Beresford tell him?!?*)*

"Oh, that," he attempts to fake. "It's nothing. That was an accident. I don't even know how it happened."

"Michael, you are insulting my intelligence. We are not children."

His cheeks turn red. They are almost glowing.

He bows his head in the discomfort and shame that his father caught him in such a blatant lie.

"How much do you know?" He raises his head slightly.

"Everything. I know everything."

Michael gasps in shock.

"Everything?!"

"Yes, *everything.*"

"Beresford told you everything?" He cannot believe his ears.

(So, this is what Beresford thinks of friendship? How could he be so stupid! Stupid!! STUPID.)

"Beresford didn't have to tell me anything. Because I knew it. Michael, I *knew.*"

Complete disbelief in Michael's eyes and on Michael's face.

Total eclipse of his mind and eyes.

"How?" he utters a question.

"Very simple. I knew it because I gave it to you. *I* gave you that gift, Michael. Neil just helped me a little."

He then tells him everything. About his dreams, about his plans, about the future he plans for the three of them—Michael, Rebecca, and himself—and about the world that lies conquered at their feet, ready to take it whenever they want.

"You are crazy!" is Michael's first reaction.

And then, "I don't want to have anything to do with it."

A storm of emotions in Michael. He feels cheated and betrayed.

Double-betrayed: by his friend and his father!

Triple-betrayed: by his friend, by his father, and by God who misled him, letting him believe that he is someone special, someone with a gift!

The wind blows again, swirling his anger, rage, and exasperation.

And then hatred.

Pain without limits and disappointment—unbearably true and painfully present.

"I don't want to have anything to do with that!" Michael cries through tears.

Hank reaches out for the bottle of beer. He forgot it was already empty.

Puts it back on the table.

"You don't want to? I thought you said something else to your psychiatrist."

"He is not my psychiatrist!"

"I thought you were pleased when you discovered your gift. That's what Beresford told me. Those are his words."

"HE IS NOT MY SHRINK! DO YOU HEAR WHAT I'M SAYING?! HE IS NOT!"

"I hear you. Why are you yelling? Do you want the whole neighborhood to hear you too?"

Michael's fury is strong and out of control.

(If I don't do something, I'll explode. I'll blow myself to pieces.

(On the other hand, maybe that's what I should do. Self-destruction is a trifle compared to all that shit. No one else would get hurt, and I'm already good for nothing. I'm no use to anyone, except Hank.)

These thoughts sober him up, bring him back to reality.

"Come on, blow up the bottle," Hank says, with a chuckle, watching his futile efforts. "You can't, can you? You don't have the power? Where's your *gift*?" He clicks his tongue. "My, my, poor Mikey. What do we do now? The bottle can't be broken—it's stronger than you!"

"Shut up! Shut up already! SHUT UP! SHUT UP! SHUT UP!"

"Or what? You will blow *me* up? Like you did those little bulbs?"

"Shut your dirty mouth! I can't listen to you anymore!" He covers his ears with his hands. "I can't listen to your voice anymore! I cannot!"

"But then you had the power. The *gift* was with you. You no longer have it. You ran out of fuel! *Oops*." He pulls his face into a smirk and covers his mouth with his hand. "Michael forgot to drink his *m-vs*. How could that happen? When's the last time you took your miracle pills, hm?"

"SHUUUUT UP!"

The bottle flies off the table, but not at Michael's willpower. His mechanical force launches it and it hits Hank in the head.

His temple splits to a bloom and blood flows.

Hank bares his teeth in a wild grin. An ugly grimace turns his face into something demonic.

He touches the blood on his cheek and licks his fingers.

"Thank you for your *gift*, Michael," says a stranger with his voice. "I *LOVE* so much everything from you."

He leaps across the table, grabs him and slams him on the floor, Hank on top of him.

Michael screams.

A slap explodes on his face and Michael's next scream is stuck in his throat.

His face burning like a red-hot poker, Michael tries to creep out from under Hank, who is sitting on his chest, straddling him.

"Well, young man, what do we do now?" His spit sprays on Michael's face. "We're saddled, huh? How about having a nice, little ride now!"

Michael's neck catches fire as Hank squeezes the air out of him. The room swirls around him, as if he is in the middle of a frantic twister. Then Hank thrusts his hand between his legs and Michael groans. Blinded by pain, he screams from the top of his lungs. His eyes cloud with tears.

Reaching for his button fly, Hank eases the pressure on Michael's chest and Michael seizes the moment. Panting and flailing with his arms, he gets hold of the unique vase and smashes it into Hank's head.

Hank moans and holds his bloodied head with his hands. Thick, dark-red blood spills over his fingers and trickles on his half-unbuttoned shirt.

I must have hit him in the eyebrow, Michael thinks, and arches his hips up. Something snaps in his back, but he manages to throw Hank off himself.

He rolls to the side, but Hank grabs his pant legs and Michael drops to his knees. The pain is sharp and short, and he feels tears well his eyes. Everything around him is like fog again.

Hank grabs him by the belt and almost rips his pants off.

Michael acts instinctively. He kicks his left leg and smashes the thick sole of his DC skateboard shoe across Hank's face. His shoe lands on Hank's nose with a crunch, followed by Hank's inhuman howl.

Michael freezes, thinking a few seconds too long about this strange cry.

Already the next moment his back slams against the glass table, not breaking the glass, but forcing the air out of him. Hank grabs him around his waist and pulls him to the floor, closer and closer to his strong, spread legs.

Michael's fingers screech against the glass in panic, seeking a handhold. They find nothing but a heavy ashtray that stands half peeking over the edge of the table. He remembers how heavy it is, too heavy to hold it, let alone swing and hit Hank on the head with it.

While he is still preoccupied with this thought, something warm sprays him across the face and neck. Without much thinking, he backs away from Hank when he lets him go and jumps to his feet.

His legs are weak and shaky and barely bear his weight.

Michael drops to his knees, then stands up again.

With dizziness and tired and exhausted and panting, he hits Hank again with the heavy ashtray. And then again and again, turning his face into a hideous mixture of blood, hair, and scraps of skin hanging down his face, at the same time wondering how the bones of his stepfather's skull can be so white in all that bloody mess.

This time the table gives in under Hank's weight and the glass bursts asunder into tens of pieces and hundreds of bits, invisible to the naked eye.

Michael doesn't wait for Hank to recover and get up. He flies toward the door, one hand holding his unbuttoned pants so he doesn't stumble over them, and with the other groping his way out to the safety of the street.

He forgets about his packed backpack, and he also fails to notice the shadow hiding behind the stairs leading to the entrance of the neighboring house when he catapults himself out of the house.

He darts past it as fast as he can, not looking back.

Running down the street,

farther

and farther away.

Chapter

19th: . . . *tail manual* (you ride your board on the back wheels and your tail is not touching the asphalt). Almost each of these tricks you can do on or over the obstacles like ramps, banks, and such. When Victor did the *mctwist* on the vert-ramp, he gained momentum and, passing the coping, . . .

SHAY FOX BREATHES IN.

Then holds his breath.

And then he breathes out.

Each time he "sniffs" something, he would resort to this breathing exercise to focus better. Being a lone hunter is sometimes not a virtue, but it is not his fault that most of his colleagues cannot keep up with him. Sharp, efficient, and cunning—his brain works too fast, leaving them several conclusions behind.

The latest case that Fox works on seems rather clear at first glance. But for a reason only known to him, Fox feels some unease about it, so he consults his breathing exercise to get a second opinion.

Breathe in—hold your breath—breathe out.

A strange feeling in his stomach—the quiet voice of anticipation confirms his initial suspicion. Something's wrong here, Fox is now almost sure of that. He wishes he weren't the only one in this belief, but no one, except perhaps celebrity agent Fox Mulder, would pat him on the shoulder and say, *Good job, buster. You got this one right.* His colleagues will only tease him about it, reminding him that no real person has such a subtle sense in pursuing the truth. This only happens in the movies.

Luckily for him, his resemblance to Fox Mulder (beside their "cunning" names and the same preference for choosing female partners—as if they had chosen them by themselves!) also ends here. Shay Fox's good looks (not that Mulder lacks anything, God forbid!) is more like a Matthew McConaughey clone in *A Time to Kill*. But the way he talks is utterly different. Fox is easier to understand, and he talks much faster.

No matter the nature of the case he works on, Shay Fox always takes his job most seriously. With the same dedication, he muses about his latest case. Somewhere in his subconsciousness is a warning sign: the moment his colleagues find out what kind of case he had been assigned to, he would be a subject of ridicule to them. He no longer cares about it. He is so tired of being teased and compared to the fictional agent that he stopped paying attention to them a long time ago.

Fox moves a few steps closer until he leans over the body of the deceased. A male in his mid-fifties lies face down on his desk, a huge, gaping exit wound in the back of his head. Dried blood everywhere.

Everything is clear. The destructive impact of a 10mm from a Glock took his life. A simple case of suicide with a farewell confession instead of saying goodbye.

Or it is not so simple, when he thinks again. Something's missing here—Fox's belly warns.

The confession the deceased left before taking his own life is not the usual way in which suicide victims say goodbye to those they love and ask them for forgiveness. This is not a last will and testament, but rather a guide that the investigation should follow.

The information found on the floppy disk provide clear answers regarding the true motive behind this suicide. However, they suggest or indicate nothing about the current whereabouts of a *special* and *dangerous*, yet allegedly innocent boy, who will need FBI protection when the truth leaks out. If the boy is in-nocent, as the former—now deceased—RIRI big shot claims, and did nothing to break the law, then there is no reason to hide that piece of information from the investigation. Those involved in the conspiracy are dead, so why play hide-and-seek? The danger is gone, unless someone else is involved in the whole thing. The third party that the late Beresford didn't know about. Or maybe he knew something and didn't want to reveal it, even now, when it is all over for him? Solving this puzzle won't be such an easy job, and it will take some time before everything falls into place, Fox realizes. He has to speak to Morgan once more and push him a little harder this time. This is not the time to play a gentleman, especially with this kind of people.

Fox dislikes people who try to indulge others in a kissing-your-ass way. This is what Morgan tried with Dawson and him when they came to the Institute for answers. Their superior, Agent Fletcher, had warned them about Morgan, but Fox didn't believe the guy could be such a sleazeball. Not only did Morgan turn out to be a hard nut to crack, but Fox also recognized the truth behind Fletcher's words that the road to hell is paved with good intentions. Fox speculates that someone from Washington, DC might have called Fletcher *asking* him to be easy on Morgan because of the delicacy of the situation. That would not be too strange, considering RIRI is also conducting re-search for the government. Damn it, Fox curses to himself, he's only seen him once in his life, and he already hates this chameleon of a man!

To kill the bitter taste in his mouth from the thought of Morgan and the smell of dried blood stuck on the walls, furniture, and his nostrils, Fox pops two pieces of chewing gum into his mouth.

He wonders what will happen if Morgan finds out about the floppy? Will he stick to his story or set in motion a chain reaction of unpredictable events? Fox decides to wait with the answers to these questions for now.

He hears his partner's voice calling him discreetly, and he turns around. Nicole Kidman's slightly changed image and persona appear before him.

Two and a half inches shorter than him, her champagne-colored hair with a tint of red pulled into a French twist, her violet-gray eyes scan his face in anticipation.

"We just got a call from Merchant," she reports. His mouth widens into a tired smile, softened by her allure. As al-ways, she ignites that undefined sense of calm within him, as if she had pulled some invisible wire and lit it.

"What does he want?" He looks straight into her eyes.

"He wants us in his office. He has mail for us." Amelia Gill Dawson is named after a famous aviatrix who disappeared somewhere above the Pacific in an attempt to fly the world.

"Mail from whom?"

"I don't know that. One of his men picked it up. He says we might be interested to see it."

"We better hurry, then." Fox scowls and offers her a chewing gum.

"No, thanks. What about our letter?" She takes a glance at the printed pages Fox pockets in his raincoat. "Will you show it to Morgan?"

"Not before he gives me some answers."

"Are you worried about the boy?"

"You could say that," he says honestly. "Actually, I don't know what to think." His gaze wanders off.

Dawson doesn't let him wander too far.

"Fox?"

"Let's go, Dawson. You're right. We don't want to let Merchant wait."

* * *

He is still moving by instinct. Everything he does, he does without thinking.

First, he must get as much distance from his home as possible, so that Hank won't catch up with him. Hurrying aimlessly, anywhere is fine, as long as it is *far* from there.

He stops for the first time, just to button his pants, when he turns the corner of St. Luke's Place. His hands and the right sleeve of his sweater are soaked in Hank's blood, hence this changes his priorities—he must wash himself and then put as much distance as possible.

He rushes into the first public toilet he comes across; he has no idea where it is because everything around him is like in a *Twilight Zone* episode. Locking himself in the stall, he vomits and clings to the toilet bowl, exhausted and with a sour taste in his mouth.

He closes his eyes and a picture of Hank projects in his mind. Bloody, disfigured, he is reaching out for him, yelling, *"You are finished, little faggot! Say goodbye to your miserable life! Say goodbye, say goodbye, say goodbye!"*

His stomach churns again and he springs onto his feet once more and empties himself. Languid and eerily pale, he walks over to the sink to wash himself.

His legs barely support him as he lets the water run a little before leaning over the sink and splashing his face. Beautifully cold water does wonders for him and his trembling body. Just when he begins to calm down, someone's hand grabs his butt, scaring him to death and making him jump.

Michael blinks the water out of his eyes and stares at the attractive man in his early forties. Expensive business suit, his face a watercolor of worries and hectic life.

The man's smile stiffens in front of Michael's murderous gaze and unwashed traces of blood on his hands. He bolts out of the toilet before Michael can tell him anything.

"Damn rump ranger," Michael hisses after him, but the man is already gone.

The blood from his sleeve doesn't wash off completely, but at least he tries. Given the circumstances, he couldn't have done much more about it.

The next thing he has to do is to call Rebecca. He must warn her not to come home *because Hank has gone mad*. It doesn't even occur to him that Hank might be bleeding to death now or already dying, because he had hit him one too many times over the head. For Michael, he continues to be a symbol of evil, a threat to him and Rebecca.

When he reaches the pay phone, he realizes he doesn't have any change. He hurries to a nearby pretzel kiosk, changes a ten-dollar bill and heads back to the pay phone. Punching in a long-distance number, he considers going home tomorrow to collect his most important things and then getting lost—forever.

He has no idea where he will go. He might go to see his grandparents for a few days. After that he may as well leave for the European Union. His life here is over, anyway.

"Rebecca!" He feels immense relief hearing his sister's voice. "Thank God I found you."

He sounds breathless, excited, and tense. Her voice becomes concerned the moment she hears him.

"Michael, what happened?"

"Rebecca, Rebecca, don't come here. Okay? I'm coming to Denver."

"I don't understand what you're talking about!"

"Don't come home before I get to you. We have to talk."

"What is it about? Tell me now! You're scaring me, Michael."

"Rebecca, I don't know how to tell you this, but . . . Dad has gone crazy."

"What!?!"

"We had a fight. I hit him. I think I hurt him."

"What are you talking about, Michael?!" Her voice quivers with the first sign of panic. "Why did you quarrel? Where are you now? *How* is Dad?"

"I don't know. We didn't agree on some things, so he attacked me. I had to defend myself. I hit him and I think I hurt him."

"What do you mean you *hurt* him? *How* much did you hurt him? Michael?"

"I don't know, Rebecca. Frankly, I don't know. There was blood..."

The scream assaults his eardrum, then dies on the other side of the handset.

"Rebecca, I didn't want to, but I had to defend myself. He went at me first and started choking me—"

"Michael, *how is Dad*?!"

"I don't know! I'm not at home. I ran away..."

Uncontrolled sighs, hesitation, and cracked voice from afar.

"Where are you now?"

"I don't know." He turns around.

"What do you mean, you don't know? Look around!"

"The Twins are a few blocks away..."

"Good. Michael, tell me, are you hurt?"

"I don't think so. But it hurts. My arm hurts and my head hurts and I feel sick."

"Do you think you have strength to return home to check on Dad?"

"No."

"Then take a cab. Do you have money on you?"

"I do. But I can't go home. Dad will kill me."

"Dad won't kill you! Maybe he needs *help*. You have to go back and see how he is!"

"I'm sorry, but I can't. Plus, I didn't hit him *that* hard."

"But you said there was blood!"

"I may have hit him in a sensitive spot. Maybe I cut or split open his eyebrow. Such wounds look much worse than they are."

"You hit him? What did you hit him with?"

"An ashtray."

"With *Mom's* ashtray?"

"Yes. With it."

"Jesus, Michael! You could have killed him!" Rebecca shrieks.

"You think so . . . ?" She spreads her panic onto him. Confronts him with the possibility he hasn't thought of and it makes him sick again. "But I didn't want to kill him, Rebecca. I just wanted him to leave me alone. I was only defending myself."

"You fool, you could have killed Dad!" she cries. The dam bursts and tears flood.

"He is going to be fine, sis. Don't cry. Now you're scaring me . . ."

"Go . . . home . . . See how Dad is . . ."

He hesitates, his heart pumping wildly in his chest.

"I'll call Alien and we'll go together."

"I don't care, just go before it's too late! Who knows how hard you hit him!"

"I didn't hit him hard! Only enough to free myself."

"Go, I beg you."

"I will, but I'll call nine-one-one first. Then I'll go get Alien."

"Do as you wish . . . Just do something, *pleeease*."

"I'm on my way. You stay there until I get back to you! Don't do anything before I call you."

"Yes! I'll wait for you to call me."

"Good. Fine."

"Hurry now, please."

"Okay." He isn't hanging up.

"Mikey?"

"Yes?"

"Watch yourself."

"I will. You too. Watch yourself."

He hangs up.

He dials 911 to give them his address and hangs up.

He then punches in Alien's number, but no one answers him. He hangs up and looks for a cab. There are none in sight. Too nervous to wait, he decides to walk to his friend's. After about twenty heavy-as-lead steps, he concludes that he is too slow, so he changes his mind again and springs into a run. Hoping he won't get sick again.

* * *

When they arrive at the charming row of Italianate houses on St. Luke's Place, the streetlight is already on. Most of the windows are also lit, but not those in Michael's apartment. The evening is nice, but chilly, and Michael is shivering even though he is wearing the sweater Alien had lent him.

There is no sign of the ambulance, and a policeman—a lonely sentinel—is on duty in front of his building and the yellow tape saying POLICE LINE DO NOT CROSS.

With a desperate, begging gaze, Michael looks at Alien, asking him for help.

"Wait here. I'll see what happened," Alien says to him reassuringly.

He squeezes Michael's shoulder in a friendly gesture and starts toward the police officer.

"Good evening, Officer," Alien greets him, pulling his earbuds out of his ears. "Do you have a light?"

A police officer in his early twenties looks Alien up and down bouncing on the balls of his heels while waiting for his response.

After studying him thoroughly, he concludes that the kid isn't a threat. "I think so," he says in a much softer voice than when he looked at Alien moments ago.

He produces the lighter from his pocket, which flickers into a small, warm flame, and Alien lights a cigarette.

"What a night!" Alien releases a few puffs of smoke.

The police officer eyes him once more. Baseball cap turned around backward, zipped-up, light-blue, snowboarding jacket with the image of an alien on the left sleeve, brown baggy pants, gray-silver-blue skateboard shoes, an attractive smile.

"You could say that."

"What happened here?"

The police officer doesn't answer him. A devoted sentinel with a heavy burden of a secret on his heart.

"You won't tell me?" Alien tries a friendlier approach.

"I won't tell you."

"Why?" He cocks his head.

"It's classified," he says importantly.

"Hey, never mind! I'll read it in tomorrow's papers, anyway."

"Then buy tomorrow's papers."

"*Should* I buy them?"

"It depends on what interests you."

Alien's gaze drifts toward the door behind the young officer.

"And what does *that* have to do with *you*?"

"My friend lives here."

"Your friend?"

"Yes, Trevor," Alien makes up a name.

"Trevor what?"

"Fry!" he recalls Michael's neighbor's last name. "Did

something happen to them?"

"No." The policeman relaxes. "I'm here for the Daniels."

"The Daniels?" Alien fakes surprise.

"Listen, did your friend report the murder?"

"The murder?!" Alien freezes. He almost burns his fingers on a cigarette.

"Someone made an anonymous emergency call, but didn't want to leave their name. Since your friend lives here, I thought he might have heard something."

"No. He didn't hear anything, I assure you. He's in Vancouver."

"In Vancouver?" The policeman becomes suspicious again.

"Yes. He went skiing last week." He tries to buy some time before he gets lost from here and tells the bad news to Michael.

"Then what are you doing here?"

"Nothing. Just passing by."

"Just passing by? Really?"

"Yeah. I live here, around the corner. Hey, if you like, you can drop by for a drink when your shift's over, so you can tell me about everything in detail." He blinks his eyes seductively, hoping the guy will turn him down.

"No, thanks. I don't think it will be necessary."

"Suit yourself. Then have a nice day?" He nods to him goodbye and gets going. Slowly, because his legs are giving out.

"Tell your friend, he better change neighborhoods. This is already the third murder in the last sixty days. If I were him, I'd move somewhere safer."

"Sure. And thanks for the tip."

* * *

"I can't stay at your place. I don't want to get you involved."

"Get involved in what? You said it wasn't your fault. That you didn't do it."

"I swear I didn't hit him so hard!"

"Okie dokie, I believe you. We'll think of something."

Michael sighs. He is still shaking, suffering the effects of a panic attack he had experienced a little before.

He takes a small sip of vodka and stretches his legs on Alien's bed, pulling the blanket all the way to his chin.

"Can you turn off the music? It annoys me."

Alien tells the radio to turn off.

"I don't know how to explain it to the police. Who will believe me? And how will I say this to Rebecca? How am I going to make her believe that it isn't my fault, and I didn't want to kill her father? Not that he didn't deserve it . . ." he adds quietly, but quickly snaps out of self-pity and lethargy. "I better go before your mom comes. I don't know if I could bear her to show me the door when she hears what happened."

"She won't show you the door, rest easy on that. When the time comes, I'll explain everything to her."

"You still don't get it? There is nothing to *explain*. Hank is dead, I killed him, my fingerprints are everywhere."

"On second thought, why do you think they shouldn't be there? I mean, you live there! That still doesn't mean you killed him."

"Who, then? Who killed him, then?"

"A burglar, for one! You said you didn't close the door behind you when you ran out?"

"I don't think so." He tries to remember.

"There you go! Someone saw the door open, thought the

apartment was empty, came in and ran into your old man. There was a fight, and he beat him to death. Simple as that!"

"And he stole nothing?"

"Of course not. He was scared! He panicked and skedaddled, just like you. He was happy to get out of there alive!"

"Thank you for the comparison," Michael says ironically. "So, he flees from the crime scene and leaves my fingerprints, that's what you mean?"

"Your fingerprints were supposed to be there! But his weren't, because he was wearing gloves!"

"Alien, sometimes I really love you. Sometimes you're like a brother to me, as if we are the same blood and the same flesh."

"Well, well! We don't have time for sentimentality now. We need to come up with a plan."

"What plan?"

"A plan for how to make the cops believe in our story."

"Our? *You* mean to convince them?"

"Who else? I'm your witness, for crying out loud! I'm your alibi. At the time of the murder, you and I were skating together."

"Alien, please don't even think about it. You know it won't work. You know they won't believe you."

"Maybe they won't believe me. But they will believe it when the two of us confirm that you were with us."

"The two of you?"

"Victor will back us up, I'm sure of that."

Michael stares in disbelief.

"You plan to get Victor involved too?"

"I don't plan to *involve* anyone, my friend. Besides, who can prove you *were* there and not with us?"

"It might work if you didn't forget one thing," Michael says after a little thought.

Alien knits his eyebrows. *(What?)*

"My phone call to Rebecca. Rebecca knows what happened. She probably already told Grandpa and Grandma. And tomorrow, the whole damn America will know too."

"Sure, and the rest of the universe," Alien adds. "But you're right when you say you made a mistake by calling Rebecca. Still, it can be taken care of."

"Yes? Don't tell me you already thought of something?"

"No. This is something you'll have to do on your own. Now you will find out how much your sister loves you."

Tears stinging his eyes, Michael asks in disbelief, "You want me to make my sister lie for me?"

"She doesn't have to lie. But she doesn't have to tell you called, either. It won't hurt anyone."

Michael is pondering. *Can he ask her to do that? Can he ask that from his baby sister? He was the one who ruined her life! Three months ago, she lost her mother and now her brother, her half-brother, has killed her father.*

Rebecca loves Michael as much as a sister can love a brother. But does she love him so much that she's ready to forget what he did to her father and stand by him?

Michael cannot ask that from her. He had already caused her too much pain.

At that moment, Alien makes himself heard again. "If you were my brother, I would do it for you," he says without thinking.

Feelings overwhelm Michael and he drowns his pride and self-esteem in the salty rain of tears and the clumsy but soothing embrace of his friend.

Chapter

20th: . . . grabbed his deck at the beginning of rotation. Why don't you try it now? You are in the air and together with your board, rotate 540 degrees (the *540 ollie with grab*). Let go of your board. Pass the coping. Extend your legs. Touch your wheels to the ramp. The difference between the vert-ramp . . .

THE NEWS ABOUT HANK DANIELS'S DEATH reach Neil Beresford in the underground levels of the Roosevelt Island Research Institute during his visit to one of his patients. This time Beresford is visiting Eric—a boy who will become a peacemaker in the future. Mankind will be indebted to him because his efforts will lead to a sudden, mass disarmament, preventing the outbreak of World War III, and in 2024 he will receive the Nobel Peace Prize.

When Beresford says goodbye to Eric, he had no idea it is his farewell to the boy. "Be good, Eric, and listen to your friends. Soon a new life will begin for you, and then you'll need their help most," he says to him on parting, calling the scientists who take care of the *children of the Institute* his friends. The mutual familiarity and friendly atmosphere between adults and their young protégés are paramount for their survival outside these walls behind which they spend their childhood, preparing to successfully achieve their goals and dreams once they embark on their missions. Because no matter how they may be prepared, they will still need the help of those at the Institute, since they will never be completely independent of them. The eyes of their creators will always follow them *as long as they all shall live or till death do them prematurely part.*

Jack Morgan—the beginning and the end, alpha and omega, and The One in Charge who has complete control over every-one at the Institute—tells him the news in person, tendering his sympathies and regrets over the murder of his colleague and longtime friend.

"When?" Beresford asks in a calm and unrecognizable voice when Morgan finishes.

"Yesterday afternoon. About five thirty."

"Do they know who did it?"

"No. The police have no conclusions yet. Everything indicates a break-in."

"Is something missing from the apartment? Something stolen?"

"They didn't say anything about it. The FBI has taken over the case."

"FBI?"

Morgan nods. "You know the procedure in such cases. Hank was a member of the nonexistent team."

"How did he die?" Beresford asks thoughtfully, suspecting something neither the police nor anyone else could have suspected.

"Beaten to death. That's all I know."

Beresford takes a deep breath, which could mean many things.

"I'm sorry, Neil. I'm sorry that happened, and I had to tell you the news."

"It's okay, Jack. Thank you for your concern."

"If there's anything I can do for you, just name it. If you need someone to talk to or if you want to take a few days off . . ."

"I don't, but thank you, anyway. I'll be fine."

"If you change your mind . . ."

"I know where to find you. But there is something else I would like to ask you. What happened to Michael, Hank's son? I believe he stayed with Hank in New York. He didn't go with his sister to Denver. Do you know what happened to him?"

"I don't know. No one knows if he was in the apartment when the murder happened and whether his corpse will soon pop up somewhere. The search for him is still ongoing. Hell, it's not ruled out that he beat Hank to death! But what would be the motive for that?"

Beresford darkens even more.

"That's a bad case, pretty nasty," Morgan continues, as Beresford says nothing. "The appearance of another corpse would be an inconvenience, you know what I mean."

"I know," Beresford affirms with sarcasm. "That wouldn't be *convenient*."

Still, he understands Morgan's concern. Soon he will have to deal with the representatives of the law, the Fourth Estate, and all sorts of weirdos curious to roam and snoop through RIRI premises to find the truth behind Hank Daniels's death.

His life is about to taste metallic and bitter, and Beresford can do nothing about it. He doesn't care. He also doesn't care if he will make his life even more miserable. It is beyond his power.

After a thirty-minute drive, he arrives at his residence in Hamilton Heights, immaculately clean as ever. It seems like no one dwells here. This time things will look different. For the first time, he will leave traces of his existence.

He settles down at his desk and unlocks the bottom drawer. In the back, hidden behind a pile of documents of various importance, he finds an envelope with a diskette. He tears it open and inserts the evidence into the computer.

Before he starts writing, he goes to make himself a quick dinner.

As he waits for the toast to pop out of the toaster, he is at complete peace with himself. An untouchable serenity descends on him, and nothing can excite him, not even the disturbing thought that his testimony might end up in the wrong hands. If it comes to that, what can he do, anyway?

A long time ago, Beresford accepted the fact that he will never receive his salary—the promised wage for sin.

There is nothing he can do to change that. In his last hours, he doesn't care at all.

Dinner is ready, and he eats it in a few bites.

* * *

All lights are out as he floats surrounded by darkness. Relaxing, meditating, and drawing conclusions without being disturbed or distracted by anyone. Peace is so complete, absolute and perfect, as if he is floating on the other side of the world of living.

Amelia Gill Dawson looked at him strangely when he told her he wants to get into the *Womb*. Although reluctant, she helps him enter the chamber and then turns off all the devices, keeping only voice-to-auditory contact. Fully trusting her, Fox relaxes. A wonderful sense of bliss fills his limbs, skin, veins, all the way to his brain cells.

"Earth to Dawson?" Her name whispered in a strange voice. "Do you read me? Are you here?"

"I read you, Fox. I'm with you. I'm looking out for you. You look good."

"Don't fall asleep."

"Roger that. I won't, and neither do you."

Fox grins the same way he grinned when Dawson stormed out of the room when he started undressing. Their friendship and mutual respect aside, there *is* chemistry and some repressed attraction between them, Fox is sure of that, and he could only regret that nothing had happened between them so far. His sense of a deeper and closer relationship with his partner has lately been teasing him with the sweet promise that not everything is said here.

"Dawson?" he calls once more.

"Yes?" slowly from the stillness of the monitoring room.

"I'm sleepy, partner."

"What am I supposed to do about that?"

"Join me."

His voice is pleasant, soft, dreamy, and kind of boyish.

She gets goose pimples all over her skin, but her voice remains professional and serious, with a note of fatigue in it.

She says to him, "So that explains those amplitudes on the monitor," and then spends a few minutes reassuring him she is only joking and that all the equipment is turned off.

Calmed again, he stretches out in the peaceful solitude of the *Womb*. His partner's voice remains his only connection to the outer world. He imagines what Michael must have felt like as he lay in this grave, alone, with the changes taking place in his body and his mind, not knowing what is going on with him. Through his eyes, he tries to see Michael's world, to better understand what is going on in the boy's mind and whether he is capable of such cruel and cold-blooded murder.

He consults with his partner on the profile of the boy from Beresford's testimony. Michael was his patient as much as his victim, Beresford didn't deny it, but Fox somehow has the impression that Michael wasn't aware of it. He probably realized it just before Hank Daniels was killed.

Did he kill him? Maybe. At that moment, anything could be going on in his head. He could have killed him in a fit of rage, without regret, or he could have killed him by accident, in self-defense. Either way, the drugs worked, which leads to the following questions that need to be answered: How aware is Michael of what was happening? How much could he have influenced the development of the situation?

Dawson agrees with Fox's theory, except for one. She immediately rules out the possibility that Michael is innocent. Unlike Fox, she has no doubt that Michael is responsible for the death of his stepfather. She doesn't believe in a breaking-in theory because there is no evidence to support it. Also, there is no evidence to support the theory that Daniels might have even known the attacker.

(Beresford!?!)

"Too impossible," she says, dismissing his idea, "there is no chance."

Beresford didn't mention that in his testimony. He didn't kill Hank Daniels, and that's why they should trust him. If they want to believe in the credibility of his words, then they must believe him completely or not trust him at all.

Beresford wasn't trying to shift the blame onto Michael to justify himself. On the contrary. He spoke in support of Michael, portraying him as an innocent victim. Only when he learned of his powers did he become dangerous.

"So, you think he used them to kill him?" Fox pushes the matter. "To give him tit for tat with his own weapon?"

"Not with *that* weapon, but with something he used as a weapon, yes."

"And so we have Michael, a murder suspect, who has these powers to kill Hank, but doesn't use them against him. Instead, he takes a risk of dealing physically with a man who is twice as strong, who can easily overcome him. Something doesn't fit in here."

"Maybe we should trust Beresford when he says that the experiment wasn't completed. Michael terminated it without knowing it, and then his powers weakened."

"Which means Michael is harmless now. He is normal, an ordinary boy like he was before."

"We can't be sure. We don't know what drugs they gave him and how far they came. We have to keep in mind that Michael may not be completely harmless. He was dangerous enough to kill his stepfather."

"What if Hank attacked him, trying to force him to continue with therapies?"

"In that case, everything is clear. Michael is the killer. He killed Hank Daniels. In self-defense or not, he killed him anyway. That doesn't diminish the fact that he is guilty."

"Don't be so quick to condemn him, Dawson. I'd rather say it was an act of a desperate man. No one can be condemned for defending their naked life. Nor can he be tried for premeditated murder."

"We need a witness to confirm this. Christ, we don't even have a suspect! All we have are unconfirmed theories."

"We have a witness, Dawson. We have Beresford's letter, and we have someone who can confirm it."

"Michael? You mean Michael?"

"I thought of him, yes, but I had someone else in mind. Morgan could help us clarify if Michael is guilty or innocent."

"In other words," she says after a brief pause, "you are saying that what Daniels and Beresford were doing to Michael has something to do with the experiments at the Institute?"

Fox's silence prompts her to come to her own conclusion.

"You think Morgan knows about Michael? And you expect he will confess everything and take responsibility?"

"Daniels and Beresford were doing research, weren't they? They couldn't do it without Morgan's approval or the blessing of someone from DC. Although I do not reject the possibility that they were working on something on their own that no one else knew about."

"Parallel experiments," says Dawson.

"Beresford has suggested something like that. What is unclear to me is why he didn't openly say that the experiments they conducted on Michael had nothing to do with their work at the Institute, if that is true?"

"Because of the nature of his research at the Institute?"

"It is possible. What if Michael is the only answer to those questions? What if there are other Michaels inside those walls?"

"You are talking about human experiments." Her voice is ice cold, emptied of emotion.

"Yes, I'm talking about experiments on humans. Doesn't that seem logical to you? Don't you think something like that is already happening somewhere in this crazy world?"

She doesn't offer him the answer to this question.

Instead, she asks him, "Do you think Morgan will admit it to you?"

"I'll deal with Morgan later, after finding Michael. He is the proof we need."

"I thought you would use Morgan to get to Michael."

"I thought about it, too, but changed my mind. It could be too dangerous for the kid."

"How can we be sure Morgan doesn't know about Michael and isn't already looking for him?"

"Because of what Beresford said and because we decided to trust him. No one at the Institute knows about Michael. And we can also be sure of that because of the thoroughness of Merchant's men."

"I still don't understand one thing. How can anyone destroy what he has been working on all his life? I can understand that when you realize you've done something wrong, you want to correct it, if for nothing else, to calm your conscience. But this has nothing to do with awakening conscience. This is much more than that, this is a completely different story."

"Of course. This became too much for Beresford to carry by himself, so he decided to ask for help. He kills himself to get our attention, leaving us to clean up the mess he left behind. What he wasn't capable of doing, will be done by the public. It is our responsibility, and it is our duty to put an end to this madness."

"And again, there's no logic to it."

"From his point of view, there is. The public opinion would condemn him, anyway; they would never fully trust him. His career would be ruined. He would lose everything. But I don't think that's the reason he did it. I don't think he killed himself for what others would think and say about him. I'm more inclined to think he did it because of Michael. He thought he could do more to help his friend dead than he could help him while he was alive."

Fox is still locked in the *Womb*, so he can't see her expression. But he senses that his words take her by surprise a little. Dawson doesn't consider the possibility that Michael might have been Beresford's friend. To be honest, neither did he until a little while ago.

"If this is true, it only confirms my doubts. Michael was the victim, and he put an end to it."

"By killing the man."

"We don't know that for sure yet."

"If you're right and if Beresford wanted to help Michael, then he made a big mistake by killing himself. That wasn't a brave man's act, Fox."

She is determined, and Fox cannot blame her. Plus, she is telling the truth.

"No, it's not," he agrees. "It was an act of a desperate man."

Fox knows from his own experience what a desperate man could do. His father was once a desperate man, when he found out that Fox's mother had cheated on him with another man. She barely survived his beating, two broken ribs, a dislocated lower jaw, three knocked-out teeth, and bruises all over her body that had not healed for weeks. She looked terrible and, when she had recovered enough to leave the hospital, she filed for a divorce, got it, and took their son with her.

Despite the court verdict, his father soon came after them again, alcohol intoxicated, not completely drunk, but with enough alcohol in his blood to point the gun first at Shay's mother and then at Shay. His mother started screaming and a few minutes later she experienced a nervous breakdown. Before she blacked out, she saw her ex-husband blowing his head off in front of a nine-year-old child.

Special agent Shay Fox remembers well what a desperate man could do. He never forgot that.

He comes out of the *Womb* and towels himself dry. During that time, Dawson is surfing the Internet, searching for skate shop addresses in New York. She is looking for a needle in a haystack, but that is also a start.

Time is not inclined to anyone; it is running out for them and Michael. Everyone is impatient, including Morgan, who called minutes ago demanding to bring the killer of his two men to justice as soon as possible.

It doesn't skip Dawson's attention that Morgan demanded justice for the killer of his *men*, and not just one *man*, which is strange given that Morgan could not have known about the link between the two deaths. Unless he knows something the two of them don't know, which wouldn't surprise her either anymore.

The chase after Michael Daniels has begun. The question is who will get to him first: the FBI and New York's police, or unidentified bad guys?

Fox sneaks up on her without making a sound and waits for the computer to spit out the last data.

She doesn't flinch when he speaks from behind her back, and that confuses him. *(Maybe he wasn't that silent, after all? Or does she have abilities he doesn't know of?!)*

"It looks like we're going to have our hands full. What do you say?" he asks, looking at the list with twelve skate shops in

New Manhattan alone.

"If we plan to visit them all. These kids spend more time on the streets than at their homes."

"I was counting on that."

"Were you?" She wheels the chair around and looks at him. The data from the screen flickers in the pupil of her left eye.

"I was. So we better start from here." He points his index finger at Supreme skate shop.

"Is that your inner voice telling you?"

"No. My inner voice tells me to start here." His finger slides a few skate shops toward the bottom of the list.

"Then why do we go to Supreme?"

"Because I would like to see something *supreme*." He tears the printout sheet from the printer and pulls his handsome face into a mischievous smile. "Ready to go?"

The skate shop he later pointed to was Division Pro Skate Shop.

Chapter

21st: . . . and the regular ramp is in its vertical part under the coping and on average it can amount from 8 to 50 inches. All these tricks you can also try on other objects, such as a bank (any sloping plane you can skate on), a grind box which resembles a box with pipes on its upper edges, while the . . .

HE THOUGHT HE WAS MUCH STRONGER. He thought Nancy would stay if he is honest with her.

He wanted so much to be honest and share his secrets with her, to open a well of sorrow before her and to show her how much he loves her.

But Nancy didn't understand.

Nancy left.

Nancy left him.

Victor is left alone because Nancy didn't understand. He opened his heart to her, and she in turn left. He could only watch with what ease and elegance she closed the door behind her and left him. As if they had been together only for a few days, as if they were strangers who had only met and not loved each other with every beat of their hearts and were comfort and a friend to each other in good and bad times.

Everything had fallen into oblivion. Everything is useless.

Because Nancy is gone. Because Nancy left, saying,

"Don't look for me. If I ever want to see you again, I'll come to you."

She hasn't returned since. Nor did she ask him how he is and if he needs anything. If he needs someone

to love him.

She disappeared without a trace, as if she had never been there. Leaving behind the shadows of love and open wounds eroded by the cold.

His grandmother died. A week ago, or maybe a little earlier—Victor stopped counting. He stopped thinking about it, because she still lives inside him with the power of everlasting love, watching him through an album of painful memories.

That is the moment in Victor's life when it all happened.

Angela Kenneth's death changed everything: his life, Nancy's life, Michael's life.

The last time he saw his grandmother, she was serene. The pain was subdued by morphine, her eyes clouded, but she was conscious. She recognized him. She recognized the boy she loved so much, his tousled, dark tufts bleached with hydrogen at the tips, his kind and warm, blue eyes, and the precious smile that had always been there for her.

She held his hand in silence and the calm of a day, and the sun was setting. Far, quiet, and soft.

Warming her heart. Warming her fragile body, her dry skin and chapped lips. Growing, becoming brighter and approaching.

She took a sip of juice as Victor held her up so she could

swallow. It didn't taste good; very few things tasted good to Angela Kenneth lately. She would have chewed dry sand, if Victor said it was good. She would have believed him it was healthy, full of vitamins and good for her, and would have eaten it without complaint. And it *would* be good to her, even though it wouldn't taste good.

This juice at least had a taste. It wasn't good, but it dampened the fire burning inside her.

The sun was getting brighter.

The sun was growing bigger.

Warming a face tired of life.

When Angela Kenneth opened her eyes again, all she saw was the sun. Only the sun.

Somewhere between this dazzling light she noticed a different hue, a different light burning with the shine of blue eyes, its pleasantly cooling warmth.

Angela Kenneth gave a gentle squeeze to the hand holding her and whispered, "I love you."

"I love you too, Nana," the hand answered.

Then she closed her eyes again because the light was too strong, too bright. Shortly after, she fell asleep.

The next day she didn't tell Victor her dream. She still dreams of it until the trumpets of the resurrection awaken her to a new life again.

Victor cried. Abandoned survivor in a cruel world.

And summer is cold.

And cruel.

Cruel to him, cruel to his grandmother, cruel to his girlfriend.

It is also cruel to his friend, who is freezing somewhere in the streets of New York, fleeing persecutors in the service of truth and at the behest of justice.

Victor wholeheartedly wanted to help Michael, but he is too weak and too scared to take the smallest step. What if he makes a mistake? Who will help him, then?

* * *

The day is turning into a beautiful one, and as the morning wears on, the sun is shining brighter. After the reign of colder days, the temperatures could rise again—if this isn't another bluff of a deceitful summer.

Alien can hardly wait for this summer to pass. He wishes for school to start again, and normal, everyday events to happen. He barely survived this summer of ninety-eight and had enough of it. Yet, something is telling him it is still not over. There is something else besides weird weather in the air. Something chilly and not too cheerful.

Breakfast is served on a table: pancakes, tea, and coffee with whipped cream. Strawberry jam, soy drink instead of cow's milk, toast, bacon, cheese, and hard-boiled eggs. An abundance for which neither Alien nor his mother have an appetite. Neither is in the mood to eat, and each has their reasons for being in a bad mood.

"Michael was here?" She takes small sips of hot, black coffee. She touches almost nothing else.

Alien nods, chewing on another pancake with little enthusiasm.

"He was here," he confirms.

Brenda Travis looks at her son over the rim of her glasses. "You should have told me about it. You should have asked me first."

"Why?" He looks at her defiantly. "He's my friend, Mom. I can bring a friend home, can't I?"

"Michael is no longer *just* your friend, Roy. At least not like your other friends."

"Then what is he? A *killer*? Is that what you meant?" In him, bitterness mixed with anger.

(You too, Mom? Do you condemn him too? Without hearing him first? Without proof? You know, Mom, Michael saw through you! He knew you would have kicked him out if you found him at home. That's why he left. Because he couldn't bear you kicking him out too!)

"I didn't say that!"

"But you meant it, I know you did!" He slams the slice of pancake back onto the plate.

"Watch your behavior! Don't you dare raise your voice at me!"

"Don't you know him, Mom?" His voice cracks. "That's *Michael* we're talking about! Michael, whom you accepted with open arms into your home a few days ago because he had problems with his father. Because you also had problems with Dad, and I had them too . . ."

"Don't you compare me to him. Don't you dare!"

(Yes, you're right. You didn't kill Dad. Even though he almost killed you.)

"Do you regret it . . . that you helped him?"

Brenda Travis puts down her cup of coffee and leans across the table to get closer to her son.

She says, "Michael did something terribly wrong, Roy. There is no justification for this. His father may have been unrighteous, he may have been tough on him, but he didn't deserve that. He didn't deserve Michael to kill him. He was a human being, for heaven's sake!"

"But Michael didn't do it! Why don't you want to believe me when I tell you so?"

"What would you have of it if I believed you? What would Michael have of it? Everyone else thinks he's guilty! What I think won't change anything. He is major goddamn news!"

"No one has yet accused him of murder. All they know is that he's gone, so they're speculating."

"Whatever! And now we're in it. Someone will dig out we helped the murder suspect by giving him shelter! Do you realize that this puts us on the wrong side of the law?"

"Screw that law! I don't give—"

"ROY!"

She yells at him, offended by his language, gazing at him as if she wants to project her thoughts into his and vice versa.

"You know something you don't want to tell me." Her voice is hoarse, her heart pounding fast with anticipation.

"I know a lot," he says, more at ease, having her attention. "But I can't tell you everything. For your own good. What I *can* tell you is that Michael is not guilty. You can trust me on that, Mom. Michael didn't kill his father. You know why? Because he was with me."

His words have the desired effect. Brenda Travis gapes in shock, disbelief, and fear.

"You're lying! That's not true! You only say that to protect him! He is your friend!"

"You're right, Mom. You are absolutely right. He's my friend. Michael is my best friend. He is more than that. I love him like a brother. But that doesn't change the fact that he was with me."

"You can't do this to me! I don't believe you! No one will believe you!"

"Ask Victor if you don't believe me. He was also with us. The three of us were skating together."

Alien couldn't believe that his mother could grow even paler. All the color drains from her face and now she looks like a freshly whitewashed hospital wall.

When she regains her breath, she demands from him, "*Who* then killed him?! He couldn't do it alone!"

"Don't you think that's for the police to find out? It could have been anyone! Break-ins happen all the time in New York." He is the image of calm, while his mother falls from one shock to another. Confusion, uncertainty, panic, skepticism, and lack of understanding mask her beautiful but tired face.

"Break-ins? Yes. Break-ins happen all the time . . . but it wasn't a break-in! No one mentioned a break-in . . ."

She is confused. Beside herself. Alien feels sorry for her, but he has to play his role to the end. The stake is large; a lot depends on whether or not she will believe him. If he convinces her, maybe he will convince others too. Michael's prospects won't be so slim then.

They won't be slim at all.

"Your colleagues have not said much on the news. Obviously, they don't know too much either. For instance, they don't know that they have an *old* photo of Michael and that Michael looks a little different now."

"An old photo . . . ? What do you mean?!"

"Sorry, Mom, for the mess we left in the bathroom. I tried my best to clean it up, but . . ." He shrugs his shoulders and pushes himself lazily away from the table, smiling victoriously.

"What?? What were you doing in the bathroom? Answer me! Roy!?"

"Don't worry, Mom. It's not what you think. He's not my

boyfriend. We haven't gotten that far yet."

"Roy, come back here! Where are you going?"

He puts the dishes in the sink and grabs his skateboard. The next minute he is at the door.

"I'm going to town. I'll take a ride and look for friends."

"You are going to town? And your job?" She loses her self-control. "Don't you have to go to work today?"

Alien stops for a moment, his hand clenching tight the door handle.

He turns around and looks at his mother. In front of him is an emotionally broken woman, scared to death and beyond. If he pushes her a bit more—no, he won't do it. Michael's situation looks much better now, and he won't push his luck. He will have time to work on his mother later. She is too terrified now not to believe him, and Alien is sure she will keep her lips sealed and remain silent about what he had told her. She's so worried about him, she won't dare say a word.

The day began much better than I hoped, Alien thinks, and answers her question. "I don't. I quit."

"WHEN?"

"Just now."

Shuts the door behind him.

Brenda Travis puts both hands around her throat as if something is choking her. Her heart pumps wildly in her chest.

What just happened? What happened to her son?! She cannot understand. *That can't be true. Roy wouldn't do that. Roy is a good boy! He could not take part in something as awful as murder!!!*

Alien's skateboard thumps against the asphalt. The sound detonates in her head.

Oh my God, he is going to get hurt! she whines.

It's hard for her to get up from the chair, and the honk of

the passing car turns her knees into a rubbery mass.

"Roy!" As if ejected by a large spring, she leaps toward the door.

With his left foot on the board, Roy turns down the Discman and looks at his mother.

"Yes, Mom?"

Grasping at the last rocks of sanity, she says a quick Thank-You-God-he-is-alive prayer.

"You didn't put on your jacket! You'll catch a cold."

Her broken voice echoes in the neighborhood.

"Oh, I forgot to tell you. I don't have it anymore."

Her mouth drops open and the morning cold rushes into it.

"What do you mean, you don't have it? Where is it?"

He comes closer to her so that none of the neighbors can hear him.

"We had a burglar last night. He took my jacket before I could stop him." He grins at her and gets on the skateboard.

Brenda Travis grabs the wall. She grips her chest with her other hand to prevent her heart from jumping out.

"Your new jacket!"

"Bye, Mom." He waves to her.

The sound of his wheels rolling away. So loud. Too loud.

"Roy!"

Impossibly loud.

"Roy, come back here!"

Before it's gone around the corner.

"ROOOOYYY!"

The soothing rustling of the *Ailanthus* trees absorb her cry.

* * *

Without exaggeration, it is a long day, one of the longest in his life. Time stood in its way to the setting of the sun, as it did thousands of years ago when the sun seemed to be motionless over Gibeon, waiting until the Israelites had defeated the Amorites. But unlike Joshua, Michael is not protected by Jehovah's blessing. The curse has followed him.

The curse and condemnation of heaven for patricide.

He slept poorly last night, very bad or not at all, haunted by Rebecca's cries and sobs of horror when he told her the truth: Father is dead; Michael killed him. It was an accident, but it didn't help Rebecca calm down. She cried, cried, and cried, until Jeremy Creek took the phone from her.

"Mikey, Mikey, son, what are you saying? What have you done, dear child?"

There is fear in his voice, too, and tears that Michael couldn't see. Despite this, Jeremy Creek stays levelheaded.

"I don't know, Grandpa. I hit Hank, and he's dead now. Looks like I killed him."

"Mikey, where are you now? Is everything okay with you?"

"Not that I wanted to hit him. I didn't want to hurt him. It happened."

"Michael, where are you now? Have you talked to the police? Are you in the police station?"

"I was defending myself, Grandpa. He attacked me first. Please, believe me, this is what happened. I need someone to believe me. I need—"

"MICHAEL, WHERE ARE YOU?"

"I, I, I'm at my friend's. I haven't talked to anyone yet."

"Good. I mean, not good, but we have to think it over. We need to think about what to do next . . ."

"Yes, Grandpa. We have to think about it. I didn't want to do it, do you believe me?"

"I trust you, Michael. I believe you. Listen to me now. What I want to tell you is for your own good."

"Yes, Grandpa. Anything. Whatever you say. I'll do whatever you say."

"Listen to me carefully, Son. This is serious. Very serious. *Don't* run away. Don't run, my child, if you think you did nothing. Don't give them a reason to suspect you."

"I won't, Grandpa. It's *not* my fault. I didn't want to kill him. I don't know what happened."

"It's okay, my child, calm down. All right?"

"All right."

"Are you calmed down? Do you understand what I'm telling you?"

"I understand, Grandpa."

"Michael, I'm telling you this for your own sake. Listen to me and remember, Grandma and I will stand by you until the end. We'll always be with you. Do you understand that?"

"Yes, Grandpa. I understand. What do you want me to do? What?"

"It's not easy for me to ask this from you, and it won't be easy for you to do that, but you have to go to the police."

"NOOO!"

"You have to do it . . ."

"NO! NO! NO! NO!"

"Michael—"

"No, Grandpa! I'm not guilty! I didn't mean to kill him! They won't believe me!"

"That's the only way they can trust you! To turn yourself in—"

"I'm sorry, Grandpa, but I'm not going to the police. I will not go until this whole thing clears out. There has to be a way to convince them I didn't want to kill Hank . . ."

"How are you going to convince them? Michael, be reasonable! How are you going to prove your innocence, if you keep hiding and running?"

"I don't know! I'll think of something. I—"

"Michael, Grandma and I love you very much. You and Rebecca are all we have. You are our only joy in life . . ."

"You want to help me, Grandpa? Do *you* want to help me?"

"With all my heart."

"Then forget I called. Act as we haven't heard from each other. Like you know nothing. Can you do this for me?"

"Michael, do you want me to tell your grandma you're asking us to *lie*?"

"Grandpa, you said you loved me! I love you too! I know I haven't shown that lately, but it's true. I love you and Elisabeth and Rebecca. And now I'm asking you, all three of you, to do me a favor and forget you heard from me. Don't lie. Just forget it."

"Son, don't you realize it's impossible? Rebecca is all beside herself. . . . How will I tell her to forget? How can I ask that from her?"

"If you don't, more bad things will happen. I feel it. I'm not kidding."

"I don't know what to do, Michael! It would be easier—"

"Do nothing. Wait. The police will contact you anyway. Just wait and pretend. I'll figure something out by then."

"What will happen to you? Where will you be during this time? What shall I tell *Rebecca*?"

"Tell her I love her and I'm sorry. Tell her it was a mistake, a big mistake. Tell her it wasn't *me*."

"You are asking a lot from me, my child."

"I know. I'll never forget that. Never."

"Michael? Tell me one thing."

"Go ahead, Grandpa."

"Will we ever see you again?"

For the first time since he got him on the phone, Michael pauses to think about answering Jeremy Creek's honest question. Once more he realizes how hard life could be, how unbearably hard, and yesterday everything seemed so simple and innocent.

"I would love that more than anything in the world," he offers him the most sincere answer he can think of, avoiding the lie.

"But you can't promise that?"

"I'm sorry. I can't make that promise. I'm no longer the only one who decides about my fate."

"Michael, wherever you are and whatever happens, know that we're with you. Both in our thoughts and our prayers."

"I know that, Grandpa. I know that. I'll call you again. To let you know that I'm alive and well."

"You don't have to call, Michael. They might tap our phone . . ."

"I don't care. I'll call you anyway. And if not me, one of my friends will call you."

"Say hello to them, Michael. Tell them to look after you."

"I will, Grandpa. You look after Rebecca, okay? Don't let her do something stupid. Don't let her come here."

"Rebecca will be fine. I wish I could say the same for you too . . ."

Once the conversation between Denver and New York

City ended, Alien took Michael to the bathroom. He tells him to take off his T-shirt and sits him on the toilet. He covers his pants with an old towel, takes his comb and borrows his mother's bleach. It took him only thirty minutes to transform Michael's brown hair into baby-blond, a shade that matches his longing and dreamy eyes.

"Man, what bad luck!" Alien exclaims satisfied, proud of his work. "I just fell in love with you, and already in the morning you have to scoot!"

Together they clean the bathroom and then retire to their respective beds. Instead of catching some sleep, they talk through most of the night. This is their last night together, and it's time to clarify everything, say what's to be said, make a big plan for the days to come and have a few more worry-free jokes.

Two hours before sunrise, Alien shares with him an intimate confession about his date with Laurie and what happened at the movie theater, her passive response to his kisses and gentle caresses. She liked him, she told him, but there could be nothing of their relationship.

"Don't be angry with me, Alien, but I still love him," Laurie said.

"But James isn't in love with you! He doesn't love you the way I love you! He is not in love with you!"

"I don't love him that way, either. But I still love him as a friend. I love him the way he loves you."

Alien grimaced.

"James considers you his friend, Alien. He is very fond of you and that's why I cannot hurt him. If it were someone else, I wouldn't make such a big deal out of it. But since it's James . . . I hope you understand."

"Of course. This is a free country and you have the right to decide for yourself. Why would you care what I think or feel?" Alien couldn't hide his true feelings.

"Alien, I cannot force you to understand, but I can't hurt James that way. I don't want to hurt him! I respect him too much."

"Then you will hurt *us*," he said ruefully.

"Maybe. But I will hurt us less than if we continue to see each other like this."

"So, this is goodbye?"

"Of course not!" She laughed at him and did something that made Alien feel stupid and immature. Laurie ruffled his hair as if he was a little boy. "We can always be friends."

"Friends? Why not? Looks like I didn't fare so *bad* after all."

She couldn't resist his sarcasm.

"Maybe I'll let you kiss me once in a while when James isn't around."

Alien seized the opportunity and kissed her with a long kiss from which she had to pull away.

"I checked. He wasn't around," he said nonchalantly, making her laugh.

She returned the kiss with such readiness that Alien thought he would melt.

To kill time, Michael goes to the movies on the recommendation of his friend, but because of one gory scene, nausea forces him to leave the show. He feels like a canary trapped in a birdcage rocked by a starving cat. Claustrophobia overwhelms him and he rushes out of the crowded theater, which screamed in unison.

In order to recover himself, he takes a long walk through

New York's districts: Chinatown, the Jewish Neighborhood, and Little Italy are first in line. When he gets bored with walking around for no specific purpose, he starts begging. He scrounges for fun and by the end of the day he *earns* a little over twenty-five dollars. If all his plans for his future fail, he will at least not starve. He will always charm someone to give him a dollar here or a few cents there, maybe buy him brunch or offer him lodging for the night. It isn't the career he is hoping for—a killer, a hobo, and a freelancer in sponging—but Michael had already learned that life is full of surprises.

This time he is curious to see another surprise: where he will spend *this* night. In a warm and safe haven or some cold dump from which New York City closed its eyes?

Eager to find that out, he hurries up to get to a secret meeting with his friends on time.

Magnificent, selfless, and full of understanding as ever, St. Patrick's Cathedral is waiting to hear another sad story in a city of rich, hardworking, and talented but lonely people.

Chapter

22nd: . . . fun box is the bank, a q-pipe (1/4 pipe), a rail and, say, the grind box together combined in one functional object. The vert wall is the quarter pipe (q-pipe) with the vertical part, while the launch ramp speaks for itself. Back to the tricks. To do the *impossible* trick, lift your front foot up off the board.

JACK MORGAN COULDN'T HAVE PEACE for two reasons.

Firstly: The investigation progresses too slowly no matter how much he pressures Fox and Dawson to speed things up. Such a development could not satisfy him, since he himself is under pressure from someone else. Therefore, no one can blame him for being so eager to change his situation. Sooner rather than later.

Secondly: Jack Morgan has the impression that he is not quite up to date and that the FBI agents are hiding something from him. As if they have a better overview of what is going on at the Institute than himself. That is, of course, impossible, ridiculous, total nonsense. But the very thought is disturbing enough for him, so he launches a small, independent, private investigation.

He does not doubt that the deaths of two of his men are somehow connected. Beresford's expression when asked about Daniels's kid corroborates that. Although Morgan is still searching for the missing link, he believes that the Daniels kid can give him an answer to this conundrum. The problem is, he is in darkness about where the kid is. The mysterious disappearance of the boy not even the FBI can locate is bugging him the most, because he could be the key to unlock the enigma surrounding Daniels's and Beresford's deaths.

"What the hell were these two doing?" he spits a curse, not too sure he will find an answer to that question inside the Institute. And just as he worries that his investigation will meet its own Waterloo, something unexpected happens that confirms Morgan's suspicions.

Elijah Peterson experiences Morgan's wrath on his own skin while he is sweating with anguish and effort to convince him he knows nothing about the death of Hank Daniels and Neil Beresford's suicide. True, he saw these two together the day he forgot the dolphin. They were engaged in a tense conversation, and the tension in the air was so thick that one could cut it with a scalpel. But he has no idea what they were arguing about.

Peterson then mentions a note—a crumpled piece of paper Daniels had hidden in his hand, and Jack Morgan's eyes shine with a wild glow.

"A note? What note? Tell me!" Morgan insists, as if Peterson knows what is on that piece of paper.

"I don't know, I swear to God, I don't know."

Morgan pounds his fist with anger into the open palm of

his other hand. The note might be the key to the answers he is looking for, and that key is lost to him as if it doesn't exist. Damnation! He knows he isn't going to shake any other information out of this lad, so he releases him.

As if caught in the hungry embrace of a deadly twister, Peterson disappears, not waiting twice to be told to get lost.

Jack Morgan forgets about Peterson the instant the door swings shut behind him, his thoughts already wandering off to the FBI agents and the answers *they* owe him. This time, however, he knows how to get answers out of them.

The air smells of *exchange*. The case will soon be closed, and a padlock put on the whole thing before the toxic waste reaches the public.

If it hasn't already leaked somewhere.

* * *

For Steven Merchant, it is encouraging to hear that the earth had not swallowed Michael and he is still somewhere in the neighborhood. He did everything in his power, and even more, to prevent him from wandering outside the city limits: JFK, LaGuardia, and Newark are alerted and supplied with dozens of Michael's photos, and Penn Station, Grand Central, and all bus lines do not lag an inch behind them. The City of New York turns into one big prison for Michael. Merchant opts for that move after a letter from Florida lands on his desk.

The letter addressed to Michael Daniels is sent by Icarus Skateboards, offering him sponsorship in two contests in the European Union: first in the Swiss enclave in the small town of Sattel, and second in the Skateboarding World Championship in Münster in the German enclave. To his great regret, Michael won't be able to accept their offer because he will not go anywhere. He is more needed here, in the States.

The last recorded call to a number in the district of Denver is made from a phone booth in Central Park. The team is sent there, but by the time they arrive, Michael is already gone. He is lucky again, but it won't last forever. Sooner or later he will make a mistake and then he will be theirs.

Then he will be *his*.

The first turn in the search occurs when a young Officer Henry reports a conversation with a young man in front of Michael's building, who he suspects might be Michael's friend. He recognizes and describes the kid as a skateboarder because his younger brother is also into skateboarding. As soon as he left, Henry informed headquarters, but they find no one who matches his description at the provided address. The kid misled them, but Merchant doesn't despair about it. Information about Michael Daniels is at once forwarded to the FBI. Michael is still in town, but he isn't alone. With him is a whole pack of his skater friends helping him. Not for long. It will be them who will lead him to Michael.

While carefully examining Michael's photo for a few long minutes: a charming smile, handsome face and very unusual, interesting, and extremely beautiful eyes—the eyes of a saint, Detective Merchant also analyzes his career at the NYPD. Each case assigned to him remains imprinted in his memory—some of these cases more clearly than others, but he remembers them all—and he finds none of them justified as much as he does in the case of Michael Daniels. Merchant could have sworn that Michael *is* the killer, that he savagely murdered his stepfather. But thanks to the material Agent Fox had sent him, he begins to look at the whole case from a different perspective. Deep inside of him, he finds understanding for what the boy had done. If something like that happens to his younger son Samuel, his promising golden boy, if someone put their hands on him like that . . . Merchant doesn't have to finish the thought, BECAUSE HE WOULD BEAT THE SON OF A BITCH TO DEATH WITHOUT FLINCHING.

On either side of Michael's photo, on Merchant's freshly polished desk, are photos of Michael's two victims. The bizarreness of the events intertwines the fates and lives of these three with an even more bizarre outcome. Two dead, one on the run. Guilty before the law, innocent before God.

He reaches for a bottle of Remy Martin and pours himself a finger of a drink. He lets the drink burn his tongue and palate before swallowing it, but the flame of life from the eyes of the boy watching him from the photograph burns him even more accusingly. There is so much suffering and sadness in these eyes, and they are still full of life, meekness, and the need for someone to understand them. So much divine beauty . . . and almost no hope for the future.

The quiet murmur of sadness splashing his heart makes him quickly pour himself another glass and drain it in a gulp. A crack opens between Merchant-cop and Merchant-gentle-father-and-friend, and in that briefest moment of truth, he acknowledges deep inside that the boy is dear to him. The crack is small, and it fills in a second, but for a moment Merchant senses the birth of a protective, paternal love in him.

Then he coughs to clear his throat, and the moment disappears like fading smoke, leaving him regretting that he had not retired when he planned to do so, and that he will have to solve this last case before devoting himself solely to protecting his own family.

***

When Fox and Dawson step into Division Pro Skate Shop, blaring sounds of screaming music blast them in the face. Masta Ace, followed by Mariah Carey, David Holmes, and Coolio, rattle their bones and rap their brains out. But the moment they flash their badges and say those three magic letters—FBI—the music stops.

Two girls and four guys eye them suspiciously, holding their breaths.

Nanoseconds later, a guy in an orange jacket and a wool beanie hat grins at them and exclaims without pardon, "Mulder! Scully! Welcome to our skate shop!"

The burst of laughter shakes the walls of the store, eliminating the tension that hung in the air. Even Agent Dawson allows herself to crack a smile, while her partner remains poker-faced and serious.

Encouraged by the laughter of his friends and the positive reaction of at least one agent, Stu continues, "What can we do for you? Are you interested in *getting* a board? Because if you are looking for inline skates, you're in the wrong place."

"Cut it off, Stu," the skater with long and rich curls silences him. Dawson recalls them being called dreadlocks.

"I humbly apologize. I just wanted to be polite and help our guests feel comfortable. You are here to buy something, aren't you?" He smack-kisses the girl sitting next to him, but she doesn't return him a kiss. One doesn't have to be super-smart to notice something is bugging her.

"How can we help you?" the dreadlocks skater asks them, ignoring Stu, and after Fox introduces himself and Dawson,

Andy introduces the others. "I'm Andy, and this is Ken, Ian, and Alex," he points at the two young men and the girl sitting on the steps. "This arrogant skater who tries to sell the board to anyone who comes to the store is Stu, and next to him is his girlfriend, Irma."

"You own the store?" Dawson asks him.

"Not really. The owner caught the flu. I'm temporarily replacing him until he gets better."

I see, Dawson nods in understanding. Sudden warming plays Fear-the-Reaper with New Yorkers.

"You need him?" Andy asks.

"Not explicitly," Fox answers. "We can also ask you."

"What's upstairs?" Dawson asks as Fox reaches into his raincoat.

Andy follows her gaze up the stairs. "Upstairs? Shoes, skateboards, snowboards, jackets, and some discount T-shirts."

"Do you mind if I take a look?"

"Be my guest." Andy spreads his arms and turns to Fox, who is showing a photo to Stu and Irma. Stu looks at it rather indifferently, but Irma turns pale when she sees it.

"Nope, we don't know him." Stu shakes his head. Irma is silent.

"Are you sure?"

"Excuse me," not answering his question, Irma apologizes and heads for the restroom.

"I don't think I know him," Stu replies. "I may have met him somewhere, but I can't remember."

"Perhaps one of you can tell me something more?" Fox shows Michael's photo to Ken, Ian, and Alex, staring without response at their friend's smiling face.

Fox decides it's time to give them a slight memory push.

"Interesting. And I was hoping you would be the ones to help me."

"What do you mean?" Confused, Ken hands him back Michael's photo.

"The Supreme guys sent us to you. A guy named Nalik told us you might know him." Silence drops like an invisible tent over the entire skate shop, muffling every sound, including already muffled beats of Coolio's "C U When U Get There." "He used to come here, according to his words."

The reactions among the skateboarders are different. What they all have in common is that everyone starts talking at the same time.

Andy's voice rises above others and Fox turns back to him again.

"Michael Daniels? You are looking for him?"

Fox nods. "Do you know him?"

"I've met him, if that's what you meant. He was here a few times to buy a deck and some other stuff. Haven't seen him for a while. Two weeks or something."

"That was before the murder happened," Fox concludes. "Are you sure he hasn't been around since?"

"I don't know if he came in the meantime or not. *I* didn't see him. I don't know about the others."

Fox eyes the rest of the skaters and holds his gaze on Stu, fixing him.

"Why are you looking at me? I don't know anything! Ask Victor and Alien! They are his buddies!" Stu has a quick tongue, but he realizes it a little too late.

"Our memory is back, Stuart Cross? That's your name, isn't it?" He glances up from a magical sheet of paper that seems to reveal all the secrets of Stuart Cross. Stu's forehead shimmers with droplets of cold sweat.

"Where can we find Victor *Kenneth*?" he persists, this time looking at no one in particular. "And who is this *Alien*?"

"You seem to know all the answers already," Andy replies. "Then why do you ask?"

"Making sure I have the correct information. Well?"

"Victor is sick. He's home, also fighting the flu. I believe you have his address?"

"Indeed, I have. And the other one? Where can I find Alien? Anybody knows his real name?"

There is a hush that lasts a little longer this time.

So does Fox's patience.

* * *

Dawson climbs the metal staircase to the upper floor. The two skateboarders doing a *line* are painted realistically on its glass walls. Impressive, she thinks, and spots three kids going through the goods; two are buying something while a third is at their service.

"Take this one, Sven. Trust me, when you hit an *ollie*, you'll fly on it like an eagle."

Noticing Dawson, he greets her with a wide smile and misses hearing Sven's next question.

"May I help you?" He is pure courtesy as he approaches her.

"I'd like to take a look around, if that's okay."

"Sure. If you find anything, just give me a call. I'll be back in a sec."

She watches him from the corner of her eye as he talks to the boys.

"Which ones will it be, then?" he asks an Afro-American boy.

"These, I suppose. I don't like that ES model."

"Okay. And you?" he asks Sven.

"I'll take this one." Sven holds out an Alien Workshop board. "Although I'm not one hundred percent sure, I'll take your word for it."

"If you're not happy with it, come back and we'll replace it. But don't crack it!" he corrects himself when a sly smile appears on Sven's face. "If you two don't need me anymore, I'd like to help this lady now."

"I'm done," Justin says.

"I still want to browse a little, but I don't need you for that," Sven dismisses him too.

"I'm all yours now." He comes to her in two swift steps, a broad smile on his face again. "Did you find something you like?"

"To be honest, I found a few things I like, but unlike my partner, I won't be doing any shopping today." She returns his smile and then produces her badge. "FBI."

Justin and Sven freeze in the middle of the conversation, wondering if they heard it well and what to do next. Eventually, they continue quietly buzzing between themselves like two dragonflies in flight, pretending to be occupied with something of *great* importance.

Alien's smile wavers as if it loses its confidence for a moment, but he continues to smile. He doesn't seem to mind talking to a representative of the law.

"How can I help you?" he asks her a third time.

The same scenario repeats as from the ground floor: the same questions, Dawson shows the same photo of Michael

Daniels, and gets almost identical answers.

Yes, Alien knows Michael, but he hasn't seen him for a few days already. He doesn't know exactly when and where he had last seen him. He knows what happened, he saw it on the news, but he doesn't believe Michael did it. Michael's okay. He couldn't kill anyone.

He promises to ask around if anyone has heard from Michael. At the end he asks her if Michael is in danger, and she confirms his worries by saying he is in danger.

"What kind of danger?"

"Why do you want to know?"

"His girlfriend is downstairs," he says in a low voice, as if trying to prevent the bad news from being heard downstairs. "Well, she *was* his girlfriend until recently. But she could still be upset when she hears that Michael is in trouble. You know, she still loves him."

"What happened?"

"I don't know for sure. Michael never talked about it. Irma tried to save their relationship, but it didn't work out. She's with someone else now."

Dawson nods. She promises to be discreet, and Alien promises to cooperate and call her if he finds out something, anything at all.

Then the small procession descends the stairs. Alien at the head, followed by Sven and Justin with serious faces and quieter than the silence that welcomes them downstairs, the FBI agent at the back.

* * *

"Have you looked at Riverdale?" the voice shatters an awkward silence.

Fox wheels about to find himself face-to-face with a new boy. His partner descends three steps behind him. He catches her gaze from behind the kid's back and recognizes the almost imperceptible nod of her head. Something is in the offing.

"No, we haven't," he replies. "Do you think we should?"

"Maybe. We often go there. You know, looking for pools to skate."

"Thanks for the information."

The skaters cannot believe their ears. They stare at Alien flabbergasted, without a clue what is happening.

"You're welcome." Alien nods and charges Sven's deck and Justin's shoes. "Don't hesitate to drop by if something else interests you."

"We will," Fox promises, and heads for the door. "Thank you very much for your cooperation."

Forced smiles respond to him. And one voice.

"Hey!" a shout stops them as the roar of traffic rushes into the store through the half-open door.

"Didn't you forget to *buy* something?" Stu continues to be Stu, now that the air is easier to breathe again.

To everyone's amazement, Fox gives him a friendly smile. "I'm sorry, Mr. Cross. If I knew you had such a marvelous offer, I wouldn't have bought shoes at Supreme. I'll correct that next time, deal?"

"Too late for that, agent." Stu grins at him and turns on the CD player.

The music theme from *The X Files* mixes with street noise.

Fox gives him a thumbs up and steps out onto the sidewalk with Dawson following him.

A moment later, Stu disappears under a pile of

skateboarders who turn a deaf ear to his cries that he was only joking.

* * *

Alien takes advantage of the ruckus and asks Andy to keep an eye on the store until he returns. He sneaks out and runs down the street. Then he returns and looks in the opposite direction.

Not too sure which way to go, he tries his luck and goes at random. He is moving fast, more colliding with passersby than slaloming between them, quickly closing the distance to the pay phone. He is careless for a second, and that is enough to collide with the man who spins around before him. The collision is strong enough to knock him down if the man he had run into had not grabbed hold of him.

He steadies him on his feet and asks him in a calm voice, "Looking for me?"

Alien swallows hard before making eye contact with Special Agent Shay Fox.

Then he looks at Agent Dawson peeking from behind Fox's shoulder and answers, "Actually, yes."

Chapter

23rd: With the toes of your back foot spin the board around that leg 360 degrees. Get the board underneath you. Roll away. The *bigspin kickflip* is basically the same as the *bigspin* (pop the *shove-it* to rotate your board 180 degrees on its vertical axis; here you spin the board 360 . . .

THE IDYL IS OVER, CRUELLY SCATTERED by the beauty of the arriving warmer summer days. And the harmony of a newly awakened nature, bombarded with a cacophony of thousands of sounds and hidden within a kaleidoscope of faded colors. Cruel. Very cruel.

The flight of a bumblebee is too loud and almost impossible to withstand.

(Cruel!)

The birds pitiless in their singing.

(Why don't they shut up already?)

The light too bright, too strong, and too warm.

(My eyes hurt! This is so cruel . . .)

The world is collapsing, disappearing in this dimension and

appearing in another. The collapse of emotions before complete misunderstanding. The defeat of sanity, with only a narrow beam of light in the abyss of darkness.

She is getting tranquilizers and sleeping pills because she needs a peaceful sleep, and the dreams she dreams are flooded with nightmares that remind her of the horrible truth.

She wakes up with the screams, bathed in cold sweat and afraid to nap again.

In the room—completely darkened—a light appears. It glows gently in her grandmother's arms and whispers comfortingly in her grandfather's voice. The light is in her room, and in her—pitch-darkness. *(Daddy's dead. Daddy's gone. Michael killed him.)*

Dry sobs stuck in the desert of her throat. Havoc smites her heart.

"Dad . . . ? *Dad?*"

(I hate you, Michael. I hate you for what you did to Dad. I hate you and I want you to die.)

The voice of conscience, acoustic and resonant, resounds without stopping. She covers her ears with her hands to soften the echo, but the voice is still there, and Rebecca surrenders.

(I don't hate him! I don't hate him! Just leave me alone!)

(I want to die.)

The laughter of voices in her head. Drinking champagne. The clinking of crystal glasses. To her father's death

(Noooo!!)

and her brother's disappearance.

Then a new toast, "Long live the killer!"

"NO!"

The sound of footsteps running up the stairs, the light scattering the darkness, and Rebecca finds safety in the arms that rock her.

* * *

This time she is dreaming of the FBI. They came to talk to her about the violent death of her father. But Grandpa and Grandma don't allow them. "She's in a catatonic state. She can't talk to anyone."

Through cracks of consciousness, she hears the car driving away. It leaves her world, swallowed by a black hole, lost in Rebecca's triangle.

She tries to open her eyes. She reaches out for the spot of light hovering above her head—at the level of her eyes, but her fingers pass through the cold light.

Rebecca shivers and gets creeps from the thought that appears in her mind before it runs away at the speed of light.

(I'm afraid. I'm afraid, Michael.)

(Don't be afraid, Rebecca. Don't be afraid. Everything's going to be fine, you'll see.)

(How, Michael? Dad's gone . . .

(Why did you kill him?)

(I had to. I had to. Dad wasn't good. Dad was bad. If I hadn't killed him, he would have killed me. Do you believe me, Rebecca? Do you believe he would've killed me?)

(You shouldn't have killed him . . . He was my dad!)

(I'm sorry. I know you loved him. But your dad went bad.)

(HOW CAN YOU SAY THAT!? My dad was good! He was good!)

(Your dad was good, Rebecca. But that was before. What I killed was no longer your dad. It wasn't HIM. Do you believe me, sis? Do you believe it's true?)

(No, I don't believe you! I can't believe you!)

(You must believe me. You have to believe me, Rebecca. If you don't believe me, I'll die. My life is in your hands. Your faith keeps me alive. Do you want me to die? Do you want to KILL me?)

(No! Don't say that! Don't, please!)

(I love you, Rebecca. I love you so much. Out of my love came our suffering. Only we are left. Only you and me. Don't kill us, please.)

(Michael, I'm scared. I'm so scared . . .)

(Don't. Don't be scared. Just trust me. You don't have to be scared . . .)

(I'm scared . . .

(Believe in me. Believe me. I love you.)

". . . for you, Michael."

Her fingers are so small, delicate and ethereal in the morning light. The glittering aura around them when Elisabeth Creek pulls the heavy drapes from the windows.

"How are you, sugar?"

"I'm better, Granny. Thank you."

She takes a cup of tea from the plate and sips from it. The tea is hot, and Rebecca burns her tongue. Makes a face.

Elisabeth Creek gives her a smile of apology. "Forgive me, I forgot to cool it down. I'm all confused."

Rebecca cups the hot drink in her hands. Pleasant warmth flows through her body, melting the ice in her.

"Grandma, can you help me to the half-moon?"

"You're too weak to go out, sugar. Can you wait till tomorrow?"

Rebecca shakes her head.

"I cannot. I had a dream . . . I dreamed that my roses died while I was in bed."

She holds her grandma's questioning gaze.

"Are you sure you can walk?"

"I am," she tells an innocent lie. She has never felt weaker.

* * *

Gentle Wind is elated, his whole body bloomed with impressions. Rebecca watches with a smile the delight on the little boy's face.

He crouches by the bed of tulips and asks, "Did you know they came from Asia?"

"I thought they were from Europe?" Rebecca answers. "Didn't the Dutch bring them here?"

"No!" he refutes, wondering at her ignorance. "They are from Asia Minor. They arrived in Europe from Turkey."

"How do you know that?"

"I know lots about flowers." He shrugs his tiny shoulders, his eyes shining with pride. "Mom taught me."

"Your mother loves you very much. It's nice to have someone who cares so much for you."

Gentle Wind gets serious. He frowns.

"Your mom doesn't care for you?"

"My mom is dead. She died this spring."

"Oh . . . I didn't know that," he says with an adult seriousness. "You must miss her lots."

"I think so. But my brother Michael misses her even more."

"My mom could take care of both of you. It wouldn't be difficult for her. And I would love that," he confesses shyly.

Rebecca smiles and ruffles his hair. "Let me think about your proposal."

Gentle Wind is smiling, too, giving her plenty of time to

build a whole new universe.

She then takes his hand and leads him to the bed of roses.

The smell is intoxicating and almost stupefying. The roses are in full bloom and never looked more beautiful and surreal.

They pause in front of the flowerbed of yellow roses and Rebecca squats down next to the boy.

"*These* are those roses?" Gentle Wind strokes the petals of one bud with his little fingers.

Rebecca confirms with a slight tilt of her head.

"Until yesterday, they wilted, and then their heads lifted by themselves and they bloomed again."

"That happened when you woke up from your dream?"

"Yes." Her eyes water her favorite flowers with love and admiration. "I don't remember them ever being so beautiful. Miraculous. Don't you think so?"

The boy cocks his head, his nostrils tasting the sweet scent of flowers.

"They are so beautiful. They know you love them."

Rebecca takes his hands in hers and turns him toward her.

She says, "You think the roses have bloomed because of me? That they came back to life with me?"

"Yes," he confirms. His eyes are big and warm. "When you were sick, they were sick too. They were dying without your love. When you were well again, they were well. Because you gave them your love again."

Rebecca pulls him closer to herself.

"Come here," she tells him, hugging him tightly.

He doesn't resist her. Content, he surrenders to her embrace.

After a while, he giggles. He rubs his cheek against hers and asks, "Do you want me to bloom too?"

She blushes and gives in to spontaneous laughter. But she doesn't let him out of her embrace, not yet.

* * *

"I'm glad you're back with us."

"So am I." Rebecca looks down, expecting to blush again. Nothing happens. She musters courage and looks into his eyes. This is their first time together since Red Sunshine proposed to her. Then she looks toward Blue Sky and Gentle Wind, who ride Vanity bareback. Excitement on their healthy red and smiling faces.

"Nothing will happen to them?" she asks, more to keep the conversation flowing than out of genuine concern.

"No," Red Sunshine replies. "Sky knows with horses. Vanity feels it."

Rebecca looks at him again. "Sunny . . ."

"Yes?"

"I don't know."

"It's okay. We don't have to talk about it now. Nothing happened between us. We are still friends."

"How did you know I was thinking about that?"

"How could I not know? Since . . . then, I thought about nothing but that. I'm sorry to ask you. Do you forgive me?"

"I wasn't angry, Sunny. Not with you. I just didn't know what to tell you. I was confused and . . . Well, I was a little angry at first, but I was also flattered."

Red Sunshine grins.

"Really?" he asks.

"I love you, Sunny." She surprises herself with the ease of translating her feelings into words. "I like being with you and I enjoy your company. It's just, we are too young to get married. And there's also something else I need to do before I even think about something as serious as marriage."

"I know. You have to go back to New York."

He surprises her.

Trying to hide her confusion, she explains to him, "I have to go because of Michael. I have to find him. Maybe he needs me. And I have to see Dad one more time . . ."

"I'll go with you."

Red Sunshine surprises her so much this time that she forgets to laugh at what he said.

Instead, she asks him in a whisper, "Why? Why would you do that?"

"Rebecca, I have to tell you this, you are the only person in the world who asks so many questions. Some questions don't have answers or don't need to be answered. I'll go with you because you can't go alone. You need someone to accompany you, and I'm not that sure your grandpa and grandma will volunteer. As a matter of fact, I think they would be much happier if you stayed here."

"You're probably right. But I still don't think we can make it, Sunny. Neither yours nor mine would agree. They would forbid us to see each other when they found out what we were thinking!"

"Then we won't tell them anything."

"That means we would have to run away. You don't think so . . . ?"

"Are you afraid?"

A smile of hope spreads across her face. "No. You?"

The truth is that she is dying of fear and excitement at the thought of what could happen to them until they arrive in New

York.

"Do you have money for the trip?" she asks, too excited to wait for his answer.

"Some, but not nearly as much as we will need. How about you?"

"The same."

"Then we will have to manage somehow."

"Hitchhiking?" she suggests, shaking again from another blast of excitement.

"Sounds exciting to me."

"They'll catch us, Sunny, I am sure of that! They'll catch us before we leave Denver!"

"Maybe."

"They'll take us back and lock us in our rooms and will no longer allow us to see each other!"

"Maybe. Maybe all this will happen. But is that a reason not to help your brother?"

"Do you really think so?"

"It doesn't matter what I think. It matters what you think. I'll be with you—always."

She thinks about the importance of what he said.

"Do you think he's innocent? Do you believe he didn't kill your father?"

"I don't know . . ." She is far, far from here, running with her brother on the streets of New York. And she is sure of one thing only: he cries for her forgiveness. *(I didn't want to do that, Rebecca. I'm so sorry.)* Nothing else matters, this is the only thing that counts. "I don't know that, Sunny, but I feel he needs me."

"Then go! Go find him. Help him. He's your *brother.*"

He's right. Michael is her brother, and nothing will change that. And no one in that damn world can force her to love him less for what he may have done.

She lost her father and shortly before that, her mother, too, and she won't allow herself to lose her brother. He is the only one she has now.

Besides Sunshine.

"Do you have a plan?" she asks.

* * *

Victor has no plan. To Michael, it seems as if he doesn't care about anything. He still has a cold, and he doesn't feel well. Michael has to do his best to persuade him to go out for a few hours and enjoy life a little, for a change.

His stomach back in shape, Michael treats himself to a beer (or two), which automatically improves his mood even more. He no longer cares that the representatives of the law are looking for him to capture him. Victor, on the other hand, is more realistic and doesn't share his enthusiasm, but still gives in to his persuasion. He takes a few aspirins, grits his teeth, and grabs his board. He lends his old skateboard to Michael and then they set off.

They roar through parts of the Upper East Side, Morningside Heights, and Harlem, as in the old days, when everything was more innocent and harmless. Then they extend their route to the Upper West Side, Central Park, and Theater District, doing stunts in the style of Rodney Mullen (especially Victor), which Michael welcomes with loud shouts. Although not successful as Victor, he also proves he hasn't forgotten to skate. He does a *bigspin kickflip* and then an *impossible* and a *double backfoot kickflip*, completely forgetting his worries and distancing himself from the problems that trouble him.

It's a little easier to handle his "exile" since Alien dyed his hair. Thanks to his new image, he can move a lot more freely, which proves useful when Brenda Travis takes a week off to stay at home and keep a close eye on her son. She doesn't care that Michael is Alien's best friend; she won't allow him to do something stupid that both may regret later.

Alien rebels against her decision and threatens to leave home and join Michael, if she doesn't change her mind. "Go ahead," Brenda Travis retorts, not impressed by his provocations, aware that her son wouldn't do such a thing if he really cares to help Michael. And Alien does just that. He comes to his senses and, though still offended, stays at home.

Brenda Travis no longer believes the story of Michael's alibi. When he first told her about that, she was terrified and horrified, succumbing to his perfect *acting*. It isn't until she thinks of everything that she realizes something is missing in his story. So, she decides to *press* Roy until he tells her everything. And she also has to talk to him and reprove him for using all of her hair bleach without asking her first!

Less than three hours later, Michael and Victor return to Victor's apartment. Still not completely healed, tired and spent all the way by skateboarding, Victor ends up in bed again. His cough is getting worse and his temperature is up again. Michael puts cold compresses on him and fills him with lemonade, plenty of hot tea, and antibiotics. He waits by his bed until he falls asleep, and then, also exhausted, lies down too. Too tired for anything.

Try as he might, he can't sleep. Too many voices yell at each other in his head; too many images flicker before his eyes, not allowing him to close his eyes.

He becomes nervous, so he gets out of bed and goes to the

toilet. When he comes back, he checks on Victor. Drenched with sweat (which is a good sign because his temperature is dropping again), he is breathing heavily, but is still asleep. Michael decides not to wake him.

He goes to the window and looks out at the street. The night is clear, and the sky is probably swimming in the stars. But Michael can only see the brightest ones. New York City lights have swallowed most of the stars this time too.

Drowning in that invisible, black sea, Michael's heart throbs, sending shivers through his body. Rebecca's scream echoes in his head, followed by a hysterical cry. It is terrifying to hear her cry like that, and Michael only now realizes how much he must have hurt her. Accident or not, Rebecca is suffering. Rebecca is in pain, fear, and agony, perhaps even greater than what he is going through. He can't stand it. He cannot live with the fact that his sister is suffering because of him. But what can he do to change that?

He is not going to walk into the police station and turn himself in, not until this mess is cleared up and everyone understands who the real victim is here. It is also out of the question to leave the country. Traps must be everywhere, and there is no safe way out of town. He doesn't mean to leave town, anyway. He is the safest here where he is. Like he has any other choice!

Thinking of his sister and looking at the void of black horizon, Michael's heart sinks into despair. He moves away from the window and slips back into the bed.

Before the restless sleep lays its heavy hands on him, a new sensation runs through his body. He sees the image of this same, though empty, window somewhere in the future, knowing that it will be a long time before he will look out of it again.

If ever . . .

He plans to leave in the morning. Although Victor still needs him, he cannot risk putting him in danger. He feels bad enough for having to leave a sick friend, but he has no choice. The world he lives in is so cruel.

As distant as the vision of an empty window and the world beyond it are also the last remnants of his *gift*. Despite this, he makes a gigantic effort to open his mind to his sister because he has a premonition she is also reaching out for him. His dying gift or intuition? All the same. That makes no difference to Michael. He keeps sending his thoughts to her, oblivious to the rest of the world lying in the cradle of darkness.

* * *

The next morning, Michael opens his eyes with the first light, but Victor is already up and taking a shower. When he is done, Michael takes his turn, and Victor returns to bed. His temperature had dropped, but he is still weak.

Michael makes an early breakfast and they eat it in silence. He puts the dishes in the dishwasher and goes shopping. The stores are just opening, and Michael is the first customer. At the grocery store he buys fresh fruit, three Vienna breads, a carton of milk, and juice—lots of juice. Then rushes to the pharmacy to get antibiotics. He supplies Victor with something to snack until Alien comes to check up on him. Michael doesn't know when he will come again. It can be later today, or in a few days.

He thanks Victor for everything and pockets the spare keys of his apartment into his Droors pants. Those are Nancy's keys that she had left when she left Victor. Apparently, she doesn't plan to return anytime soon, if she will return at all. They will come in handy for Michael because now he can get into the apartment, even if Victor isn't home.

Victor suggests that he takes his old skateboard, too, but Michael refuses. He can come back for it if he wants to skate. Now, he has the keys, right? No need to raise suspicion; the police might look for a boy with a skateboard.

He sprints down the stairs, skipping two steps at a time, and brakes to a stop when he erupts out on the street. Ponders for a moment which way to go. He was in Central Park yesterday, and he wouldn't mind seeing again a modern performance of William Shakespeare's tragedy *Romeo and Juliet*, which he liked a lot. But that won't be smart, will it?

The courage and daring that alcohol had poured in him last night melt this morning. Michael is again a lost, young man with no home and so many places to hide. Fleeing from the sins of the past, denying the present, and being a stranger to his future. Leaving a sick friend behind, leaving everything he has and had, and waiting for a miracle to happen. When will he see Victor again? What will the future bring to the two of them?

(Cold is the world we are living in . . . And it doesn't care much.)

He consults his wristwatch how much time he has before calling Alien at their pay phone. It'll be a call at noon. Until then, anything can happen. He just has to be careful not to get caught. Time works in his favor, but one day he will have to stop running. Guilty or innocent, he will have to face justice. The verdict he will get depends on two of his friends and whether or not they will succeed.

With almost four hours left, Michael heads south. New Brooklyn seems as good to him as any other place under the sun.

Chapter

24th: . . . degrees as your body rotates 180 degrees), while the difference is in flipping your board so that it flip rotates too. To do the *double backfoot kickflip*, first do the *ollie*. Then level out your board and flip the tail with your back foot.
All good? We still have to do the *fakie*. Without much . . .

THEY ARE ONE STEP BEHIND HIM, but luckily on the right track. It's only hours, a day at worst, when they will have him, Dawson thinks. Michael is still one jump on the skateboard ahead of them, but with less and less space to run. The circle around him is closing, and Dawson is increasingly convinced that they are breathing down the neck of the right culprit.

To paraphrase it, the whole city is on its feet. Everyone involved in any way with the case is searching for Michael Daniels. The information Michael possesses (or may keep inside of him) is of national importance. If it were not so, Dawson is further thinking, Fletcher would not have sent two teams on this mission, nor would the entire NYPD be alerted. She doesn't know if anyone else is involved in the investigation, but she wouldn't be surprised if that is the case. Hank Daniels and Neil Beresford are very *important* names, and working in such conditions is almost impossible. Especially in the presence of media praying for their piece of cake.

Apart from public pressure, things are heating up at the Institute too. Rumors circulate that Beresford and Daniels were working on a secret project for the government or a secret organization. Whatever the case, the phones at the Roosevelt Island Research Institute don't stop ringing, and many of them come from DC.

Even though Dawson knows what activities caused the deaths of Beresford and Daniels, she doesn't buy Morgan's explanation that the two were researching genetically modified drugs that would suppress and prevent AIDS. They didn't actually work on a *cure* for HIV-infected people, but their discovery would be a giant leap toward complete victory over a vicious disease if they were to succeed.

She is more inclined toward a theory that Beresford and Daniels worked on some medicine or drugs, but not to be used for medical purposes. Their main preoccupation was finding a cure (or some types of drugs) that will help people raise their awareness to extreme heights, the majority of social stratum, burdened with everyday problems, have no time to even consider. These experimental drugs are used on pre-teens, who are trained to challenge, manipulate, and control their new abilities. To what purpose, why, and against whom—Dawson doesn't know. Is it a new future of mankind created in the laboratories of the Roosevelt Island Research Institute? Or is it just another in a series of secret labs where a new type of perfect weapon is worked on: a soldier, a common man from our neighborhood?

Is *Michael Daniels* the prototype of that perfect soldier in the dawning of the genetic warfare of planetary dimensions? She indulges in her imagination so much that she sounds like Fox to herself.

But she isn't Fox, so she doesn't resort to chewing Juicy Fruit to improve her concentration when something big appears in front of her. She has no secret powers or abilities or sixth sense to help her solve the case she's working on. But that's why she *has* an above-average high intelligence quotient, a stubborn tenacity to persevere through the end, and guts like a man—as Fox would say.

Combining the three, she comes to the following conclusion: the fact (not the premonition) is that she spoke to Victor Kenneth at his apartment twenty-eight minutes ago. The guy has a bug, but his health is improving. Despite his exhaustion, fatigue, vitamin deficiency, and weight loss, Victor was surprisingly ready to talk to her, even though he had been interviewed by two FBI agents, some fifty minutes before she arrived.

Yes, he reaffirms, seeing her bewildered look, two, early-thirtyish men in expensive, dark Armani suits—a hulk with a shaved head and his spooky, skinny partner with neatly trimmed, short, black hair and dark, pencil-thin mustache, who seemed a little intimidating. The hulk introduced himself as Casper Dillon, Victor recalls, and he has a nasty scar on the left side of his neck. Probably a knife cut. He forgot the name of the skinny one; his last name could be Haim or Ames or something. This guy has an ugly habit of swallowing syllables and no visible marks to identify him. Fortunately, Dillon did most of the talking.

Victor furrows his brows while answering her next question. They inquired about Michael. They were not only interested in his whereabouts, they also asked him a whole series of weird questions. Victor told them the same thing he answered Dawson forty minutes later: he saw him on the day of the murder, but not only saw him—he *was* with him. The three of them—Michael, Alien, and Victor—were skurfing together *all* afternoon and early evening. So it wasn't strange Michael wasn't home when Hank was killed, because he was with them! Victor was sorry he couldn't name anyone to confirm that. No salesmen, no greengrocers, no waiters; they carried their food and drink with them in their backpacks. Considering that Michael was in no mood for a bigger crowd, they were just the three of them. Agent Dawson would have to take his word for it because there was no way she could check it.

"Then why is he hiding from the police, if he was with you? He has an alibi, if you are telling the truth."

"You will have to ask him that. Maybe he doesn't trust the police? Maybe he thinks they already found him guilty? You know better than I do."

"To indict someone, we need evidence. We don't work like that."

"Do you have evidence? Do you have something to press charges against him?"

"You should know better than to ask that."

"Sure, you cannot talk about an ongoing investigation. But let me tell you something. You think you have evidence because you found his fingerprints? You think you have evidence just because Michael is hiding and doesn't want to talk to you? Well, ma'am, you're wrong. You're dead wrong. Michael *didn't* kill his father. Michael is as innocent as a lamb, and you better figure this out before someone gets hurt again."

"We also want to close this case as soon as possible. It's also in Michael's interest that we find the killer as soon as possible."

"Maybe so, but it's more in your interest. Personally, I don't give a crap about this circus. But I care about Michael and I want him to start living normally again. If there is anything I can do to speed it up, I'm ready to cooperate with you. Anytime, anyhow, just say it."

When she was done with him, Dawson calls her partner to check out if he knows anything about the backup duo the Bureau had assigned to work with them on the case.

* * *

He'll be damned if he knows anything about it, Fox answers her, but he'll ask Fletcher when he gets off the phone. He is in his office, because a murder eyewitness popped up. Also, about forty minutes ago, just as he was on his way to where Juanita Dolores lives, Merchant called him from there. Merchant confirms that the two agents, Dawson inquired about, had already visited Juanita Dolores, but they don't belong to the FBI New York. Hence, Fletcher finds himself talking to Washington, DC to find out who sent them without first informing him of their arrival.

"A lot has happened in the last two hours," Fox concludes. "Things have started to unravel."

"Fox, I'd like to ask you again, do you still think Michael is innocent?"

She hears him take a deep breath on the other end of the line.

"I don't know what to tell you, Dawson. Not with this eyewitness who appeared. When I first heard about him, I was convinced you were right. But then I saw her, and you told me about our mysterious colleagues . . . I'm not sure anymore. One thing is certain, though. If Michael is to blame for the death of his stepfather, I don't think he is the only one to whom credit goes. More and more I get the impression that someone else is pulling the strings here."

"Do you suspect Morgan?"

"Maybe. I wish I knew that for sure. The time has come when we get some real answers."

"Interesting. Victor told me something like that a few minutes ago."

Fox breathes out into the receiver. "Did he? What else did he tell you?"

"Nothing we already didn't suspect by ourselves. Except he gave Michael an alibi."

"Excuse me?!"

"According to him, the three of them—Michael, Alien, and Victor—were skating together around the town at the time of the murder. They didn't leave each other's sight."

"And, I presume," Fox adds cynically, "no one can confirm if he's telling the truth." Not waiting for her to tell him he is right, he continues, "Correct me if I'm wrong, but this Alien kid is popping out everywhere. Like we're looking for him and not Michael. I think we'll have to put the screws on Roy to sort things out. The kid is self-confident, but something tells me he might have a lot of interesting things to say to us if he makes a little effort."

"You want me to visit him? I'm done with Kenneth, and I don't have much to do right now."

"I'd prefer to meet you at Juanita Dolores's." He gives her the address. "We'll go together to see him when we're done with her. Unless the invisible two don't get ahead of us again."

"Right. See you there, then."

"If you get there before me, hold Merchant till I come. I need to talk to him about this eyewitness."

"One witness gives him an alibi, the other one refutes it. Which one is telling the truth?"

"I can't answer that right now. Fletcher is coming back, so I'll talk to you later."

"Got it," she says. "And don't forget to tell him that those two FBI guys are thorough at digging in someone's dirty laundry."

"Why do I have a hunch he won't like your information?"

"Because it's you."

* * *

Although he was looking for them, Alien was surprised to come across Agent Fox. The collision with him was strong and sudden, and Alien would have fallen had Fox not grabbed him. Alien only managed to mutter, "Ugh."

Alien recalls that Fox then asks him, "Looking for me?" and he replies, "Actually, yes."

Fox casts an I-told-you-so look at his partner, and she returns him the same you-told-me-so look instead of answering.

Only then does he release Alien and say, "I think it would be best if we sat down and had a chat."

"I'm sorry, but I can't. I have to go back to the store. I only have a little time."

"Then let's take a walk?" Dawson suggests, and that's more acceptable to Alien.

"But just a short one. I don't want the guys to see me with

you."

They set off and Alien explains to them.

"I couldn't tell you at the store, but I think you should know. It may be relevant to your investigation."

"I'm listening," Fox encourages him to carry on.

"You do understand I couldn't talk about this in front of the others? Someone could tell Alien and he would avoid me then. And that wouldn't benefit Michael. No, sir."

"What wouldn't benefit him?" Dawson asks.

"If Alien got scared, he might not want to testify for Michael."

FBI agents exchange glances.

"You probably didn't know, but Michael has an alibi for that day. He wasn't alone when the murder happened. More precisely, he was nowhere near his home. Alien told me he was with him."

"Can you prove that?" Fox wants to know.

Alien turns around to look for familiar faces, but there is no one in sight.

"I can't. You'll have to trust me. Of course, that's your decision."

Not impressing them much with that answer, Alien tries to fix it.

"Maybe I could talk to him one more time and get him to meet you? Whaddya say?"

"That won't be enough," Fox replies. "If Michael is innocent, it's in his best interest to have Alien talk to us."

Alien shakes his head no.

"I have to prepare him first. Alien doesn't want to deal with the police. Nothing personal, no offense."

"We're not the police," Dawson corrects him.

"Whatever. Look, this is what we'll do. I have to go back now, and you give me a few hours to talk to him. Then I'll let you know how it went. But I can't promise anything. Fair enough?"

"Better be sure to tell him he's committing a felony if he's holding back something from us." Fox hands him his business card. Dawson had exchanged phone numbers with him earlier in the store. "You can reach me here. Don't hesitate to call me. *Anytime.*"

"Thanks. I'll do that." He hurries away, and the next minute the crowd swallows him.

He pulls his cell phone from his pants and calls Victor's number. Victor didn't leave his apartment, so he asks Alien to bring him shaving gel and some food of his choice. He is tired of soups and teas. Alien promises to take care of it, then adds, "Vic, it's time. Do you think you can step into a scene, or do you want me to stall a little longer?"

"You spoke to them?"

"I threw the bait, and they swallowed it."

"Good. Don't stall anymore. Let them come. I'll make a statement."

"Thanks, man. Sorry again for dragging you into this, but I don't know what else to do."

"Don't be silly. Just stick to our plan and in two or three weeks the three of us will laugh at all this."

Eighty minutes later, he makes a call to Agent Fox, whom he finds at lunch.

"Never mind," Fox assures him that everything is fine when Alien starts to apologize, suggesting to call him later. "We're almost done anyway. You have something for us?"

"I talked to Alien. I think I have something that might

interest you."

"So fast?" Fox winks at his partner. Something was going too smoothly here. "Didn't you say he went to Riverdale?"

"He changed his mind. He stopped by the skate shop first."

"When can we see him?" Fox gets to the point.

"I'm sorry to tell you this, but I'm afraid you can't talk to him yet. He wants to be in touch with you only through me. He has had some unpleasant experiences with authorities in the past, so—"

"And he might have them in the future if he continues to obstruct the investigation," Fox interrupts him, becoming more serious.

"I know, I know. I explained it all to him, but he will take his chances. He doesn't want to obstruct the investigation; he just doesn't want to meet you. But he's ready to cooperate because of Michael."

"But only through you, Roy, right?" Fox concludes. "I'm not sure if we can agree to that. Tell your friend you don't set conditions with the FBI. Even better, you give us his address and we forget the whole thing."

"I . . . I can't do that. I'm sorry, I promised him. I can give you the name of someone else who is ready to talk to you, if you want. He's also Michael's friend. His name is Victor Kenneth . . ."

* * *

"What a coincidence!" Dawson comments after her partner hangs up.

"Just when we were about to visit him," Fox adds.

"I wonder what *he* has to say to us?"

"Maybe he wants to give him an alibi?" Fox says, joking. "Or maybe he'll take us to Alien. We'll find that out soon."

They don't get too far when Fox's phone rings again. Dawson gives him a curious look. "Roy again?"

Fox grins. "Could be."

Less than two minutes later, Fox hangs up again. With a straight face, he says briefly, "Fletcher. Wants me urgently back in HQ."

He glances at her. "You go ahead as planned, okay? Visit Kenneth and call me when you're done with him. By then we'll know what to do next."

She nods in agreement with his proposal and fishes the car keys out of her pocket. "Who will do the walking?"

"You take the car. I'll take a taxi."

He does as he says.

* * *

She thought she would get to East 11th Street much faster, but the traffic is so dense—a total gridlock—and it takes her almost an hour to cross those thirty streets. When she finally arrives, Fox is already waiting for her, and Merchant is getting ready to leave.

Juanita Dolores is still very excited and upset. Neither government forces could calm her down. Dawson had never seen her before, but she instantly recognizes the corpulent woman dominating between her three daughters and the bunch of grandkids. All of them have gathered here to give her support in these difficult times.

"I telling you, young Daniels looking for devil, one day he find devil. Now I find him too. Because young Daniels not want listen to me."

Giving her a tired smile, Merchant greets Dawson on his departure. "I've been listening to this for more than half an hour. If I stay a minute longer, I'm done for. This woman sucked the life out of me. If you get lucky, give me a call."

"Of course, Sergeant." Dawson smiles back at him and joins forces with Fox dancing around Juanita Dolores with the enthusiasm of a newcomer.

"What else do you know? Can Michael be held responsible for his father's death? Did he provoke him with something?"

"What idea!" Juanita Dolores is astounded. "Young Daniels good boy. He never do something like that! Never! Young Daniels can not kill. He very nice boy. Good-behaved boy. Polite. He not kill his *padre*."

"You said he was looking for troubles? What kind of troubles?" Fox isn't giving up yet.

"He looking troubles with board! That kind of troubles!"

Fox gasps in surprise, while Dawson gives a laugh in her sleeve.

"With the board??" (Or maybe he is going to give up, after all.)

"Everything begins when he crack his board. Bad omen—I tell you. Bad omen. Young Daniels very unhappy because that. Very unhappy without his board. Either he ask his *padre* for money or he not see Europa!"

"Michael asked his father to give him money?" His interest returns. Maybe she isn't a hopeless case as he thought at first.

"*Si*. He ask, but not get. Old Daniels not want hear about that. Young Daniels very unhappy. Young Daniels leave his *casa*."

Dawson and Fox exchange glances. This is something new.

Neither Fletcher nor Merchant have any information about Michael's escape from home. Fox's patience is rewarded.

"When did it happen? Can you remember exactly when Michael left home?"

"Some days before death. *Tres* maybe, I not remember."

"Did he return home after that? Did you see him coming home?"

"No. I not see young Daniels. I only hear when he call. He want to come to make peace with his *padre*. I always be in fear for him. Where he is. What happen to him . . ."

"Mrs. Dolores, please, listen to me carefully. This is very important. Try to remember. Did Michael return home to make peace with his father? Did the two meet before Hank Daniels was killed?"

"That I not know. . . . I not there. No one talk with me. Old Daniels tell me I must not tell anybody. I must be silent. . . . He order to me."

"What did he forbid you? What were you not allowed to tell anyone? That they had a fight? Or that Michael left his home?"

"*Sí, sí*, both. He drink very *mucho*. And when he drink, he be very bad. . . . I worry so much for young Daniels. . . . That very hard, Agent Fox. That very hard for me."

"How do you know all this? Did Michael tell you he had a fight with his father? He told you that Hank didn't want to give him the money?"

"I maybe not speak English good, but I not blind! Someone has take care of him since his *madre* die. I his *secondo madre*," she starts to cry. Her words are hard to make out through tears. "Everything begins with that board. Damned board guilty for everything!" She makes the sign of the cross for letting out the curse.

Alarmed by her tears, her family surrounds her.

Fox and Dawson quietly retreat. She told them everything she knew. She is drained, and Fox doesn't want to bother her anymore.

Descending from the ice-blue sky, the sun is warming East 111th Street. It's finally too warm for coats, so Fox slips out of his raincoat and carries it over his arm.

"Everything begins with that board, Fox. Too bad she didn't warn you before you bought those shoes at Supreme," Dawson teases him. "I hope *you* not look for devil."

She makes him laugh and is glad about that. He is tired and needs something to relax him. Too bad she cannot do more than that for him. Perhaps take him in her arms and hold him like a little boy before she tucks him in to sleep. Once, many years ago, she did something similar and later regretted it. She was an inexperienced girl at the time, but matured very quickly and in a rather crude and cruel way. The young man she was comforting got it all wrong. They made love, even fell in love with each other, but when she told him she was expecting his baby, he disappeared from her life. Like she had never existed. She almost took her baby's and her life when her wealthy, but conservative parents gave her money for an abortion and threw her out of the house as a family disgrace. She killed her child, and with it the best part of herself. To stop thinking about the home they left her without, she applied to the Police Academy and started a new life among the men she hated so much. This time, however, she was smarter, and she built a high wall around her that protected her so they could never hurt her again. Oh, how she despised their vulgar jokes, flirtations, and stupid laughter. How she hated everything about them. But she beat them all, thus defeating her past, until she had the grace to meet a man who differed completely from the others, the man of her girl's dreams, her Prince Charming, who had embodied himself in her partner.

Shay Fox doesn't react to her joke and says, "It looks like our Michael has gotten into the habit of running away from home."

"Provided he returned home after he first escaped and before Hank was killed," she corrects him.

"I didn't know you took his side. When did that happen?" He looks at her.

"I didn't take anybody's side. I am just more open to other options," she says, not acknowledging that she hates Hank now even more than when they were just starting to work on the case. "What's new with your witness?" she says, changing the subject.

On their way to Patchin Place, Fox tells her about an elderly woman walking a dog when she saw a young man walking out of the building where the Danielses lived. As she thought the case was closed, she didn't inform the police before, but then saw Michael's picture in the news. She thinks it was Michael, though she couldn't give his exact description when Fletcher asked her. She was too far away, the man was too fast, and her sight didn't serve her best. Fletcher nevertheless promised her he would summon her for identification when they brought Michael in.

"That's our eyewitness," Fox concludes.

Dawson says nothing. She is too confused, and her premonition that something is wrong is growing stronger. The premonition that something is *very* wrong.

Fox continues, "Fletcher talked to Washington, and they

also know nothing about the other agents. Somebody else is conducting the investigation passing themselves off as the FBI."

"Anything else?"

There is sarcasm in her tone, but Fox cannot blame her for being sarcastic.

"Actually, there is. But it's more a premonition than something I can say for certain."

She looks at him. The dance of the sunbeams on her face.

"Tell me."

"I think this case will be closed soon, with or without Michael."

"But they can't do that!" she protests, frightened by her own reaction, which leaves Fox as calm as if he has expected it.

"They can if they think they have enough evidence. Once they find him guilty, who will reopen the investigation? Michael? His sister? His grandparents? This case needs a scapegoat, and Michael is best suited for the role."

"And there is nothing we can do to prevent it!"

"Maybe there is. If we find Michael and get him to talk to us before someone else comes to him who won't have so much understanding."

"Then what do we do?"

"We will visit Roy and take the burden off his back. He is dying to give us the answers we are looking for—I can feel it. If we persuade him to put the key in the right keyhole, everything else will fall into place."

Chapter

25th: . . . explanation, the *fakie* is riding backward. Let's summarize everything now. You can do *ollies, kickflips* and *heelflips* either on the flat or on objects and obstacles, you can *grind* them, *slide* them—anything. You can *nollie* them, or ride them *fakie, switch,* or *regular.* There are many . . .

FEAR GROWS IN MICHAEL like an impending tidal wave. The smoldering spark of restlessness turns into a gentle flame, which first flickers and then flares up.

Hank was right; it hurts Michael more than anything. Michael himself is to be blamed because he allowed him to be right.

(How did he not see it? How did he not sense it? How did he not suspect?)

Well, he suspected something on several occasions when strange things began to happen to him, but he has never suspected that Hank could be the cause. Hank was capable of anything—Michael knows that better than anyone—but he still didn't believe Hank could go that far. This is too much even for Hank.

Hank played with Michael's trust; Hank betrayed him. Hank did something a normal person wouldn't think of, let alone do. Hank did something terrible, and that's why he had to pay.

He took Michael's innocence, humiliated him—many times, beat him, lied to him, and more than once made his wounds bleed as he wept quietly in the solitude of his room. Hank had to pay for humiliation and disgrace; for all this he had to pay.

And he paid for everything. He faced the music, for all his sins and all his crimes. But in the end the price is a little too high, even for him. One blow too many cost him his life and deprived Michael of his freedom.

And maybe his life too.

Because Hank's blood is screaming for revenge.

Michael didn't want to kill Hank. He only wanted to bring him to his senses, but Hank wasn't ready for that. No, he wasn't ready to cooperate. He was *unreasonable*, deaf to Michael's pleading and cries, blind to his son's tears. Hank had a goal in front of him and no one in the world could do anything to divert him from it. Michael tried, and that's why he is now on Coney Island, fleeing from the law. Before he even knew what happened, he becomes a renegade.

Hank wanted to beat the hell out of him again, rape him, and force him into something Michael didn't want.

So Hank reaches for him and STARTS to choke him and Michael ALMOST loses consciousness BUT then he sees his HAND moving of its FREE WILL and grabbing SOMETHING grabbing an ASHTRAY and hitting Hank with it hitting him HARD once twice MANY TIMES until Hank's GRIP loosens and Michael RUNS away.

That's all he can recall, that's all his gray cells memorized. The vision of Michael the killer symbolized by the whirlwind disappears with Hank, erased from Michael's memory, forever. Had he still been alive, Neil Beresford might have drawn some conclusions from all this through therapy. But he is also dead. Good old Beresford won't help him anymore. Michael saw his picture next to Hank's in the newspaper and so he finds out about his death. Although Beresford is no less guilty than Hank of Michael's miserable situation, Michael feels sorry for the man.

Deep down, Michael believes that Beresford wanted to help him and be his friend. But Michael wouldn't let him. That's why he is now wandering down Neptune Avenue with-out a single, almighty dollar in his pocket. Because he was too smart to listen to others.

The pain tears his knee as if someone is driving a nail into it. His abdomen suffered many kicks, and his stomach sounds vomiting alerts. False alerts, though, because Michael threw up what he had.

Several delinquents gave him a licking at the corner of Surf Avenue and West 23rd Street, emptying his pockets' contents.

Michael could blame this on his father and his sick idea of making him a superhuman. Because of his stupid urge to play God, Michael loses faith in the Maker. For a moment, however, he regains his faith when he discovers his *gift*. For a while, Michael believed that God had given it to him. How wrong he was! Dear God doesn't care the least about him. To Him, he is worthless, like a grain of dust, and the universe is so large. Somewhere in its vast expense, there must be creatures more worthy of His attention, love, and compassion than Michael.

Because otherwise all that wouldn't have happened to him. Having this in mind, Michael decides that God no longer exists for him.

He dies the same day Hank Daniels dies.

Michael kills Him with a blow that beats Hank to death, which results in Neil Beresford's death.

Hank's death ruins Michael's life, paving it with corpses. Wherever he places his foot, he leaves behind a bloody footprint, marking the trail for his pursuers to find him.

If it weren't for Alien and Victor, Michael would have already stopped running and turned himself in. They are the ones who keep his hope alive, though he doesn't have the slightest idea how they intend to prove his innocence since he is guilty. Since he killed Hank.

Anyway, he's too tired to bother himself with that now. Tired of life, tired of hiding and waiting, his morale is very low. He has had enough of his life on the streets, restaurants and various diners, and enough of secretly watching skateboarders and inline skaters, envious of their freedom.

Wrapped in black thoughts, he remembers his mother. She is closest to him now, because never has he smelled death so intensely as he does now. If only he could visit her and talk to her briefly. . . . Alien explicitly ordered him to stay out of places where an ambush might wait for him. Melanie Hope's grave is a critical zone.

His animal instinct for self-preservation wins, and Michael clings to his dear life again.

He cannot visit his mother, but no one is stopping him from looking with his mind's eye for his father—the real, biological one. Michael has no memories of Larry; he disappeared when Michael was only eighteen months old. When his mother remarried two years later, Michael took his stepfather's last name, and newspaper clippings, photos, and video footage remain his only link to Larry Cohen.

The mission to Mars led by his father failed, but his name and the names of the others from the Roswell crew remain remembered to this day. A year later, a new Roswell 2 mission was launched in a carefully planned attempt to rescue the survivors, but it failed to reach its destination because of a mechanical failure on the spacecraft. Only in the second attempt did Roswell 2 land on the desolate surface of Mars. But the bodies were never found. The secret still lives among those who look at the sky, sparking their imagination.

Not Michael's, though. Not anymore. Michael has long ago ceased to be interested in how his father died. What still bugs him is the question of what would have happened if his father stayed on Earth that morning. Michael's mother would not then marry Hank and die of the viral pneumonia she had caught while exploring Peruvian excavations. She would still be with them and Michael would not go to visit her at Woodlawn Cemetery. He wouldn't have met Neil Beresford and fallen victim to a conspiracy. Nor would he have killed Hank and be on the run now. Instead of that,

MICHAEL WOULD BE HAPPY.

He would be with Rebecca, following her on his skateboard as she inline skates along Park Drive and then passes The Band Shell and further east into Central Park before climbing Andy's Hill. The images flash faster than he can recognize them.

If Larry were still alive, they wouldn't have been separated and Rebecca wouldn't hate him for what he did. BECAUSE REBECCA WOULDN'T EXIST THEN.

Yeah, right! Rebecca would exist, Michael is sure of that,

except she would be called differently. But it would be her, his baby sister.

Slowly advancing to Old Brooklyn Bridge, Michael stops for a moment in Joralemon Street, where he catches sight of a billboard depicting a skateboarder kissing his girlfriend somewhere in Midtown New Manhattan. The girl is standing on his skateboard, her hair braided in two blue braids, and she is wearing a tight, yellow T-shirt that stretches to her navel, and a silver miniskirt. She pulls up the skater's dark-blue T-shirt, exposing his Dennis Kay boxer shorts. The traffic is in total collapse, and a mounted policeman in a hurry struggles his way toward them, waving a truncheon at them to move away and blowing the hell out of his whistle. But the boy and the girl, Alien and Laurie, pay no attention to him. *You don't need any protection—except for Dennis Kay men's underwear.*

Michael feels a lump in his throat and his eyes moisten. Life is all around him and everyone is entitled to it . . . except him.

He pulls himself together. Soon he will talk to Alien. Until then, he must endure. But first he should eat something. With no money for even some chewing gum, he prepares himself for sponging again.

The first passerby doesn't even stop to look at him. Michael lets a young couple madly in love and oblivious to the world around them to pass him by, as well as an angry guy looking for trouble and an elderly lady who drags a worn, wheeled shopping trolley behind her, and then approaches a dressy woman in her late thirties wearing heavy makeup. He puts his best smile on, and she smiles back at him.

* * *

Alien takes every precaution that no one follows him to Victor's apartment.

He finds Victor in his favorite armchair, screwing the truck on the skateboard. In front of him a table that chokes under the weight of scattered magazines, dirty glasses, and plates with the cold remnants of something that looks like food. Nancy's absence is felt in every corner, on the dirty windows and in the kitchen where a heap of unwashed dishes waits. Several layers of dust cover everything, including Victor's expensive Aiwa stereo.

Alien takes the groceries to the kitchen and then returns to the living room and sinks into a big reclining chair opposite to Victor. He thinks about playing some music, but he changes his mind, not much in the mood to listen to D-Mand today.

"I had to do something," Victor explains to him. "I couldn't just lie in bed anymore, watch TV, and do nothing."

"I can see that. Getting ready to skate?"

"If I fix this baby."

"Why don't you buy a new board?"

"For sentimental reasons. We're still head over heels in love."

"I heard from Michael. He sounded depressed."

"I don't blame him."

"You don't look much better, either."

Victor stops working on the board and gives him a long look.

"Sorry. It was stupid. Forget I said it."

"What does he say?"

"He is considering turning himself in. He can't take it anymore. I barely persuaded him not to do anything until I call him after talking to you."

"It means we have to do something to get things going."

"Any idea?"

"I have one, but I'd rather not talk about it yet. It's just an idea. It might turn out to be a bad one."

Alien shrugs his shoulders. "As you wish. Just tell me in time."

"Of course," Victor says, a shadow of concern flitting over his eyes.

"Do you have any news from Nancy?" Alien asks.

"Nothing yet. Did you buy the shaving gel?"

"I put everything you ordered in the kitchen. Speaking of the kitchen, when do you mean to clean up this garbage? This place is total chaos. Tell me which day suits you and I'll come help you."

"Can we talk about it later?" He drops the skateboard to the floor. "I appreciate your offer."

"No biggie. Hey, how did it go with the FBI?"

"With that Dawson chick, pretty good. But I didn't like the other two."

"*What* other two?"

"I thought you would have no idea about them."

"About whom?! What are you talking about?"

"Relax, Alien. I didn't tell them anything. Things are still somewhat under control."

"Under control? With four FBI agents—two, whole teams!—who work together to find Michael? I wouldn't agree with that! What the hell was Fox doing if he wasn't with her?"

"I don't know. But I know Michael is in bigger trouble than we thought. Especially if those two aren't the FBI."

"Holy cow! What do we do now? I can still handle Fox and Dawson, but with two others more, I'm afraid that's too much for me."

"We stick to our plan, that's what we do. I'll think of something. In the meantime, talk to Fox and Dawson. Maybe they will know something that might help us, though I doubt it. It surprised Dawson when I told her about the other two agents."

"I like this less and less, Vic. I have to be honest, I don't like this at all."

"We should have expected this when the three of us decided to mess with the FBI and the police. To put it mildly, it was daring. And now there is someone else in the game. I believe you realize it's the two of us left now, because we can no longer count on Michael."

"Yeah, I do. So what's your idea? How do we get out of it?"

Victor doesn't answer him immediately. He sits like that for a while, just sitting and thinking. Somewhere he heard that the first time is the hardest. And it's much easier next time. Almost as easy as breathing. But is it really so? What if he's wrong, and no one believes him? What if he makes things even worse?

He looks at his friend, trying to fathom what he will say if he tells him about his plan. He thinks he already knows the answer, so he decides to tell him nothing unless he figures it out by himself.

"Listen, Alien, I feel like having pizza. Let's reason it out over dinner?"

"No problem. If we have anything to reason out."

* * *

"Do I know you?"

"I don't think so. I don't think we've met before."

The woman smiles at him again.

"It doesn't matter now, does it?"

Michael smiles back at her, not knowing how to ask her.

"You need money?"

She is straightforward and makes Michael uncomfortable. She penetrates his soul through his eyes. Seeing everything.

"If you have any change . . ." he replies reluctantly.

"Come with me. My car is on Remsen Street. Denver-blue Ford Taurus. Follow me, but not too close," she gives him brief instructions and, not waiting for his reply, sets off.

At first, Michael doesn't know what to think, much less how to act. While he is hesitating to follow her or not, the woman disappears. More driven by his instinct than his own will, he hurries after her.

The engine is already running, and when he reaches for the passenger door, she instructs him again, "To the back seat."

Michael listens to her and climbs into the back seat as he is told.

The woman adjusts a rearview mirror and joins the traffic, taking the route to New Manhattan Bridge.

I'm coming home, Michael thinks.

"You can turn it on," she says, alluding to the small screen in the back of her seat, connected to the computer on the dashboard. "It will take a little while to get where we are going to."

Michael listens to her again and after a few seconds immerses himself in *Riven* fantasy world.

"You have beautiful eyes." She looks at him in the rearview mirror.

Michael meets her gaze; the colors from the screen play their own game on his face.

"Thank you."

"You're welcome!"

He is in *Riven* again when she speaks to him for a second time, "You remind me of someone."

"It's possible. People keep telling me that."

She looks at him once more. "How is it going? Are you scoring anything?"

"Not bad. This is a good game."

They cross the New Manhattan Bridge and turn toward the Lower East Side.

"What's your name?"

"Mike."

"I like you, Mike."

"Thank you," he mutters in a quiet voice.

The woman lights a cigarette, waiting for the green light.

"Do you like me too?"

Michael switches off the game. She is taking a turn onto Park Avenue.

"You are pretty."

She smiles. "That's good. That's very good. Are you hungry?"

Yorkville is approaching them.

"A little," he admits.

"Do you like Italian cuisine?"

"I'm not too picky."

"Fine. I like simple men." She turns around. Waiting for the traffic jam to clear, she reaches out for his Zoo York baseball cap. "Practice truth. Fear nothing," she reads from a label on the inside of Victor's cap. "Do you *always* practice truth?" she asks, teasing him.

"Well, mostly . . ."

The woman laughs. "You don't have to answer me! I didn't

mean it seriously. But I like your cap. Can I keep it?"

"Uh, the cap isn't mine. A friend lent it to me—"

"Never mind, Mikey! I was just kidding!" She fixes the cap back onto his head. "You don't have to take my every word seriously. Besides, it's not the cap I'm interested in."

Then she turns back in her seat and stubs out the cigarette. They are moving again and minutes later she parks the Ford Taurus on East 89th Street.

Near the street where Victor lives. Painfully close and yet so far away.

* * *

"What do you do except go to school?"

Michael swallows the mouthful of spaghetti topped with sweet basil sauce before replying, "I skate and write poetry a little."

"You don't say! That must be exciting!" she exclaims.

"What? Skateboarding or writing poetry?"

"Both! Will you dedicate one of your poems to me?"

"Maybe." He grins. "All right."

"Oh dear, I cannot believe I have a poet here. You'll recite some of your poems later, won't you, cutie?"

Michael coughs in mid-bite. *(Cutie?!)*

"Well, if I have to . . ."

"Of course you have to! Don't even try to argue with me about that. Remember, I *always* get what I want."

"Really?" Suddenly, he has trouble breathing.

"Be patient and you'll see. Tell me, who is your Number One Poet? You have a Number One Poet considering you writing poetry, don't you?"

"Sure. I think Rimbaud is awesome. He's totally cool."

"So the Europeans interest you? I adore Whitman. Did you know Rimbaud was homosexual?"

"I've heard, watched, and read about his relationship with Verlaine, but I don't think he was gay. People like to make things up."

"You're right about that." She eyes him above the rim of her glass. Red wine shimmers in it like sacrificed blood. "What about you? Are you gay, or do you prefer women?"

"I have nothing against women. I just let everything come in its own time."

She doesn't understand the message. Or maybe she doesn't *want* to.

She reaches out her hand to him and says, "Come. We'll finish the dessert in my room. I want to show you something."

Michael looks around. "What's for dessert?"

"Apricot ice cream," she retorts, drawing him closer. "You smell nice." Without a warning, she peels his T-shirt off and breathes in the smell of his freshly bathed neck.

"It's shampoo."

She drags him to the bedroom, sits him down on a large double bed and kneels in front of him.

"How did you like your lunch?" she purrs like a cat.

"It was . . . excellent!"

She unbuttons his pants and works her hand through his fly.

"Am I a good cook?"

"The best . . ."

"I don't know about you, but I'm crazy about apricots," she murmurs and takes him in her hand, and he can do nothing to stop her. She thrusts her tongue into his mouth and releases him from his pants. Tosses his boxer shorts into the corner of the room and climbs on top of him.

No doubt, she's a good cook, but she's just as crazy about apricots. Any normal man would appreciate, with the knowledge of a gourmand, her obsession with this fruit. Any normal guy, which Michael isn't.

(*Irma . . . Irma, forgive me.*)

He wants so much to be a *normal* guy—he doesn't want to *pretend* to be normal, but *tries* to be normal, doing his best.

(*I'm sorry, Irma. I'm sorry about everything . . .*)

Giving more than he could, but to no avail.

Michael fails. He cannot do it.

He cries, aware that everything is over. His hopes sink like ships with broken masts. No more self-deception. No more pretending. He will never again be happy with a woman because they have taken it away from him.

Mad with passion and lost in ecstasy, the woman keeps reaching for him and trying for him. And then she stops too.

Then it all stops.

What to say to her silent gaze, shaken by surprise, disappointment, a sense of deceit, and the accusation of a rejected woman? How will he explain that it's not her fault? Why didn't he tell her before she made a fool of herself? WHY?

"I'm sorry . . ." He crawls out of her embrace and grabs his boxer shorts. He jumps awkwardly into them.

"*Who* is Irma?"

And another rush of pain. Her eyes demand an answer, not accepting silence or lies.

"Irma is . . . my girlfriend. My ex-girlfriend."

His voice cracks and he turns away from her.

"What happened?" her voice is soft, almost motherly.

"What happened, Mikey?"

This confuses him. And scares him a little.

He expected her to slap him and punish him for embarrassing her, torment him with a torrent of derogatory words of condemnation, *Incompetent! Impotent! Fairy!* Humiliate him and finish him off. Instead, she comes to him, puts her arms around him, and comforts him as he cries.

"What happened, Mikey? Everything . . . tell me everything!"

And he tells her everything. Not keeping anything secret from her.

It is difficult, it is painful for him to say out loud what he confesses to himself only minutes ago, but he has to do it. No matter how much he suffers, whether he bleeds to death because of it, Michael can no longer remain silent. He spills his whole life out, all his suffering, pain, and misery. He tells her all about his nightmares, unhappy childhood, and the rare moments of brief happiness, his kisses, screams, tears, and smiles, unfulfilled dreams. He spills everything out in front of the woman he barely knows, confessing.

Putting himself with confidence in her hands.

Now he's all hers. She is the mistress of his destiny, his good fairy and evil witch; his friend and lover, a woman who smokes cigarette after cigarette before breaking the silence.

"You are Michael Daniels?"

"I am Michael Daniels."

She puffs out another smoke and says, "You probably think I'll report you? Maybe I should do that, but I won't. I can't. Because one part of me tells me you told me the truth, and the other part hates your stepfather. But despite that, you can't stay here. I'm sorry."

Michael nods. He understands. He didn't ask her for a favor, just some money to buy himself a sandwich.

"It will be best for both of us if you leave now and forget you ever met me."

He wipes the remaining tears from his face with the back of his hand.

"Do you understand that I have no choice?"

"It's okay. Thank you for listening to me and . . . everything."

She watches him as he dresses. And then halts him at the door.

"Hang on. Take this." She produces forty dollars from her purse. "That's all I have with me."

"Thank you, but I cannot accept those . . ."

"Take them!" she insists, and shoves the money into his hand. "I won't ask you twice."

"Thanks," he says in a small voice. He hates himself for doing this, he hates himself for needing money and getting it that way. "Well, goodbye, then."

"Michael?" she stops him one last time.

"Yes?"

"I'll pray you smooth things out with Irma."

She closes the door behind him, saying nothing more.

Maybe, Michael thinks to himself, *if a miracle happens, and the world disappears for a moment and then it is born again, pure and without sin, then maybe I will. And if miracles do happen, which I didn't notice because they most likely happen to someone else, why would it be any different this time? The world will continue to be the same—cruel and without mercy.*

Chapter

26th: . . . combinations of these tricks. If you are an experimental type, you can also do them *gnarly*, over the bigger ledge, bigger rail, the crazier the better! In *A Note from the Author* I explained that the *tail grab* is a trick in which the trailing hand grabs the tail of the board. On the other . . .

THEY MAKE ONE MISTAKE, they only make one wrong step, and because of this they don't arrive in time at the Travises' home. Before Patchin Place, they go to RIRI and lose precious minutes there. By the time they reach West 10th Street, the Travises are already alerted.

Their visit to the Institute turns out to be futile and unnecessary because Morgan is unobliging, aggressive, and touchy, not in the mood for any discussion.

The two agents work fast, he has nothing to complain about that, but they are *ineffective*. There are no *results* of their work; not even the Daniels' maid nor Michael's friend, Kenneth, bring him an inch closer to the answers he is looking for. Not to mention Peterson, who turns out to be completely useless about that Daniels's letter. And that letter troubles him more than anything, getting to the top of his priorities list.

There's no point in guessing now what might happen if it falls into the wrong hands. Morgan is not afraid for his position if that happens. He already has other offers on the table. But he is afraid of what will *precede* the loss of his job if someone digs a little deeper—something that he already has to take seriously. He doesn't like the directive from Washington, DC, according to which he has to carry out a complete and extensive evacuation. It will be a hell of a demanding job—to relocate three underground floors to the facilities in western Wyoming in the strictest secrecy and in a very short time. If he fails to do *that*, his status can be compromised in the eyes of power brokers in Columbia. *That* is his greatest concern, and that's why he is so harsh on the two agents sent here to help him. Because of this, he swallows aspirin without dissolving it in a glass of water and then rudely chases them away, *demanding results.*

The shaved-head agent doesn't like Morgan's attitude and blacklists him, knowing that orders from Washington, DC will soon stop arriving. Before he and his partner return to the District of Columbia, they will also conduct a private job here.

He is looking forward to settling the score with Jack Morgan.

* * *

Special Agent Shay Fox doesn't like to snoop on the private lives of the people whose cases he works on. Some agents enjoy it, but Fox doesn't belong in their flock. In this case, however, he is forced to make an exception to that rule. Moreover, he will snoop around in the absence of a person who trusts him and therefore disgusts himself. But another voice, different and louder than his conscience, tells him that this is the right moment, and if he means to do it, he better do it now or he will never do it. Then he may as well drop the whole case.

Therefore, after exchanging surprised glances with Special Agent Amelia Dawson, Brenda Travis indulges his request and takes him to Roy's room.

Pausing in front of the door to Roy's room, Fox thanks her with a genuine smile, and says, "Thank you, Mrs. Travis. I'll take it from here. I'll call you if I need anything."

Clearly, she doesn't like the idea of a stranger, even if it is an FBI agent, nosing around in her son's room. Even she doesn't do it herself because she knows how sensitive Roy is about his privacy. He always makes his bed alone and cleans and dusts his room, and to his mother's amazement there is always some order in his room. It isn't the order she wants, but Roy's room has its character. That is also the case now, when an FBI agent is about to inspect it.

What the hell, she thinks, *Roy cannot blame me for this! This is the FBI! It's his fault they are prying into his stuff now. I didn't invite them! They're not here because of me. He should thank me for not telling them Michael was here. Only then would they have reason to search his room. They are just doing their job now. It's a routine procedure because Michael is Roy's friend, and this is not unusual. Is it?*

Yes, that's it. It's just a routine procedure. Nothing more. NOTHING.

Brenda Travis nods her approval, calmed that at least she doesn't have to worry about the look of his room. Then she returns to Agent Dawson, upset that she might pry into *her* things while she entertains her partner there.

***

Darth Vader's frightening mask, eying suspiciously every intruder, is the first thing that strikes his eye when he crosses the threshold of Alien's room. Below, it says, MAY THE FORCE BE WITH YOU. Capital letters as a screaming warning sign. *You can enter here, but no one guarantees you to leave from here. So think twice before making a call. And may the Force be with you, because no one else will hear your screams.*

A model of the Millennium Falcon floats in the air, suspended on invisible threads, preparing to take off in a hyper-jump into the distant universe. Its crew—miniaturized to the size of figurines—is stacked on shelves, along with chronologically-ordered, Bantam, *Star Wars* books, several novelizations of sci-fi movie screenplays, and all published sequels of *The X Files*. Luke Skywalker, Han Solo, Princess Leia, Wookie Chewbacca, and robots R2-D2 and C-3PO. Obi-Wan Kenobi, Jedi master Yoda, Anakin Skywalker as Anakin Skywalker, and Anakin Skywalker as Darth Vader.

The latest DVD technology with a plethora of DVDs, including the *Special Edition of the Star Wars Trilogy*, occupies a corner by the window, while the wall facing the window is covered with maps of space and posters of *Contact* and *Gattaca* blockbusters.

Below them is Roy's desk with his computer and accessories, its drawers full of newspaper clippings and photos from *The X Files* show, a few personal photos that have nothing to do with the extraterrestrial, and a photo of Roy kissing a girl in a Dennis Kay men's underwear ad. On the back of it the dedication signed by James Stowe.

Under the table are two boxes of skateboarding magazines,

on top of them a skateboard—or rather a deck with no trucks and wheels that Roy no longer uses.

Overcome with fatigue, Fox sits on Roy's bed, turning his back on a copy of a poster from Fox Mulder's basement office I WANT TO BELIEVE.

He stares blankly at the telescope that stands under the window and gazes at some distant point in the sky beyond the clouds, far beyond the distances that the naked human eye can reach, and the slow tide of comprehension splashes him. He realizes how lucky Dawson and he are to get to the Travis place first.

The whole thing is getting more serious every minute.

And that intrigues Fox even more to get deeper into the investigation.

Once he identifies "Dillon" and "Haim" or "Ames," he will deal with Morgan. But this time, more careful and in its own time. Because Morgan is not the type of man to deal with lightly—Fox realizes that as soon as he sees him. Thanks to Beresford's confession of what he did with Daniels in his spare time, Fox has a somewhat clearer idea of what they worked on at the Institute. And thanks to him, Michael Daniels still has slim chances of not being found guilty and stored in the FBI archive. Fox and Dawson will see to it. They will do their best to get Michael a fair trial and to protect him from Morgan, because it is plain as day that Jack Morgan is looking for him too. The boy poses a threat to him, and Fox won't be surprised if the two agents are working for him. Because of this, Fox must find him first, not only to save the boy's life, but to make Morgan talk.

The eyewitness of Hank's murder is not now his main concern because the woman doesn't pose a major threat to

Michael. Besides, there is always the likelihood she has mistaken him for someone else. To clear this out, he must first find Michael.

And he must do it *fast*, especially after the discovery at the Travis home. It is sheer luck or God's will that he didn't listen to the voice of his conscience. Fox is almost hyperactive with excitement and is eager to share his secret with Dawson. Still, he cannot barge in like that in front of two women. So he pops two Juicy Fruits into his mouth in order to compose himself a little, takes a few deep breaths, then closes the door of Alien's room.

At parting, Fox gives a piece of friendly advice to Roy's mother, "If someone else claiming to be with the FBI visits you, you don't have to talk to them. You owe them nothing because you've already talked to us. Have a nice day, Mrs. Travis."

The relief that appears on Brenda Travis's face when the two agents rise from their chairs and walk toward the door fades in the face of doubt and controlled fear. "Somebody else might visit us?" she asks in a quivering voice.

Agent Dawson calms her down.

"You don't have to worry. They have informed us that someone other than us is also investigating. Since we spoke with you, my partner does not see the need for our colleagues to disturb you too. You don't have to open the door for them if you don't want to."

"I don't have to open the door for them? What in heaven's name is that supposed to mean? Will anyone tell me what this is about?!"

"Please, Mrs. Travis," Fox's voice has a soothing effect. "Tell your son to call us. We urgently need to ask him some questions."

"How about . . . you wait for him here a little longer? He should be home for lunch soon." She considers her options and rather chooses Fox and Dawson over the two unknown men she should not even let in.

"Very kind of you, but we have something else to attend to." Fox gives her a reassuring smile. "Just give him the message that a witness with a bit of a different story appeared. He will understand."

"Witness with a different story?"

Brenda Travis grows so pale that Fox asks himself if she isn't telling them something. But now he has no time for that kind of doubt. He's finally on the trail of someone who will take him to Michael Daniels.

"That's right. Thank you for your time, Mrs. Travis."

The door shuts behind them, and the deadbolt locks it.

Fox and Dawson drive off, passing by a parked car with two men ducking down in it. One of them wears a thin, dark mustache while the other one's head is clean-shaved.

* * *

Rebecca and Red Sunshine are lucky. No one notices their disappearance, no one suspects or raises the alarm.

And, most importantly, no one stops them.

They thumb for a ride for half an hour until the first vehicle pulls over—a pickup truck heading to Abilene, Kansas. A jolly fellow in his late forties sold all his cattle and doesn't mind bringing a young, teenage couple part of the way back home.

After parting with him, a retired, married couple—still in love the same as fifty years ago—who are in the middle of a tour of all the places they had visited when they were much younger, picks them up. Unfortunately, their destination is Arkansas, which is off-route to New York City, where a brother and his younger sister are going after spending unforgettable vacations on their grandparents' ranch. A nice old couple parts with tears in their eyes, but also keeping with them Rebecca's wallet she dropped while climbing out of the gleaming, white Plymouth.

She only realizes this when she reaches for it to buy bus tickets, and the thick darkness is already hovering over their heads. They didn't want to thumb their ride during the night, and they also didn't want to spend the night in a motel so as not to raise suspicion. Rebecca couldn't sleep, anyway. She is too upset about her wallet.

Red Sunshine also cannot sleep, but for another reason. The journey he took in the role of a protector and a friend (and a patient lover) turns into an adventure he could only dream of. He feels phenomenal, and he catches himself thinking with sadness about ending the trip. It's hard to believe he could experience something so exciting, alluring, wild, reckless, and extraordinary anytime soon. Luckily for him, the excitements for them don't stop even when they leave Kansas City.

At two after midnight, they reach St. Louis. They are about halfway to New York City, and they don't have enough money even for a room for the night. They can barely afford a decent, hot meal. Had Rebecca not lost her money, they would have been much farther now, far closer to their final destination. But she lost it, and because of that she keeps fretting over it.

It takes very little for her to lose control and snap at Sunny, who cannot do anything to calm her down. Besides, he also has to be careful so that police don't find them. The Creeks and his parents have already reported their disappearance for sure.

Sunny doesn't believe much that the letters they had left will calm them. His mother is the most wonderful person in the world, but when it comes to her children, anything can be expected. Sunny can imagine her packing the rest of her family and moving them to the Creeks where they (all except Blue Sky and Gentle Wind, who are already in bed) will watch in anticipation of a life-saving phone call. Either Rebecca and Sunny will let them know that they have safely arrived in New York or the police will tell them that someone has attacked, raped, and killed them and dumped their mutilated bodies into a nearby ditch or one of the old car dumps.

Imagining the picture of two families gathered together in fear and hope, an idea is born in him. When he first proposes it to Rebecca, she automatically rejects it. That is out of the question. They will come for them and bring them home. This will be the end of everything: their trip, them, and Michael.

This time Sunny doesn't give up. He persists until Rebecca eventually relents and empties her cell phone battery, which she forgot to recharge, on one call to Denver—first, last, and final.

They are lucky this time, too, because already after the first ring Rebecca's grandfather answers the phone.

"Rebecca, dear child, where are you? *How* are you? Is everything okay with you? How's Sunny?"

"We're fine, Grandpa. We just ran out of money. Are you mad at me?"

"I'm not mad at you, my child. I'm just *worried* about you. Are you sure you're okay?"

"Yes, Grandpa, we're fine. In fact, we need your help. Will you help us?"

"Of course I will. Tell me where you are, and I'll be right there for you."

Ear glued to the back of the phone, Sunny resolutely shakes his head no.

"No!" he whispers in case she doesn't understand.

"I can't tell you that," Rebecca says to the phone. "We can't go back. We have to go on, but we have no money left. I wanted to ask you—"

"Listen to me, child. Have you thought the police might eavesdrop on this conversation?"

She didn't think about it, and neither did her astonished friend.

"They may have already traced you and may have already located where you are calling from. I just need to call them. But I want *you* to tell me."

"Grandpa..."

"Tell me where you are." His voice is determined and authoritative. Rebecca couldn't remember when her grandfather insisted so much on something from her.

She asks through tears, "Promise you won't bring us home if I tell you! I need to see him. I've got to see Michael..."

"Rebecca..."

"I *have* to see him, Grandpa! *I just have to!*"

"... you to New York."

"I beg your pardon?" She wipes her nose. "What did you say?"

"I said, I'll take you to New York! Ted and I will get in the car and come for you, and then we will all continue to New York."

"GRANDPA!"

"Easy now, child, I'm not deaf!"

"Are you serious? Are you seriously going to take us to New York?"

"I'm giving you your grandpa's word. If I knew you cared so much, I would have taken you. Why didn't you ask me?"

"But I did! I've asked you so many times!"

"I guess you did, but I didn't listen to you. Maybe I was afraid you'd get worse if I let you go to New York. Maybe I was afraid New York would hurt you, as it did Michael . . ."

"Waiting would hurt me, Grandpa! Waiting! Not New York. Not Michael, never . . ."

"Now I know that . . ."

"Grandpa! I'm calling you from my cell phone. My battery's dying, I'm losing you! We'll have to hang up—"

"Quick, where to pick you up?"

"St. Louis. Missouri. Wait for us by the Saint Louis Arch. We will look for you in case the police are faster than you."

"Take care, both of you. And tell Sunshine his mother loves him very much and that she is worried sick about him."

Red Sunshine hears it himself, so he claps his palm to his forehead. *(When will she let him grow up already?)*

Rebecca giggles and hangs up.

It is her first laughter since they began this adventure.

* * *

Fox's strokes are slow and synchronized. The sleeves of his impeccably white shirt are rolled up above his elbows, his tie loosened. Dawson and Alien sit opposite him; Dawson in a linen jacket and matching, beach-sand-colored pants while Alien has a white, Alien Workshop Clone Technology T-shirt and his baseball cap is turned around backward.

The weather had improved, and most New Yorkers crawl out of their homes to enjoy a warm and pleasant sunny afternoon. The calm waters of The Lake in Central Park are dotted with boats.

Low temperatures and stormy weather with snow move eastward and disappear somewhere over the Atlantic on their way to the European continent, defeated by the warm Arctic currents and heat that ravages Europe. Heavy fires devastate the old continent and wrap in thick smoke that blankets the sun and diminishes daytime visibility. People are sick across the continent—besieging hospitals and wearing masks over their mouths and noses in futile attempts of respiratory protection.

In New York City and all along the East Coast, though, the bad weather draws in its evil claws, and again the song of the birds and the racket of many gleeful voices can be heard in the air, as if they had returned home after a long journey through the galaxy.

Alien watches the blooming of life around him, listening to the splash of Fox's oars. Fox declines his offer to replace him in rowing; he will have plenty of time to show his rowing skills. Alien doesn't complain. Reaching the middle of the lake, Fox pulls out the oars to prevent them from accidentally slipping into the water.

"You're probably wondering why we met like this?" he asks him. "That's because we need to talk in peace. What we are going to say to each other is very confidential, and my partner and I think this is an ideal place for this type of conversation."

"And here I thought you dragged me all the way here because you're afraid I might escape," Alien makes a joke. "I'm a pretty good swimmer, just to let you know."

"What made you think so?" Dawson asks him, a thin smile dancing in the corner of her lips. "Do you have a reason to jump into the lake and swim away?"

"Of course not. That was a joke. What's up? Mom told me you had to tell me something. She was pretty upset about it."

"What else did she tell you?" Fox asks.

"The two guys visited her just after you left. They were also from the FBI. She was pissed off because of that."

"What did they want?" It's Dawson's turn to be curious.

"I don't know because she didn't let them in. She allegedly heeded your advice and slammed the door in their face. Did you really tell her that?"

Fox laughs heartily while Dawson greets with a smile the young couple rowing past near them. The young man and the girl wave back to her, beaming with joy.

"Not literally. We only explained to your mother that there was no need to talk to them since we already visited her. That's all."

"There's something else, partner," Dawson corrects him. "We *did* advise her not to open the door to strangers. These are dangerous times. But we didn't tell her to slam the door in their face."

The wind plays with her hair and Alien notices she is attractive for her age.

He smiles at her. "And why did you need to see me?"

"We have news for you," Fox satisfies his curiosity. "But first we have to ask you two questions."

"First news then questions," Alien tries his luck.

"I think we can agree to that." Fox looks at Dawson and she nods in agreement.

Then she says, "We wanted to warn you that Michael is in danger."

"Thanks for the info, but I already know that!"

"He is in greater danger than you think. *That's* what we

wanted to tell you."

Alien closes his eyes for a moment. "People who visited Mom? Two from the FBI?"

"*If* they are from the FBI." Fox looks at Dawson again. *I had to tell him*, his gaze speaks.

I think it won't hurt anyone, she replies the same way.

"That's what I thought! I knew they weren't the FBI! I told Victor that something was wrong there, that I was suspicious about these guys. I saw through them!" He is bursting with pride.

"You mean—Victor Kenneth? The skater you told us to visit?" Dawson asks, trying to clarify things. "When did you see him?"

"I was with him today. I brought him some groceries and other stuff from the store. It isn't a crime to visit a sick friend, is it? Why do you want to know?"

"Never mind. Just asking."

"Did you talk to Alien?" Fox adds. "We wanted to see you, among other things, to tell you we have to meet with him. If he knows anything about Michael, he better tells us before it's too late."

Alien gets serious, as if considering this for a moment, then shakes his head.

"Unfortunately, I didn't. Last time I saw him was in the skate shop. But I'll buzz him and tell him what you said. If he's Michael's true friend, I'm sure he'll talk to you."

"I wouldn't rely too much on that, if you ask me," Fox retorts. "I mean, you don't have to buzz him. We have information that he'll be here, in the park."

Alien tenses up. The little hairs on his neck stand up from cold shivers running down his spine.

"How . . . how do you know that?"

"FBI," Fox states modestly, shrugging.

"You saw him?" He feels his throat tighten even more.

"Well . . ." Fox lets him sweat a little longer. "It depends how you look at it."

"Someone *showed* him to you?"

"Actually, we expect you to do that," Dawson jumps in. "Someone anonymously informed us he would be near the Bow Bridge . . . about now." She consults her wristwatch.

Only now Alien notices that their boat is drifting toward the Bow Bridge. He starts to sweat a lot under his armpits and becomes alarmed that the two agents will notice it.

Fox continues, "Since we don't know him, we were hoping you would show him to us," and then he follows Dawson's example by consulting his wristwatch. "He should be here by now."

Almost completely panicked, Alien looks again in the direction of the bridge and people strolling across it. He nervously yanks at his earphones, almost plucking them out of the Disc-man.

Dawson touches him on the shoulder and he jumps, rocking the boat.

She says, "Not on the bridge, Roy. We were informed that he would be in one of the boats."

Sweat trickles down his forehead, his hair is matted under his cap.

"A man in his early thirties, accompanied by a very charming lady, would also be with him," Fox concludes.

Alien yawns helplessly like a fish out of water.

Then Dawson gives him a detailed description of a man fitting Fox's description, and when Fox starts to describe

Dawson, Alien cuts him off.

"All right, all right!" He takes off his baseball cap and runs his fingers through his wet hair. "I got the point! How did you know it was me? How did you figure it out?"

He looks at them with anticipation, in a way, relieved that he no longer has to hide from them. *If everything else were so easy*, he thinks.

"Your mother showed me your room. Quite a nice place," Fox gives him a compliment. "Don't blame her for that."

Alien nods. "I see. That was you. I thought she was *making order* there, but I didn't get to ask her because I was in a hurry to meet you."

"Why didn't you tell us straight away, Alien . . . or maybe Roy? How shall we call you now?" Dawson asks.

"I prefer Alien. Everybody calls me that, except, of course, Mom. I'm kind of used to it."

"All right, Alien. Why didn't you tell us the truth? We just lost valuable time. What's even worse, Michael wouldn't be in such danger because he would be under our protection."

"*Protection?!* You're kidding me! If I had told you earlier, Michael would already be behind bars!" he shouts, gasping for breath. "Sorry. I just want to help Michael. I want someone to listen to his side as well, that's why I didn't tell you earlier. Maybe I was wrong, I don't know."

"Alien, you just admitted that you broke the law," Fox says cautiously. "Are you aware of the consequences for you?"

Alien scratches his head. "I think I am. But I don't see why I would have to bear the consequences when I did no harm? I didn't hide the killer or anything. I was only helping a friend who, incidentally, is an innocent victim."

"First of all," Fox corrects him, "Michael has not been

charged yet. And second, it's up to the jury to decide whether Michael is guilty or innocent. That's not up to you, me, or Agent Dawson to decide. Are we understood?"

"Maybe. But it's up to me to help a friend in need, just like it's your duty and obligation to bring a suspect to justice and gather evidence of his guilt. Do you have evidence Michael is guilty, Agent Fox? If not, you cannot accuse me for breaking the law."

"Actually, we have a witness who claims that Michael was inside the house when Hank Daniels was killed. She saw him leave in a hurry."

Alien turns pale, then he turns gray. He resembles one of the aliens in *The X Files*.

His voice is quiet, tired, and hoarse when he whispers, "That's not possible."

"Come again?" Fox doesn't hear him well.

"I said, that's not possible. Michael was with Victor and with me. If Michael killed Hank, then we killed him, too, because we were together. In that case, you will have not *one* suspect, but *three*."

"I gave a thought to that as well." Fox also looks tired.

"What??" Alien is shocked. "You must be joking!"

"Can anyone confirm that? I didn't think so. Then why are you surprised?"

Alien is more than surprised; he is deeply concerned. It is only a matter of time before the FBI agents will catch him lying and unmask this little conspiracy. So he plays his last card—he bluffs one last time, and what happens, happens. He did everything he could. He runs out of ideas.

"I do not deny, this may all be true, but it isn't. If anyone had a reason to take revenge on Hank, it's Michael. If I had a stepfather and if he did to me what Hank did to Michael, he wouldn't fare well. He wouldn't fare well at all. I'd chop his balls off—excuse my language—before he'd get to sodomize me again. But Michael isn't me; Michael is too good. He couldn't do it. He is not a cold-blooded killer."

"If I understood you correctly," Dawson responds faster than Fox, "you claim that Hank sexually abused Michael?"

"That's what I think. What? You didn't know that?"

"No, we didn't." She shakes her head. "Who would tell us?"

Alien frowns. "I found that out by accident. Michael doesn't know that I know that, and I want it to stay that way." He waits until both agents promise not to disclose their source. "When Michael ran away from home a week ago, he slept at my place. He was distressed and restless, he slept poorly. He would wake me up at night without being aware of it. He sobbed in his sleep and that's how I found out he was . . . what Hank was doing to him."

"Maybe it was just a bad dream?" Fox suggests. "Perhaps his worst fears came to life in his dreams, creating a convincing impression of reality?"

"Fears of what? Needles, or Hank raping him again?"

"Needles? What needles?" Dawson furrows her brow.

"I'm not sure, but it seemed like Hank was giving him some injections or something. So that Michael wouldn't resist him while raping him?" He shrugs. "I really wouldn't know. As I told you before, Michael said nothing about it to me. I made my conclusion after putting the pieces together. But something had to happen there. Something bad. When Michael had those dreams, his eyes were wide open, but he was not conscious. But I managed to get some answers out of him. He didn't remember talking to me in the morning, and I didn't ask him about that later. I was afraid he would lose confidence in me, when he found out what I had done."

He then tells them about Michael's gift—which is the reason he went to see a psychiatrist even though he didn't want to. He argued a lot with Hank about this, but Hank forced him to do so, convincing him he isn't normal, that he is dangerous and stuff. He cried a lot, calling for his mom and Rebecca, threatening to kill himself . . .

"But at no point did he say he would kill Hank," Alien concludes. "If you ask me, the one who killed the bastard has done a tremendous favor to the whole world. They should reward him for that, not punish him."

"Does anyone else know about this?" Fox asks, ignoring Alien's remark.

"No," he hastens to say, not admitting that Victor also knows about Michael's dreams.

"Good. Let's keep it that way for now," Fox says.

"Why?"

"Because it wouldn't be in Michael's best interest. And neither in yours," Fox says briefly.

"You don't believe me, do you? You think I made up everything to protect Michael? Well, you are wrong!"

"We trust you, Alien. We don't know how much you have been telling the truth about Michael's alibi, but we believe this. Don't ask *how* we know this because we cannot disclose it to you in the interest of the investigation."

"In the interest of the investigation? Don't you think I know too much already?!" He looks desperately from Fox to Dawson and back.

"You know, but you'll keep quiet about that."

"And if I won't? Then what? Will you bring me in?"

"Only by our good will, you are still as free as a bird," Fox says coldly.

"And not because you need me? Not because only I can take you to Michael?"

"I'm sure Michael will be happy to turn himself in when he hears you are arrested for the murder of his stepfather," Dawson says. "I don't think he would leave his friend in the lurch."

Alien wants to scream in anguish.

"If you want me to shut up, then I'll shut up," he squeezes through his lips. "But at least tell me *why*."

"Because we need you," Fox says, his patience running thin. "Because we need both you and Michael alive. You are of no use to anyone if you are dead. Is that a good enough explanation for you?"

"I think so," he says in a sad voice, his shoulders sinking. "What else do you want from me?"

"Just one thing," Fox retorts.

"Michael."

"Yes."

Alien sighs. "I'll talk to him tonight. Can't promise he will see you, but I'll try to convince him it's in his best *interest*."

Dawson gives him a smile that says, *"Good boy."*

"Can we be there while you talk to him?" Fox asks unobtrusively, but Alien knows he has no choice.

"What happens then? What happens to Michael if he meets you?"

"It depends on what he tells us. If it proves his innocence and your alibi as reliable, you can all go skateboarding soon. But if it proves his guilt, he will be tried. In that case, I would sleep with one eye open, if I were you."

"And in neither case can you guarantee us we will be safe. You cannot guarantee that we will live to see the end of the investigation."

"I guarantee your safety is our priority. We'll do everything in our power to protect you. Remember one thing, Alien. As we tracked you down, we'll find them too. That's not a promise, that's a fact."

"You are lucky to have the best FBI agent working on your case," Dawson tries to cheer him up.

"And with the best partner helping him out." Fox smiles at her. "Alien, are you still in the mood for rowing?"

"Sure. Might be the last rowing in my life. I wouldn't miss that for the world."

He plops his baseball cap on his head, grabs the oars, and without a word turns the boat toward the shore.

Chapter

27th: ... hand, you do the *boardslide* by performing a slide along an object or obstacle. There are many tricks which are not mentioned here, and there is no need for that. Talented skaters around the world regularly invent, "patent" and "place to market" new tricks. Like there's no end to ...

THE MOMENT THEY FINISH THEIR conversation, Fox's phone starts to sing its tune again. Indifferent to everything, including Merchant, who is informing Fox about a call from a guy named Elijah Peterson, a RIRI employee, who wants to talk to him about the case, Alien keeps rowing toward the place where they rented the boat forty-five minutes ago.

After saying goodbye to the sullen boy, with the promise of seeing him later, they rush to an incognito meeting with Peterson, who will be waiting for them at the south entrance of Flushing-Meadows Corona Park. The recognition sign will be a folded Sunday edition of *The New York Times* that Peterson will hold under his right arm.

On their way to Flushing-Meadows, Fox briefs Dawson of

what Merchant had told him over the phone. Merchant visited their eyewitness at her home to show her six photos of underage drug dealers with a record, including a photo of Michael Daniels. It is interesting that the woman doesn't recognize him this time, though she claims to have seen Michael's photo on television. Michael's hair is much brighter, almost blond, than the ones in the photos. This only confirms to Merchant that he cannot rely on her statement—as he suspected from the beginning. The woman could easily accuse some innocent kid who probably never heard of Hank Daniels, much less killed him. So he thanked her for her cooperation and promised—just to say something—that he will be in touch with her.

If he got this news an hour ago, Fox might have celebrated it with fanfare. He is still annoyed with Morgan, whom he didn't stop suspecting even after talking to Alien. But Fox is a realistic person, and he has to admit to himself that Michael very likely killed his father. In spite of his "alibi" and Fox's wish that it isn't true, his usual ninety-five-percent-correct hunch is telling him that Michael is guilty of murder. It may not have been a planned murder, but it is a murder just the same.

Before speaking with Alien, Fox was inclined to suspect a conspiracy within RIRI that sought to eliminate Hank Daniels after learning the shocking truth about Beresford's and Daniels's personal project. The plan is simple: kill the father and cast doubt on the son. The perfect solution for the perfect plan. Only there is no such plan. Because there is no conspiracy.

As it turns out, Elijah Peterson—a slender, tall, and not-heartbreakingly-good-looking, young man with an intelligent and charming smile—had only recently arrived at the Institute but, ironically, had no intention of building his career for long. As soon as this investigation is over, he is out of the game and looking for a new job in a friendlier environment. He would have done that already if he hadn't thought it is too dangerous for now. Elijah Peterson isn't ready to take *that* much risk and reveal himself as Fox's source.

Hiding the truth from Morgan about contacting the FBI, Peterson has little satisfaction as revenge on the man who has picked on him since his first day at the Institute. As a rookie with no friends in high places, Peterson could do nothing about that. This time, however, the situation is a bit different. He has something Morgan is desperately searching for: Michael's letter he found in Hank's overcoat when he accidentally mistook it for his own and put it on. That same letter is now in Fox's hands, writing a big, front-page story. Several gaps of which the letter doesn't offer explanation, Peterson himself fills in in exchange for FBI protection and immunity.

As soon as they are done with Peterson, Fox calls Merchant to ask for help from his department. Getting his full support and cooperation, Fox consults with Dawson on how to get a confession from Morgan.

Less than three hours separate them from meeting Alien, when they will finally talk to Michael. They will give him only a few hours to think it over before deciding whether to cooperate with them. Even though he is a killer, Michael is just a small-timer. The victim—a tool in the hands of two scientists—who accidentally found himself on the wrong side of the law.

A boy without a future, yet aware that despite all the pitfalls, fears, and insidious secrets the world consists of, life *can* be beautiful.

* * *

It isn't easy for Michael Daniels to open himself before a stranger. It isn't easy for anyone to open their heart and soul to a stranger, as Michael does before Georgia. And in return gets money from her before saying goodbye to her.

Michael is still a child of fortune. A few hours ago he was flat broke, but now he is okay again. He won't have to spend this night outdoors, exposed to the gangs' moods and low temperatures. Thanks to Georgia, Michael can now afford lodging. He isn't fantasizing about luxury rooms with splendid views and fragrant baths. Modest as he is, he will settle for a warm *bed*.

He is dying to meet a familiar face, especially his sister's. That is impossible. Plus, seeing him or talking to him may only hurt her. And Michael doesn't want to hurt her again. He already did too much damage.

So he thinks of Victor, a friend in need and a buddy, the best skater he has ever encountered and in whose company he is privileged to be. What would he say if he knew Michael had told all about himself to an unknown woman? Georgia, the first woman he tries to sleep with and fails completely. Which is no wonder, considering the hell of abuse and threats he went through lasted for years. He doesn't remember exactly when his father first came to his room, wanting to have sex with him. He was too young to understand what he needed to do when he forced his penis into his mouth. He was so scared that he wet himself with fear. He was crying for his mom, but Melanie Hope was not there to protect him. Hank knew that. Hank waited for the moment when the two of them would be alone and once he started, he couldn't be stopped. The roots of fear are too deep in Michael and he couldn't pull them out so easily. When he finally succeeds in doing so, he also cuts Hank's life with them. It's the story of his life.

It took time for Michael to understand why his mother had to travel and why she left him alone with Hank. He often thought she did it on purpose, so Hank and he could do *those things*. He thought she *expected* it from him. But when he realizes that it isn't so, it was too late. Michael was afraid of Hank. Then he enters his teenage years—fear gives its place to shame, and Michael continues to please Hank so he won't tell anyone what kind of boy Mikey is.

Somewhere during these difficult ordeals of youth, Michael comes across several books about children sexually abused by their own parents. Emboldened by this discovery, but still feeling uneasy about their contents, he reads them on the spot instead of taking them home with him. The most important thing he learns from these books is that he is not *alone* in going through such experiences and that he could fight it. So, on the first occasion, he threatens Hank that he will tell everything to his mom, and if that doesn't help, he will go to a social worker and tell her everything. And if *that* doesn't work, he will contact one of the institutions that care for abused children and ask them for help. Hank had the answer to everything. He warned Michael that he better not do it because Rebecca could bear the consequences of his foolish act. He didn't need to say it again because Michael believed him. He opened the door to his room for him again and greeted him without resistance every time Melanie Hope was out of town. That went on for years, a lifetime, until he killed Hank.

The irony is that Hank helped him break free by crossing the line of Michael's patience. Giving him the *gift*, he signed a death sentence for himself.

Although Michael didn't want his revenge in *this* way, he

has no regrets. He only regrets making Rebecca's life miserable and unhappy and dragging his friends into all that. But they agreed to it on their free will, it was their choice. And no one—neither he, nor Alien's mother, or anyone else—could dissuade them from that once they decided to stand by him.

Michael slides into Alien's jacket, but doesn't zip it up. The air is crisp, but not too cold. Temperatures will soon drop as the sun sets behind the skyscrapers—painting shadows.

Alien's jacket is still in good shape despite the beating. It's a miracle it survived all that kicking and dragging without tearing up.

It is also a wonder that Alien doesn't have dozens of such jackets. He could have had as many sponsors as he wanted, but Alien isn't interested in that. He doesn't skate in contests because he doesn't care about skateboarding for money. He skates from pure pleasure and because he likes it.

Michael draws a parallel in his mind. Neither does he skate for money, but, on the other hand, he wants to make better use of his talent. He wants people to see how good he is; he wants to make some money, meet new people, and travel the world. What's wrong with that?

Nothing, except that in all likelihood he won't see the contest in Sattel. Sponsors also have not contacted him yet. He is sad because of Independent, while he only sent his video footage to Icarus Skateboards and Doghouse Production as a backup. He didn't dare to write to Victor's Blackout. They are too good, and they only sponsor the greatest talents. Like Victor.

Just as Michael is about to draw a parallel between Victor and himself, a familiar face comes into his view. Fortune favors him again.

He is glad to see Justin as much as he would have been to

see Alien, Victor, or Rebecca. But it seems to Michael that Justin isn't so happy to see him. Nothing at this moment, however, can spoil his mood.

"Justin! What are *you* doing here?"

Justin grins nervously at him.

"Yo, Michael."

"How are you?"

"Fine, I think. I'm waiting for someone."

"Anyone I know?"

"I wouldn't say so."

"Some girl?" Michael winks at him.

"No," Justin replies quietly, blushing.

"Well, I'm glad to see you, Just. Have you heard about me?"

Justin nods.

"Yeah. How have you been, Michael? What happened to your leg?"

"Nothing terrible. I got into some brawl. I'm fine now."

"The guys are wondering what happened to you. There is no news about you. We know Alien is in touch with you, but nothing more."

"Tell them I'm fine and say hello to them all, will you?"

"I will."

"Alien informs me what's going on. Hey," Michael changes the subject, "did you find out the snitcher? Who called for the raid?"

"The rumors are it may have been Nando. No one knows for sure."

"You are kidding me!"

"We don't see him much after the raid. The dude has evaporated." His gaze wanders in the direction of the metallic-gray

Mercedes that is approaching them.

It pulls to a halt and the passenger-door window rolls down. A husky, male voice calls out, "Nas?"

Justin gets fidgety. He says to Michael, "Excuse me. I'll be right back."

"What was *that*?" Michael asks when Justin returns.

"Sorry, Mike. I'd like to chat with you more, but I gotta go. It was good seeing you."

"It was good seeing you too, Just." Michael can't stop staring at the Mercedes. "Who is this?" he asks. He is not comfortable with the sudden change in Justin's behavior.

"You don't know him. I have to do some work for him. I owe him."

Work, it echoes in Michael's head. *I have to do some work.*

His stomach turns when he realizes. *(Justin, don't. Don't!)*

"You need money? Is that it? How much do you need? Tell me how much you need, and I'll give you money. Just get rid of the guy!"

"Michael, it's not that simple. Besides, you need money more than I do. I'll manage, I've done it before."

"Nas, are you coming?" a nervous voice calling from the car.

"Why does he call you *Nas*? What a freak!"

"Michael, trust me. Everything will be okay. I'm going now."

The agony on Michael's face. Newly experienced painful moments.

"Justin . . ."

"Bye, Michael. Please, don't tell anyone you saw me. I beg you."

"I won't. Goodbye, Justin. Take care." He nods and walks

away. He cannot watch Justin get in the car.

Seconds later, the Mercedes is on the move and it passes him by. Michael looks at its heavily tinted windows once more, but sees nothing through them. He only senses that Justin looks back at him for a moment before the car drives him away.

* * *

After meeting with the FBI in Central Park, Alien goes straight to Victor's place. They urgently need to adapt their plan to the new situation. But when he rings the doorbell, no one answers him.

A piece of paper carried by the wind is fluttering on the street and Alien picks it up. He scribbles a message, informing Victor that he will arrange a meeting between the FBI and Michael.

Then he rings at Victor's neighbor to let him in, but no one answers him there either. He tries another apartment and again nothing. Only on the fourth attempt does he find someone at home who lets him in after he introduces himself as a friend of Victor Kenneth, for whom he has an urgent message.

Alien sneaks into the building when a buzzer sounds on the intercom and pushes a piece of paper through the mail slot on Victor's door. Then he calls Victor and leaves him a message on the answering machine in case he doesn't find the written message.

To be on the safe side, he heads to Division Pro Skate Shop, hoping that maybe someone knows where Victor might be. Only then he goes home. He is hungry and drained. He needs to take a thirty-minute nap before he meets the FBI for the second time today.

Michael's fate is in his hands, and he must not screw up.

* * *

Michael looks into himself, but he doesn't find that trace of light that had given him hope not so long ago. The dark is in him. Complete, pitch-black, palpable darkness. The encounter with Justin finishes him. He is again haunted by the memories of Hank and they make him sick. Everything makes him sick, and he leans against the wall of the building next to the Polish Consulate and empties the contents of his stomach onto Madison Avenue: a crab-burger, a cheese pie, and cherry juice. Then he hurries from the scene before the Poles take it personally and heads for the Grand Central Terminal.

His plan is to surprise Alien and meet him in person. Whatever the risk, he wants to see him. He must see him after the shock with Justin.

Like clockwork, he spots him walking toward the telephone booth. However, he is not alone. Michael doesn't know the two people who are with him, but he has an idea who they might be. G-man and G-woman fit to the detail the description Alien gave him.

He hides in the crowd among the commuters, waiting for the first pay phone to be free, then dials the pay phone number next to which Alien is waiting. Two agents haven't noticed him so far, and that's good.

Alien jumps when the phone rings and waits for it to ring again before he picks it up.

"*Who* is with you?" Michael asks, though he knows the answer. "And *why* are they here?"

"Hey, Michael! How was your day?"

Alien's voice trembles a little—a sign that his friend is scared. But he is sensible enough not to answer Michael's questions directly. Not while the FBI is around, listening to their conversation and watching people come and go.

(How stupid of him to ask him something like that!)

"Alien, answer me *yes* or *no* when I ask you a question. Okay?"

"Yes, that's good. My day was also interesting, but I'll tell you about it later."

"The FBI is with you?"

"Yes."

"Are you in trouble?"

"Nope. It's nothing that bad."

"They forced you to come with them?"

"Not really. I already told you."

"Did you bring them by yourself?!"

"Yes, in a way. Michael—"

"You're crazy! Alien, do you know where I am now? You could hear me if I sneezed loud! What if they see me?"

He can imagine Alien turning pale.

Alien asks, "Where? Where did that happen . . . ?"

"Never mind. Just don't turn around! Talk to me like nothing happened."

"Of course. You don't have to worry about *that*!"

Fox and Dawson look at him curiously. *(What happened?)* Alien's grip is melting the handset in his hand.

"Forgive me, I didn't stick to our agreement. I wanted to see you. I *had* to see you."

"Well, it looks like you did one hell of a job with that," he says, trying not to arouse suspicion. "What are you up to now?"

"Don't have a damned clue! Got a suggestion? It's obvious

we can't talk like this. Shall we meet . . . say, in an hour in the same place as yesterday?"

"Sounds good to me. But first, I have to ask you something."

"I'm all ears. Just hurry."

"There's someone with me who wants to have a word with you."

"What do they want?"

"Agent Fox and Agent Dawson from the FBI are with me."

"I know who they are! I asked you what they want!"

I know you know, you fool, but they don't know it! he almost hisses into his handset.

"They would like to hear from you for a minute. They want to tell you something."

"That's all? They won't ask me to meet them? Shit, they could tell me to my face what's on their mind, if they only knew!"

"They won't. They just want to hear you."

Both Fox and Dawson now stand so close to Alien that he can feel Fox's breath on his neck.

"Are they alone or there are others too?"

"No. Just the two of them," Alien waits for their confirmation. *We are alone. No one followed us. This is not an ambush.*

"Okay, I believe you."

"Very generous of you," Alien says sarcastically.

"What now? What do we do now?" Michael asks.

"I'm going to give you Agent Fox now, and you listen to what he has to say. After that, it's all up to you. If you ask me, I think you can trust them. *I* trust them."

"Okay, okay. What about us? Talk to you in an hour?"

"Yes. There should be no problem with it unless my

boogie-board cracks," he reminds him using their secret code in case something gets complicated and he won't be able to come. In this case, Michael calls Victor for further instructions.

"Yeah, I know." Michael sighs. "Thanks for everything, man. And sorry if you got the impression that I doubted you."

"Sentimental bullshit," Alien retorts. "Hang in there. Here's your G-man."

"Hello? Michael?"

"Good evening, Agent Fox. Alien told me you wanted to tell me something?"

"That's right. Why don't you call me Shay? We'll both feel more comfortable that way. What do you say?"

Dawson and Alien exchange astonished glances. (Where does this sudden intimacy come from?)

"If that's what you want, Agent Fo . . . Shay."

Shay Fox smiles and starts talking. He speaks for several minutes without stopping, and several telephone booths away, Michael is listening to him and occasionally nodding in understanding.

When Fox is done, Michael says, "I'm sorry, but I have to hang up now. People are already waiting in line for the phone."

"So what are you going to do, Michael?" Fox asks him in the end.

"I'd like to think about it. Can I call you in the morning? I promise to give you an answer then."

"All right. Just don't put it off too much because if they find you before us, we won't be able to give you any protection. And my offer will be ended, in that case."

"Forgive me my asking, but is this really true or are you telling me this just to lure me?"

Fox laughs. "Your friend here asked me the same thing. It's

true. But we don't want to let our fellow citizens wait any longer, do we? Alien will go into details with you later. You'll see him, won't you?"

Blood rushes to Michael's head, while Alien pretends not to hear Fox's comment. But his scarlet ears betray him.

"Don't worry, Michael. I will respect our agreement as long as you do the same. You double-cross us, we'll be singing to a different tune. You got that?"

"I won't double-cross you. I'll call you. I promised, didn't I?"

"Do you have something to write our phone numbers with?"

"I do. Go ahead."

Fox tells him first his, then Dawson's number, and Michael repeats the numbers before memorizing them.

"If you make up your mind earlier, give us a call. You don't have to wait until the morning. You can call anytime, because we haven't been sleeping much lately."

"Okay."

* * *

The digital clock shows 06:59 when the phone rings and wakes Fox. As soon as he realizes where he is, Fox snatches the phone and leaps to his feet. It is a matter of habit, for Fox has no reason to panic.

He waited until late at night for Michael's call, and now he wholeheartedly hopes it is him.

"Good morning. I apologize if I woke you up."

(It's Michael.) Shay Fox is relieved.

"No problem, Michael. Tell me. What have you decided?"

"I'll meet you, but on one condition. I don't want anyone but you and Agent Dawson close. I want to talk to you off the record and tell you everything I know. After that, we will decide what to do next."

"I think we can agree to that. Dawson and I will come alone. But later you'll have to talk to others, you know that?"

"We'll talk about it when the time comes."

"Very well. Where shall we meet?"

"Can you be at the Riverside Skate Park at eleven o'clock? Do you know where that is?"

"I think I know. But it wouldn't hurt to refresh my memory."

"It's in Riverside Park near One Hundred Eighth Street. You can't miss it. If you get lost by accident, ask any skater and they'll instruct you."

"We won't get lost. So, we will find you there?"

"No. I'll find *you* there."

Chapter

28th: . . . skateboarding stunts! It's not important which of the tricks *you* will decide to master and *whether* you'll master them. It's not important if you'll *kick ass* and amaze others doing stunts and become a pro skater or you'll simply enjoy skurfing or cruising to your school, work, or to the store.

VICTOR FINDS BOTH ALIEN'S MESSAGES, but he doesn't respond to any of them. Better not to tell him anything until it's over.

Instead, he takes his skateboard and goes for a ride. That's when he does his best thinking. Some guys he knows need to be focused on their ride, but Victor doesn't have that problem. Skateboarding is something normal for him, like walking or breathing.

Most of all he loves the night rides when the traffic is rare, and the streets are wide, open, and empty—just waiting for him. The air is also more pleasant, fresher, and easier to breathe.

The sea smells stronger then.

Victor doesn't return Alien's call for a simple reason: he

may try to talk him out of his idea, and that won't be good for Michael. Alien will forgive him that. Maybe not right away, but over time he will. He will realize that there is no other solution. Victor's way is *the only way*. Unfortunately.

Among a dozen other skateboarders also skurfing and enjoying the night ride, he comes upon Justin. Justin gives him Michael's regards and tells him that Michael was in some kind of trouble. Victor thanks him and rolls away, trying to control his emotions.

For a while, he is just riding, ignoring the sound of the wheels following him in his tracks. He is ignoring his friend's shadow sliding parallel to him, while at the same time he would give anything for just one more ride with him.

A ride that won't happen.

He does a huge, mountain-like *ollie* across the street, by a hair's breadth avoiding a collision with a fast-approaching car furiously honking at him. He safely lands on the opposite sidewalk and slows down almost to a stop, *(Calm down, bro, everything's fine.)*, waiting for the pleasant sound of his friend's wheels to join him.

Michael's shadow lands at the same spot where Victor had landed moments before and screeches his wheels to a halt beside him.

"What does your grandma like to eat the most?"

"Why do you ask?"

"We could buy her something before we visit her."

We could buy her. Before. We visit. Her.

(Michael. Of all the people in the world, why does this have to happen to us? Why, my friend?)

Michael doesn't answer him. He just smiles, keeping up with the pace Victor imposes again.

They pass St. Mary's Heart nursing home in which Victor's nana spent her last days. And when she died, something in Victor died with her. *(If he only knew her death would affect him that way . . . Well, he probably would have done the same thing. He probably would have done it again, if she had asked him. But if he had only known . . .)*

"You could have known that," Michael's spirit says to Victor's spirit. "You could have guessed."

"You're right, I could. But what can I do now?"

"You can do something. And that is not to do the same stupid thing again. Do as I tell you, and we'll ride together every night."

"I can't, Michael. I have to do that. You know there's no other way out."

"But there is! There is the other way. There is a way out for all of us to stay together."

"You think so? I'd like to believe that . . ."

"Then, believe! Believe, Vic, never lose faith. Because I believe."

"I believe."

"Believe and tell me what you see."

"I see the door. I feel the summer behind that closed door."

"Summer?"

"Warm and lazy summer that never ends. I hear the rolling of the wheels and the blasting sounds of the boards on the surface of the asphalt! There is joy everywhere. Can you believe that, Mikey? Can you believe that?"

He returns home with the first rays of a still sleepy sun. He takes a shower, makes himself a sandwich, and then goes out again. Leaves the skateboard at home this time. And the folded sheet of paper across it—a message for Michael.

He is scared, and with each new step his determination weakens. Yet he drags himself up to the New York FBI headquarters. With his thoughts finding comfort on his nana's gentle face, he approaches the first agent he sees.

"I'm sorry, but neither Agent Dawson nor Fox is here, at the moment." Agent D'Antonio looks at him curiously. "Maybe I can help you?"

Victor gives him a short look before answering. "I have information regarding the Daniels case. I would like to speak with them personally. Do you know where I could find them?"

Agent D'Antonio's eyes sparkle briefly. The crow's feet disappear around his dark-brown eyes for a moment, and now he seems much younger to Victor than before. A quick twitch across his face and, "Can you come with me? This way, please."

They stop at the door of Damon Fletcher's office, the FBI director, it reads. D'Antonio asks him to wait here and disappears behind it. Seconds later, he leads him in and introduces him to a corpulent man in his early fifties with a determined look and a firm, long handshake.

"Damon Fletcher," the man's deep voice thunders and shakes the windows.

"Victor Kenneth," Victor replies, insecure, and casts a glance at Agent D'Antonio leaving the room.

Fletcher motions him to a chair, then settles himself behind a massive desk opposite Victor, littered with papers, pencils, a telephone, and a laptop, and two family photos. A golden tiepin on a dark-purple tie with a yellow pattern glints on his chest with the power of cherub swords at the gates of the Garden of Eden.

"Agent D'Antonio informed me you have information about the Daniels case? Is that correct?"

"That's right. I would like to discuss this with the agents who work on this case."

"I understand. Suitably to your wishes, Agent D'Antonio

has already notified Agent Fox, and he is on his way. You can wait for him here in my office. Can I offer you coffee or something, if you like?"

"Thanks, I'd rather not."

"You know, this case has already taken us too much time, hence we appreciate any reliable information. May I ask what kind of information you have for us?"

"Well, I have information on the identity of the man who killed Hank Daniels."

Unlike agent D'Antonio, Fletcher remains calm. His lips are sealed tight, his eyes penetratingly radiant.

"But that's not the only reason I'm here. I want to report another murder. My conscience tells me to report the murder of Angela Kenneth."

The black rings under Fletcher's eyes turn a few more shades blacker. His eyes lose their questioning glow for a moment—as if a big and dark shadow passes over them. Before he can say more, they blur into the silent tears of Victor's confession.

* * *

Meeting Michael at 11:00 cannot fit better into Shay Fox's plans, because he has just enough time to visit Jack Morgan before he sees Michael.

He isn't surprised by Morgan's restrained reception, but he is amazed to see a large swelling under his left eye. His mouth is distorted—someone did a good job in whacking him. Morgan barely pronounces the words.

That doesn't prevent him from continuing to be a smartass, though. It also doesn't make it harder for him to deny every possibility that researches at RIRI are conducted for some purpose other than the food products' quality improvement and finding the cure for AIDS, Alzheimer's disease, multiple sclerosis, arthritis, cancer, and other incurable diseases. That research is far from what Fox and Dawson insinuate and suspect.

"You claim you don't conduct such experiments on humans?" Dawson wants to make sure.

"Of course not!" he gasps, horrified by such a thought. "Nothing like that is happening at this institute! Not to my knowledge and certainly not with my approval. We conduct numerous experiments here every day, and I have heard nothing so scandalous throughout my practice. We monitor each of our employees, and there is not an inch of the space that isn't covered by cameras. However, there is always a theoretical possibility that something goes unnoticed. So far, that's just a theory."

Fox lets him speak, even though he knows Morgan is lying. He isn't lying, though, when he said that he doesn't know beans about Beresford's and Daniels's activities outside their working hours.

"So you don't reject the possibility that some of your people might have worked on their own research without you knowing about that?"

"There's *always* a possibility of something like that, Agent Fox. But that didn't happen here. How many times do I have to repeat it to you?" His face pulls into a painful grimace.

"Sir," Dawson tries when his face retraces to its former pre-painfully-distorted look, "a man of your achievements and reputation has surely heard of a significant number of drugs that manipulate human consciousness and subconsciousness? Changing people's identity is no longer science fiction. Of course, such people do not officially exist in the real world, which is not the least surprising to me. But what is happening unofficially in this real world of ours? Give someone a sufficient dose of electroshocks mixed with certain drugs—and you have a walking machine. You have created a person with a new personality. Although physically of the same appearance, their past and present are so altered that they no longer have any memory of who they really are and where they came from. The perfect weapon for espionage projects and terrorist actions. Do you agree with me?"

"No offense, Agent Dawson, you're talking about science fiction! The Cold War is long over. What would be the purpose of these weapons? Or do you think there is some conspiracy against the whole human race? Spooky." He pretends he is shuddering from the very thought of such a thing.

"Let's consider it from a different angle," she continues, not discouraged by his mocking. "What if these half-humans and half-robots are not created for terrorism and conspiracy against governments, but for the purpose of changing this world *for the better* . . ."

"Any insinuation that something like this is happening in my institute is insolent, insulting, and utterly unfounded! You cannot be further from the truth! I could sue you for this! Do you have any idea *who* is behind the research we conduct here? Probably not! Because if you did, you wouldn't dare to think something like that!"

"Is that a threat, Mr. Morgan?" Fox asks calmly. "Do you think you can intimidate us?"

"For God's sake, I don't mean to intimidate anyone! I'm just trying to reason with you! You're both barking up the wrong tree. You live in the clouds, dear lady."

"Is that so? Do you think Michael Daniels lives in the clouds too?" Dawson's voice quivers in the heat of debate, and Morgan's face stiffens like frozen in an ugly grimace.

"What do you mean by that?"

"My partner wants to say that it wouldn't hurt to ask Michael Daniels what he thinks of people with artificially implanted *abilities*, and especially those who created them," Fox jumps in. He knows that they had just turned Michael into a sacrificial lamb if something goes wrong. But they are so close to him now that they can take their (and his) chances. Besides, Morgan's response to Dawson's provocation could bring them to the last missing parts of information.

"Daniels!" Morgan hisses, his forehead gleaming with perspiration and he thrusts his trembling hands into the pockets of his pants. "Are you accusing one of my best men of experimenting on his son? This is ridiculous!"

"We don't accuse anyone. We have *evidence*." Fox produces a bundle of papers from his inside jacket pocket, but he doesn't show them to Morgan. "Do you know what this is? Can you imagine what I have in my hand? This is a statement Neil Beresford wrote before he died. This is an acknowledgment of the experiments that Daniels and he conducted on Michael. Don't bother. This is just a copy. The original is with the Bureau."

Morgan opts to remain silent, not sure if the FBI agents are bluffing or not.

"I presume you knew nothing about it, did you?" Dawson's question is like a sting in a painful spot.

"I didn't know . . . This is the first time I hear about it," he says quietly.

"Surprise, surprise, but we believe you!" Fox exclaims. "Then why did you send your men after Michael? What did you want from him?"

"What men?"

"The two men who claim to be the FBI." Fox gives him their description.

"I heard about them. But they are not my men."

"No? Then who do they work for? They are certainly not Slovak tourists playing FBI."

"I don't know."

"You don't know? And who, if I may ask, *knows*?"

"You are the FBI."

This time Morgan didn't lie, though Fox has a hunch he is holding something back from them by hiding behind someone very powerful and beyond their reach. He feels safe there, and nothing they say can upset him.

Before attempting a different approach, Fox asks, "Do you know what they wanted from him?"

"And what do *you* want from him?" Morgan asks him in return, pretending to be clever.

Fox then goes full force at him, "I wonder what you can tell us about the *controller*?"

Fox and Dawson learned about this miniature device, which is implanted in the brain of a person to be monitored by the Institute, from Peterson. No matter what the distance, it works like a clock and there is not a chance for *missionaries* or *entities* (as those with the implants in their heads are called at the Institute) to abandon their missions without successfully accomplishing them before. In case of rebellion, they will be declared dysfunctional and then destroyed.

Although the controller isn't implanted into Michael, Fox lets Morgan believe that Beresford and Daniels did just that. Morgan swallows the bait and, when Fox is about to give him the final blow, he receives an urgent call from his boss.

In the nick of time, his greatest enemy saves Morgan. Their conversation is over. And it won't continue next time because the killer of Hank Daniels is finally found.

Nevertheless, as soon as the FBI leaves the Institute premises, Morgan calls Washington for further instructions.

* * *

At ten minutes after ten o'clock, Fox and Dawson split. Dawson goes to an appointment with Michael while Fox returns to the New York FBI headquarters to deal with Daniels's killer.

Although burning with a low, blue flame for interrupting an important meeting with Morgan, he fully dedicates himself to new priorities. Later, he will take care of Morgan and his lies, and resolve the matter once and for all.

Now, he has to take care of another liar. Frustrated by Victor Kenneth's fabrications, he once again questions Michael's innocence. Having enough lies for one day, he is badgering Kenneth to get him to withdraw his affidavit and force him to admit perjury. Fletcher gives him thirty minutes to break Kenneth; that is how much Dawson needs to bring Michael in and then confront the two of them.

"I'm not covering for him!" Victor is defending himself. "They were covering for *me*!"

"That means you lied in your previous statement?" Fox is attacking again.

"I wouldn't agree with that. We lied when we said that all three of us were together all the time. The truth is, I joined them later."

"After killing Hank Daniels?"

"Yes."

"Prove it!"

"I can't—"

Fox slams his fist on the table, startling Victor and making him jump from the chair.

"Prove it, big shot! I won't fall for it twice! Do you hear me? I WON'T."

He paces up and down the room. Then he looks closely into Victor's face, his breath smelling of Wrigley's Juicy Fruit.

"Tell me. I want to know. I want to *understand*. *Why* did you kill him? Why did you kill the bastard?"

"Because he deserved it! It was him or Michael. If I hadn't killed him, he would have killed Michael. Someone had to stop him!"

"So you decided to be Michael's Good Samaritan. You missed the point, my friend. The Samaritan killed *no one*."

"Hank was insane! That was the only way to help *Michael*..."

"You're not a judge, and neither are you a jury," Fox spells into his face. "Although, I promise you, you'll have to deal with both soon."

"I know that, and I'm ready to face the consequences. I have nothing to lose anymore."

He is tired, and Fox sees that. Still, he cannot leave him alone until he withdraws his confession.

"Do you think Michael will be proud of what you did? Do you expect him to thank you for ruining his life and the life of his sister?"

"You forget that *I* didn't ruin his life. Besides, I'm not asking Michael to thank me for anything. What matters most to me is that he's *alive*. That's all I care about."

Fox looks at his wristwatch. And then into Victor's eyes, scrutinizing him. "I want you to tell me again everything from the beginning. Once again, I want to hear what happened there."

"Do I have to?" Victor says, on the brink of despair.

"*Do you have to?* What kind of question is that?! Of course you have to!"

"*Why?* I've already told you everything. I wrote everything down! I even signed a damn confession!"

"But I don't believe you! I don't believe your confession. That's why you will repeat your story. From A to Z. You got it?"

Victor silently watches him, heavy bags under his bloodshot eyes, his whole body screaming for sleep. His mind drifts away, searching for the path to nirvana.

"I'm listening," Fox says, and Victor starts narrating again. What he knows, what he learned, and what he believed to have happened.

"I knew Michael wouldn't be home because Alien told me he had moved in with him . . .

"Michael was sleeping in Alien's room, while Alien and I were talking in his kitchen. Alien didn't want Michael to hear what we were talking about."

"Alien told me he didn't tell anyone about it," Fox interrupts him.

"He told you that? I don't know why he did it. I knew because he told me. Anyway, you have to ask him.

"Michael had nightmares, he talked in his sleep, and Alien spent hours lying awake and listening. He didn't want to wake him; he knew how much Michael needed sleep. That's how he found out what Hank was doing to him. Do I have to go through this again?"

"You can skip that part," Fox shows him some compassion.

"While Michael was sleeping, the two of us agreed that something had to be done to stop Hank. We couldn't count on Michael to do it because he just couldn't do it. He was a wreck; that much was clear. And we also knew what caused it.

"Our plan was that Alien would stay with Michael, while I would go to his home and talk to Hank. And it was like that. Michael and Alien were in town, waiting for me to join them. Michael knew nothing about what was going on.

"No one saw me when I got there. Now I regret that, because then you would believe me. Hank was surprised to see me; I was probably one of the last people he hoped for on his doorstep. He let me in, anyway. He was drunk; I knew it the moment I saw him. He had been drinking a lot lately.

"We settled into the living room, trying to have a conversation. There was not much to talk about with a man in this condition. I told him I knew everything about him and Michael and warned him to leave Michael alone. Otherwise, I'd press charges against him. He laughed in my face. He didn't believe a word I said and started to poke fun at me. He said ugly things about Michael. You know, how that little fag has a cute butt and that I should also try it sometimes, stuff like that. He wanted to provoke me at all costs.

"I admit, I didn't owe him, either. He went too far. Michael, Alien, the guys, and I also use all kinds of language between us, but what Daniels said then was vulgar. I told him to shut up or I'll slug him so he would remember what he said. Before I could do anything, he attacked me . . .

"He jumped on me and grabbed me across the table. I gave

him a punch while we were still in the air toppling over, and when we hit the floor, he punched me back. We crashed something; I heard it shatter. Even drunk, he was pretty strong, and I could hardly handle him. I thought of Michael, how it must have been for him to endure being with that man. Michael is much gentler, and there was no way he would handle Hank. My situation was getting worse each second, but I knew I did the right thing when I got there. Someone had to show their teeth to that man.

"Hank was like a bully, probably the alcohol gave him extra strength. He was hitting me everywhere, almost beating the hell out of me. He threatened I'd find out what it was like to be Michael when he tears my ass up, saving no words to tell me what he was going to do. I won't be able to walk for a week after he's done with me. I don't remember exactly what happened then . . . I think he pushed his knee hard between my legs. I writhed in pain as he reached for my belt. When I realized what he was trying to do, I blew a gasket, snatched the first thing that came into my hand, I think it was an ashtray, yes, it was an ashtray—your boss asked me about it—and whacked him over his head. I kept hitting him until he let me go. I was scared, hurt, and humiliated, and didn't even think I was hitting a man. Instead of Hank, I saw a monster lying in a pool of blood, a monster that must be destroyed. Beaten to death before it hurts someone else.

"His blood was all over me, and the room looked like a slaughterhouse. For a few minutes I sat by his body, pondering what to do next and how to remove evidence that would later point to me during the investigation. First, I took my bloody clothes off and put them in my backpack. Then I washed myself and borrowed clean clothes from Michael's closet. They weren't my size—they were too small for me, but Hank's clothes were three sizes larger than what I wear. Besides, I didn't want to wear anything that belonged to him. After that, I trashed the apartment. I flipped the lamp over, scattered pillows, books, and magazines to give the impression that it was a burglary. Then I bolted out, leaving the door open behind me, which was also supposed to indicate a burglary.

"When I got out, the street was empty except for one woman walking a dog in the park across the street. I don't know if she saw me or not. But if you make the effort to find her, she might confirm what I told you. She's the only person who can tell you I was there. I think that would be all."

"What happened to your bloodied clothes?"

"I tried to wash them, but the blood wouldn't come out completely, so I had to throw them away. Wrong thing to do, right?"

Fox sighs deeply. Eleven had passed twenty-five minutes ago, and Dawson had not arrived. Regardless of her, Fletcher would get here any minute to take Victor with him.

Fox forces himself not to think what will happen in that case. Instead, he returns to the day the murder happened and Victor's witness.

Yes, the woman recognized him as a young man leaving the crime scene at the time of the murder. However, Fox isn't sure if the woman really *saw* him or *decided* to see him. On the other hand, if she didn't see Victor and Victor didn't see her, how could Victor know about her?

To be sure, Fox once again asks, "One thing is not clear to me. How come your fingerprints are not there? I mean, *nowhere.*"

"Because I wore gloves."

"You wore *gloves*? Why?"

"I guess I was cold. I wasn't planning on staying long, so I didn't feel the need to take them off."

"Daniels not once asked you why don't you take them off? He didn't find that weird?"

"He was drunk. I could have had a fur cap on and sit in an astronaut suit, and he'd be okay with that."

"And I'm supposed to believe that?"

"I'm just telling you how it was."

"I suppose you also threw your gloves away with the rest of the ruined clothes?"

"Certainly. Would you be walking around the neighborhood with bloody gloves?"

"Tell me, what does it feel like to kill a man?"

Sensing a trap, Victor thinks for a moment before answering.

"You probably expect me to tell you how awful you feel the first time you kill a man. And that it is not so bad when you kill the next time because you get used to it somehow. It's not like that at all. Only a sick mind can think like that. It's hard every time. Because you never forget the faces of the people you killed. They stay with you forever. They never leave you. They continue to live in your nightmares."

He is breathing heavily, getting lost in his thoughts and disappearing into nothingness. Before losing him, Fox asks him one more question.

"Do you consider yourself a murderer, Victor? After all, you killed two people?"

"Agent Fox, I would be happy if you understood two things. I killed Hank because it happened. I didn't *plan* on killing him. As for my grandmother . . . she was dying. She was dying in pain, and when she could no longer bear the pain, when she could no longer stand the *dying*, she asked me to help her. She asked me to kill the pain. That was the last thing I could do for her. That was the last thing she asked of me. Would you deny one last wish to your dying grandmother?

"No. You don't have to answer that . . . *I did it, not you.* It was my choice. My decision. But for that, I do not consider myself an angel or a saint. I feel remorse and I have nightmares. In that moment I could not have done otherwise. . . . It was the only choice Nana and I had.

"I did it because I loved her . . . Because I wanted to help her. You will have to discuss the morality of my actions with someone else. . . . I did it for love . . ."

Chapter

29th: Everything counts as long as you do it with passion, fervor, a wild gleam in your eyes and the wind on your face! If you wish to learn more about this sport, grab the first skater on the street, visit your local skate shop, and look for info about the contests in your area or close by. Spend your . . .

A TALK WITH SHAY FOX BRINGS BACK THE LIGHT in Michael. It shines in him with a soft and gentle flame of faith that takes him to the immediate neighborhood of Victor Kenneth. Before meeting with federal agents, Michael is longing for another ride. One more time he wants to feel the rolling of the wheels and the bouncing of the board under his feet—perhaps for the last time. Who knows, maybe this will be his last ride? What happens thereafter, he cannot say. He doesn't know that.

He unlocks the door of Victor's apartment with Nancy's keys. Victor isn't there, but he left him a message.

Michael,
When you stop by, take this board. I will no longer use it and that's

why I give it to you. Be careful not to crack it—we had some unforgettable moments together. I wish you the same.

Take care, my friend.
BCNU,
Victor

Michael is staring at the sheet of paper in his hand, not believing his eyes. He reads Victor's letter again, but he still cannot believe that Victor had given him his favorite board. And just yesterday he fixed it!

He finds a pencil and on the other side of Victor's message scribbles:

Thanx, Vic.
The most beautiful thoughts always remain unspoken. I hope we both justify your trust.
BCNU, buddy.
M.

He leaves the message on the kitchen table and, putting the skateboard under his arm, out he goes.

Down Fifth Avenue and farther south, all around Central Park. Over Columbus Circle he comes to Broadway, approaching Riverside Park. But not directly, because he still has plenty of time. So he skurfs the neighboring streets.

He slaloms between passersby, skateboarding faster and faster, his T-shirt and the legs of his pants fluttering around him.

The wind is in his tousled hair, fervor in his eyes. Wild glow.

Where are the cops? he wonders, dashing across the

intersection.

Everything is working in his favor. The whole town is waiting for him. And he takes it.

* * *

Ted Atkins and Jeremy Creek are not very comfortable in the too-loud atmosphere of Hard Rock Cafe at 221 West 57th Street, packed with teenage kids. Rebecca often goes there with her girlfriends from school, so it's not unusual that she chooses it as their meeting place.

Red Sunshine and Rebecca are visiting the places where skateboarders gather and skate, while Ted Atkins and Jeremy Creek went to St. Luke's Place only to find out that the Daniels apartment is still under police surveillance. A police officer on duty sends them to the man in charge—Steven Merchant, and the two of them went to look for him. But even he doesn't help them much because he doesn't have any information about Michael himself. He offered to let them know as soon as he finds out something.

Jeremy Creek gave him the name of the hotel where they will stay and asked him to leave a message at the concierge, because they will be in town looking for Michael. They'll contact him again in an hour, whether or not he calls them sooner.

After visiting Division Pro Skate Shop, Rebecca phones Alien and Victor, but neither are available. It looks like everyone has disappeared without a trace. No one knows anything about them, and because of that, Rebecca is increasingly restless.

Red Sunshine is already uneasy since they arrived in New York, confused and a little scared of the hail of new impressions. For him, it is a world diametrically different from his own world, a world from a tale or films about the future. The rivers of cars; people rushing in the streets like bees around a hive or ants in an anthill; buildings that reach so high that their peaks scratch the clouds. The sky boils with airplanes, helicopters, airships, and balloons of various colors. It is a world of glass, light, noise, and commotion. People of all colors, ages, different and extreme dressing styles, and the craziest hairstyles Sunshine has ever seen merge into one mass on their way to their goal: SUCCESS (and success only).

Skateboarders are a story for themselves, looking ridiculous in their oversized clothes,

(His mom would give him a beating if he showed up dressed like that at the door: with his pants down, his underpants peeking out, and the back of his pants hanging just above his knees.)

and talking in jargon he doesn't understand. What little did he understand baffled him so much that he had to mention it to Rebecca. To his surprise, Rebecca laughs at his innocence. She likes them and thinks they are cool despite their language. Each time she sees a skater cruising around town, she points to him.

They reach Washington Square and only then Rebecca manages to explain to him what the catch is in riding on a piece of wood, as Sunshine complained. Gaping in disbelief at two kids, no older than him and Rebecca, doing madcap stunts, Red Sunshine is expecting any moment to see one of them breaking his bones. Nothing like that happens. The boys keep riding and doing tricks, bathed in sweat and pumped with adrenaline.

Rebecca smiles at her friend and takes him from Washington Square Park to Hard Rock Cafe.

Mustering courage and risking being ridiculed again, Red

Sunshine asks her, "Your brother is also like that . . . ? Like these two?"

She doesn't laugh at him this time. "Michael is *better*. He is very, very good. He is looking for a sponsor to become a pro. He will skate in contests soon."

"You mean, they will pay him for it? He will get money for . . . *hopping* like that?"

"Yes!" Rebecca chortles. "He will get money for *hopping*! That's right!"

Then she gets serious. "How do you like New York?"

This time Sunshine thinks twice before saying anything. He stares once more at the tall buildings and skyscrapers around him, then looks down at the wide streets that branch before him and looks back into her curious eyes.

Arriving at their destination, Red Sunshine experiences another culture shock. He wishes to take back what he had said about New York a moment ago. To his surprise, his father and Jeremy Creek also share his opinion. Impatient and already half deaf, they couldn't wait for the two youngsters to show up.

Rebecca takes a seat opposite Ted Atkins while Red Sunshine sits opposite Jeremy. She glances at him to find out what he thinks of her favorite place. As usual, his face says it all.

To Jeremy's and Ted's hurry, Rebecca and Red Sunshine finish their burgers and chase them down with Cola. To Red Sunshine they look artificial and unhealthy, but he is too hungry to complain. Finishing lunch, they exchange information. No couple learns anything about Michael, which saddens Rebecca. Her self-confidence weakens, but she isn't thinking about giving up yet. She didn't travel that far to quit now. She still believes that she will track down Michael sooner than the FBI and the police, she only has to get in touch with Victor or Alien.

They will know what happened to him.

She slurps the rest of her cola through a straw, and so does Red Sunshine. Unaccustomed to such a diet, something unpleasant happens to him. His stomach swells and he lets out a loud burp. Rebecca bursts out laughing, as do the four girls at the next table.

Red Sunshine turns purple-red from embarrassment and springs to his feet. "Are we going or not?" he asks in a hoarse voice, ashamed.

Ted Atkins says to Jeremy Creek to let him through to pay the bill, but Jeremy Creek insists it's on him. While they're arguing over who will pay the bill, Red Sunshine and Rebecca head for the exit.

Getting out on West 57th Street, Red Sunshine stops suddenly, blinded by the sun. (Or is it a subconscious reaction?)

The wheels rattle close to him, missing him by a whisker.

A second later, Rebecca bumps into him from behind and pushes him out into the street. And then, guided by instinct, she leaps to the middle of the sidewalk, craning her neck after the sound of a skateboard moving away. (Or is it a conscious reaction, after all?)

"What the hell!" she hears Red Sunshine uttering a curse before he bites his tongue. She doesn't give much thought to that it is his first curse she hears him say in front of her, perhaps his first curse ever. She is looking at a blond skater in a fluttering and a little-too-large, Zoo York T-shirt.

(Michael?)

Her eyes widen as the skater pushes himself farther down West 57th Street. Then he jumps doing a trick, an *ollie*, and Rebecca shouts after him,

"Michael?!"

The skateboarder doesn't stop at her yell, but it doesn't confuse her. There is something so familiar about his appearance. Something so much *hers* . . .

"MICHAEL!!!"

She breaks into a run, leaving behind Red Sunshine, and Ted Atkins and Jeremy Creek, who dash out of the cafe hearing her shouts.

* * *

Michael is happy that he is still in good shape and not rusty despite not skating for *hours*. He is riding Victor's Prime board for the first time, and he knew immediately that it is right for him. Although narrower than the boards on which he normally skates and with a smaller concave, it fits him well as his earlier boards.

He does a few *ollies* and *manuals* while turning from Broadway to West 60th Street, and then to Eleventh Avenue. He goes all the way to West 57th Street, and then turns eastward again. Here he repeats the same tricks as on Broadway, only *fakie*.

He thinks of Victor and regrets he's not here to ride with him now.

He *ollies* again, jumping over a manhole, and skirts a couple with a stroller. He pushes himself a few times with his foot, gaining acceleration.

He cruises through Ninth and Eighth Avenue, still having a little over half an hour to meet with the FBI.

His plan is simple: across Avenue of Americas, to East Drive in Central Park, and then to Riverside Park. But something distracts him from that.

Somewhere between Broadway and Seventh Avenue, he

barely escapes collision with a pedestrian on West 57th Street. Not paying attention, a guy rushes out of Hard Rock Cafe and Michael almost runs him down. Without stopping to see if he is okay, Michael shouts an apology over his shoulder and speeds up again. He thinks someone is calling after him, but how many Michaels are in New York? So he doesn't stop.

He also doesn't turn around to check if it is someone he knows, for a group of Japanese tourists appears out of nowhere in front of him. He slows down to get around them, then pushes himself faster again. The voice is still calling his name, though, not leaving him. In fact, the voice is *following* him.

Someone is running after him. He looks down the streets ahead . . .

"MICHAEL! MICHAEL, WAIT FOR ME! STOP!"

Only twenty yards to Seventh Avenue, and the sidewalk is clear.

He turns around, doing *fakie*, and gapes in disbelief.

"Michael, wait for me . . ."

She is out of breath, with tears streaming down her red face. Her long, blonde hair flies behind her as his baby sister collides with passersby and stumbles.

She reaches out to him and smiles.

"Michael . . ."

He smiles at her smile, that lovely smile, and feels the blow from behind.

Michael knocks down the passerby, but doesn't fall himself. He keeps his balance and continues to ride *fakie*, slowly.

He looks proudly at Rebecca and forms with his lips, "Did you see that? I didn't fall!"

Her smile then disappears. Turns into a grimace of pure horror.

***

Shay Fox is relentlessly stubborn, but Damon Fletcher is even more stubborn. He is determined and inexorable. Fox and Dawson will not continue their investigation, period! Everything is clear. End of story.

"That's exactly the point! Nothing is clear," Fox persists.

Fletcher then grabs him by the jacket and, like a schoolboy, drags him to his office. With a slam, he shuts the door behind them.

"I said, the investigation is closed. We found the perpetrator. In Washington, they are pleased. Am I clear?"

"What about Morgan? What about the research he conducts there? Dawson and I have—"

"You have *nothing*, Agent. You saw nothing, you heard nothing, you didn't talk to anyone. Nothing is going on at RIRI. Nothing to panic about. Someone fooled you. Do you understand?"

Fox is all beside himself from anger and helplessness.

"We have a witness who will confirm that this is not the case! We have evidence to show there is cause for alarm."

"Which witness? What evidence?"

"Elijah Peterson," Fox decides to break his promise and reveal the man's name. "Elijah Peterson talked to us."

Fletcher frowns. "In that case, I have bad news for you. Elijah Peterson is on the list of three victims. A fire broke out at the Institute. It is already localized, but the damage is enormous. Evacuation is underway."

Fox is thunderstruck. His head is drumming, his abdomen convulses so much that even his breathing exercise doesn't help him. He feels instant weakness, and he needs some fresh air now.

He only utters, "Morgan?"

"He's alive. They probably already evacuated him."

"Where?" Fox whispers.

"The Washington FBI has taken over control of the evacuation. Even I don't know all the details."

Something human, paternal, and friendly awakens in Fletcher at that moment. He says to Fox, "I'm really sorry, Shay. I know how much that case meant to you."

Fox doesn't answer him. He leaves his office, not even bothering to close the door behind him.

* * *

Alien watches the skaters from a discreet distance while practicing in the skatepark built by Andy Kessler, a member of the former original Zoo York Team. Although helmets and pads are the requirement in contests while skating on the vert-wall, vert-ramp, quarters, and other elements, most of the skaters now don't have them. Neither did Alien on the day James Stowe spotted him while practicing in extreme weather.

An acquaintance with a successful photographer changes a lot in Alien's life. Not only did he make money and become famous thanks to Dennis Kay's men's underwear ads, he also falls in love truly for the first time in his life. Laurie officially ditched him, true, but that won't stop Alien. His life depends on her being his girlfriend. Alien agrees to the friendship compromise only because it is not the moment to insist on more. He has too many things on his mind, and even with best intentions, he has no time for his love life.

Watching the skaters jump, slide, and grind, Alien is making yet another sacrifice. He keeps watch in case something goes wrong for Michael. The only problem is that Michael isn't there. At least Alien doesn't see him.

At five minutes to eleven o'clock, he catches sight of Agent Dawson. Fox isn't with her and this surprises him. Dawson is behind the east fence of the skatepark waiting for Michael to show up, while Alien is hiding behind some guys on the opposite side. When, even after twenty minutes, there is no sign of Michael, Alien becomes concerned. Preoccupied with alarming thoughts, he forgets about Fox because Michael has a habit of never being so late.

At 11:25, Dawson answers her mobile phone. She speaks to someone briefly before leaving in a hurry. Alien is now certain that something must have happened. Just in case, he waits another ten minutes. He no longer enjoys watching the skaters and their stunts, so he forces himself to leave too.

Something dark and cold creeps into him while he is leaving Riverside Park.

* * *

Adrian Wood is one of the most reliable, skillful, and agile New York cab drivers. With ease he avoids gridlocks, knowing every corner of the city as his own pocket. He learned as a teenage addict and former drug dealer about every street, every cul-de-sac and every intersection, because he needed to know his surroundings as the palm of his hand if he wanted to survive. Times are changing, though.

And with them, people.

Adrian Wood decides to change and become a model

citizen. He severs all ties with his infamous past, fully aware that it isn't at all simple and easy in New York. He becomes convinced of this when he picks up his old buddy this morning, just as he had been convinced of it many times before. He is nostalgic for a moment and, for sentimental reasons, he lets him in his taxi, as if he is asking for trouble.

The truth is, Adrian needs money, but he isn't going to make it the way his old buddy offers it. He doesn't want to get into the drug world once more; three times is enough.

His friend is persistent, and had Adrian not remembered his brother Ricky, who fell a victim of poorly purified and bad quality Big Harry overdose, he might have relented. But he remembers his brother and the promise he had made to him and himself that he will never again resort to drugs. After two failed attempts, he stays clean, mostly thanks to a picture of dead Ricky he couldn't squeeze out of his mind.

Once again resisting the temptation, he starts to think about how to get rid of his buddy before something he doesn't want happens. He doesn't want to argue with him and throw him out of the cab just like that; that's not Adrian's style. But he also won't think twice if forced on that. The memory of Ricky, though distant, is still very much alive in him.

Lost in thought and burdened by his buddy's coaxing, Adrian hears a soft thud and instinctively hits the brakes. The sound is not loud, he almost doesn't feel the impact. But the body of the man he hit is flying in a high arc before it lands on the sidewalk.

In two swift moves Adrian is out of the car, forgetting his old buddy, who sneaks out on the other side and disappears in traffic.

He runs to the boy lying unconscious, his head resting

against the curb, as if asleep. The boy is lying on his stomach and Adrian cannot see if he is badly injured or not. He takes the boy's pulse, and when he pulls his hand under his neck, his palm is red with blood. The blood is now soaking the boy's blond hair.

A girl screams out the boy's name. His girlfriend? Maybe his sister?—Adrian doesn't know. She makes her way through the gathered people and looks hysterically for an answer from him.

(Is he alive?? Is he alive?! Tell me he's alive!)

Adrian steps away from the motionless boy, too scared to say anything. He just looks back at her, overcome with sudden sadness.

His eyes must have been full of pain as the girl screams again.

"MIIICHAAAEEEEL!"

Why must history repeat itself? Adrian thinks, heaving a deep and sad sigh. The girl kneels beside the boy and takes his head in her lap. Silently sobbing, she rocks him gently.

"Everything's fine, Michael. Everything's fine. I'm back, little brother, I'm back. All is well . . ."

* * *

When the car strikes Michael and tosses him in the air, traffic doesn't stop. It takes a whole minute for people to comprehend what had happened. Not even fifteen minutes later, traffic doesn't stop completely, though it slows down almost to a crawl.

Michael is stopped while riding a *fakie* and is thrown back toward the sidewalk. Seconds later, he is lying in his sister's arms. More seconds later, Red Sunshine, Ted Atkins, and Jeremy Creek arrive at the scene of an accident. Petrified by the sight of a limp boy's body, they don't remember to look at what had happened to Michael's skateboard.

As Michael was falling, pulled by gravity, his board continues rolling on its own. Under a second taxi which stops with a squeak, under the other cars slowing down on Seventh Avenue, until it hits the sidewalk at the other side of the avenue. Undamaged.

A ten-year-old boy picks it up there after following it across the street and stopping right in front of him. He looks around for its owner, but not seeing him anywhere, he carefully puts his right foot on the skateboard. He has never held a skateboard in his hand before, let alone ridden on it. But when he pushes himself, it comes naturally to him.

He pushes himself again and again, making slow progress toward East Drive in Central Park. One step at a time, by pushing his left foot after another, getting hooked, getting elated, getting enthusiastic.

In four years, that same boy will become one of the best skateboarders in New Manhattan. Many sponsors will scramble for him, but he will only be interested in skating for Independent.

The filmmakers will also notice him and offer him engagements. Two years later, he will make a movie about New York skateboarders, and a few more movies will follow, which will bring him fame. His fame will bring him plenty of money, a large percentage of which he will donate to the institutions for the care and protection of children abused by their parents. With the second part of the money he will start a foundation for young, talented writers and poets to help them publish their first books. At twenty-five, he will publish his first collection of poems titled *Dream Collectors*.

The first city to host its promotion will be Paris, and the whole event will turn into a huge success for the young writer. It will also be the success of a carefully prepared and launched project that started more than a decade ago, on a small island in the very arms of the City of All Cities.

Upon his return from the French enclave, Mikey R. will continue to support humanitarian efforts throughout the States. Wherever he makes a speech, he will express his deep gratitude to the unknown skater whose unexpected gift has helped him find his place in the world and thus enable him to help other people.

Although he is in his late twenties in 2017 and with very little free time, he will use every precious moment to grab his skateboard and hit the streets of New York in the company of his old friends.

Thuuunderooously!

Chapter

30th: . . . time in skateparks and with local skaters. Watch the video footage and read everything you find on the subject.

One day you might be teaching others about the art and challenges of skateboarding! What's most important, grab that board and enjoy the sound of the rolling wheels! Break a leg!

THE GREEN OASIS OF BRYANT PARK at the back of the New York Public Library. The murmur of the fountain water is pleasant and soothing. The only ones who look tense in this yard of peace and quiet are Alien and his companion. Their heads are full of worries and questions that seek answers.

So many questions, and there are no answers to every one of them. Some questions are too complex to answer, others are too dangerous to insist on being answered. Alien and Shay Fox know that.

Alien mostly answers Fox's questions, while Fox hesitates to offer answers to Alien's queries. Maybe that's how it's best for him. The truth sometimes can hurt, be too dangerous.

Unlike Fox, Alien could hardly wait to unload the burden

of truth. The case is closed, and this informal conversation is what he needs to unburden himself before he can return to normal life.

Fox's partner is not with them. She's on vacation, away from New York City. And Fox is officially on vacation, but there is still something left to finish. His private investigation.

The FBI has a killer to be tried for his crimes. Victor Kenneth will be tried for the death of Angela Kenneth, despite the *merciful nature* of his act. However, Fox is worried that he could be held accountable for something he didn't do. Because: Michael Daniels committed involuntary manslaughter; he killed his stepfather, Hank Daniels, in self-defense.

Roy Travis, nicknamed Alien, acknowledges this when he tells Fox the real truth about the events that led to Hank Daniels's death.

"I was coming back from skateboarding when I found Michael waiting for me outside the house. He was all beside himself and blabbering about having a fight with Hank and injuring him. He said he thought he had killed him. I pushed him inside so someone wouldn't hear us because he was loud. I gave him something strong to calm him down and then he told me what had happened.

"Michael went home to mend fences with his father—you already know that. But when he explained what was bugging him, Hank began to mock him and disagreed with Michael. First, they quarreled about Michael's therapies, then exchanged heated words about their *private affairs*. I remind you, I guess so, because Michael never told me that. But he told me something that led me to that conclusion. He threatened to leave home if Hank did not leave him alone. He meant it seriously, his backpack with his personal belongings the police found confirmed this. Then Hank attacked him. They got into a fight, Michael grabbed the ashtray and hit him. Not waiting to see how badly he had hurt him, Michael ran away. He was in panic and forgot his backpack in fear. He didn't dare to take the risk and come back for it, fearing he would not escape Hank a second time.

"He washed himself in one of the public toilets and then called Rebecca. He confessed to her what he had done, and Rebecca begged him to go home and check up on her dad. Instead, he called 911 and went to my house. The two of us returned to his home together, and I talked to the officer on duty. That is where the story of Michael ends. Michael had been hiding from that moment and he had nothing to do with what was happening later. *I* am responsible for that.

"When I saw how things were, it wasn't difficult for me to conclude that Michael was in danger. He killed a man, and he wasn't even sure about that! Anyway, the law was on his heels, so I thought I had to do something to help him. I knew a lot more than Michael knew I knew. I also knew that as the only witness, I could not give Michael an alibi. Especially when they find out we're friends. So I involved Victor. Victor didn't hesitate for a moment when I explained to him how things were. He at once said we had to help Michael. I even told him that Hank sexually abused Michael, and Victor also thought Hank must be stopped. I didn't tell you this before because I thought this information might be of use to us later in the investigation. But in the meantime, Victor screwed up, and Michael is gone, so it doesn't matter anymore. The problem was that Victor and I didn't know how to stop Hank. While we were figuring out what to do, Michael took care of that himself. He stopped Hank once and for all. Hank challenged him and Michael accidentally killed him. If you ask me, sooner or later one of them would be hurt, anyway."

"Both were killed in the end," Fox concludes. "Tell me, how could Victor Kenneth know what happened in the Daniels apartment that day? Where did he get the information? Why did he take responsibility for Hank's death since Michael killed him?"

"I don't know that. His confession surprised me just as much as Michael's death. He may have been depressed after giving his grandmother a drink of liquid morphine. He hadn't been the same since his girlfriend left him. And Michael's situation was hopeless, so he had to come up with an idea—"

"By confessing a double murder, he calms his conscience and saves Michael. Because he had nothing more to lose," Fox recalls Victor's words.

"Exactly. There is no other logical explanation. He could admit that he killed Hank because I told him what I heard from Michael. Apart from that, he was indeed in their apartment that afternoon. He admitted to me only after two days when we were already too deep into this to change anything in our plans. And I've told you already. I was angry with him for not telling me earlier, but he said that it wouldn't change things, anyway. I believed him. But now, when his head is at stake, I can't help but question it. That's why I'm telling you all this. Because I believe something could still be done for Victor. Michael is dead and he won't mind us. On the contrary. If he were alive, I think he would also want to help Victor.

"So it turned out that both of them were there that day. Victor was hiding out in the park across the street and under the steps of neighboring buildings, waiting to see what would happen to Michael. Michael didn't appear for a long time, and Victor was already thinking about leaving, when Michael dashed out of the building and missed him only by a few steps before fleeing down the street. Bloody, holding his unbuttoned pants so he wouldn't lose them and trip over them.

"For a few moments, Victor remained hidden in the shadow, then went to see what made Michael escape like that. He had no idea what he would tell Hank, he just knew he had to do something. Michael was a total mess when he ran past him.

"The apartment door was open, so he went in without knocking. The lights were on inside and it was unusually calm. *Too* calm, as Victor described it. He went straight to the living room and found Hank there. You know that part anyway. He checked if Hank was alive, but he was already dead as a dodo.

"Since there was nothing he could do for Hank, he no longer wanted to stay there. He headed for the door, but then he remembered something. He returned to the living room and simulated a burglary. Then he came out. He left the door open behind him as he had found it before.

"He was in no hurry. The street was empty, except for one woman walking a dog. Victor saw her, and she saw him too. That part is true, only Victor wasn't the one who killed Hank. The woman had to take the dog for a walk only after Michael had run away and while Victor was still in the apartment. That's why it came to confusion.

"As for Victor's fingerprints, the situation is also pretty clear. Victor really did wear gloves. He was telling the truth about it. It was pinching cold, and when he saw what had happened, he thought it was better not to take them off. That's what you didn't know. The rest is an old story for you."

Alien falls silent and Fox takes his word. He speaks to him in a relaxed manner, studying his face closely.

"We agreed that this would be an unofficial conversation.

However, I have to ask you if you would be ready to testify if the investigation into the Daniels case is reopened? Would you be willing to make a signed statement that you and Victor have interfered with the investigation by misleading it? Don't rush to give me an answer. Think it over. You have to be aware that in this case you may be tried."

"I've already thought about it. I thought you would ask me that, so I thought about it beforehand. My answer is yes. I'm ready to take on that responsibility."

"Are you sure? Are you one hundred percent sure of that?"

"Yes, sir. I'm fully aware of the consequences. And I also know that I will not be punished as much as Victor would be punished for being tried for murder. I'm still a minor, and you can also offer me, as you offered Michael, immunity. Because I cooperated with you, didn't I? When I consider everything, I can't lose as much as Victor can gain if I testify in his favor. Am I right?"

Fox smiles at him. The kid has *potential*, he has to give him credit for that.

"You're right. But you will still have to take responsibility. If you decide to cooperate, there's no escaping it."

"I'll take my chances. I'm not a coward. And I don't leave friends in the lurch."

"Thank you."

"I should thank you."

Fox reaches into the pocket of his jacket, which he keeps folded over the back of his chair, and forks out a few sheets of paper. Holds them out to Alien.

"I would like to ask you something else. This has nothing to do with the investigation. Can you tell me what this means?"

Alien accepts the papers and unfolds them.

He flips through the positive responses of Doghouse Production and Icarus Skateboards to Michael's requests to represent them in amateur contests.

He manages to smile, but it is a smile which fights back tears. Because Michael lived for that moment. If only he had lived long enough to see it.

Suddenly, Alien feels the need to explain to Fox what it meant to Michael, even though he could not yet skate like a pro (with his name printed on the boards on which he skated). It doesn't matter that much because Alien knows amateur skateboarders who are better than some pros. Michael was one of them. Which isn't important anymore. Because Doghouse and Icarus are late. Forever.

Instead, he suppresses his enthusiasm and just says, "That means Michael was a good skater. A badass skater."

Then he changes the subject and asks Fox if he had learned anything about the two mysterious guys. He is also interested in how the investigation ended, because it is still not completely clear to him what was Michael's role in Beresford's and Daniels's plans.

Fox thinks carefully before deciding what to say to him and begins with the news of the fire that happened at the Institute. Sooner or later, Alien will hear about it in the news, so he sees no reason to keep it secret from him. However, he doesn't tell him about the two agents, because he also isn't sure what to think about them. He is still undecided whether they work for the FBI Washington or some secret organization. The same goes for the nature of the research conducted within the closely guarded underground laboratories equipped with state-of-the-art cloning technology only the personnel involved in the *Project Messiah* had access to.

Down there, deep underground, somewhere up to twenty yards below the surface, lived and grew in-vitro-born children, whose cells were genetically manipulated from the cells of felons and criminals serving life sentences across the States. The aim of these experiments was to create good offspring from bad seed. In other words, to clone the bad seed with a high IQ and turn it into a human who would contribute the society once it grows up and becomes a model citizen, thus repairing the damage its original did to that same society. Monitored by a *controller*, a genetically manipulated *copy* is guaranteed to function and serve its purpose or otherwise be destroyed.

Once they finished their educational program at the Institute, these children would be given for adoption to selected couples for the purpose of integrating them into daily life and society. Watered by parental love, their hearts and minds would flourish with a strong sense of affiliation and responsibility to the nation and their homeland, where their true mission would begin. Fifteen of these children have already successfully completed their missions, just ordinary children for those who know them, whilst special and extraordinary children for those who created them.

Not wanting to satisfy the boy's vivid imagination too much, Fox tells him, "Beresford and his stepfather tried to develop Michael's ability to use his mind energy. It's called psychokinesis. Until recently, science didn't acknowledge its existence. It was considered a parapsychological myth. Thanks to numerous experiments, this opinion has changed. Ordinary people can also use the mind energy, not only people with so-called supernatural powers. Beresford and Daniels wanted to *give* Michael that ability, to teach him on a conscious level to use psychokinesis. If he passed the test, those abilities would also develop with Rebecca. We don't know if they had any other motives besides money and gaining power. We can only speculate, but we won't get far in guesswork. So it's best to forget all that."

"That means, you don't know the *reason* Michael is dead?"

"We don't know the reason, but we have an explanation. Michael and Rebecca should, to put it bluntly, have become *superhumans*. We do not know *who* or *what* Daniels and Beresford wanted to control by them. It could have been anyone. The fact is that they almost made Michael a very dangerous weapon. And that weapon could, with the power of his mind, move objects and control people by projecting his thoughts into theirs. And no one could stop him."

"What you just said explains the black cloud Victor was talking about."

"The *black cloud*?"

"Yeah. Victor told me he had a feeling . . . He told me he had a weird feeling about Michael. He saw Michael see *him* disappear into the black cloud. Of course, that didn't really happen."

"Michael saw Victor disappear into the black cloud and that's what Victor saw Michael see?"

"Something like that," Alien confirms.

"Was it any particular cloud? Was there any meaning in all this?"

"Maybe it has to do with his grandmother and everything that happened later. Victor had that *experience* the night before he killed his grandmother."

"Hence, he gives his grandmother morphine and a black cloud of remorse, guilty conscience, regret, sorrow, and everything else swallows him up and turns his life into a nightmare,"

Fox concludes Alien's thought.

"Soon after, Nancy leaves him, and he becomes even more depressed. Then Michael kills his stepfather and Victor takes responsibility for Michael's act," Alien finishes.

"And everything fits."

"Agent Fox? Do you really believe that? Do you believe this really happened?"

Fox rests his hand on Alien's shoulder. "Where there is evidence, we don't need faith, do we?"

"So you believe Michael had those powers? That he could get into other people's thoughts and convince them that his thoughts were theirs?"

"I believe Beresford and Daniels were on their best path to make it happen. How far they have come will remain a mystery. We can only speculate whether it is good or bad that they failed to do so."

"What do you mean?"

"Consider this possibility, Alien. If it is true that we have these abilities and powers, then we have been on the best track to discovering a new part of ourselves. And I emphasize *if*."

Then he gets up, grabs his jacket, and throws it over his shoulder. It's time for him to go.

"I'm not going to do anything about what we talked about today until I talk to Victor. Either way, prepare to testify. And, be smart, Alien. Don't do anything stupid. I hope you've learned a lesson from this."

"I won't. I promise." They shake hands. Alien is looking after him until he is gone. Ready to scream, yell, explode, eating his heart out. Preventing his emotions from erupting to the surface. On the outside, Alien is calm as the oil spilled on the sleeping surface of the sea. Beneath that, a storm is raging.

WHY DID MICHAEL HAVE TO DIE?!

More than ever, Michael's death seems meaningless to Alien. Hank Daniels was a sick man, Hank Daniels hurt Michael, but he didn't want his death. Maybe he really wanted to help Michael, help him discover a part of himself he didn't know he possessed. Maybe he wanted to help him become someone *special*.

(Or maybe not? Or maybe he wanted the exact opposite?)

Who cares! Indirectly, Hank killed Michael in the end. And he *didn't* have to die!

He jolts so abruptly that he flips over the chair. *(He must calm down.)* There is one thing left he has to do, and he must not blow it.

This time he will persist to the end. *Laurie will say yes when he kisses her. She will agree to be his girlfriend.* And she will be with him in the days to come, when he will need comfort. Those days will be all but easy for him. Only Laurie will make them happy, only with her will he make it through them. With Laurie standing on his boogie-board, with Laurie caressing him under his T-shirt, with Laurie kissing him.

* * *

There are more people at Woodlawn Cemetery than in previous days, but it's still very quiet. Even the birdsong is more discreet, the tears speechless, and the rustling of the leaves too timid.

Rebecca is standing in silence beside the grave, emotionless, with tears already dried on her face. Her heart cold like a marble tombstone in front of her, three names carved into it.

Melanie Hope Daniels.
Hank Daniels.

Michael Daniels.

Years of their births and common year of their deaths. 1998, toward the end of the millennium.

In front of the tombstone, a bouquet of yellow roses. Nineteen roses in total. One for her mother, one for her father, and seventeen roses—one rose for each year of Michael's life.

In one day, which is two days ago, she buries two bodies. The killer and his victim sleep in the same grave, the same earth covers them and offers them common peace.

In one summer, Rebecca loses her family and the fall of her life ensues. Even the leaves had not yet come to bloom in colors and are already wilting on the grass.

Red Sunshine slips his arm through hers and pulls her gently. She doesn't resist him. She lets him lead her, take her wherever he wants.

She doesn't care. Everything she needs is with her.

All her memories: a light, summer, dark-blue dress her mother bought when she was in London, an amber brooch in a honeybee's shape her mother loved most, her father's gold Rolex and Michael's backpack full of dreams and poems. She will publish them one day, soon. They will be as successful as Rimbaud's poems and the whole world will find out how good Michael Daniels was. Best brother. He loved poems very much, but more than anything in the world he loved skateboarding.

The wind blows and ruffles their hair, bringing with it the scent of freshness and a hint of distant cold.

Despite the weather change with the drop in temperature, New York's late-afternoon hours are still pleasant and warm. Heavy rain with showers is expected, and snow on the heights.

Summer is passing cruelly fast.

(Or maybe it is coming back?)

Instead of an Epilogue

*My mind is collapsing under the
weight of the night.
The burden is heavy and tiresome.
Rest won't come.
Sparkles of illusions and
a world of troubled thoughts.
Blizzards of snow-born sorrows.
Flight of the sparrows
in frenzied flocks.
Coming and going away.
Into the night.
Into surrender.
Into oblivion.
Into the dark fogs of eternity.
I saw Death on my window.
It was gray.
And it was dancing . . .*

Michael Daniels, *Death Can Dance*, 1998

The Appendix to Cruel Summer

Postcards from Beyond Reality: The Selected Poems of Michael Daniels

Courtesy of Rebecca Daniels, here you can read a few poems from the collection of selected poems *Postcards from Beyond Reality* by Michael Daniels, first published by his sister two years after the author's death. Initially, this collection circulated from hand to hand among his closest friends, before the general public recognized and accepted it.

For, as the author says in one of his poems, *Despite the present coldness, indifference, and apparent cruelty, the world exists and goes on, with or without us.*

Bernard Jan

CRUEL SUMMER

A plastic sea, heaving with purple tulips;
Coral reefs overgrown with skyscrapers;
Asleep sun behind the red sky that guards over the charred forests;
Phoenix pierced with a crossbow plunges over New Queens;
Clouds swallowed by the flames of morbid torches of the extinct KKK;
Dreams turned into reality;
Faces of New Yorkers painted with smiles;
The streets of New York—free skateboarding zone;
Resurrection of Titanic with fanfares and fireworks;
I walk on the Red Planet (fresh footprints in the sea of silence);
The meeting with my father;
Return of innocence;
Mornings smelling of buds of late changes;
Daybreak of tolerance and victory of equality;
Locked fears and the pogrom of nightmares;
Rainbow in my eyes;
Peace among men.

(17 iMAGES) fROM bEYOND rEALITY

BERNARD JAN

The man believes in what he wants to believe.
                I want to believe that Love exists.

                fAITH

CRUEL SUMMER

I am screaming to the boiling point!
Voice rough like sandpaper.
Asphalt sings a symphony under
the dancing wheels.
And I'm sweating . . .
It's summer.

sUMMER sYMPHONY

When I open my eyes,
mornings tend to be soft and sickly gentle,
offering absolution on a gold platter of
oblivion, hope, and New York's madness.

When I open my eyes, a day seems cuddly
despite frustrated haste
of unsmiling faces. The colors are unspeakably clear
while I slide through the streets on the board.

(The envy-green of Central Park; the gray-blue
of the high, opaque-sky-like, tired eyes
of a young addict, jealousy-purple of the bruises
on my body; vibrating lecherous-red glow
of the nightclubs, blood, and sin; platinum bodies of the surfers
on the Coney Island beaches; electric-blue
of the rebellious sky pierced by lightning.)

I enjoy and absorb every movement,
each reflection from the window glass while
the night slowly descends. The morning gives way
to the evening, joy hides from despair.

It's dreaming time . . .

Darkness covers the city losing the battle with
the lights of the city. But it wins my
soul chained with anxiety. Fear.
And predictability of forthcoming . . .

CRUEL SUMMER

Dream . . . Time to dream.
The only beauty of New York I feel at night
when I can ride. Far. Long. Free.
Without thinking. Relaxed. Wild. Suicidal . . .

I appreciate that. I respect that. I LOVE that.
I reject the dream that will bring no rest or break
before the new ride. (I know that.) I refuse to dream
because I remember the earlier dreams. I remember them too
well . . .

I don't rest tired limbs tightened with hard,
healthy, and inflamed muscles; I stay up at night and
like a watchman near the end of the shift I count minutes.
I remember, I count, and turn into one of . . .

dream collectors . . .

And I remember . . .

uNFINISHED pOEM

BERNARD JAN

I know I am good for nothing anymore:
17 awakenings (toward the end ever
longer and weary)—wasted time.
I don't regret what *never*
happened, I don't mourn what
I *didn't* have.
With the fate of a fallen angel I stand
in the sunset and look at the summer,
in the waters of Bethesda rinsing the salt
of my tears.
Somehow I know I will not breathe
the smell of Central Park asphalt again.

aWAKENINGS

CRUEL SUMMER

The East River has begun to weep
Spilling its sorrow over the shallows
Of New Manhattan

Swaying algae on the anchors of sleeping giants
And gnawing at the rusty steel of their hulls
Looking for me

Knowing I won't be here soon

A little longer . . .
And my body will disappear from these banks
Awoken with mornings with no future
And lulled to sleep with restless nights

A little longer and I am leaving without a trace

A pair of worn-out Droors pants
Is left in SoHo
And discarded memories
No one took notice of

tHE eAST rIVER hAS bEGUN TO wEEP

BERNARD JAN

Once I believed in You
and my life wasn't a farce
Once while I slept soothed
on the feeding breasts of my mother

Now, now I don't know anymore what it means
to be calm, and I don't try to understand
lofty goals they taught me
I should respect

So I am taking a running start and escaping from everything
Hasting away from the eyes and alien looks
Eager to be different
Eager to be my own
Like a tattoo of the cross I carry on my leg
eager to be

iNDEPENDENT

Did you like my story? If your answer is yes, please follow me on Twitter, @BernardJanWorld, and tweet what you think. Don't forget to include #CruelSummer. Say hi, and I promise I'll respond.

Please continue reading now and find bonuses you may like.

Share What You Love
(About the Author)

If you liked my writing and enjoyed reading my novel *Cruel Summer*, please visit my website, where you can find other books I wrote and stay in touch with me by subscribing to my mailing list, reading my blog Muse, or just emailing me.

www.bernardjan.com

I encourage you to also check out my other novel *January River* and two novellas *Look for Me Under the Rainbow* and *A World Without Color.*

Besides being passionate about books, I'm also an animal rights advocate and environmentalist. Helping others and spreading kindness, love, and empathy toward every living creature plays an important role in my life.

If I'm your kind of guy, you are welcome to connect with me and follow me on my favorite social networks: Twitter, Goodreads, and LinkedIn.

There is no greater joy than to share what you love with

those who appreciate it.

Thanks for your time, love, and support!

BJ

Reviews

Thank you for reading *Cruel Summer* and spending, I hope, a few quality hours or days with it. Please consider leaving an honest review on Amazon and Goodreads. It doesn't have to be long. Even a sentence or two make a huge difference, and I will appreciate them.

I'm sure you know how much indie authors depend on you. You're the reason why we write and publish, strive to improve and do our best.

Your honest review generates a beacon of light to other readers seeking books to enjoy. Books that take them elsewhere, into different worlds and other lives, as they get lost between their pages.

Thank you for that. Thank you for sharing our stories.

Please also leave your honest review for *A World Without Color*, *Look for Me Under the Rainbow*, and *January River* on Amazon and Goodreads.

Acclaim for Bernard Jan

A WORLD WITHOUT COLOR

"I recommend this short story to anyone who has ever lost a beloved pet, but also to the elevated reader who enjoys a story with a strong undercurrent of social responsibility and a dystopian reflection of our world, as I often view it myself."
—Bibiana Krall, American novelist and short story writer, author of over twenty books

"The power of this book is that it opens an old wound, a wound that you don't want to close, a wound that itches and needs to be scratched. You need to bleed!"
—Peter Donnelly, founder of The Reading Desk and top reviewer on Amazon, Goodreads, and NetGalley

"Jan's writing is raw with grief yet also beautifully sentimental."
—Stephanie Jane, author of *Finally a Vegan: My journey to Veganuary and beyond* and reviewer for Literary Flits book blog

"It is a wonderful story for fans of animals, especially cat lovers. Reading about the desolation and the loneliness of the narrator,

the reader understands the place that Marcel occupied in his life as a companion . . . It is a story that explores themes of loss and grief and that celebrates a connection with a cat, a connection that brought meaning to the life of the narrator."
—Christian Sia, reviewer for Readers' Favorite

"Wow. Such an incredibly touching story. My heart ached with emotion. Those who have never had a beloved pet would never understand the gravity of losing one, but if they read this, it would be impossible not to glimpse the pain associated with the loss of one. Well written and bittersweet."
—Vicky Whedbee, author of *Things He Hadn't Told Her*, *Sarah's Song*, and *Sarah's Home*

LOOK FOR ME UNDER THE RAINBOW

"From the beautiful cover to the **elegant prose bordering at times in poetic**, you can tell there was lots of care into this narrative. This is the kind of story which will make you question why we hunt our fellow creatures."
—Ingmar Albizu, a Puerto Rican science fiction author

"I loved this book from beginning to end. It really hit you in the feels . . . The worldbuilding and descriptions are basically spectacular . . . I became lost in the icy world the author created . . . Honestly, I would have this book in schools everywhere, because it really teaches people (and kids) the cruelties of humans."
—John-Clement Gallo, author of *The Shadowverse* and *The Shadowverse: Vengeance*

"Bernard Jan writes with unique and captivating prose a journey of a harp seal pup named Danny. I enjoyed the adventure and was gripped until the very last page . . . Great story, good moral underpinnings, and fantastic writing make this story not one to miss out on."
—Jordan Ring, author of several books, book marketing and launch guru, freelance copywriter, writing coach, and consultant

"This story almost brims over with beautiful language. It has been long since I read such an incredibly well-written story. Few writers possess such advanced writing skills. Mr. Jan definitely belongs to the top league of authors."
—Edvin Palmer, author of *You're My All* and YouTuber

"Without getting into any gory details or making it uncomfortable, Jan has truly shown a different side of life in the ocean. Death is never easy. Loss is profound. Through wonderful imagery, lyrical text, and strong emotions, he's got a winner with Danny's story."
—James J. Cudney, author of *Watching Glass Shatter*, *Hiding Cracked Glass*, *Father Figure*, and *Braxton Campus Mysteries* series

JANUARY RIVER

"The beautiful landscape of words and emotions will grab you and won't let you put the book down till you reach the conclusion. The words flow smoothly through the page and highlight how passionate the author's is about his subject . . . What a compelling story told by a true master."
—Toni Osborne, book blogger and reviewer

"*January River* was blind journey for me and I really enjoyed the twist and turns and flow of the story. Bernard Jan is a writer with heart."

—David Sharp, author of *The Wild Boys, Escape from Dolphin Street*, and other punk fiction, queer, and horror books

"Bernard Jan never ceases to amaze with his emotionally packed, so 'true to life', and well written books. The characters in this latest novel, *January River* are life-like and jump out of the pages at the reader. This is truly a story you won't want to miss. Engaging, heartbreaking at times, and filled with passion throughout. Highly recommended!"

—Starjustin, reader and book reviewer

"*January River* by Bernard Jan is a wonderfully written and richly descriptive novel with brilliantly drawn characters and settings. It's a unique work that will captivate the reader from the opening chapter. Skillfully constructed, this well-written life affirming tale will have you turning the pages from beginning to end. There's also plenty of imagery in the writing style that makes you feel you are right there in the story, and that's something I look for in a good book. When I stopped reading to work, I found myself wondering what happened in the book, and replaying parts of the novel in my head to see if I could figure more out. It has been a while since I enjoyed a book this much."

—Píaras Ó Cíonnaoíth, poet and author of books for both children and adults and reviewer for Emerald Book Reviews

"**Bernard is a writer who can evoke deep emotions with his excellent writing.** He uses the perfect wordings and well-chosen metaphors to paint a scene and give us a look into his characters' deepest feelings . . . I really enjoyed reading this book, as Bernard has the wonderful quality to take you on an emotional trip through some beautiful locations and great memories. Looking forward to his next work already!"

—Koen Van den Eeckhout, Belgian information designer,
reader, and Goodreads book reviewer

A World Without Color Extract

You curl up in your new hideout, and the soft light of the April afternoon washes your worn-out body. You are aware of my closeness. You confirm that with a gentle sigh while my palm tenderly slides down your fur. You still like my touch, although pain is what you now mostly feel. And uncertainty—but for how long?

Against the tracksuit pants I wipe a lock of your hair which is stuck to my palm. I try to take a better position, crawling next to you under the table. I hate the sentimentality of people who want to capture with photos the beautiful moments in life because they believe that's the only way they can remain part of their memories. Ironic, because I myself resort to this now. Nothing else is left for me. Another day, week, month at best is the most optimistic prognosis.

Only this time. I will make an exception.

Your chest is rising and falling, fighting for every breath. It's not easy for you, I know, and I would love most if I could breathe for you. But I can't. Even if I breathe a new life into you, it probably wouldn't help. You wouldn't even let me.

Because you are a fighter. Besides, it seems to me you don't like people taking pity on you, as you didn't like it when they laughed in your face. This is why I control myself when I'm around you, poorly disguising the true nature of my feelings in a lame attempt to preserve your dignity. Panic hits me because of what is coming!

A tidal wave rushes from within, forcing tears to my eyes, which stream silently down my face and drip-drop onto your colorful blanket. Jolly green, purple and beige squares support your long, thin and distorted body like a gentle cloud. The shadow of what you used to be.

I support myself on my elbows, taking the first snapshot with my cell phone in my left hand. You hear a click and crack open your eyes. Your gaze rests on me, warming me with the heat of the hearth fire that fades away. I take another picture, producing another click, and then my hand trembles; I have to dry the tears that, undecided, stop and pause in the corners of my eyes.

You raise your head, not ceasing to look at me. Your good eye caresses my soul, while the other, sick from cataracts and inflammation unsuccessfully treated with ointments and drops, looks into the unknown. I'm stroking your hair, matted around it, waiting for you to be ready to continue our little photo session.

Again you accept me and indulge my whim. Gently as a newborn, you push your head along my hand, responding to my caress. First you rub your little nose into my fingers, and then you push your left ear against my hand, wanting me to scratch and massage it. When you become bored or you think it is enough, with amazing vigor you start to wash yourself. You surprise me a little because I don't remember when was the last time I saw you wash yourself. (It was a long time ago, just as eons have gone by since the days when you would happily nestle in the most comfortable seat in the apartment, after successfully sponging an abundant meal, and start to clean yourself. An invisible clock, or timer in you—as we used to joke—woke you up and led you, with your tail raised, to your bowls, where you patiently waited until, usually Mom, capitulated before your determination and persistence of the winner.) I smile, encouraged by a false hope and strong mental images awakened from the past. How little it takes for the Phoenix to resurrect in me and clatter the wings of joy. How dishonest I am with myself (and you) and subject to self-deception!

    I leave you for a moment and hurry into the kitchen to show the photos to Mom. You continue sprucing up, as you know it's time for Saša's arrival. As always, you want to show yourself to him in the best light. You care about what Saša thinks of you. I don't think you do this so he can pet you and lavish words of praise on you, calling you Viola, Love. No, you accept Saša because you know you will be better each time you see him and you want to give something back to him. You want to show him that his visits really make you feel better. And so you do that. I don't know with which words I can express more clearly what I feel for you, so I will repeat: *Viola, my love*.

My thoughts come rushing back like raging currents of mountain rivers that do not stop for anything or anyone. Hurrying with a roar to their finish line, completely self-sufficient. Each word I make immortal here must be engraved with the dedication of a blind stonemason who, just by sense of touch and guided by indestructible faith, creates from the shapeless mass a work which present generations, but also those who come after, will admire. Those who are alive today, and their children who are just born, setting the foundation for new generations. This is our written monument and I snuggle up against it, blinded by the pain inflicted upon me by every minute that takes us into the future. The future is what I want to avoid at any cost, selfishly keeping the present so these moments last as long as possible. Not thinking about you and the relief it will bring you. We are both on the road of no return. Do you think so too? Do you also feel at least a fraction of regret we will part soon, with no guarantee and no promise that, in the blink of an eye or the distant future, we might meet each other again? Tell me, dearest . . .

Please leave your honest review on Amazon and Goodreads.

Look for Me Under the Rainbow Extract

The sea was unusually calm, even the deep currents seemed to stand still. As if suspended in the hushed stillness of dawn. The blue darkness of the night sky began to recede as the pale daylight washed over the horizon. Helped by the frail rays of the wintry sun shimmering through a cloud of fog. In the cold air, the coat woven out of the drops evaporated from the sea, turned into small crystals of ice.

The fog crept along the surface of the sea, dragging like a tired traveler, and spread in the direction of the land. Thin in places, thick in others, it occasionally revealed a glimpse of the blinding whiteness that covered most of the land.

If you looked at the right moment, when patches of fog dispersed enough to reveal an endless vista, you could see that it was, in fact, not land. Enveloped by the gradually disappearing fog, huge icebergs loomed, huddled atop the ice crust covering the sea of blue. At first glance, one might easily mistake them for a continent. It did, in fact, exist. The outline of the coast etched against the distant horizon was all part of nature's optical trick to fool a casual observer. Swathed in a mist of crystals, countless icebergs of various sizes stacked next to each other merged into the image of an ice mountain. The anomaly, carried by deep but weak currents, traveled the ocean almost imperceptibly.

If not for the sound of the icebergs clashing and breaking piercing the sleepy air, the entire scene would appear lifeless. A white wasteland. Even the scattered groups of seals dozing lazily on white sheets of ice, seemed motionless and almost unreal. Their dark, slick bodies struck a sharp contrast with the surrounding harmony of whiteness. As if they were unwanted intruders. Now and then a seal would move, usually a female. With a sharp sudden spasm, one cried out in pain struggling to bring a new life into this icy world of cruel beauty.

Having left her group, she lay on her side trying to find the most comfortable position to endure the labor pains. Growing stronger and more frequent, they produced searing pain. She felt the restless pup kick and strain to come out into a whole new world. A world of breathtaking beauty, yet fraught with danger. She wanted to help it. She matched the pace of her breathing with his efforts to break the thin membrane that divided him from the outer world. She synchronized her heartbeat with his, but to no avail.

She knew it was going to be a difficult birth. Still not full term, her offspring was in a hurry to leave her body. She nevertheless hoped the two of them would somehow succeed.

When the pup suddenly started to writhe and push inside her, she could not help howling in pain. Her cry resounded over the ice, eclipsing the muted groans of other mothers-to-be who were to begin labor in a few days. They were rested and ready, prepared for the hardship of giving birth, while she had only just arrived and was still exhausted after the long swim from the north. A journey she would again take several months from now with her pup, back home to the winter-bound land of eternal snow and ice. That is, *if* the birth went well and all ended happily.

As time went by, her fears seemed well founded. The last obstacle that separated her baby from the outer world was removed. Splashes of red blood stained the ice around her, slowly freezing in the bitter cold. But the pup still did not come. Not moving, exhausted and weary, it braced itself for another attempt.

She wondered whether it was male or female. If a male, would he look like his father who had just woken and proudly sniffed the air? If a female, would she, like her mother, one day have to go through this pain to bring her baby into the world? After carrying it lovingly inside her womb for months and months, only to . . .

A new wave of excruciating pain slashed through her body and interrupted her thoughts. The pup pushed its way into the world, this time with more force and determination. The mother again synchronized all her bodily functions with its efforts to break free. Though united in their struggle, she wondered whether they felt the same pain. Or if only she suffered? Though it did not matter. She would gladly endure all the pain it took, if only to let it live.

As cry after piercing cry woke up other seals, they grew agitated, particularly the females about to become mothers in a few days. They timidly lifted their small heads to listen to the cries until they gradually abated. And then, one by one, they softly stretched on the ice that glistened in the sun. Silence fell, and everything was again hushed and motionless.

Please leave your honest review on Amazon and Goodreads.

January River Extract

1

Ethan McCoy lay in the grass, stretched out to his full length. He flung his head back and unbuttoned his shirt, exposing his neck and the pale skin of his chest to the sun. His rolled-up sleeves were already drenched in sweat. Perspiration ran off his forehead, dripping onto the jacket folded under his head in a faux pillow.

Ethan removed the light-sensitive glasses from his nose and wiped the sweat off with a handkerchief. Inhaling deeply, he stared at the sun through unprotected eyes. The scent of Greenfield invaded his nostrils, conquering his throat, lungs, and heart. Inside him the memories were waking up, ignited by familiar feelings from the past.

In the strong light he felt a pain in his eyes, forcing him to close them. So that he might suffer too, he didn't move to escape into the protective shadows. Determined to stay exposed to heat that reached him from the vast distance with such strength, he willed the sun to cause him pain. Wanted it to numb his senses and make him oblivious to any and all experiences—both pleasant and unpleasant. Most of all, he wanted to let go of the internal pain that refused to leave him alone after all these years.

He wished one pain could soothe another. The physical could annul the emotional. Even as he thought it, he knew it was in vain. He also accepted there was no cure for that pain. At best, it might be blunted some day and become just a painful reminder of his past.

But it would never disappear.

Because if it did, Greenfield would no longer exist. The artificially created grove beside the river in which he now rested, would vanish too. The same for Willy, then Jason, Derrick, and Sarah. Riv and . . . Susan. Could they evaporate, all of them? Did he have the right to ask that?

Or, what if it were possible for *all of them* to remain in their reality where they belonged? While *he*—Ethan—disappeared? Both could be possible only by some supernatural phenomenon. Something that could never happen.

Eventually moving into the shadows, he took off his shirt, shoes and socks and continued with his fantasy. Recalling. Or gathering up the strength and determination to do what he intended. Well, that's what he planned on saying if someone asked him why he was there. So far, nobody had. Nobody knew. He arrived less than an hour ago. He hadn't gone to the town, but had come straight to the river. To the place where everything had begun. Therefore, it only seemed fitting that it be where the beginning of the end transpired. The place where he would insert a period at the end of a life story. If he got lucky, he'd tear out a blank page and start anew. No memories. No past.

Without the bad memories, he could live in peace.

However, if he were honest with himself, that would be equally impossible to achieve.

In the still air, the river flowed quietly. Steadily. Innocently. Nothing about it had changed as if nothing happened. Effortlessly and seemingly without concern, the river continued to give life to all around it. But also taking it. . . .

Ethan watched the river and felt as though the river also observed him. Two silent witnesses, side by side again after so much time. Ethan had often wondered what this moment would be like. Would he find the river repelling, disgusting even, carried by the ravages of time and pressured by anxiety heavy as storm clouds? Or would it be seductive like it had been long ago when he was still a child?

Removing the rest of his clothes, he stood on the sand along the riverbank. The sunbeams warmed his naked body—a body weakened and slimmed by an avalanche of past events. He walked into the cold water up to his knees and shuddered. Almost icy. Or was he too hot after basking in the sun?

He barely hesitated before plunging in. He knew he wouldn't be able to resist the temptation. Love between the river and him could not dissipate that easily. As he swam, he wondered if this love would ever dissolve. Would another separation be even harder than the last?

Not far away, a dog gave up chasing a butterfly. Pricking up his ears and staring toward the woods, he searched the spot where his guardian had lain only a moment ago. Except for a heap of clothes tossed on the grass, the spot was empty. Sniffing the air, the dog moved toward the river—slowly at first and then breaking into a run.

Reaching the riverbank, he looked at the water. He gazed at the other bank. No sign of life on the river. Only the nature, butterflies, and the twittering of the birds. He wagged his tail and whined. Then he barked. Soon, he ran up and down the riverbank not knowing what to do. His barking became louder and uneasy. He decided to jump and was already in the air when Ethan surfaced, with no way to avoid the collision.

The sound of the dog's whine mingled with a yell of surprise filled the air before it was swallowed and disappeared in the splash of water. The waves rippled its calm surface.

A bit later, the sun warmed their bodies, drying them. Unlike the golden retriever's thick hair, Ethan was already dry as dust. Holding the dog's head in his lap, he babbled to him, "Riv, you big, mischievous, hairy maniac. We could both have been killed. What came over you? Why did you do that?"

The dog murmured away contentedly, positioning his head for Ethan so he could scratch the itching spots. Gone were the uneasiness and worries that made him jump. He enjoyed every one of Ethan's strokes feeling both safe and beloved, and returning those feelings of love and safety in the same measure.

Ethan leaned in and kissed his forehead. "I love you, buddy. What would I do without you?" You are the only one who didn't desert me, he said to himself with sadness.

He closed his eyes. The breeze tousled his brown, but graying hair. For a moment, the welcome freshness of the air invigorated his soul full of melancholy and sorrow.

Please leave your honest review on Amazon and Goodreads.

Made in the USA
Middletown, DE
07 December 2021